TWO HEADS ARE DEADLIER THAN ONE!

Even Dalvenjah had never seen a demon anything like this. It looked somewhat like a large, flightless dragon in the middle, with a thick, slightly flattened body supported by eight pairs of legs, and its heavy armor looked more like the segments of a centipede. The most curious thing was that it had no tail, but segmented necks growing out of each end. Each long neck ended in a massive head with fanged jaws that worked from side to side and immense powerful claws like those of a scorpion jointed at the back of the head, perfectly located to pull its prey toward those jaws.

All in all, it was an extremely unpleasant thing to discover in the garden before breakfast. . . .

Ace Books by Thorarinn Gunnarsson

SONG OF THE DWARVES
REVENGE OF THE VALKYRIE
MAKE WAY FOR DRAGONS!
HUMAN, BEWARE!
DRAGONS ON THE TOWN

DRAGONS

on the Town

THORARINN GUNNARSSON

ACE BOOKS, NEW YORK

This book is an Ace original edition,
and has never been previously published.

DRAGONS ON THE TOWN

An Ace Book / published by arrangement with
the author

PRINTING HISTORY
Ace edition / December 1992

All rights reserved.
Copyright © 1992 by Thorarinn Gunnarsson.
Cover art by Walter Velez.
This book may not be reproduced in whole or in part,
by mimeograph or any other means, without permission.
For information address: The Berkley Publishing Group,
200 Madison Avenue, New York, New York 10016.

ISBN: 0-441-15526-X

Ace Books are published by The Berkley Publishing Group,
200 Madison Avenue, New York, New York 10016.
The name "ACE" and the "A" logo
are trademarks belonging to Charter Communications, Inc.

PRINTED IN THE UNITED STATES OF AMERICA

10 9 8 7 6 5 4 3 2 1

DRAGONS
on the Town

❧ PART ONE ❧

Bones to Pick

Wind Dragon drifted quietly through the night sky, passing like a dark cloud above the lights of Bennasport. She moved effortlessly without a sound, her magical lift and propulsion vanes operating in complete silence. Autumn was settling once again over this hilly coastal town and the air was cold and fresh, the night so deep that the red and blue stripes of the ribbed stabilizing sails behind her four lift vanes and the smaller steering stabilizers rigged to her bowsprit were faded to bands of grey. Although she was a small ship, hardly more than a schooner, her dark shadow passing before the stars appeared vast and menacing. And yet she might well have passed completely unnoticed above the sleeping town, unless someone had happened to look up at just the proper moment.

From her position at *Wind Dragon*'s helm, the esteemed sorceress Kasdamir Gerran had much the same point of view. Seen from above on a dark night, Bennasport looked like just so many lights scattered across a rolling black landscape. An airship was actually quite easy to fly at night, as long as navigation was limited to charts and compasses. Finding one house in an entire city, when she could not even see the city, was another matter altogether.

"Here they come, Lady Mira!" Dooket, the taller of her pair of young hired mercenaries, called from the bow.

Mira looked over the side of the ship, and almost immediately she saw the dark forms of the faerie dragons, their broad wings spread against the night as they hurtled past. A moment later they circled back and came up the other side of the ship, slowing greatly to match speed. They stood off a short distance

1

to *Wind Dragon*'s starboard side for a moment until they were certain that they had Mira's attention before they began to drift slowly away to the side. Mira understood their message and turned *Wind Dragon* slowly to follow them, spinning the rudder wheel only a couple of turns so that she did not overshoot them in the dim light. It was hard enough even to see them.

Sir Remidan came up the steps from the middle deck, his armor clinking softly as he walked. As a Knight Errant of the Loyal Order of Stewards, that being a very elite group and not entirely obsolete even in this modern age, his armor and weapons were magical in origin and curiously light, cool and comfortable to wear. Which was just as well for Sir Remidan, since he insisted upon wearing his armor at all waking hours. He even wore the damned thing to bed, for all Mira knew. Plate armor had one universal disadvantage, particularly for those who were not wearing it themselves: almost every armored warrior that Mira had ever met tended to smell rather bad, at least as the day wore on. Remidan was one of the very few exceptions, and even he tended to smell a little shabby at times.

"Help me to keep an eye on those dragons," Mira directed. "They can see so well at night, they tend to forget that we cannot."

Remidan paused and leaned well out over the siderail, staring out into the night for a long moment. "Bless me, but I don't see them at all."

"Perhaps not," Mira agreed. "Boys?"

"Dragons, ho! Dead ahead!" they shouted back. They normally stood duty somewhere near the front of the ship, where they could be at hand for either lookout or to tend the ropes and cables of the stabilizers in *Wind Dragon*'s bowsprit. Airships were fairly massive flying machines built almost entirely of wood and ropes, and the only magic was involved in making them move and not in keeping them together. Flying them was best done with a great deal of blind trust and a certain amount of reliable help. Mira had to trust in luck.

"Staemar will be happy enough to be back on the ground," Remidan remarked as he walked over to stand beside Mira at the wheels. "He is a bold and loyal steed, but this has been a great trial for him. He hardly knows which he fears more, the flying or the dragons."

Mira glanced at him. "Where did he learn to talk? I've never heard of familiars taking the forms of horses."

"He is enchanted, of course," Remidan explained softly, for this was obviously a delicate matter. Staemar was standing on the middle deck, and he had excellent ears. It helped that they moved. "He used to be a knight like myself, until he fell afoul of a common enemy."

"The Dark Sorceress Queramael?" Mira inquired succinctly. Remidan and Queramael had been mortal enemies all their adult lives, and apparently for the latter portion of their childhood as well. The ill effects of a poorly aimed spell of uncontrollable lust had improved their relationship for only a few hours, and a certain lingering side effect on Queramael's part had caused matters to deteriorate very quickly from that point.

"Down slowly," Erkin, the shorter of her barbarians, called out.

"Right, boys!"

"Staemar . . . Sir Staemar, I suppose I should say, was caught unawares at a time when he did not have his magical armor and its protection against most magic. That is why I hardly ever remove my own. So it was that Queramael turned him into a horse." Remidan caught her dubious glance and shrugged. "Actually, she enchanted his mortal spirit into the body of his own warhorse. That of course left the horse as the new tenant of his former residence, as it were. The poor, stupid thing proceeded to eat grass with its former appetite and soon died of a bowel obstruction. Thus, with no human body to inhabit, he is stuck with the horse."

"Left fifteen degrees!" Dooket called.

"Right, boys!"

"No, left!"

"Clowns," Mira muttered to herself. "So how did Queramael manage to catch him outside his armor?"

"Well, yes . . ." Remidan coughed, looking very uncomfortable. "After her slight miscalculation with me, it seems that she managed to refine that spell of overwhelming lust. It is quite a spell, I assure you. A temptation well beyond even knightly restraint."

"Yes, quite," Mira agreed quickly.

"Alas, poor Sir Staemar." Remidan paused to wipe a noble

tear with a silk handkerchief. "He is now subject to various mortal fears that one encounters upon finding oneself a domestic animal. He does fret so about being eaten. And as for having him shoed, I fear that I must first get him fairly tipsy on wine. The nails, you understand."

"You might try glue," Mira suggested.

"I dare not even mention the word to him."

Mira would have never suspected the tragic and frankly preposterous tale of how Staemar had become a horse, but it was very much along the line of the thoughts that she had been contemplating for the last three days. Her young protégé Jenny Barker had been evicted from her own body without the benefit of a true destination, and still lingered in partial life because she now shared the body of the faerie dragon Vajerral Foxfire, her first cousin by adoption on her father's side. But Jenny was only a silent partner in the arrangement; she could only move or speak for herself when Vajerral allowed. Mira had been considering a replacement body for Jenny, but that meant either a body that had no inhabiting spirit or one that could be accommodated. In the former case, she had certainly met a great many people in her career whom she suspected would be none the worse for having no souls, but she knew of no one already in that state. And as for the latter case, that involved evicting some other poor soul from its rightful home. Again, Mira could think of many people who would benefit from the process, but the only practical answer was to use an animal.

That always brought the debate back to the same conclusion: it would be best to do nothing until they consulted Dalvenjah Foxfire, Vajerral's mother and perhaps the most capable of the faerie dragon sorceresses anywhere. Her command of dragon magic was strong, and the possession of dragon magic in itself gave her a tremendous advantage over Mira's relatively simple mortal magic. The only trouble that Mira anticipated was finding the illustrious and all-knowing Dalvenjah Foxfire, who was a very busy dragon indeed. The last that Mira had heard, Dalvenjah had been trying to talk to a dead dragon. That was not so strange as it may seem, since the dead dragon in question had been loitering about with Mira's group. With that in common, Mira was almost surprised that Dalvenjah's path had not already crossed her own.

Which was just as well for Mira, considering what she had been doing the last few weeks.

"Down, Lady Mira!" Dooket called.

Mira looked up, perplexed. "How much down?"

"Until we say stop."

Mira frowned fiercely, knowing that this was no way to fly an airship. It was not the airship she distrusted as much as her two barbarians. The ship needed time to react to a change in the angle of the control surfaces, especially at such slow speeds, and she doubted that the boys could judge such matters accurately enough. *Wind Dragon* had been through a lot herself lately, so much that Mira was already worried about her frame. The airship might not take another hard landing, and it was easy enough to lose a vane to a tree at the best of times. The tree had the advantage of bulk over a fragile vane or bowsprit, and there was not very much in nature which lived and grew that could beat a tree for traction. Or stubbornness: trees never got out of the way.

A grey form glinting with metallic gold shot past the ship and circled tightly to move up close beside the helm deck. Mira recognized Vajerral, the smaller and rangier of the two dragons, still a slightly immature example of the species. Faerie dragons were as a rule extremely clever, and telepathy helped to make up for anything they might have otherwise missed. Vajerral had perceived the need and dropped back to direct the ship. Ordinarily Mira would have had as many misgivings about that, knowing Vajerral's remarkable talent for poor judgement. At the moment, the young dragon did benefit from having Jenny on board, with her own experience at flying the airship.

Now there was a possibility, Mira thought. Two minds were said to be better than one, and stupid people might stand to benefit from sharing their bodies with someone as bright and well educated as Jenny, to provide ready advice and information. There might actually be a market for this.

"Descend slowly five hundred feet," Vajerral called, struggling to keep herself not only flying but balanced at such a slow speed. There was a faint glow of lift magic surrounding her, since her wings were not getting enough lift of their own. "Turn left some fifteen degrees or slightly less."

"Flying by approximation," Mira muttered as she spun both

of the wheels. This was better than Dooket's instruction, but hardly perfect. She wondered just who was giving the advice.

Wind Dragon responded very smoothly, considering her size, even at such a sluggish speed. Fighting a strong wind, she could feel like a hundred feet of dead bulk. There were of course massive freighters and flying battleships nearly six times her length and ten times her weight, twice the size of any wooden ship that had ever ridden the waves. Surprisingly, the larger airships were considerably more stable, too massive to be bothered by normal winds.

"Jenny says to straighten out," Vajerral reported, although her doubt was obvious.

Mira decided to trust Jenny's judgement and spun the rudder wheel about. The girl knew *Wind Dragon*'s ways from long experience at the helm, that it took a brief moment to straighten the rudder and a longer moment before the mass of the ship agreed to stop rotating. The result seemed to please the dragon, who was watching ahead carefully but declined to comment. Mira was far from satisfied, however. She was still flying blind, and her guide had turned out to be a committee. It was up to her to figure out which of the two was actually talking and to decide accordingly how much she trusted the advice. Vajerral dropped back just behind the ship and suddenly darted in, catching hold of the rail and pulling herself aboard. She hurried to the front of the helm deck, on the starboard side above the steps leading down to the middle deck, and hung her long neck over the siderail so that she could peer straight down. Sir Remidan, overcome by curiosity and a misdirected idea that he was being helpful, leaned over the rail beside her.

"What do you think?" the dragon asked.

"Well, I don't . . ." Sir Remidan began in a voice that tried very hard to deny the fact that he did not know a thing.

"Not you. Jenny," Vajerral said, and paused. "Slow up."

Mira stared expectantly, aware that this odd scene meant that Vajerral was conferring with Jenny, a process complicated by the fact that they were in the same body.

"What, so soon?" the dragon asked herself. "Unless you want to circle around, and we were very lucky to get Mira on course so easily the first time. Well, I don't know . . . Will you just keep quiet and let me do this? I've flown this ship, and you have not. If you insist."

She lifted her head and looked back over the shoulder of her wing. "Level the ship and begin slowing. You will be hovering at a full stop in about five hundred yards."

Mira considered it a miracle that they were able to work together well enough to make one dragon fly, let alone guide an airship.

"Slower," the dragon warned.

"I don't see anything," Sir Remidan complained.

"Neither do I," either Jenny or Vajerral replied, not looking up. "Steady now. There is not much of a wind, but it must be dead behind us. Now, cut your forward thrust and let her drift to a stop. Perfect."

"Are you satisfied?" Mira asked blandly.

"Yes, I believe so. Now, begin to drop the ship straight down."

"Winch down the wheels, boys!" Mira shouted. "We seem destined to land somewhere."

Mira decreased the lift thrust until *Wind Dragon* began to descend, so slowly that she could not even feel the motion. That suited her perfectly; she was mostly flying by sound, waiting to hear the cracking of branches or perhaps even a roof. As she watched, the dark shapes of trees began to rise about her on all sides, although she still did not hear the protest of anything from below. Then she peered forward, realizing that the massive shadow just ahead of the bowsprit was *Wind Dragon*'s shed, and the airship settled smoothly to the ground a moment later. Tally up a point for the faerie dragons and their keen eyes. Vajerral leaped over the siderail, spreading her wings to break her fall.

A storage locker against the siderail opened and J.T. the cat lifted his head, looking around. "Are we down? Thank goodness!"

"Boys, take down the rigging and fold back the lift vanes," Mira directed as she set the brakes. "You can roll *Wind Dragon* into her shed with the winch when you are done."

"Right, Mom!" they called back.

Mira hesitated in her stride, pausing to reflect that she was going to slay a certain male dragon for starting that business.

Then she sauntered blissfully down the steps to the middle deck and to the boarding ramp, still folded up against the ship as a part of the siderail. She needed only a moment to release the latches and lower the ramp to the ground. Then she turned and stared meaningfully at Staemar. Sir Remidan stood at her side and stared also. Staemar, a large white stallion decked out in equine plate armor and chain mail, just stood in the center of the deck with his legs braced solidly on the boards and his head down.

"We are on the ground, Staemar," Mira told him. "Are you feeling better?"

Staemar rolled one eye, peering out through the opening in the steel armor of his faceplate. "You just go ahead."

"There really is no reason to be afraid," Remidan told him.

"I am not afraid," the horse declared proudly. "I just want to go down that ramp in my own good time, with no one watching."

"As you will," Mira told him. "Have the boys show you to the stables as soon as you are ready, and do have them bring you anything you require to make the place suitable to a horse of your station."

"I will be around shortly to undress you," Sir Remidan added.

They descended the boarding ramp, finding the two dragons waiting for them at the top of the path leading to the house. Mira paused a moment to glance back. "That poor horse is nervous about everything. Pride goeth before a fall, they say."

"Pride goeth after a fall, I believe, is what worries Staemar," Remidan explained. "That ramp is very steep, and he is in armor."

"What did you mean, that you would be around shortly to undress him?"

"He cannot remove his armor by himself, of course. And he is very sensitive about who sees him naked."

"Really? I can't imagine that!" Mira exclaimed. Then she noticed that the knight was affording her a very curious stare. "A horse being nervous about being naked, I mean. As you point out, he is only a horse on the outside . . . Oh, never mind."

"Dalvenjah Foxfire is going to undress the whole lot of us right down to our bones when she finds out what we've been doing," Kelvandor reminded them. He was the largest of the two faerie dragons, although Mindijaran, as they were called in their own flowing language, were the smallest of all breeds of dragons. And generally the most civilized. "We tried to do something we knew better than to even attempt, and it turned out about as wrong as possible. She is going to be furious, and I can hardly blame her."

"I am not afraid of any dragon," Sir Remidan declared proudly.

"You have never met my mother," Vajerral said softly. "She is not going to be pleased. Oh, no, my precious. Not pleased at all."

Mira paused a moment, staring up at the dark form of her house. There were more lights in the windows than she thought should be normal, considering that only Dame Tugg and possibly Adenna Sheld were at home. Mira was thinking about her great, gaudy, comfortable home and what it would be like to run away and live in the wild for the rest of her life. That whole ill-conceived plot of tempting the Prophecy of the Faerie Dragons had been her idea.

She sighed heavily and led the way to the back door. "Unfortunately, the august and ill-tempered Dalvenjah Foxfire is exactly the one we have to see, and as soon as we can get away. We could leave in the morning, if we must. But I would prefer to take two or three days to have *Wind Dragon* checked out and some of her parts replaced, after all that she has been through. The one question is, where can we possibly find Dalvenjah? The last either of you two had heard, she has been on some quest of her own, looking for the ghost of a dragon who was looking for us."

"All I can think of is to go home and wait for Mother to show herself," Vajerral offered. "If she is moving through different worlds, then she will be coming and going from there. If you want to follow, then you will need Kelvandor to open a Way Between the Worlds for you."

"Yes, that is quite beyond any mortal magic that I know," Mira admitted as she opened the back door, pausing to look back at them. "And if you do find her first, you might begin breaking the news to her. After all, you do have Jenny with you. She isn't likely to want to kill the two of you, whatever dire fate may be in store for me. But above and beyond all else, there is one thing that Dalvenjah Foxfire must not know for now. . . ."

"And just what is this bit of news that Dalvenjah Foxfire must not know at the cost of your life?" a voice asked from the darkness within the house. A moment later, the very dragon in question moved forward into the light, a golden Mindijarah with a sapphire blue crest and jade green eyes.

Lady Mira took one look at the dire glint in those large eyes and drew back in alarm. She was not the only one contemplating a hasty retreat, and she might have already made her escape if the way had not been blocked by dragons, a cat and a knight in armor. In her hesitation the moment was lost. Two large golden hands reached out and took both Mira and Vajerral firmly by the ear. Vajerral's ear was large, pointed and very mobile, but even that did not help it to escape.

Commanding her captives by such a tender rein, Dalvenjah marched the pair of them through the dark corridors of the house. Kelvandor, Sir Remidan and the cat followed behind, too surprised to know what to do and too fearful of their own lives to intervene. As the procession made its way through the halls of the mansion, Mira happened to see Dame Tugg retreating judiciously into a corner. The elderly housekeeper, wearing as always the habit of a Wansorian nun and riding boots, appeared for perhaps the first time in her life to be quite speechless. The retired Abbess had been trapped in the house with the dragon since her arrival.

"Tea, Dame Tugg!" Mira called after her. "Lots and lots of tea!"

"Where will you be?" Dame Tugg asked.

"Just follow the screams and shouting."

Dalvenjah propelled her prisoners mercilessly around a corner and into Mira's own office. The lamps were lit and Allan, Dalvenjah's mate and a dragon slightly larger even than Kelvandor, waited expectantly in the middle of the room. Sir Remidan, J.T. and Kelvandor retreated as far as they were able into one corner of the room, into the windowed alcove that overlooked the garden, first the knight and then the dragon bumping into the small table and chairs. Vajerral and Mira were given no such chance to hide themselves, for Dalvenjah did not release their ears until they were in the center of the room.

"Now, where is Jenny?" she demanded, glaring first at Vajerral and then at Mira.

"Oh, well. Jenny." Mira, who had never been intimidated by anything in her adult life, did not dare to look the dragon in the eye. "Ah, yes. No problem there, I assure you. Jenny is still with us."

"Outside?" Dalvenjah asked suspiciously.

"No, inside. Inside Vajerral, to be precise."

Dalvenjah glared at Vajerral, who grinned sheepishly. On a dragon, that expression came across as nothing but exceedingly ridiculous. Then she glanced at Kelvandor and Remidan, who were still arranging chairs around the table as quickly as the dragon's tail and the knight's sword would knock them aside. "Come over here and sit down, all three of you. That includes you as well, cat. Unless you want to take up the violin the hard way."

They all three looked at each other, the dragon and the cat with their ears laid back and Sir Remidan's drooping mustache mimicking the gesture. They meekly walked over and sat down, Remidan and J.T. on the sofa while Kelvandor sat back on his tail on the floor beside Allan. The two dragons glanced at each other. Even Allan looked quietly subdued, and he was not in trouble.

Mira turned her head and frowned at Sir Remidan. "Do you use oil on your joints?"

"Yes, certainly."

"Then get your armor off my sofa."

Dalvenjah took Mira by the collar and drew her close until they stood nose to nose. "There was something you wanted to explain to me."

"Did I?" Mira found herself looking up the dragon's long nose and right into a pair of large green eyes that were glaring hard enough to crack ice and frighten large dogs. "Ah, yes. This is one of those proverbial long stories. Would you care to hold me by the neck the whole time, or may I proceed at my own pace?"

Dalvenjah let her down. "I will not hold you by the neck, just as long as you proceed at a pace which suits me. Would you prefer to relate your little tale hanging upside down while I tickle your ass with my flame?"

Mira just stood and blinked stupidly, at a complete loss for words. She was used to being on the other end of a sharp tongue. "Ah, well now. It all sort of began like this. One night several months ago I was hosting a party, when this rather strange girl named Jenny Barker and this dragon who claimed to be her cousin arrived. Jenny was to be my special student, while I never did quite figure out why Vajerral was here except to eat prodigiously. You arranged it all, so you should remember."

"Yes, I do remember," Dalvenjah agreed coldly. Then she turned to glare at Sir Remidan. "Sit down!"

"Where was I?" Mira mused.

"About to be hung upside down for failing to proceed at a pace which suits me," the dragon told her.

"Ah, yes. Well, a friend of mine, Adenna Sheld by name and a fine concert singer, had recently toured in the South. When she came back with tales of the new Empire and barbaric doings, and I recalled what Jenny had told me about the Prophecy of the Faerie Dragons, then I thought to myself, 'Ah-ha! We should stand up to that silly prophecy and kick it right in the nose, and have a good look about down South at the same time.' But first I thought that we should visit my old teacher, the Sorcerer Bresdenant, since he is the leading expert on the doings of the old Alasheran Empire and the Dark Magic due to a lifetime of research on the subject. But on the way to see him, *Wind Dragon* was attacked by an Imperial airship and a group of winged demons, and that was a very fierce battle, I can tell you, but we prevailed through fortitude, cunning and excellent leadership, if I do say so myself. And it was a most enlightening experience in a way, since we did not know until then that the Empire had airships of its own, even if they did have to steal them. And the winged demons as well, if you take my meaning."

Dalvenjah rolled her eyes. "If you don't mind."

"Not at all. I mean, I am trying!" Mira protested, then turned her head to glare at Sir Remidan. "Get your tin britches off my sofa!"

"Allan, fetch me a rope!" the dragon declared.

"This is all very complicated, but I will be as brief as possible," Mira assured her. "You see, it was from Bresdenant that we first heard about the prophecy of someone else whose name I don't offhand recall, but it was very important."

"Maerildyn," J.T. offered quietly.

"Yes, the Prophecy of Maerildyn. You know:

> 'Dragons gold and dragons black
> Seek to gain what each may lack.
> White and black, red and blue,
> Fortune hangs between the two.'

"That was what Bresdenant told us, anyway. Of course, we could not at the time begin to make sense of what it was trying to say."

"I doubt that the lot of you could interpret the signs correctly if your pants were on fire." Being a dragon, Dalvenjah could not help but think about setting fires when she was angry, and she seemed to have a fixation about just what she wanted to roast. She glared at Sir Remidan. "Sit down."

"We returned home then, which was where we found Vajerral and Kelvandor, and then we were off again. Except that this time we were attacked not by one Imperial airship but three, and a whole flock of flying demons. We did get the better of them, of course, but *Wind Dragon* was a mess. Oh, yes, and Jenny was wounded by an arrow and needed a couple of days to recover. We put in at Woody Bog for needed repairs . . . to the airship, of course. And we met the biggest damned demon you could imagine, lurking about in the basement, but Jenny had such a way with dragon magic, it was no problem."

"Had?" Dalvenjah asked politely.

"Has, of course," Mira hastily amended. "Then we found old copper-bottom and his neurotic horse—Blow your butt off my sofa!—stranded on a deserted island. We continued on to Alashera and were warmly received by an old friend of mine, Dasjen Valdercon, who actually turned out to be the most recent incarnation of the High Priest Haldephren. Well, he kidnapped Jenny and was about to sacrifice her to the Heart of Flame inside the neck of the volcano, but I arrived with Sir Remidan and the boys just in time, and then the two dragons came at them from the other side. Jenny and I sent both him and the Heart of Flame into the volcano, which had the unexpected effect of causing the whole damned island to explode. That was a close one, and we barely got away. They had hidden *Wind Dragon* inside an underground tunnel and we had to follow that all the way down to the sea with lava just behind us, and then we had to ski the airship across the harbor on her struts as the volcano exploded, and we just barely got the lift vanes rigged before the tsunami got us."

"Is that it?" Dalvenjah asked suspiciously.

"Well, you actually did forget the part about *Wind Dragon*'s brake cables being cut while you slept," Sir Remidan offered. "I was not yet with you at that time, of course, or things might have turned out different. . . ."

"Things turned out just fine, thank you!" Mira said hastily to shut him up. "And sit down."

"Pardon?"

"But not on my sofa!"

Dalvenjah sat back on her tail and lifted her head as she sighed loudly, supplication to the Dragon Gods for patience. Dragons generally were not known for their patience, at least not when they were angry, and certainly if there was no promise of food or sex involved. "Now just why do I get the impression that you have not told me the whole dirty story?"

Mira looked hurt. "Would you think that I would hold out on you?"

"If you thought that you could get away with it. Let me put it to you this way. On this one little airship of yours, there was yourself, Jenny Barker the Immensely Curious, Vajerral of the Profound Blunders and Kelvandor, Blithe Spirit of Good Intentions. A boundless potential for misfortune, and you tell me that that was all the trouble you got into?"

"Oh, well. I just did not want to bore you with the small details, and you did say to keep it brief."

"You have not kept it brief, and you have already bored me to distraction with the glorious highlights!" Dalvenjah declared, picking her up again by the collar. "What did you do with Jenny?"

"That is a bit more complicated, and you really should hear it all," Mira protested, and the dragon released her reluctantly. The sorceress straightened her collar and swallowed loudly. "That dead dragon you were looking for, your half-brother

Karidaejan. He has been hanging about Jenny from the start and muttering cryptic warnings. The night after Alashera exploded—what was that, three or four nights ago?—Karidaejan approached Jenny again. He explained to her he had gone into her native world and discovered that the original object of the Prophecy, Jenny's uncle Allan, had been born male and therefore ineligible to fulfill the Prophecy. Then he had taken mortal form as the one you knew as James Donner and sired Jenny himself; he was her real father, and so she had always been a faerie dragon in mortal form and never aware of it. Then Haldephren came and they fought. Karidaejan was able to defeat Haldephren and force him to withdraw, but Haldephren stole his body and forced his spirit to serve him. That night, the Emperor Myrkan forced him to distract Jenny until the Emperor came himself. He expelled Jenny from her own body and gave it to the Dark Sorceress Darja, to return her to life."

"And Jenny?" Dalvenjah demanded. "He must not have captured or released her spirit, or you would be even more frightened."

"No, I have her," Vajerral said.

"You do?" Dalvenjah asked, and she relaxed into a fairly decent mood for the first time that night. "Perhaps you have finally outgrown that blundering phase you were going through."

Mira paused in mid-squirm, too dumbfounded to remember to be properly terrified. Dalvenjah Foxfire might be a dragon of mercurial moods, but this defied explanation. Just when Mira was certain that Dalvenjah would roast her fanny without even waiting to hang her up, the dragon almost seemed pleased.

"You don't seem particularly surprised," Mira observed, even though her hindquarters began to sweat in anticipation. "I thought that was the most surprising part."

That, she thought to herself, and Jenny's explanation of how to make love to a dragon.

"I had always suspected something odd about Jenny's origin," Dalvenjah explained. "She was able to perform dragon magic from the start, even when I first met her years ago. You know yourself that no mortal should be able to perform even faerie magic, while dragon magic is the highest and most elusive form. Then more recently, when I discovered that Karidaejan had been in her world, I began to suspect the truth. That was the real reason why I was trying to find Karidaejan. That, and to give the two of you time to set the Prophecy of the Faerie Dragons properly into motion."

Mira thought about that for a moment, and a little bell rang inside her head. "That was why you sent Jenny to be my student, when there was nothing about magic that I had to teach her? You knew at the time that I am the other half of the Prophecy."

"Exactly," the dragon agreed guilelessly. "Now ask the last important question."

Mira looked as if she had been hit between the eyes by a stone. "What last important question?"

Dalvenjah sighed again; the Dragon God of Patience was feeling generous. "When things were looking the worst and you would begin to regret that you ever got yourself involved in this business, what question did you ask yourself most often?"

"Why me?"

"Precisely," Dalvenjah declared, her ears standing straight up. "What was your part in the Prophecy?"

Mira made a face that looked more bewildered than thoughtful. "I assumed that I was along to help, perhaps to provide mature guidance."

"You were the true object of the Prophecy," Dalvenjah told her bluntly. "Jenny was the distraction. Having the Dark Emperor and his allies focused on her kept all attention away from you. She was never the one they should have been after, but you. Now they have been tricked into making their first major mistake."

"What?" Mira demanded incredulously. She felt weak in the knees and light of head; she had gone too long without tea. Either it was not yet ready, or Dame Tugg did not dare to face Dalvenjah's wrath to bring it.

"The Emperor Myrkan, the High Priest Haldephren, the Dark Sorceress Darja, indeed the entire Alasheran Empire, were products entirely of your own world and the native magic of that world," the dragon explained. "There are the four magics: natural magic, mortal magic, faerie magic and dragon magic, but never entirely the same in any two worlds and most often very different. That was a tie with you, a common ancestry as it were, that they never could have with Jenny. Doubly so, since she never was mortal but a dragon, even if she did not know it. And who, I ask you as objectively as you can possibly manage, is the greatest sorceress alive in your world today? The Sorceress Darja was meant to have your body."

It all made tremendous sense, which was why Mira had to sit down on the sofa for a moment to think about it. Unfortunately, thinking about it only caused it to make even more sense. And now she had a double measure of guilt to bear. It had been her idea to face the Prophecy bravely and engage in some spying in the South, the last place that Jenny should have gone. And now she learned that Jenny had paid the terrible price of the Prophecy in her place. She glanced over at the other end of the sofa and saw J.T. staring up at her, looking as miserable as she felt. At least the cat chose to be gracious; his kind usually preferred a smug "I told you so."

Mira stared up at Dalvenjah. "Why do you seem so pleased with the way that things have turned out?"

"Pleased is not entirely the correct word," she explained. "Things are progressing the way they must. I sent Jenny to you for the very reason of having the two of you together, knowing that trouble would come to you soon enough. I did not anticipate that you would go looking for trouble, but the result has been the same."

"What result? You could have kept Jenny safe in some other world. Did you send her as bait to distract them from me?"

"Although it turned out that way, I did not know until this night that not Jenny but you are the object of the Prophecy. Only when I was certain that Karidaejan was indeed her father did it occur to me that the Sorceress Darja would not want her body, if she knew. And as for keeping her safe . . ." Now the dragon began to grow angry again, although her rage was now directed at her own pain and frustration. "The time was past for keeping her safe. Do not think that I have failed to examine my motives. I am compelled to do what is best, at any cost."

And what was best, Mira realized, was not necessarily best for Jenny. Or for Mira. Or even for Dalvenjah herself; she had already lost her half-brother to the cause. Mira also realized that it was time to keep her mouth shut on that subject. This game was very ugly and unpleasant, and the stakes were high enough to demand sacrifices. Punishing Dalvenjah—or herself—would

only slow them down, and they were already beginning to fall
behind.

"The point now is that Jenny's misfortune is also the misfortune of our enemies," Dalvenjah continued when Mira said
nothing. "History tells us that Darja was unique among sorcerers. She is in some way a creature of magic herself at the same
time that she is mortal. She possesses the ability to control and
channel any source of magic no matter how great, and in the
past she could command the great crystals of power such as the
Heart of Flame, something not even the Emperor himself could
accomplish. But because of her nature she lives a dreamlike existence, lacking any desires or ambitions or even much sense of
personal identity. She is subservient entirely to the will of the
Emperor, living vicariously through his desires and passions,
but even he cannot compel her will.

"Darja lives again, and the magic at the Emperor's command
has increased at least a hundredfold because of her ability to
identify and command any source of natural or accumulated
magic. But she is in the wrong body, one less able than she sus-
pects. More importantly, one that is a creature of magic alien to
herself but tied to the dragon magic, and one that is not even in
its proper form. These are disadvantages that we may be able to
use against her."

"How?" Mira asked.

Dalvenjah twitched her ears. "I wish to hell I knew!"

Mira sat at the table in the alcove of her study, looking out her
window as she enjoyed her morning tea. The early sun was
bright but it looked cold, and there were no colorful flowers in
her garden, only leaves that were beginning to turn brown and
grey. Winter was coming, and that was generally a very productive time of year. The snows of Bennasport could be deep and
lingered long into spring, and Mira would be given a good deal
of time for her research and practicing her magic. She was
pleased to have a long winter to attend to some necessary work,
since the rest of the year was entirely too interesting to spend
days and weeks at a time locked inside her study. That was why
the first thing she had done when she had moved into this large
house was to have this alcove built onto the study, so that she

could have her favorite place for working in the same room as her favorite place for thinking.

But now Mira had every reason to suspect that this winter would not be so simple. The dragons would be moving on soon, probably this very day, and she could not yet guess whether Dalvenjah Foxfire meant for her to go with them. She was not entirely sure what she had to offer. She was still a part of the Prophecy. Indeed, she had turned out to be the most important part of the Prophecy, but the possibility was that her own part was done now that the Dark Sorceress Darja had made off with the wrong body. That all depended upon what Dalvenjah should happen to think best. And considering what Dalvenjah Foxfire thought about a certain Kasdamir Gerran, it did not seem likely. Upon reflection, Mira was even less certain that she even wanted to go.

Mira paused and looked up, seeing that J.T. had entered the study. The cat was ambling along in the slow and sleepy manner that his kind practiced to perfection, hesitating halfway through the room to stretch first one long hind leg out behind him and then the other. He leaped up on the other side of the table and seated himself daintily, then began to wash his face for breakfast.

"Tea?" Mira inquired.

"Yes, please."

"Two lumps?"

J.T. glanced up from his washing. "Three, if you don't mind. After last night, I need my fortification."

"You have a sweet tooth worthy of a dog," Mira remarked as she removed the lid from a tray. "Dame Tugg has already brought your kipper."

J.T. bent his head and sniffed the grilled fish daintily before returning to his washing. He delighted in his kipper for breakfast, a beloved delicacy, but being a cat he could never allow himself to demonstrate the slightest interest. Cats saved their enthusiasm for those rare times when they could make complete and appalling asses of themselves.

"So what about it, Jay?" Mira asked. "Did we blow it?"

"That depends entirely upon your perspective, I suppose," the cat answered without looking up.

She stared at him, surprised. "Perspective? I am sure that the

Emperor is pleased with how things have turned out, although he probably could have done without our destroying Alashera."

"That was one perspective that I was not considering," J.T. said shortly. "I was referring to your level of objectivity. If you consider the matter entirely from the perspective of the Prophecy, then it is a good thing that the Emperor made off with Jenny's body rather than your own. If it is any consolation to you, then you might think that you were fated to be an agency for placing Jenny in danger to fulfill the Prophecy to that desired end. In other words, it is better in the long run that it was her rather than you. On a more personal level, of course, it was not a desirable end at all."

Mira frowned, thinking about that very carefully for a long moment. She glanced over at the cat. "Did Dalvenjah know enough to stop this? Or did she want this to happen?"

J.T. paused in his exploration of his kipper. "That is the part that I cannot fathom, for it makes no sense however I turn it. I agree with putting the two of you together, but Dalvenjah seemed to know that something would happen. Her anger last night, however, indicated that she never expected that you would act the way you did, taking Jenny into the South when you knew about the Prophecy. All I can say for certain is this. If she knew that she could not protect both you and Jenny forever, and if there was real danger that the Emperor or the High Priest would realize their mistake and come looking for you, then she had to, in a sense, toss Jenny to them to prevent a far greater disaster."

"What do you suspect, even if you are just guessing?"

J.T. twitched his ears. He was a familiar, a creature of magic that exits to provide information, and he disliked having to guess. "Dalvenjah seems to have been appointed by fate to unravel the Prophecy, and she has to remain objective in her judgement. If she is to resolve the Prophecy and defeat the Emperor and his ilk forever, then she has to play it through to the end. The only way she can control the Prophecy is to invite the Emperor to steal the wrong body for the Sorceress Darja, a potentially fatal mistake on his part if she can then exploit his mistake."

"Then why is she so angry?" Mira asked.

"Because you sprang the trap too soon. The Emperor has

made his mistake, but Dalvenjah was not yet ready to act upon it." He paused, lifting his ears in alarm. "And speaking of a certain malevolent Mindijarah, you are about to have company for breakfast. If you would just open a window?"

"Certainly," Mira agreed.

She rose and turned the latch on the nearest window, then lifted it a short distance. J.T. leaped through, carrying his kipper in his mouth to enjoy in the seclusion of the garden. Mira closed the window and sat down quickly, lifting her cup and saucer to pretend that nothing had happened. Dalvenjah and Allan entered a moment later, and Mira moved to the other side of the table to make room for them.

"Your familiar left without his tea," Dalvenjah said, indicating his cup. "He also had nothing to say that you did not already know. Stupidity is not one of your faults."

Mira frowned fiercely. "There are no secrets from you, are there?"

"Faerie dragons are tremendous natural telepaths," she said. "Your cat knows that perfectly well. He was not trying to hide from me, but to leave you to face any potential wrath."

"The traitor!"

"I have expended my wrath for the moment," the dragon continued. "In fact, I feel in the mood for questions. I might even force myself to answer most of them."

"Oh, my!" Mira had been anxious enough about meeting Dalvenjah again this morning that she could have followed the cat out the window. Now it seemed that she was to be rewarded with privileged draconic information. She hardly knew what to ask. "Was J.T.'s little guess on target?"

"Close enough, considering his limited information," Dalvenjah explained. "Curiously enough, our battle so far has been based entirely upon the direction and misinterpretation of various prophecies. Our enemy has been acting largely upon what they could determine from the Prophecy of Haldephren, made two thousand years ago during the final defeat of the old Alasheran Empire. My understanding is that Haldephren himself does not remember making the Prophecy, but he did die almost immediately afterward."

"It was fortunate for him that someone thought to write the damned thing down at the time," Allan remarked.

Dalvenjah nodded. "That of course is exactly their problem. Not only is their copy of the Prophecy of Haldephren second-hand, but there is that added confusion of meaning inherent in trying to cast a Prophecy in verse. Mortals seem to have this need to cast their prophecies in verse, as if that gives them an added magnitude and veracity. I guess simple prose sounds entirely too mundane to be a warning of future disaster. That is also the problem of the Prophecy of Maerildyn. They have surely heard of that prophecy by now, but I suspect that it seems to them like nothing more than a lot of gibberish."

"Exactly the point," Mira agreed. "I now understand White and Black, Red and Blue. My hair is red and Jenny's is blue, so the final triumph of Light or Darkness depends of course upon which of us got stolen by the Dark Sorceress Darja. But Dragons Gold and Dragons Black Seek to Gain What Each May Lack is beyond me."

"The Gold Dragons are obviously the Mindijaran," Dalvenjah said. "The Black Dragons might not be physically black in the sense that we are gold in color, but Dark Dragons in general. But as far as I know, the Emperor has not yet dared to attempt an alliance with the Dark Dragons. Above all else, he is still mortal and they are not. He will have to command a great deal more power than he has already if he expects to approach them as an equal, for his magic is still very much subservient to their own."

"Even then, he would not get anything from them," Allan added. "He can offer little to entice them to serve him, even if their pride allowed, and he would need control of tremendous magic indeed to be able to command them."

The dragons sat in silence for a time as Dame Tugg arrived, bringing their breakfast in covered dishes on a rolling cart. She set their plates before them and left again without saying a word. For Dame Tugg, not to say a word was so astounding and unusual that Mira stared in amazed silence. The two dragons lifted the lids to their plates and found to their consternation that they each had a dozen kippers.

Mira stared. "My word! Cat food!"

Dalvenjah took a fork and poked at a kipper cautiously. "And on that same subject, they did not know about the Prophecy of the Faerie Dragons until very recently, if they know it even yet. They certainly cannot know how to interpret it."

"You dragons never cast it in verse?"

"In words," she said. "Dragons foresee in their dreams, the gold dreams. The Prophecy of the Faerie Dragons exists only in the form of a dream, a complex series of images that tells its story much better than a few choice words. When you tell the story to someone who has not seen the dream, then only the words are left."

Mira reflected upon that. "Yes, I suppose I understand what you mean. Another question?"

"Yes?"

"What next?"

Dalvenjah laid back her ears, considering that briefly. "I do not know where the Emperor has taken the Sorceress Darja, but I have discovered some disturbing ties between the Empire and the world of Jenny's origin. That is the best place I know to look. But the first problem is to get Jenny's spirit out of Vajerral and into a more permanent form of her own."

"You can do that?" Mira asked.

"I cannot give her a physical body," she explained. "I can restrain her spirit from attempting to find its way into a new life, as the Emperor did with my brother Karidaejan. She is, after all, a faerie dragon in spirit, and that is now her natural course. But I think that I can do much better for her than to leave her a weak and insubstantial ghost. Vajerral and Kelvandor will be leaving with me this very morning for my own world."

"I will not be going?" Mira asked.

"Not to my world, no. Allan will take you and your airship into Jenny's world, where you will wait for us to join you. You will spend that time with Jenny's parents, learning to speak the local language. Then we will see what we can do to resolve this matter."

She paused, seeing J.T. streak across the garden and leap completely over the flowerbed, landing on the outside window ledge so hard that he slammed into the window pane and fell back into the shrubs. She wiggled her ears. "I suspect that your cat wants in."

Mira reached over to open the window, and the cat hurtled through as if he had been kicked. He ran straight up Mira's

shoulder and sat on her head. Then he reconsidered, leaped
across the table and ran up Dalvenjah's back, where he held on
tightly to her horns with all four legs.

"I always wondered why these creatures were called familiars," Dalvenjah said, staring at the cat with crossed eyes.
"They presume upon their familiarities."

"There's a demon in the woods," J.T. insisted, shaking so
hard with fright that Dalvenjah's ears wiggled.

"If you piss on my head, I'll give you to Allan to make
strings for his cello," she said. "Now what is this business about
demons?"

"A big demon," J.T. insisted. "A very big demon."

"What does it look like?" Dalvenjah asked patiently.

"A dragon demon," the cat said. "A real dragon, that is. Not
like you."

Dalvenjah removed him from her horns and tossed him
across the table into Mira's lap. She shook herself, as if to rid
herself of the contamination of idiocy, or at least stray cat hairs.
She turned to Allan. "When was the last time you hunted demons before breakfast?"

"A quarter past three in the morning, last Wednesday," he answered without hesitation. "That was the last time that we were
attacked by demons. You were there. Friday night, it was just
after dinner. And yesterday morning, not half past nine, we
found five winged demons sitting on Mira's own roof like a
flock of crows."

"We did dispatch them," Dalvenjah added, and glanced at
Mira. "Emperor Myrkan seems to think that I represent a major
nuisance. He also seems to think that he can get rid of me with
demons. Well, even vile masters of the Dark Magic can't be
right all the time."

"Yes, Jenny and I happened across one or two demons in our
travels," Mira agreed. "Nasty things, demons. No manners at
all, frightening poor cats."

"Yes, quite." Dalvenjah turned to Allan. "Do you suppose
that we should deal with this very big demon, before it makes a
complete shambles of Mira's shrubbery?"

Allan frowned at his kippers. "What, before breakfast?"

"Yes, I'm afraid so."

"Very well, but let's not make a habit of this."

There was certainly no point in getting the cat to show them where to find the demon. By the time they stepped outside, the demon had found them. Or at least it would have found them if it had been facing the right direction. Even Dalvenjah had never seen a demon anything like this. It looked somewhat like a large, flightless dragon in the middle, with a thick, slightly flattened body supported by eight pairs of legs. Of course, no real dragon had ever had eight legs, and its heavy armor looked more like the segments of a centipede. The most curious thing was that it had no tail, but segmented necks growing out of each end. Each long neck ended in a massive head with fanged jaws that worked from side to side and immense powerful claws like those of a scorpion jointed at the back of the head, perfectly located to pull its prey toward those jaws. All in all, it was an extremely unpleasant thing to discover in the garden before breakfast.

There remained of course the question of how a monster with a head at each end could have been facing the wrong direction. At the moment, it was bent around in a circle with both heads contemplating the problem of eating an ornamental stone cherub. As they watched, one end of the demon bit the head off the cherub and chewed it up whole.

"If two heads are better than one, I wonder how stupid that thing would be with only one," Mira commented. "How does something like that crap?"

Dalvenjah glanced at her. "Would you want that in your yard?"

The other head took a bite from the cherub. The crunching of stone from two sets of jaws sounded like gravel in a cement mixer.

"Are you going to do something?" Mira asked impatiently.

"Should I fetch the pink flamingos?" Allan asked.

Dalvenjah seemed to be considering the problem carefully. "Do you think that we can dispatch it quickly, or should we lead it away for an extended battle?"

"This beggar must be eight to ten times the size of the largest that we have ever fought," he said. "Is its size going to make it that much more resistant to our magic?"

"That has not been the case in the past, but I hesitate to predict with types that I have never seen," Dalvenjah said. "All the same, I think that we should give it a try."

"I might sneak around to the other side of the garden and provide a distraction," Allan offered.

"Be very careful. Distracting a monster with two heads is likely to be a complicated and dangerous task."

Allan moved quietly down the steps, walking gingerly on all four of his long legs. Mira watched him with growing curiosity. If this was his idea of being unobtrusive, then he had to have no idea just how large he really was. Being the smallest breed of dragon by over a ton, perhaps Mindijaran thought of themselves as far more dainty than they actually were. But if Allan's technique lacked subtlety, the stupidity of the demon seemed to balance the scales. The beast was too preoccupied with Mira's lawn ornaments to notice.

Realizing that he might actually slip by unnoticed, Allan stopped short and seemed to consider his options. He coughed, then waited a long moment to watch the demon. When nothing happened, he rolled his eyes and coughed again. One head of the demon spied a marble sundial and both ends moved in with deep, rumbling demonic cries of delight, purring with a noise somewhat like a long train rolling slowly past. Allan looked over his shoulder at Dalvenjah, his ears standing straight up. Getting a demon's attention had never before been a problem that they had encountered; in the past, they usually found it just about impossible to avoid the attention of demons. None of the demons that they had ever met were especially bright, but they did what they were designed to do very well. Ordinarily they would have liked nothing better than to eat little golden dragons. Admittedly, not even Dalvenjah would have ever thought of baiting them with lawn ornaments.

Mira came out from behind the shrub where she had been hiding for a better look. The sight of a faerie dragon teasing a giant demon in her own garden was something that she was likely never to see again.

"You could put on a pointed hat and pretend to be a stone garden gnome," Dalvenjah called softly, watching from the top of the steps.

"You just be ready," Allan called back.

He aimed himself at the middle part of the demon and took a

deep breath, obviously about to release a tremendous blast of flames. He was just at the deepest point of his inhalation when one end of the demon suddenly whipped around and hurtled straight toward him. Caught by surprise, Allan leaped back with a startled cry and fell over on his back, and in the next instant the tips of both pairs of the demon's claws buried themselves in the ground to either side of him. That did not necessarily make Allan feel particularly safe, since those powerful, cherub-chomping jaws were now coming up through the middle. It was such an alarming situation that Allan exploded; all of the fire that he had been saving erupted like Vesuvius. The demon's entire head disappeared in a flash of flames.

Allan was up and running in the next instant, making a very hasty retreat on all fours, although his tail was tucked so far up between his legs that it stuck out in front while his head was bent all the way around to see where he had been. There was perhaps something to be said for having a head at both ends, but not much. Dalvenjah, of course, had not been idle during this time. As both ends of the demon oriented on Allan, she spread her wings to glide to the bottom of the steps, then lowered her head and hurled a fireball directly at the middle of its tremendous bulk. It was no simple dragon-fire but some of her strongest magic, for the fireball was a blue so deep that it was almost black. The demon was consumed almost instantly, burning away in misty blue flames.

"Well, it worked!" Dalvenjah sat up on her haunches, looking immensely pleased with herself. "I am dragon. Hear me roar!"

"You sent it back where it came from?" Mira asked.

"What would be the point in that?" she asked. "I dematerialized it. That is the quickest and most certain way of killing them, and also the easiest. How do you dispatch demons?"

"In actual practice, I've always had Jenny to do it for me," Mira admitted frankly. "The best that I've been able to do is to set spells on our weapons. That, and I can make your clothes disappear."

"Then I should consider myself lucky that dragons are not in the habit of wearing clothes," Dalvenjah said, then turned to Allan as he came up the steps from the lower yard. "You really should be more careful."

❧ PART TWO ❧

The Spirit Is Moved

Evening was just beginning to settle dark and silent as the three dragons descended to the landing outside Dalvenjah's home in the mountains of the world of the Mindijaran. They had left Lady Mira's ostentatious abode more than twenty hours before. Since the Ways between the Worlds delivered the traveler to a corresponding point in the second world and not to his desired destination, by the expectations of their internal clocks it should have been dawn; such was the result of time changes between worlds. Dalvenjah had waited just long enough to see Mira, Sir Remidan and the Trassek twins in *Wind Dragon* follow Allan through the Way Between the Worlds that he had opened. Dalvenjah had her doubts about the quality of her mortal allies, and she thought that she would have little need of them unless she found the need to establish a circus. But Mira was still a part of the Prophecy, and Dalvenjah did not yet know whether or not she might yet be useful.

Dalvenjah's house was an abandoned fortress that she had adapted for her own. It was far less ornate and conspicuous than Mira's great gaudy palace but a good deal more cozy and comfortable, better suited to a dragon's more civilized tastes. It had certainly been home enough for herself and Vajerral, and even better when Allan had come to live there too. Dalvenjah had been fond of Allan from the start, but turning him into a dragon had helped her decide that she wanted to take him home. But now this place reminded her most of Jenny, for reasons that she did not entirely understand. Certainly Jenny had lived the second half of her childhood here, but the girl had been gone, away first at college and then to study with Lady Mira, for nearly the past five years.

Dalvenjah trotted quickly to the front door; faerie dragons were very long-legged and short of body, and they trotted on all fours very well. She stepped inside and silently ordered the magical lamps to full brightness, then glanced about quickly as if to assure herself that no part of her household had escaped in her absence. She turned back at Vajerral and Kelvandor, who were standing about aimlessly just within the door.

"Amuse yourselves quietly," she told them. "I must consult my books on the care and manipulation of disembodied entities. It is not a common subject, since there are not that many dead dragons needing manipulation. Since we have been away for so long, you might see if the kitchen needs any attention."

Vajerral waited quietly, her ears alert, as her mother disappeared into her study and closed the door behind her. "Do you get the impression that the children have been dismissed?"

"I sometimes get the impression that your mother looks upon herself as one of only a very few adults in whole worlds full of children," Kelvandor said as he opened the curtains over the long bank of windows in the back of the main room, looking out from a high cliff into darkness. He frowned. "I know that it is time for breakfast in Mira's world, but why do I have this idiotic craving for kippers?"

"Well, I for one am grateful to be home," Vajerral said as she sprawled her full length on a pile of cushions, her long neck hanging limp. "Mortals are fine, as far as mortals go, but they all smell a little funny. All except for Jenny."

"Jenny was from a more civilized world, from what I understand. Nor was she in the habit of wearing metal and leather," Kelvandor reminded her. "Have you noticed that the ones who wear armor are the least fond of bathing? Except for Sir Remidan, of course. But Jenny was also secretly a dragon, and that might have affected her scent."

"Perhaps. Even Jenny's mother smelled funny, so . . ." Vajerral paused, and her head shot up in alarm. "Hey, watch it! Sorry, I tend to forget about you. And stop talking about me as if I was already dead."

"Jenny, I hardly ever hear you speak anymore." Kelvandor

gently interrupted their odd argument of two people with one mouth. "Why do you never have anything to say?"

"I feel somewhat guilty about asking Vajerral to surrender herself for me," Jenny explained, turning her head away in a reticent gesture. Vajerral had withdrawn herself, allowing Jenny full command of her body. "And, I have to admit, even I tend to forget that I am not already dead."

Kelvandor settled silently on the cushions beside her. He did not want her to know how alarmed he was that she was losing her sense of identity so quickly. Her spirit was doing as well as ever, but her mind, perhaps even her sanity, was reacting to an almost completely passive state of existence. She needed to be separated from Vajerral into some existence of her own, so that she could be able to enjoy at least the freedom of independent motion and the ability to speak and interact for herself. But she ultimately needed the return of a physical form and all the actions and sensations that were familiar to both mind and spirit.

"You have never told me what you think about being a dragon," he said.

"I always knew that I must become a dragon to protect myself from the Emperor," Jenny replied vaguely. "Dalvenjah always insisted upon it, but never enforced it. I see now that it would have likely alerted them to the true nature of the Prophecy."

"Perhaps. But now you know that you always were a dragon, regardless of the form you wore."

"Well, that was surprising," she admitted.

Kelvandor smiled to himself. Jenny was and always would remain Jenny. The prospect of changing form or even existing disembodied did not upset her too much, not when her insatiable curiosity welcomed almost anything that happened to her as a new and challenging experience. A lesser, or more normal, person would be holding up much worse under the circumstances.

"I never worried too much about us, about you and me, because the answer seemed to be a part of the problem," she continued after a brief moment. "The Prophecy had come between us, but I had the assurance that protecting myself from the Prophecy would eventually force me to become a dragon, and that would solve any awkwardness in our relationship.

Finding out that I always was a dragon in spirit actually took away the guilt about the rightness of the whole situation. As I see it now, my heart knew something that was hidden to the rest of me."

Kelvandor made a vague gesture. "What was my excuse for debauchery?"

"Well, get on with it!" Vajerral declared suddenly.

Jenny turned her head to glare at herself, failing in the attempt. "Vay, what the deuce are you talking about?"

"You know where my room is," Vajerral said. "This is your first chance to keep company as one dragon to another. I won't intrude. I promise!"

Her brightly eager expression turned abruptly into one of outrage. "What do you mean, you won't intrude? How can you not intrude? It's your damned body!"

Her long dragon's face underwent another of its instant transformations. "I'll be good. I will just keep quiet and enjoy myself."

Her face returned to infuriation mode. "Enjoy yourself? What the hell do you think the problem is? I don't mind making use of your body, but I don't like the thought of you loitering in the background drinking it all in. I know you promised, but I also know you better than that. You could never keep your damned mouth shut, especially during the hot and heavy parts."

The innocent face returned. "How could I say anything? You would have my mouth otherwise engaged."

"Vajerral!"

"Well, you know what I mean."

The annoyed face returned, but it slowly softened to an expression of consternation. "It's just not that simple. You are a fine dragon, and the best friend I have. But there are simply some things . . . Kelly, you tell her."

Kelvandor had been sitting quietly, looking bemused and wiggling his ears one after the other. "Why can't you ever call anyone by their real name?"

One of them, most likely Jenny, turned to stare at him, so he thought about that very hard. "Vajerral, you simply are not welcome."

"Aw, nuts!" Vajerral muttered, looking vastly disappointed.

"There is more to it than just that," Jenny added as soon as she regained possession of their mouth. "I feel so remote and insulated in your body. No matter how much control you allow me of your body, everything remains so distant. My hearing is muffled and my sight is dim. I hardly have any sense of touch or smell at all. I cannot make love to Kelvandor in your body, regardless of your presence."

"Oh." When Vajerral returned, she made their face look even sadder. Then she lifted her head and perked her ears. "Then can I make love to Kelvandor, and you watch?"

"Vajerral!"

"You sound like my mother," Vajerral said, amused. "Right now, you even look rather like my mother. I was just trying to change the subject."

"Excellent notion," Kelvandor agreed.

They just sat quietly for a long moment, three dragons, two mouths, and nothing to say. Admittedly, the circumstances were a little difficult. Jenny and Kelvandor could not even enjoy a private conversation, much less anything more adventurous. And Vajerral was still just young enough to occasionally find it difficult to relate to adults, at least in quiet conversation. Having been to Jenny's world from time to time, she had learned to appreciate the passive company of the television. Kelvandor, of course, had no idea what a television was, and would have denied that such a thing could possibly work without the aid of magic.

"Do you know what worries me more than anything?"

Kelvandor turned to her, shifting his ears. "What is that? Ah, Jenny?"

"Yes, it's me," she said. "I was just thinking that it is about to start all over again. I had tried to tell myself that I would have a rest from being frightened and anxious. But being stuck inside Vajerral only reminds me over and over that the hard part has only begun."

"Well, there is one important difference," he reminded her. "This time, Dalvenjah and not Mira will be in control."

"Mira does have her methods," Jenny agreed, with obvious reservations. "She does manage to get a lot accomplished, although never quite what she had intended. The worst part is that she seems to be contagious. I recall the sight of you hanging by just your horns from the bottom of that Imperial airship."

"I recall that as well, although by no means fondly."

"How did you get yourself into that one?"

Kelvandor frowned fiercely, laying back his ears. "The last thing I remembered was looping around the back of *Wind Dragon* and seeing you standing completely naked at the ship's wheels."

"I never knew that you were the type of dragon who would harbor a taste for human flesh."

"Ordinarily no, but I always found yours interesting. Of course, I do prefer virgins." He saw that she was regarding him skeptically, and he made a vague gesture. Dragons tried, but as a rule they were miserable at telling jokes. "Vajerral has told me the legends of your world. Actually, the sight of you flying an airship while standing naked in a snowstorm was a startling sight. Of course, a naked human is a startling sight at the best of times."

"You did not object before," Jenny observed.

He bent his neck so that he could rub the side of his muzzle against her own. "Now you can never doubt that my love was true, if I could ignore the way you used to look."

She smiled demurely. Then she suddenly turned her head away, stuck out her long tongue and made an incredibly rude noise. She followed up by trying to glare at herself in outrage. "Vajerral! I am sorry, Jenny, but that was the most sorry excuse for love-talk that I have ever heard. Well, you can still keep your little opinions to yourself."

"And we were doing so well," Kelvandor added, looking so ridiculously dejected that Jenny, although not Vajerral, knew that he was up to something. "You know, if you were to stay quiet long enough, we might forget that you are even there."

Vajerral brightened. "Say, yes!"

A large, tapered hand appeared suddenly, taking Vajerral firmly by one ear and hauling her up from her seat on the cushions. Dalvenjah paused only long enough to glance at Kelvandor. "If you will excuse us, I suspect that I can solve at least part of your problem."

Kelvandor stared, but he remained where he was and even more wisely elected to say nothing. The expression that Vajerral was wearing suggested a very strong desire to protest, but she had the weight of long experience to teach her what Kelvandor

only guessed. Her mother led her quickly and rather unceremo-
niously into her study, pushing the door closed behind her with
a quick sweep of her tail. The study was a fairly large room with
all the things a dragon sorceress needed to ply her trade. All of
the walls were lined with shelves upon shelves of books, and
there was a pile of cushions where she could read, a large drawing table, a selection of her favorite weapons and a large barrel
of cider. The very image of the scholarly dragon at home.

"Take the two of you over there and look in that mirror,"
Dalvenjah told Vajerral, although she went herself to collect a
book from the table.

The young dragon looked around quickly, spying the large
mirror that stood in one corner of the room. It was not a magic
mirror as far as she knew, and it had been in the house for as
long as she could recall. There were no magic mirrors as such,
but a mirror could be a useful tool for the manipulation of visually oriented magic, and some mirrors were magically prepared
for optimum use. Apparently Dalvenjah had already prepared
this mirror for some purpose. Vajerral did not see her own reflection at all but the image of Jenny's lean and rather long-
limbed form. There was room to spare for the girl, since this
was a full-figure mirror for a dragon.

Vajerral sat back on her haunches and hid her long nose behind her arm, as if holding up a cape. "Blah! Blah! Do not be
afraid. All I want is to use your phone."

Then she paused, fascinated to see that every move she made
was copied exactly by the reflection, just as if it was her own.
She lifted one arm and put it down, then the other. Mindijaran
differed from all other dragons in the fact that they were mammals, bearing live young and suckling, although their breasts
were usually fairly small except when they were nursing. Jenny,
being so slender and rangy, was not greatly endowed even as
mortals went. Vajerral jumped straight up, just enough to set
things in motion, staring in amazement as Jenny's breasts jig-
gled in a manner that was strange and slightly horrible to a
dragon. Delighted with the effect, Vajerral began to hop up and
down, flinging out her arms and legs first to one side and then
the other.

Then she hesitated, seeing the reflection of her mother's face
staring into the mirror behind her. Dalvenjah was wearing one

of those quiet, pensive expressions, so it was hard to tell whether she was equally fascinated in the reflection, or containing an anger that was building to an explosion like a volcano, or if she was wondering whether her little dragonet had dried up her brain breathing fire out her ears, or if she was just waiting to make some particularly cutting remark. One of the latter explanations seemed the most likely. Vajerral slowly lowered her head almost to the floor.

"Are you quite finished?" Dalvenjah asked.

"I suspect that I am," Vajerral agreed quietly.

"If you like your ears and wish to keep them, then you just stand right there and do not move until I tell you otherwise."

Vajerral suspected that the threat was serious, for she had certainly feared for her ears often enough in the past, once her mother took hold of them. Dalvenjah made a few magical gestures in the direction of the mirror and muttered the appropriate words under her breath. Then she reached out and snapped Vajerral very firmly on the top of her tail, where a dragon would have otherwise had a rump.

"Now run along, and close the door quietly behind you," she said. "And tell that amorous friend of yours that no one but Allan is to come through that door until I say so."

"But Jenny. . . ."

"She is here with me, now."

Vajerral turned away and made a fairly hasty retreat toward the door. When her mother told her to go then she went, and was glad to be making her escape. But even after she was gone, the image of Jenny lingered in the mirror.

"As fond as I am of Vajerral, I am glad to be rid of her," Jenny said, her voice thin and distant. "At least I think so. Can you hear me?"

"I can hear you just fine," Dalvenjah insisted as she turned back to the mirror.

"Can I ask just one question?"

"And what is that?"

"What happens if the glass breaks?"

Dalvenjah laughed to herself. "You will be safe enough. For one thing, you will not be in there that long. And I am here to intercept your spirit if it should escape."

"And now?"

The dragon frowned fiercely, having a talent for it. "I really should leave you in there to punish you for behaving foolishly."

"Did I really have any choice?" Jenny asked.

Dalvenjah knew what she meant, and considered that carefully. "I do not know what to say. Faerie dragons do not accept the theory of predestination on moral grounds. We are, as you may have noticed, strongly independent and determined creatures. That leads to one of the greatest incongruities of being a Mindijarah, because we are all subject to the gold dreams. From time to time we all dream of the future and know, to varying degrees of detail, what is going to happen. I dream a great deal more than is good for me, and my dreams have the bad habit of coming true."

"Are you explaining or avoiding?" Jenny asked.

"Is it hard to tell?"

"Digression is another of your special talents."

"Then I will be brief, which I find difficult. And I will tell you one of my greatest secrets. Can you handle all of that at once?"

"I am an evicted spirit in temporary residence inside a dragon's mirror, one short step from being honestly dead. I feel that I can handle anything."

Dalvenjah nodded. "Have you ever wondered why I seem to know so much more about the Prophecy of the Faerie Dragons than anyone else?"

"Because you cheat?"

"Right. The Prophecy of the Faerie Dragons was assembled from the dreams that all the Mindijaran had on the same night. My dream was just a whole lot more detailed than anyone else's. So the answer to your question is yes."

Jenny concentrated very hard. "What was my question?"

"Did you have any choice but to act in any way other than you have. So the answer is really no. My mistake. But you have to promise me that you will tell absolutely no one else."

"I promise," Jenny insisted. "But why?"

"Well, there is one thing, of all the monsters and horrors of the hundred worlds, that your Auntie Dalvenjah fears. Your mother."

"Why?"

"Because she is family. I cannot just kill her and be done with it."

Jenny smiled, the idea appealing to her enormously. "But there are a few more things I would like to know."

Dalvenjah arched her long neck, looking surprised. "You seem to think that this is your lucky day. What would you know?"

"Why are you so secretive? I can understand why you could not interfere with the Prophecy before now, but I get the feeling that you still have a few secrets left to play."

Dalvenjah shook her head sadly. "I honestly wish I did. I enjoyed a certain confidence in knowing that the Prophecy was actually working according to plan, as hard as it was to encourage apparent disaster by allowing matters to follow their proper course. You see, I was not allowed to see the conclusion of my gold dream."

"What?" Jenny demanded incredulously. "There was more? What happened, did the gods of good dragons withhold the important part?"

"Not exactly," Dalvenjah admitted, looking decidedly uncomfortable. "You see, I woke up at that moment with an overwhelming need to piss."

Jenny stared in disbelief, then rolled her eyes impatiently. "Do you mean to tell me that the fate of whole worlds hangs upon the capacity of a dragon's bladder?"

"You must understand that Allan had only just become a dragon, and we were still learning how to be romantic with each other. We had stayed up late that night, throwing darts and drinking mead." Dalvenjah made a small gesture of helplessness. "Perhaps even that was meant to happen. Prophecies are notoriously elusive in nature. Perhaps we are not allowed to see exactly what we should do from start to finish so that we may maintain our sense of free will. You wait right there, and I will see about getting you out of that mirror."

"Am I going anywhere?"

Although she had said that facetiously, it did start Jenny thinking about her present situation. From her point of view, she was standing in a perfect replica of Dalvenjah's study, although the wall she faced was missing and a sheet of glass prevented her from stepping out into the real world. She certainly was not frozen in place as she feared she might be, but could move about freely. The fixtures of the room were solid to the touch but she could not feel their texture; there was carpet beneath her bare feet, but it might as well have been smooth floor. But she could not figure out if that was because her room was a visual reflection, an illusion, or because she was only a ghost, with no physical form to respond to anything solid.

Lured by her own curiosity, Jenny crossed the room and cautiously opened the door leading out into the main room. But the room beyond was completely dark, illuminated only by a strip of light through the open doorway. The real main room was of course brightly lit, and Kelvandor and Vajerral might have still been there. This was only the portion that could have been seen in the mirror when the door was open, and the reflection must have been captured at that time and remained hidden after the door was closed. There was even a back of the door, which would have been seen when it opened. But when Jenny reached around the doorframe her hand encountered no obstruction even past the point when half of her arm should have emerged through the wall beside her, which of course it did not. She closed the door quickly and backed away, fearful of what might have happened if she had stepped through, particularly if she had closed the door behind her. She suspected that it would have been far worse than white rabbits and tea parties.

Then the door suddenly opened of its own accord, and no one was there. Jenny was so startled that she jumped back and nearly screamed, although that would have embarrassed her so much that she elected to blush instead. She turned back to the glass wall and saw that her uncle Allan had entered the real study.

"Well, that is safely done," he announced, then paused when he saw Jenny standing in the mirror. As she moved closer to the glass, her apparent height returned nearly to full size. He stared critically. "Hello, Jenny. Nice to see you, I suppose. Do you realize that you are naked?"

Jenny did not see fit to answer, knowing that he was teasing. Allan was a dragon in all ways, which was to say that he hardly cared about her nudity on either a personal or an objective point of view, although some dragons might have had something to say on the topic of aesthetics. She had also lived with these

dragons for years and she had not always been in the habit of
wearing her clothes even then, at least until the novelty itself began to wear off.

"Mira, Sir Remidan and the boys are safely delivered to Dr.
Rex's cabin at the lake," he continued. "Rex and Marie were not
there, but I did talk to my sister briefly on the phone. The faerie
centaurs will see that they stay out of trouble."

"Did you explain matters to Marie and Rex?" Dalvenjah
asked.

"Yes, well enough," Allan agreed vaguely, although he lowered his head and laid back his ears. Even Dalvenjah professed
to be afraid of Marie, Jenny's mother and Allan's sister, although Jenny privately doubted that.

Dalvenjah twitched her ears. "What do you mean, well
enough?"

Allan shrugged. "I told her that Mira would explain."

"But Mira does not speak English."

"Yes, I know," Allan said, beginning to look slightly mischievous and self-satisfied. "Marie is not yet aware of that, of
course. Mira has only a few days to be ready for our arrival, and
magic alone does not seem to be enough. I thought that she
would learn most quickly if she had a very good reason, such as
having my sister standing over her all day and half the night
beating the language into her. Marie is going to be furious to
find out what happened, and I admit to dropping certain hints
that something was up."

"And it will have the added benefit of leaving Mira tame and
biddable by the time we arrive," Dalvenjah agreed. "That was
very sneaky and even slightly cruel. I must say that you have
certainly learned how to be a proper dragon."

She turned abruptly to Jenny. "Why do you look like that?"

Jenny almost flinched from the challenge in the dragon's
voice. "Because I cannot find anything in here to wear?"

"What are you?" Dalvenjah insisted.

"A ghost?" she ventured, knowing that her answer was not
enough.

"Whose ghost?"

"My own ghost, I suppose."

"And what are you?" the dragon asked again. "Are you any
less or any different in thought or mind than you were when you

were walking about in a hundred and some odd pounds of animal? Was the true definition of what you are to be found in the flesh that you have lost, or in the spirit that can never be taken from you?"

"I am still me," Jenny agreed pensively. "Memory does seem to be largely a function of the flesh. My memories already seem distant, and I fear that I will begin to forget if I remain in spirit form too long. But I believe that the essence of what I am will remain forever."

"So it shall be, even after you pass from this life in truth and are reborn," Dalvenjah assured her. "Now, what are you?"

"I am . . ." Jenny paused, knowing that the answer would not be the most obvious one. Then she thought that she understood. "I suppose that I am a dragon."

"Then why do you look like that?"

Jenny frowned as she thought about it. "Strictly speaking, I am the ghost of a dragon. This is the part of me that always has been the same, even for all those years that I thought I was something completely different. But does the spirit really have a form, or is that entirely arbitrary?"

"It is," Dalvenjah agreed. "You appear as you do because this is the way you imagine yourself to look. In your imagination, you do not yet think of yourself as being a dragon. Indeed, you have never seen your physical form as a faerie dragon, so you cannot know how it looks. But for all practical purposes, it hardly matters."

"Then why did you bring it up?"

"To give you something to think about. And to begin the process of teaching you to think of yourself as a dragon. That is now more important than you might think. You must assume the form of a Mindijarah, any form that you might wish, and wear that form from now on. You must learn both the gifts and the limitations of what you are."

Jenny frowned. "So what does that have to do with getting me out of the mirror?"

"You can leave the mirror any time you want," Dalvenjah told her. "I just do not recommend it. When you are outside the mirror you will be nothing more than just a ghost, and subject to the two dangers that any ghost most face. One is the fact that your spirit could easily be captured and commanded against your will."

"What?" Jenny asked, alarmed. "Here, even in the world of the faerie dragons?"

"At this point I will put nothing beyond the Emperor and his minions, and I no longer have the means to predict his actions. Keep in mind that there are very few faerie dragons in this world, which is as large as any. And if the Emperor happened to discover two very disturbing facts, that he stole the wrong body for the Dark Sorceress Darja and that we have maintained your spirit, then he might want you."

"Would he not rather go after Mira and the body that he needs?"

"Of course," Allan agreed. "I have also arranged for fifty of the most capable Veridan Warrior-sorcerers of the Mindijaran to guard her from a very discreet position. Your mother would have a fit if she knew that the woods around the cabin is crawling with dragons. She was having trouble enough accepting Mira, a knight in armor, a talking cat and two adolescent barbarians."

"And the second danger?" Jenny asked.

"Yourself," Dalvenjah said simply. "The mirror protects you from your own natural need—your spiritual instinct, if you will—to complete your passing from this life and seek rebirth."

"Then I have to stay in this mirror forever?" Jenny asked, dismayed.

"No, not forever," Dalvenjah assured her. "I can work the magic that will give you a more solid and secure spiritual form, although not an actual physical body. That is a very difficult thing. It must be done at a very special place of magic, far from here, and I will need the help of a great many dragon sorcerers. That will take some time to arrange, ten or perhaps fifteen days."

"That long?"

"Would you like to go back inside Vajerral?"

Jenny kept quiet, aware when she was well off.

The moon of the dragon world rose full and golden, pouring its cool, magical light into the depths of the dell, illuminating the dozens of faerie dragons that sat patiently on the many stone ledges and steps that ringed the steep walls. Allan stood patiently with Vajerral and Kelvandor as they waited in a silent group a short distance behind Dalvenjah, all of them looking up from the small grassy glade that filled the bottom of the dell, in form very much like a natural amphitheater. Allan had never been here before, but he knew the history of this place. Dragons had been coming here for thousands of years, once as a forum of law and government and always as a place of strong and unique magic. He was certainly dragon enough to feel the electric tenseness that seemed to flow through the ground and fill the air.

It said much about Dalvenjah's reputation, as young as she still was, that so many dragons had not just answered her request for assistance but had come eagerly, willing to help in any way they could. Even Dalvenjah knew only half of them from personal experience, the other half only by name and reputation. She had not requested anyone specifically, and even she was surprised and a bit flattered by the ones who had responded. For his own part, Allan still felt occasionally daunted in the company of true dragons, especially by such a large and august body as represented here, more than four dozen of the wisest and most capable sorcerers and the most powerful Veridan Warriors. It was true that he was now a very capable sorcerer in is own right, and warrior enough to make himself valuable to Dalvenjah in a fight. But such meetings served to remind him that he had not begun life as a faerie dragon, and he had often been fearful that someone would say that he did not have the right to the power, the magic or the immortality that Dalvenjah had made possible for him when he had taken this form.

Of course, that immortality was only theoretical. Considering the lives they led, there was a very good chance that either he or Dalvenjah would be gone within the next century. And considering the struggle they faced in the Prophecy of the Faerie Dragons, there was a strong possibility that neither one of them would survive the next few weeks. Dragons accepted that, secure in the knowledge that they would always be reborn, knowing that the only harsh price that death demanded of them was the loss of old loves.

Dalvenjah stepped forward to the center of the glade, holding a large stoppered bottle of colored glass. For a long moment she stood staring up at the moon as if she awaited a sign, her broad wings folded on her back and her long, sinuous neck lifted. At last she set the bottle securely in a small nest in the deep grass and pulled the large wooden stopper, then took a couple of steps back.

Allan watched with quiet interest, half expecting that a fountain of smoke should emerge from the bottle and slowly take the form of a genie. Because he had actually seen the process before, usually at least once a day since the start of their long journey a week earlier, he knew what to expect. Jenny arose from the bottle after a long moment, flying straight up, at first so small that she fit through the neck with room to spare but expanding in the blur of an instant to her normal size. She settled to the ground to stand beside the bottle and facing Dalvenjah, still wearing the appearance of human form, meaning of course her usual skinny and naked self.

After a few initial jokes about the Jenny that lived in the bottle, they had all become fairly used to the situation. Except of course for Jenny, who considered existing in an immaterial state in a magically protected glass bottle to be only slightly superior to being trapped inside an adolescent dragon. The mirror was better than this; there are few abodes more boring than the interior of a glass container.

"You are not thinking of yourself as a dragon," Dalvenjah admonished.

"Perhaps not very well, but I am learning to do a fine imitation of an imported champagne." Jenny shrugged. "I will do what I can."

"Save yourself the effort for the moment," Dalvenjah told her. "The time has come that we can give you a more durable form. Are you prepared?"

"Is it going to hurt, or anything?"

Dalvenjah hesitated only briefly. "I cannot say how this will seem to you, since magic of this nature is hardly ever needed. It was not recorded how you should expect it to feel. There might be a certain amount of stress, for it is violent magic. But I doubt very much that it will hurt, for you lack the capacity to feel pain as such. Courage and resolution are needed, and in that respect I ask you again if you are prepared."

"In as far as I can be prepared, for this is also beyond my experience and I cannot know whether my courage is equal to the test until the task is done," Jenny answered, then had to try very hard to keep from frowning. Dalvenjah Foxfire's manner of speaking was sometimes as contagious as it was eccentric.

Dalvenjah did not answer, lifting her head high and arching her long neck around to stare up at the moon. It seemed almost to respond to her call, and if it could not pause in its journey then it granted her request, sharing its gift of magic freely. The light that poured down into the bay became brighter and even more golden. The dragons waiting on the ledges lifted their heads as well, staring up toward the stars. The night became tense, filled with magic and a sense of expectation. Then, after a long moment, the dragons all turned their heads as if at an unspoken command, looking down at Dalvenjah.

But Dalvenjah turned her own head suddenly to fix Jenny with a sharp, commanding gaze. "Who are you?"

Jenny drew back a step, so great was her surprise and confusion. She had apprenticed for years in the daunting presence of Dalvenjah Foxfire, and her fearful response was a part of the acquired instincts of her childhood. She remembered too well those spontaneous quizzes, stern questions to be followed by thunder and lightning if she did not know the answer. But this was a part of the magic, she was sure, and important.

"I am Jenny," she answered uncertainly. "Jenny Barker."

"That is only your name," Dalvenjah said sharply, even as a cool breeze moved through the dell, brushing softly through the leaves of the trees. "Who are you?"

"I am just me, a person."

Dalvenjah shook her head impatiently. "That is not enough. Who are you?"

"Right now, I'm a damned ghost," Jenny answered bitterly, then wished that she had not used that particular combination of words.

"That is not true," the dragon insisted. "Your spirit is forever a part of you. Now tell me the truth, and tell me all that you know. Who are you?"

"I am a dragon," Jenny said, remembering what Dalvenjah had been trying to teach her for the past few days.

"You are indeed a dragon," Dalvenjah agreed. That finally

seemed to be the right answer, but not yet enough. "That is the essence of what you are, even if you never knew. You must now take that form as your own, even if only for the sake of the appearance. In your present state, appearance is almost as important as reality."

Jenny had to concentrate very hard, learning from experience that forcing a continuous change in her visual aspect was far more difficult than a momentary illusion of change. This was a matter of changing the way she thought about herself, rather than a convenient form as she wanted others to see her. After a moment her form began to waver and then collapsed suddenly in upon itself, expanding rapidly into the long-limbed, winged shape of a faerie dragon.

"Now at least you seem to know what you are," Dalvenjah remarked. "Now, again, who are you?"

"I am Jenny the faerie dragon," she answered. Then she almost felt herself leave the ground, as if a powerful hand had suddenly taken her in a crushing hold. She could still feel no pain, but she was acutely aware of the tightness that encircled her. For the first time ever, she became aware that she did not breathe.

"For the final time," Dalvenjah insisted. "Who are you?"

"I am Jenny Barker, Sorceress and Veridan Warrior of the Mindijaran," she proclaimed, forcing those words against the weight that was threatening to crush her with increasing force.

It was as if the golden light of the moon had merged and concentrated into a single lash of lightning that reached down, not to destroy her with a sudden blast of immense power but to gather her up in its fiery embrace and make her a part of itself. Jenny twisted frantically in its hold, suspended in that crackling shaft of golden light a few feet above the ground, clawing uselessly with her long arms and legs and moving her wings in long, slow beats. She felt as if she was being taken apart, bit by bit, and then put back together again in the next instant, like a wave moving slowly through her entire being.

Then the pressure returned, not crushing her this time but bearing her down. She drifted back to the ground and, as the pressure increased, she bent her back and long neck beneath the unrelenting stress, bracing herself on her haunches with her long arms spread wide against the ground. She still had no material form, and she could not understand what was happening. She knew only instinctively that she must fight, that the magic would not release her until she overcame it. The magic pressed down upon her even harder, a waterfall of golden light battering her draconic form before it spilled in waves across the grass, vanishing into mist. But Jenny fought back. After a long moment she shouted some inarticulate cry of fury and denial and thrust herself upright, her arms lifted and wings spread. The magic retreated from her, a rush of golden lighting ascending into the clear night sky.

"My, that was certainly theatrical," Dalvenjah remarked. "Jenny, are you well?"

Jenny was not entirely certain, as it happened. She slowly folded away her wings as she lowered her head and peered about in a confused and rather self-conscious manner, as if she had just managed to embarrass herself without even trying. She no longer felt any stress or discomfort, of course. In fact, as the first few moments passed in long silence, she became aware of small, unexpected things. She no longer felt empty and vaporous, but as though she possessed a sense of mass that was in some odd way different, as if she still lacked weight. The ground felt solid beneath her, and a slightly numb sense of touch, of heat and cold, had returned to her. The sense of being isolated, of being a mind without a body, was nearly gone. She still lacked any physical form, but at least she now had the illusion of one.

"Now you are protected," Dalvenjah continued when it became obvious that Jenny had made the transition well. "No one can now capture your spirit and command you against your will. I also doubt very much that anyone could hold you captive physically, since you still have the advantages of your immaterial form. Now we are ready to continue."

"Ready for what?" Jenny asked fearfully.

"Ready for our most difficult task yet," the sorceress explained. "Now we must face your mother. And collect that . . . that Mira person."

❧ PART THREE ❧

Detectives and Dragons

The rift opened with a single point of flame that burned away quickly in a widening circle of fire, filled within by the unending night that was the Way Between the Worlds. The flames were not as easily seen against the cool, bright morning sky as that deep pit of blackness, suspended in the air just over an open, grassy ridge surrounded by the tall pines of the mountain forest. The Way Between the Worlds opened just enough to allow the forms of four faerie dragons to slip through, bright golden with crests of sapphire blue, and the passage closed quickly behind them.

As the dragons gained altitude and circled around, Jenny very quickly fell behind. Inertia wanted to treat her as three hundred pounds of dragon while the wind considered her as insubstantial as tissue paper; Jenny was trying to bend the rules of Newtonian physics, and Newton was out for revenge. She was beginning to appreciate the real reasons just why ghosts were known for their generally bad dispositions. Everyday existence became very annoying when you could walk through a wall but not a stiff wind. She was only able to fly in the direction she wanted by crabbing at a very pronounced angle into the wind, and she gave the surprising and very ungainly appearance of flying sideways. In fact, she was flying sideways.

Kelvandor quickly dropped back to fly by her side, having a hard time himself keeping pace with her uncertain aerobatics. He was in a very awkward position all his own, compelled to offer help, knowing that there was nothing he could do for her, and aware that she might not be in any mood for him to start behaving more like a fearful mother than an understanding mate.

His own situation was not any better for the dream that he had had the night before. He had imagined that Jenny no longer liked him now that they were both dragons. She had declared that she wanted a mixed mating, and had run off with a dwarf.

It was, of course, a ridiculous notion. Dwarves did not associate with dragons of any breed even to this day, not if they could help it. Love did not necessarily conquer all, at least when it came to guarding one's hoard.

The dragons circled out over the lake and came in around the cabin from the side. The place still looked very much as it had when Dalvenjah and a very young Vajerral had come there for the first time, years before. There was one car parked in the usual place, a white imported sports car that could only belong to Dr. Rex, Jenny's father. That reminded Jenny that her mother would be there, and the thought of Marie Barker frightened her so much that she lost her balance and nearly fell. *Wind Dragon*, Mira's airship, was settled in the clearing in front of the cabin. Assuming that the language lessons had gone well during the last three weeks, at least Jenny would be spared the dire necessity to trying to explain things to her mother. Marie would have had time by now to adjust to the fact that her daughter was not only a dragon, but the ghost of a dragon.

Of course, Jenny did regret missing her mother's reaction upon learning that she had once been married to Dalvenjah Foxfire's half-brother.

Kelvandor landed ahead of Jenny and then stood ready to help her if she needed it, knowing that she had the same troubles getting back on the ground as dirigibles and other things that were lighter than air. The thought was well intended but hopeless; Jenny passed right through his arms and landed in a sprawling pile on the ground.

Dalvenjah glanced over her shoulder, wearing one of those adult looks that mothers did best, one of slightly impatient disapproval. She punctuated that by twitching her ears, one after the other. "Put on your monkey suit, Jenny. We do not want to alarm your mother too much."

Jenny concentrated on her monkey suit, wishing that Dalvenjah could find a more beneficent term for Jenny's human form, and after a moment her shape collapsed in upon itself and expanded quickly into the appearance of the person that she had been most of her life. Jenny concentrated again and was able to summon jeans and a light sweater for herself, something that would help in the process of avoiding causing her mother alarm. The illusion of clothes was an easy one for Jenny to manage, since she was used to thinking of herself in clothes. She hoped that she would not be forgetful now that she was once again in mortal company.

When the dragons held back, watching her, Jenny realized that they were expecting her to enter first, another part of the process of avoiding alarm. Jenny had her doubts, but she also doubted that it was important enough to argue. She opened the door.

Of all the sights she might have expected when she stepped inside the cabin, Mira still managed to surprise her. Mira was seated in a large easy chair in the middle of the room as she watched the reruns of *The Jetsons*, a bottle of Bailey's Irish Cream and a bag of Snickers bars at hand. The second surprise was that Mira had shrunk considerably, looking like a child in that large chair. Sir Remidan was nowhere to be seen, but Dooket and Erkin were seated on the floor making castles with the same building blocks that had once been so entertaining to a four-year-old Vajerral.

"Jenny!" Mira exclaimed in English, although somewhat imperfect English. She leaped straight up, standing in the seat of the chair to recapture the height she had lost. "Bosom buddy! Lifelong pal!"

Something about that greeting seemed immediately familiar. Jenny glanced at the television, and remembered *The Flintstones*. Barney Rubble had been fond of saying that. Jenny knew now where Mira had been getting a large part of her language lessons. In her time, even Dalvenjah Foxfire had communed with Kermit the Frog.

Jenny's mother Marie entered at that moment from the direction of the kitchen, still drying her hands on a dish towel. Almost in quiet contempt of Dalvenjah's concern, all she seemed to see was the dragons. "So there you are. If I had known you were coming, I would have cooked a ox."

"I see that everything has gone well enough," Dalvenjah remarked.

"And just how do you imagine that?" Marie asked.

"Well, both of you are still alive," the dragon said, although she was staring uncertainly at Mira. "Indeed, you have, as they say in your world, cut Mira down to size. What did you do, wash her in hot water? Tumble dry?"

"You reverted!" Jenny exclaimed.

Mira shrugged. "There is so little magic in this world, I had to let go of the spell that made me taller. I thought that I should save my magic for more important things."

"Do you mean that this is Mira's actual size?" Allan asked.

"Yes, she used to be a midget in the circus," Jenny explained, forgetting for the moment that Mira might not wish to have that part of her past discussed, at least not in front of the dragons. "They found her doing magic tricks and working as a clown, and took her away to the Academy. Once she had learned enough magic, she decided that she was tired of being so short."

"Tired of being stepped on by dragons," Kelvandor added in his own broken English, which he had been learning from Jenny and Vajerral over the past few weeks.

"Hey, watch it, dudes!" Mira snapped, becoming irritated.

"These smaller breeds are known for their short tempers," Dalvenjah said glibly. She could be a very glib dragon, when she was in the mood.

Marie afforded her a stern glance. "We are not finished with you. Indeed, we have not even started. Certain glib dragons should not be so cocky."

Dalvenjah twitched her ears.

"Now, we are going to have a very lengthy explanation," Marie continued. "There was this funny thing. Allan brought me this flying ship of fools with barbarians, a knight in armor, and a shrinking sorceress who, he declared, would explain everything. But lo, none of these strange people speak a word of the indigenous patois."

"I beg your pardon?" Marie said, looking confused.

Marie paused for a moment as Dr. Rex and Sir Remidan entered the room from the kitchen. The honorable knight was now dressed in a tweed suit complete with a sleeveless sweater and light jacket that had leather patches on the elbows, looking for all the world like an Oxford professor. They were both drying their hands on towels, having been conscripted by Marie as slave labor in the kitchen. Galley slaves, as it were.

Marie turned back to the others. "So after considerable effort, I was finally able to piece together the report that someone had stolen Jenny's body but that she was doing well enough inside Vajerral, and that it all had something to do with the fact that she had been talking with her real father, and that it turns out that I was once married to a dragon who was Dalvenjah's brother, and that you were trying to do something about it. Is that essentially correct, or did I simply misinterpret the message?"

"Half-brother," Dalvenjah corrected her.

"I am half relieved to hear it," Marie said. "But now Jenny stands before us, looking very much the same as always. She does not appear to be a ghost, and she certainly does not look like a dragon."

"Actually, it is a lot more complicated than that," Dalvenjah admitted. "At this time, Jenny is a ghost and able to assume any form that she desires. For as long as she is in this world, it is convenient for her to be human."

"Why is that?" Dr. Rex asked.

Dalvenjah shrugged. "Easier for her to get through your narrow doorways. Allan and I should perhaps have been there to protect her, but this was fated to be. And we were distracted by tracing the source of a secret stronghold of the Emperor and his Dark Sorcerers in a place that we should have never expected. This world, I am afraid to say. For now, it is important that you call Wallick and Borelli and make arrangements for all of us to go to New York. There is someone there whose help I need very much."

"Who is that?" Marie asked.

"Sherlock Holmes."

"Oh." Rex looked perplexed. "Don't you mean London?"

By the time Dave Wallick arrived the next morning, he was by no means alone in wondering if the worthy Dalvenjah Foxfire was completely out of her gourd. She had been in this world often enough to know that there was no Sherlock Holmes. The others tried to tell her that there was no Sherlock Holmes, and that even if there had once been a Sherlock Holmes, he had gone into retirement decades before, way back when Miss Marple was only middle-aged and before Lord Peter Whimsey's habits had gone out of style. Wallick tried to sit her down and have a good talk with her. Surely she would listen to an FBI agent.

He was not successful.

"But you do agree that Sherlock Holmes was a character invented by Sir Arthur Conan Doyle a century ago," Wallick insisted.

"Yes, of course," Dalvenjah agreed easily enough.

"Then of course he is not real."

"That does not necessarily follow. I am a dragon and real enough, and yet you yourself would have once said that I could not exist."

"That is not at all the same," Wallick said, and sighed. "Sherlock Holmes is and always has been just a character in a book, not real like you and me."

"My argument is that he is both, and I must find him," Dalvenjah answered simply.

Wallick watched her for a long moment, and he could see that he was not going to be able to talk her out of this. For her own part, Dalvenjah was watching him just as closely, and she could see that Wallick was not convinced that the necessity of this outweighed the trouble involved. Taking Dalvenjah Foxfire and her Magical Misfits to New York to look for someone who did not exist was asking for endless amounts of trouble; not only could she see this, but she agreed with his concerns.

"The matter is this simple," she said. "The Emperor and his Dark Sorcerers have come into your world. Why?"

Wallick looked surprised, and troubled. "There is either something here he wants, or he is looking for Jenny."

"He was establishing his base in this world long before he captured Jenny the first time," she said. "I doubt very much that he has discovered his mistake, much less looking for either her or Mira. There is something here that he wants."

"Technology?" Wallick asked immediately.

"The obvious answer," she agreed. "But I do not consider that very likely. There is nothing of this world that would be of any use to him. Your technology is too easily subverted by magic."

Wallick glared at her suspiciously. "Are you serious?"

"Yes, quite," she insisted. "By magic, I can deflect bullets or divert ballistic missiles. Anything electronic, especially computers, is very easy to defeat or even control."

Dragon hackers. Wallick found it an especially frightening thought. "So what do they want here?"

"I have no certain idea. That is why I must find Sherlock Holmes."

Wallick had known even before he had started that he was going to give in, if he could not convince Dalvenjah that she was making a mistake. He had been with her during her battle with the steel dragon Vorgulremik and he felt compelled to trust her, even in the face of certain logic. Indeed, everyone was inclined to go along with her quest for fictional detectives, even if certain members of the party doubted the results. Allan trusted her, as did Jenny, based mostly upon long familiarity with her ways. Kelvandor trusted her, but he did not understand this matter of people who did not exist, and he would have been just as willing to set out for Camelot to find Captain Nemo or Peter Pan. Vajerral had no opinion one way or the other, while Dr. Rex was hoping that they did find Sherlock Holmes.

Getting four dragons, much less all the rest of this retinue, to New York was in fact the hardest part. Wallick would have preferred to make arrangements to fly them all to New York in a cargo plane, and he would have left behind as many members of this menagerie as possible. Dalvenjah Foxfire, of course, had other plans. She wanted everyone present and accounted for, and *Wind Dragon* near at hand in the event that they had to move quickly into another world. The only ones who would not be going along were Marie and Rex, who were given the task of staying behind with the faerie centaurs and the mortal students at the school of magic and guarding against attack. In other words, Dalvenjah had invented an excuse to be rid of them.

Wallick considered briefly the thought of disguising *Wind Dragon* as a blimp; her length was adequate, but her four wide lift vanes made that difficult. The only solution seemed to be having the airship flown by a polar route, as it were, flying only at night and along a carefully plotted course that kept her away from areas of large population and bright lights, until she was well into northern Canada. Then she would proceed east until she reached the Atlantic and finally south over open ocean until she came to the area of New York. The fact that *Wind Dragon* moved fairly swiftly and in complete silence was very much in her favor, while the fact that she was the size of a small airliner was not. There was no point in trying to arrange for an escort, since planes or helicopters would have only attracted attention with their noise. As long as the military was warned to leave her alone, *Wind Dragon* should be safe enough.

The next problem was the matter of a pilot. Mira was now too short to see over the siderails well enough to steer the ship safely, and she could no longer command enough magic to keep the ship in the air for long. She had already had to release the spell that kept her tall for absence of magic, for mortal magic was in very short supply in this world and even a sorceress of her caliber was suffering from the lack. She had not been expecting it when she had brought *Wind Dragon* through the Way Between the Worlds following Allan, and she had nearly lost control of the ship before she could get it landed. The dragons would have to pilot *Wind Dragon* on this journey, since their command of the dragon magic had not been as seriously effected.

Not only was Jenny on the duty roster, she found herself at the top. Being dead had not seriously interfered with her abilities as a sorceress. Indeed, it had not been nearly the inconvenience that she would have expected. And she was the only one of the group with experience at flying the airship, something that the other dragons were curiously hesitant to attempt. Of course, it was presently a little hard for the others to think of Jenny as one of the dragons, even the other dragons. For as long as they were in this world, Dalvenjah agreed that it was best for her to remain in her "monkey suit."

Wind Dragon remained Mira's ship, and she was still the captain. She remained on the helm deck with Jenny through the night, helping in any way she could with navigation, evasion and simple companionship. Since Jenny no longer had any need for sleep, and was immune even to tiring physically, she ended up flying the airship through most of the night. Mira would stay devotedly at her side, or at least in the near vicinity. She explained that since she now weighed about half as much as she had at her full height, she needed only half as much sleep, and she could do that during the day easily enough and avoid the company of Dalvenjah Foxfire.

"It is also a very effective plan for losing weight, half of what you weigh in only three weeks," she added. "The way that everyone in this world worries about losing weight, I could bottle it and make a million dollars. But then, what would I do with a million dollars? Dollars mean nothing where I come from."

"With the side effects of your diet plan, you would have to get out of this world in a hurry," Jenny remarked. "Besides, I have a better diet plan. I don't weigh anything."

"Dragon, ho!" Dooket called from the bow.

Jenny could see the dark form of a dragon approaching rapidly out of the night, circling wide around *Wind Dragon*'s bow and then moving up to fly level with the helm deck. The three dragons had been taking turns flying ahead of the ship and scouting the way. She finally recognized Allan.

"Lights ahead. A small town, at least," he reported. "Turn some twenty degrees to north."

"Right away!" she answered as she spun the rudder wheel, and Allan hurried on ahead to scout the way. Jenny watched the compass as the ship came around, then straightened *Wind Dragon* in time to stop her slow turn at twenty degrees. She saw that Mira was watching over the side, having to stand on a wooden box that she kept handy. "We will be out of this world soon enough. Then you can restore your height."

"Oh, I don't really mind being short," Mira insisted.

"You don't?" Jenny regarded her skeptically. "For something that you don't really mind, you went to some trouble to do something about it."

"That spell is completely passive, and no trouble to me at all," Mira insisted as she turned to lean back against the rail. "I will admit I used to be very embarrassed about being short, especially when I was a child. The worst was when I was in the circus. Then it seemed that my main worth to the world was as a freak, an object of mirth and self-ridicule. Doing a few magic tricks allowed me to be something besides just a clown. But I got over that very quickly once I went away to the Academy at Tashira. Given the chance, I soon discovered that I was very happy with myself. I never would have bothered to do anything about it, except for one thing."

"What is that?"

"Being very small in a big world is damned inconvenient,"

she explained. "It kept getting in the way of the things I wanted to do and enjoy. I had learned that I no longer hated being a midget, but I can't say that I ever became particularly fond of it either."

Everything went well enough. Jenny was pushing *Wind Dragon* as much as she dared, getting more than sixty knots out of the ship. Dalvenjah had the dragons scout their way carefully, so that the airship could take to the sky late in the afternoon before it was completely dark, and continuing on sometimes an hour or so after sunrise. Fortunately it was autumn, and the nights were getting longer.

Dalvenjah considered that they were far enough north at the end of the third night that they could go on through the day, flying now without stop, and she even took the wheels herself for a while. She insisted that at least two dragons fly ahead of the ship during the day, looking for areas of habitation. She was also less worried about being seen, as long as *Wind Dragon* was out of range of most guns. Wallick had already arranged for both the American and Canadian military to ignore the airship, and the civilian authorities along *Wind Dragon*'s flight path had been discreetly warned that no one should be alarmed if they happened to observe the test flight of a special "stealth aircraft." Mira had been instructed to keep her ship high enough that no clear details of her unusual design could be seen.

Jenny still found herself piloting *Wind Dragon* almost the entire time. She did not tire either physically or magically, and so she also had no need to rest or recover. Flying the ship was less boring than hovering about watching someone else fly it. And as long as she was at *Wind Dragon*'s wheels, the dragons were free to scout ahead or to rest.

The last part of the journey had promised to be the most difficult, but the answer turned out to be simplicity itself. *Wind Dragon* settled into the sea just out of sight of New York Harbor and waited for night. Then, with her lift vanes and stabilizers carefully packed away and her running sails raised to catch the wind, the airship slipped quietly into port surrounded by an escort of Coast Guard cutters, looking very much like any of the other sailing ships from a past century that occasionally came to call. The sails were of course only for show, since *Wind Dragon* was not a sailing vessel and could not easily be tacked. Jenny was actually driving the ship with its propulsion vanes, and her only problem besides fighting the drag of the wind on the sails was holding the ship's speed low enough to keep her landing struts hidden in the water. *Wind Dragon* was a functional hydrofoil, whether or not that had been the intention of her builders.

Mira was standing on her box at the siderail, captivated by the lights of the city. "My word, I must have died and gone to heaven. This place is bright and gaudy beyond my wildest dreams."

"I have died," Jenny remarked. "Spending the rest of eternity in New York is one thing, but I don't know that I would call it heaven."

They were directed to a dark and remote section of the naval shipyards, their destination illuminated in a sudden wash of lights. Jenny held the ship dead in the water for a few minutes while the Trassek twins furled the sails and unstepped the masts and cranked down the wheels in the landing struts; then she drove *Wind Dragon* straight up a concrete launching ramp and into the open doors of an empty warehouse. The two FBI agents Wallick and Borelli came aboard as soon as the boarding ladder was released, along with a tall man none of them recognized.

"So, you made it," Wallick declared. "Any trouble?"

"None at all," Jenny insisted.

Dalvenjah Foxfire emerged from the hatch leading below, turning and ascending the steps leading to the helm deck. The tall, quiet man who had come aboard with Wallick and Borelli took a step back as she approached. He had obviously been warned about the dragons, but he understandably found the sight of his first dragon to be a little overwhelming . . . or at least disconcerting. Dalvenjah was much larger than most people, as small as she was for her kind, but also a creature of rare beauty in bright gold with emerald eyes and a sapphire crest.

"Everyone, this is Clark Bowenger, with the FBI locally," Wallick said as dragons continued to emerge from the lower deck. "He is here to help convince you that there is no Sherlock Holmes."

"I hope that he is also here to help me find Sherlock Holmes," Dalvenjah remarked tartly.

"From our point of view, it is the same difference," Wallick assured her. "The only thing that worries us is how long you intend to look for Sherlock Holmes before you're ready to admit that he does not exist."

"If things go well, I will only need a couple of hours," she insisted. "I will need some way to travel unobserved about the city. Myself, Jenny, also Allan and Mira, if that can be arranged."

"That should be easy enough," Bowenger assured her. "I already have a large delivery truck standing by. When do you wish to start?"

"It is very late tonight," the dragon mused, mostly to herself. She seemed to come to some decision. "Tomorrow, then. What is a likely time that two dragons can move between your truck and a building without causing too much trouble?"

"Right now, actually," he said. "It really is not that late, only just past seven-thirty. Do you suppose that Mr. Holmes will still be receiving visitors at this hour? If you're not ready tonight, then I would recommend waiting until this time tomorrow night."

"I am ready," Dalvenjah said, then looked around at Sir Remidan. "Would you mind making certain that the boys finish settling this ship? I am going to take the ghost and the midget to meet Sherlock Holmes."

Hardly half an hour had passed before a large, brown delivery truck came to a stop at the main doors of a small but very expensive apartment building in a fashionable part of the city. There it sat for a long moment, dark and silent. The driver, Clark Bowenger, glanced at his companion in the front of the van. Wallick shrugged, and they both turned to look over their shoulders at Dalvenjah Foxfire.

"This is the place," she insisted.

"Are you absolutely sure?" Bowenger asked.

"Have you ever known me to be wrong?" she asked.

"Not in my half-hour of experience, no."

"I was asking Mr. Wallick."

Wallick sighed heavily. "When you asked that question, I was thinking of the first time you came into this world and went looking for the most powerful sorcerer you could find."

"Was I wrong?"

"No, but you couldn't have convinced me of that for the

longest time. That is why I went along with this business, no matter how certain I am that you must have kibbles in your brain."

"Thank you for that unqualified vote of confidence," the dragon remarked wryly. "Why do we not just step inside and see if your good faith is to be rewarded, no matter how certain you are that it will not be."

Wallick and Bowenger stepped out of the truck and stood for a moment looking around, trying so hard to look inconspicuous that anyone watching would have probably called the police. For one thing, people who drive delivery trucks do not normally wear business suits. There was no one else to be seen on either side of the street on that block, although there were a few farther along in either direction. Since things were unlikely to be any better any time soon, they hurried to the back of the truck. Jenny was waiting outside the closed doors.

"How did you get out?" Bowenger asked.

"I stepped through the doors," she said. "I am dead, you know."

There did not seem to be any point in arguing. Wallick opened the rear doors of the truck and the dragons leaped out, hurrying to the main doors of the apartment building that Bowenger held open. Last of all Wallick reached in and lifted out Mira, setting her on the ground. It was undignified, but so was climbing down the bumper.

"So this is what you FBI agents out west do," Bowenger remarked as they followed the entourage into the building.

"When we aren't after horse thieves and other odious desperados," Wallick said.

"Don't you mean ornery?"

"That is a word I save for dragons."

They entered the main lobby of the building just in time to see the elevator door close on the two dragons. That was enough to lead the two agents to the edge of panic, especially Bowenger. He had assumed that his role was that of supervisor or at least guide and he was beginning to feel that he had lost control of the situation, a common complaint of people who had to deal with Dalvenjah Foxfire. Bowenger was beginning to think of some of his own words for dragons. Even admitting that there was not enough room in that one small elevator for them all, he still thought that he should have gone first. Of course, there was also some virtue in getting the dragons out of the lobby as quickly as possible. Fortunately Jenny had the second elevator waiting by the time they arrived.

"Follow that elevator?" she asked as she waited for them to enter.

"How do you know which floor?" Bowenger asked.

"Mystic divination or logical deduction?" Jenny inquired, and pressed a button. "Dalvenjah said that they would be waiting on the fifth floor. I thought we might look there first."

The two agents were both beginning to have the same thought at about that same time. How did Dalvenjah know where she was going? They had both thought that she would wander about the New York area for a while looking for a person who did not exist, but she did seem to have a very definite idea of her destination. The doors of the elevator opened at last and they found the dragons waiting just beyond. Wallick pushed out quickly ahead of the others, hurrying to intercept Dalvenjah.

"Don't you think that I should go first?" he asked. "Just in case . . . I mean, perhaps I should warn Mr. Holmes about you dragons first, so that we do not startle him."

"Perhaps you should, if it makes you feel any better," she agreed. "And just in case there is no Sherlock Holmes, we do not want to frighten some unsuspecting person unduly."

So much for trying to put anything over on Dalvenjah Foxfire, Sorceress and Veridan Warrior of the faerie dragons. Wallick remembered being told not to make the common mistake of talking to crazy people as if they were stupid; it only upset them. Just then the nearest door opened and a portly gentleman in white hair and a three-piece suit stepped out, then stopped short when he saw the company that was keeping in the hall.

"Ah, Watson?" Wallick asked cautiously.

"No, Svensen," the gentleman said in an accent that was not English. He nodded politely and stepped back within his apartment. Then, with a final glance at the two dragons, he closed the door.

"Perhaps I should lead the way after all," Dalvenjah said impatiently.

Wallick stepped back to allow the others to pass. Bowenger

stood quietly at his side. "Watson, indeed. I'm not entirely certain, but I think that we just frightened the Swedish Consul half to death."

"Well, he reminded me somewhat of Nigel Bruce," Wallick said defensively. "That's all I know about Sherlock Holmes."

"Are you saving any new words for your dragons?"

"Exasperating comes to mind," he said. "It's a fairly common word, but it has the virtue of five syllables."

By that time Dalvenjah had reached the door she wanted, and she knocked boldly. There was the wait of a long moment, enough time for the two agents to arrive, and then the door was opened by a most unusual man. He gave the appearance of being tall, for he was very light and lean of build, but graceful and strong like a dancer. If this was indeed Sherlock Holmes then the descriptions of him had not been quite right. His eager, hawkish look was mostly a matter of expression, for the true delicacy of his features was hidden by a demeanor that was alert and cunning, even predatory.

"Ah, so it has come at last," he said sadly, seemingly not at all surprised to find a dragon on his doorstep. "I suppose that you should come in quickly."

"It is perhaps not what you think," Dalvenjah told him as the others filed in. "I am not of your world."

"You say that as if you mean it to be reassuring," he remarked as he closed the door, although he was obviously surprised. "The faded Realm of Faerie of this poor world had only limited contact with the other worlds, and the gates closed as the last dregs of faerie magic died away, long ago."

"But there were survivors even yet," she assured him. "I have myself sent most of them to safety, years ago."

Their curious host afforded the group a slow, appraising stare as they took their seats in the main room of the large apartment. The furnishings of the room were elegant enough in a rather stolid sense, the furniture itself heavy and primarily in dark woods. The room, although large, had a cozy, almost self-contained look, giving the sense that the cold wind of a winter's night howled outside.

"You two gentlemen are Federal agents, probably FBI, although I would not put this matter beyond the CIA, when dragons are involved. You are definitely local," he said to

Bowenger, then turned to Wallick. "But you are not, and I would suppose that you have come here recently from some very different climate, possibly one of higher altitude."

"Sherlock Holmes," Wallick muttered to himself. "I am Dave Wallick, and this is Clark Bowenger. FBI."

"This young lady is of Scandinavian descent," he continued, turning next to Jenny where she sat beside Mira on the sofa. "I also perceive that you are a sorceress, that you are not mortal despite appearances, and that you are doing a very good imitation of life when you are in fact a ghost."

"Bingo! Jenny Barker. My father was a dragon."

"How did you know that she is a ghost?" Mira asked.

"Because she has no scent, as your dragon friends could probably tell you. And you, my most remarkable woman." He actually bowed to her, and kissed her hand. "You are mortal and a sorceress, but not of this world. Are you perhaps responsible for this dear girl?"

"I am indirectly responsible for her current condition," Mira admitted, unexpectedly blushing from the chivalrous attention.

"I see. Are you a medium?"

"At the moment, I happen to be a small."

"Ah, Mira," Dalvenjah interrupted. "If you will excuse her, she has a very limited familiarity with the local language, and an attention span to match."

"And I hope that you will excuse me as well," he added. "You do know of my habits, I am sure, even if only indirectly by reputation."

"Are you Sherlock Holmes?" Wallick asked, unable to contain the question any longer.

"No, I am not, nor have I ever been," he answered directly. "For all practical and convenient purposes, I am Malcolm North, an English expatriate who has been living in this country for some years. Some ninety years to be specific, although that is not commonly known. But you may call me Sherlock Holmes, if that is your wish. I suspect that you will anyway. Would anyone care for tea?"

"Oh yes, please," Mira agreed eagerly, and turned to Jenny. "Did you know that they have tea in this world? Well, of course you do."

"Since you seem to be the one who knew where to find me, perhaps you can explain things to your friends," he suggested.

"Yes, certainly," Dalvenjah agreed, pleased to explain her own brilliance. "I became acquainted with the stories of Sherlock Holmes during my past visits to this world, and I had noticed something unusual from the first. In every description of Holmes that I have read—the original Holmes of Arthur Conan Doyle, of course—everything about his appearance and manner suggested to me an elf. That led me to realize that the literary Sherlock Holmes had to have been based upon an elf, in particular a wise and learned elf lord, one who had grown old with the world and knew all its secrets. Someone who had lived among men for a thousand lifetimes and knows them better than they know themselves."

"That is so," Holmes called from the kitchen. From the sounds, he had just set a kettle of water on the fire. "In a very distant past I was Lord Alberess of the northern kingdom of the elves. But my kingdom was crushed beneath the ice of the north, the advancing glaciers of the last Ice Age as you mundanes would say, long ago. That left me homeless and without purpose. Then, as the first kingdoms of men arose in the south, a certain remedy to my boredom seemed to suggest itself."

"To make a long story short, you eventually found yourself in England just over a hundred years ago," Dalvenjah continued. "Just in time to meet a young writer named Arthur Doyle. Whether you intended it or not, you must have made quite an impression upon him. Your centuries of wisdom, logic and learning were far beyond those of mortal men, the exact qualities he wanted for his perfect detective. The Sherlock Holmes of the stories, of course, had to be mortal to seem believable, but that only made his abilities seem even more amazing."

"What do you mean, an elf?" Bowenger asked. "I thought that elves were tiny, cute little things, and naked. I've read Xanth novels."

"Xanth novels?" Wallick demanded incredulously. "Get real, man! Go read some Tolkien."

"I may have outsmarted myself on that account," Holmes said, ignoring them both. "Sir Arthur had already published the first story by the time I knew what he intended. Then he kept writing more and more. He insisted that I should not worry, that this Holmes business was just a minor fad that would pass soon enough, and everyone would have forgotten the name of Sherlock Holmes within the year."

"But it soon became awkward, I suppose," Dalvenjah said. "Your resemblance to Sherlock Holmes was obvious enough to those who knew you, especially those who knew that you were acquainted with Arthur Conan Doyle. Soon, even people you had met only for the first time began to notice. Changing your identity did not help. Eventually you thought of coming to America, where everyone thinks of all Englishmen as unusual."

"Precisely so, although I fear that I am never entirely free of the name of Sherlock Holmes," he said as he returned with the kettle and a tray of cups. "If you will excuse me for remarking upon it, but you seem to possess a keen intellect equal to that of my literary alter-ego."

"Thank you," Dalvenjah replied. "It is a great pleasure for me to say that you are certainly no slouch yourself. If anything, Arthur Conan Doyle failed to do you justice."

"If the two of you are quite through preening like a pair of hens," Allan suggested. He was not entirely sure whether this had turned into a meeting of their mutual admiration society, or if they were simply sharing a private joke between them.

"As odd as this may seem to outward appearances, your particular command of the language clearly identifies you as a native speaker," Holmes told Allan as he poured a cup of tea. "For you, little lady, I would anticipate two large spoons of honey with your tea, and a small amount of Irish Cream."

"How did you know?" Mira asked suspiciously.

He glanced over at her. "Admitting that you are not familiar with the tales of Sherlock Holmes, I thought that you might have guessed by now from our conversation."

"Conversation?" she demanded. "I can't understand half of what you say!"

"Jenny could translate everything into words of one syllable," Dalvenjah remarked.

"She could as easily translate into my own language," Mira remarked testily as she accepted her tea. "I speak the language as well as anyone could hope after only three weeks of magical memorization and daytime television, and I endure enough insults from this dragon as it is."

Holmes frowned. "My good woman, surely there is no reason for you to be so short."

Mira just glared.

"A poor choice of words, I agree," he admitted. "It takes no great feat of logic to conclude that you are here for my help. What may I do for you?"

"That is a very long story, as they say," Dalvenjah replied.

"And one that will have to wait," Bowenger added. "We need to get these dragons back out of here while it can still be done without their being seen. We do have very fine accommodations prepared for them down by the shipyards. The rest of you are free to come and go as you need."

Holmes regarded him suspiciously. "If you don't mind, I think that I would first like to know just who is in command of your little expedition."

Bowenger sighed heavily. "I've been firmly instructed to assist Dalvenjah Foxfire any way I can and not to question or interfere in her actions no matter how strange they may seem."

"All of the resources of the FBI?" Holmes asked.

"As well as the CIA, various New York area police departments, the postal service, the armed forces, and the United Nations Security Council."

"The postal service?"

"They make wonderful spies."

Holmes looked thoughtful. "Is this situation as dire as all that?"

"Apparently so."

"Excellent. Sherlock Holmes should not come out of retirement for anything less."

They certainly had not expected trouble that night, but they found it waiting for them when they returned to the warehouse at the docks. Dooket and Erkin, Mira's two allegedly barbarian henchmen, had decided to make a trip out on the town and had simply disappeared from the area of the warehouse. There were three essential problems with their little wenching expedition. First was the fact that they barely spoke a word of the local language. To make matters worse, they were still dressed as barbarians, including weapons and armor; that was their idea of how to impress girls, and it tended to work in certain worlds.

Last of all was the fact that they did not have the slightest idea of how to conduct themselves among the natives. Dalvenjah had not considered it necessary to instruct them in such matters, rightly believing that they did not have the wit or subtlety for the task.

Bowenger got on the phone immediately. As a credit to his abilities, he had them tracked down in only four calls. As he returned to the others, it was hard to tell from his expression whether he was appalled or amused.

"They must have been picked up only minutes after they left here," he said. "They went straight to the nearest bar and made such a spectacle of themselves that someone called the police right away. It was an Irish pub near the waterfront, and they were too strange even for that crowd. Dooket was throwing daggers at the dartboard, while Erkin was telling women that he was a federal mother's milk inspector."

"They went along peacefully?" Mira asked.

Bowenger nodded. "They apparently thought the policemen were taking them somewhere to pick up girls. When the police tried to get some story out of them about who they are, it seems that they got scared and decided to tell the truth. Right now, they have a suite all their own on the sixth floor of City Hospital."

"The mental ward," Allan explained to Mira and the dragons.

"Well, they should feel right at home," Jenny quipped.

Mira engaged one of her quaint little expressions. "I know that I will regret this for the rest of my unnatural life and probably a good deal longer than that, but I suppose that I do need them back. Is that possible?"

"It can be arranged," Bowenger said. "Would you be willing to testify that they are sane?"

"Heavens, no!" Mira exclaimed, then she looked chagrined. "Well, if I cannot say that they are sane, I might as well turn myself in also. People have been telling me all my life that I must be insane, but I always assumed that sanity must be a state of mind."

"Then we should . . ." Bowenger paused and stared at Mira, wondering if she had meant exactly what she had said. "Then we should hurry. You will have to come along with me. Can you be discreet?"

"My word, the questions this man keeps asking!" Dalvenjah exclaimed.

Mira glared sullenly. "Oh, piffle!"

Retrieving the truant barbarians was simple enough, once Bowenger showed his credentials and invented an elaborate story to explain their obvious eccentricities. Dooket and Erkin, he explained, were the sons of the Ambassador from Ruritania, very new to the country and not yet aware that they should not wear their native costumes and weapons in public. Their unusual stories were the result of a practical joke that had been perpetrated upon them in their innocence; their English was actually so poor that they had not known what they were saying.

"Ruritania, eh?" the doctor remarked as he signed the release. "You know, their story sounds better than yours."

"Truth is stranger than fiction," Bowenger said tightly. Something had gone wrong with his little plan, but he hoped to bluff his way through with that tough, no-nonsense professional attitude that agent cadets were required to practice in front of mirrors until they had it right. Department motto: Posturing Saves Paperwork.

"If you're going to go to so much trouble to convince me that this is none of my business, then I'll take your word for it," the doctor said. "If those two are of any worth to you, you can have them."

Jenny and Mira were waiting outside with Holmes; Sir Remidan had elected to remain with the airship, not really trusting the locals, and the dragons had no choice. Jenny had been telling Holmes what she could of the history of the Alasheran Empire and of the schemes of the Emperor Myrkan and the High Priest Haldephren, especially of Mira's and her own journey to Alashera, where they had unintentionally destroyed the entire island/city and Jenny had become a ghost . . . in separate incidents. The matter of the Prophecy of the Faerie Dragons was a difficult one to relate, since she did not understand it completely herself. Holmes did, once she had explained everything she knew. In fact, he seemed more impressed than ever with Dalvenjah Foxfire's cold logic.

Bowenger returned at last with the two barbarians, who were looking both confused and contrite. They were also dressed in more conventional clothes, which Bowenger had wisely re-

membered to bring along, their various pieces of armor, mail
and leather packed away in canvas bags that they carried.

"So there you are!" Mira declared. She took the boys aside
and proceeded to chastise them thoroughly in their own language.

"She reminds me oddly of the Empress Cleopatra. They are
of very similar stature, although Cleopatra was more tall and
more round," Holmes mused. "If she finishes any time soon,
there is a certain restaurant I know that should still be serving. I
do not intend to ask much for my services, but a dinner or two
should not be out of the question."

"Of course. I have a company credit card," Bowenger said.
"Strictly off the record, what would you ask for your services?"

"Two things only. First, I intend to stay with these dragons
for as long as they will have me. Second, when the quest is done
and the dragons return home, I wish to accompany them."

"You will be leaving us forever?" Bowenger asked. "I feel
like we've only just found you."

"Perhaps not forever," Holmes answered, choosing his words
carefully. "I have been in this world for more centuries than I
care to recall. I will not say that familiarity has bred contempt,
but it has engendered a certain degree of boredom."

"I think that I can assure you that no one on this end will attempt to interfere with your plans. But you will have to convince Dalvenjah Foxfire. She seems to be very much in charge
here."

Mr. Holmes's restaurant was still open. It was not particularly
large, not particularly expensive, and not at all crowded at that
time, all very important considerations as far as Clark
Bowenger was concerned. A couple of tables were quickly
pushed together, mostly so that the Trassek twins could be located as far as possible from the adults. Mira stared in consternation at her menu, her passing familiarity with the language
not quite up to the task as far as reading was concerned; Dooket
and Erkin put their menus on their heads and pretended to be
Chinese. Jenny just looked quietly distressed.

"Are you not hungry?" Bowenger asked discreetly.

"That is an understatement of vast proportion," she explained
quietly. "I not only lack the need but the capacity to eat. One advantage to being dead is that you will never starve to death."

"Order an appetizer," Holmes suggested. "Something that the rest of us could quietly remove from your plate."

The waiter came to take their orders very quickly, in the process somehow quietly removing the breadsticks, crackers, and little packages of sugar and coffee creamer from within easy reach of Mira's two bodyguards. He returned a couple of minutes later with their drinks. Mira regarded her glass cautiously for a moment and even sniffed it, but she did not dare drink.

"What is this?" she asked at last.

"Tea," Jenny said.

"Are you sure? There's ice in it."

"That's iced tea. People here like it that way."

"Tea with ice in it?" Mira mused, and made a face. "And just when I was beginning to think that this was a civilized world."

"That brings us eventually back to the discussion at hand," Holmes reminded them, then blinked as a soda straw wrapper hit him in the nose. The twins, who had been aiming at Mira, giggled nervously, but he chose to ignore them. "The whole matter seems to focus on this Dark Sorceress Darja. Why does the balance of victory or defeat rest upon her return to life? Who is she?"

"The records are unclear," Mira said. "In the days of the ancient Empire, she appeared suddenly long after the Emperor Myrkan and the High Priest Haldephren had already come to power. She spent a lot of time standing about at the Emperor's side, and she traveled around with Haldephren learning to do really atro . . . attol . . . nasty things. The only really funny thing was that in the defeat of the Empire, they killed her themselves and left her spirit in some safe place to await their own return."

"There was something different about her," Holmes said, speaking mostly to himself. "Her spirit was something valuable. Something to be protected. But how in the world does the fact that she is in the wrong body alter her influence upon the future? A body should, for her purposes, be just a body, once the previous owner is evicted."

"Nothing about my body would be an advantage to her," Mira said. "At the moment, I have to ask waiters for phone books to sit on."

Holmes waved that aside impatiently. "That we know already. It is not a matter of any advantage in having your body, although I am not as convinced as the Sorceress Dalvenjah seems to be that the unexpected disadvantage of inhabiting Jenny's body is quite that important. You misunderstand my question because I did not say aloud exactly what I was thinking. What is Darja going to do that will be upset by the fact that she is not aware that she inhabits an immortal form? It has to be something magical, and of prime importance to their cause. That is the thing that we must discover."

"I'd have thought that you would have it all figured out by now," Bowenger said seriously.

Holmes nearly laughed aloud. "I might allow you to call me by that name, but I am not the Sherlock Holmes of legend. Even if he was here at this very table, we would both withhold judgement until we have heard everything there is to know. So, what do we know so far? They wanted a very specific body to return the Sorceress Darja to life. They have the wrong body, and they do not know that. They are apparently doing something in this world, the very reason that Dalvenjah Foxfire has come to consult me. Now, put it together and what have you got?"

Mira shrugged. "Bippity Boppity Boo?"

"Where do we begin?" Jenny asked, ignoring her.

"Right here, in New York," he said. "Dalvenjah says that her own trail has led here. They are at a disadvantage here, unaccustomed to the ways of this world, lacking in magic and unable to move freely. If we can discover what they want here, in a world without magic, then the other answers will be much easier to find. I just wish that Dalvenjah had some clue about where specifically we might begin."

"Ah-ha! We know!" Dooket declared, and then both of the Trasseks began babbling furiously in their own language.

"What is it?" Holmes asked.

"I'll try to make sense of their ravings. I've had a lot of experience with that," Jenny said, and she and Mira both spoke with the two barbarians for a long moment. She turned at last to Holmes. "They say that when they were in jail, they overheard two men in the cell next to them speaking in the Alasheran language."

"Are they certain of that?" Holmes asked suspiciously. "From Jenny's story, I suspect that it is a language that none of you actually speak."

Perhaps Erkin understood what he said, for he quickly pulled out a folded piece of paper and passed it to Mira. At the same time, Dooket was offering some explanation.

"Dooket says that they recognized too many words for it to have been a coincidence," Mira reported. "They wrote down everything they heard, and it happens that I do speak the language."

"Well, they are not only clever but reasonably literate," Holmes remarked.

Mira read through the page quickly. "It's mostly a lot of nothing about lawyers and such. Yes, here we have something. When they get out, they are expected to return to the warehouse of the blue fish."

"That makes no sense," Bowenger mused.

"No, you must remember the circumstances," Holmes said. "If these people are indeed servants of this Emperor Myrkan, then they are most likely of very little importance or they would not have foolishly gotten themselves arrested. They might speak the local language well enough to get by, but they would have little reason to learn to read. They probably find their way about the city by visual references of their own invention. If there is no warehouse known by the name Blue Fish, then I would suggest looking for a warehouse that has the symbol of a blue fish somewhere about it."

Bowenger nodded. "I can get on that first thing in the morning."

"Find out from those two barbarians which cell this was in relation to the one they were in, and discover for me who they were—or at least who they claimed to be—and why they were arrested," Holmes added. "Then we may have to pay a visit to their lawyer and threaten him with anything from heresy to high treason, as long as we get him to talk to us."

"It might be easier to send Dalvenjah to him in the middle of the night, just like the ghost of Jacob Marley," Bowenger said. "I've had a fair amount of experience with lawyers. The smart lawyers are almost always the honest ones, since they make a better living winning cases for honest clients. The stupid lawyers have to bite and scratch and get themselves involved in dirty games, but they tend to be too cocky and stupid to know when they've gotten into more trouble than they can handle."

"I could go," Jenny offered. "Being a ghost, I can poke around his office all night if I have to. If I can't find what we need, then Dalvenjah and I could try Scrooging him at home until his bell cracks."

Bowenger frowned. "That is breaking and entering, at the least."

"That's only half right," she told him. "I don't have to break anything to enter, and I'm immune to alarms, cameras, and all forms of personal injury. Besides, if he is in deep with the Empire, then Dalvenjah might not frighten him quite as much as you expect."

❧ PART FOUR ❧

The Battle of New York

One of the disadvantages of being a genius super-sleuth is the pressure of live performance. A great detective operating in real life is like a magician on a stage: unless he pulls the rabbit out of the hat on clue, he feels that he can lose his credibility with the audience very quickly. The greatest problem faced by the Elf Lord Alberess, alias Malcolm North, alias Sherlock Holmes, was that he was competing with the reputation of the greatest fictional detective who had ever lived. Well, who had ever lived on paper. The fictional detective has the advantage of having a writer who already knows how the crime was committed, the identity of the villain, and how the story ends, and who can even invent new witnesses and clues along the way should his sleuth run into trouble. Mr. Holmes envied his fictional counterpart. At the same time, he would not have wanted to have been Sam Spade.

The trouble from the first had been a lack of information. Agents of the Alasheran Empire were in this world; they had even been found in New York. Holmes had been given the problem of discovering where they were and why they were here, and he simply had nothing to work on. The two agents that the Trassek twins had overheard in prison had been rescued by a lawyer who firmly believed that his services had been retained by an international shipping firm, and his statements had survived the careful probing of both lie detectors and dragon magic. The names and addresses supplied by that same lawyer had led nowhere. The one thing that remained was the possibility that the warehouse of the blue fish could be found.

Holmes had long since moved into the apartments that had

been arranged for the off-worlders, meaning of course the dragons and Lady Mira's strange crew and company. Such was the state when Clark Bowenger arrived early in the morning of the fourth day with no idea how to proceed. The apartments were in fact a group of unused offices in one portion of a building, decked out with inexpensive and rather dated-looking furnishings so that it had the appearance of some cheap hotel. The first thing he found was that Holmes was playing his violin, just like in the story. What was surprising was that Allan was accompanying him on the cello, although the only way that the dragon could play it comfortably was to sit back on his tail and hold his instrument up to his shoulder like a violin. Not wishing to interrupt, Bowenger went into the next room to discover that Mira, J.T. and the Trassek twins were watching *Yogi Bear*. Jenny was sitting on the ceiling.

"What are you doing up there?" he felt compelled to ask, knowing that he would not like the answer.

"Pennants," she explained simply.

"Penance?"

"No, pennants," she insisted, and showed him. She was trying to attach a Mets pennant to the ceiling with tape.

Bowenger had to step aside as Dalvenjah Foxfire came shuffling into the room, walking slowly and heavily on all fours, dragging her tail and almost dragging her head, it hung so low. He knew that the dragons had been flying over the city at night, hoping to sense the presence of Dark Magic somewhere below. She looked more like a dragon who had tipped a few too many bottles. Dalvenjah ignored him completely and kept going, eventually disappearing into the kitchen.

Bowenger turned to Holmes, who had just arrived from his impromptu concert with the dragon. Both of them were still carrying their instruments. "Did the fictional Holmes learn to play the violin from you?"

"Of course," Holmes insisted. "Before I became Sherlock Holmes by accident, I enjoyed a very successful career as a concert violinist. You have heard, perhaps, the name of Paganini?"

"Used to play shortstop for the Yankees?" Bowenger asked suspiciously. Holmes often teased him about having been famous people of history, since both he and Wallick had wondered about that. Holmes also insisted, when he had answered that very question frankly, that he had always preferred to take an interesting but anonymous role in history.

Dalvenjah came shuffling back from the kitchen at that moment, this time walking awkwardly on her hind legs so that she could carry a mug of cider and a large roll stuffed with cheese and roast venison. A nutritious part of this complete breakfast. She glanced up only briefly at Jenny, who was still sitting on the ceiling, and sighed heavily.

"New York, the town that never sleeps," she said, and stuck out her long tongue to make a rude noise. She glared at Allan. "All of us were flying all night long."

He shrugged. "I awoke to the sound of strings. I just had to join in. Do you have any idea how long it's been since I've played Mozart?"

"I awoke to the sound of strings. I just had to get up, whether I wanted to or not." Dalvenjah paused a moment to stretch her neck in a long, slow wave that began at the top of her neck and rolled down the full length of her tail. "Is there any hope in asking if there is any news?"

"No, there is not," Bowenger told her simply.

Dalvenjah stretched her wings, spreading them both as wide as they would go and then holding them half-open while she fanned them furiously, working the deep flying muscles in her chest. The exercise created quite a little bit of wind. Jenny, who had been drifting back down from her perch on the ceiling, was caught by surprise and sent tumbling across the room and through the door, tossed like a piece of paper.

Dalvenjah frowned. "I resent every passing day that Jenny must be left in that disembodied form. I must do something about it."

"I am going to do something about it," Holmes said. "The nightly reconnaissance of the dragons is a good idea, in as far as it goes. Your advantage is in your command of dragon magic, the strongest magic any of us have. Your disadvantage is that you are obliged to keep yourselves some distance above a rather large and brightly lit city. Now, I believe, is the time that the rest of us who possess some magic go out for a closer look of our own. I possess some small faerie magic even yet, and Mira has held her remaining magic in reserve. But most important, J.T. is a familiar with the ability to detect all sources of magic, and Jenny still possesses her full dragon magic."

"Not only that, I have the ability to go anywhere and move unseen," the girl added eagerly.

"Besides, it is time that Sherlock Holmes takes a more direct part in the solving of this mystery," he continued. "Since the real Sherlock Holmes is not here, then I must do my best."

Bowenger looked very concerned. "Do you mean to say that you intend to search this entire city in the company of a talking cat, a midget sorceress and a ghost?"

"No, just the waterfronts."

"Oh, well! I cannot tell you how much happier that makes me feel."

Jenny had made the acquaintance of elves of many types in her travels, and she knew they were capable of many great and wondrous things. She did not normally think of elves as driving cars, certainly not the white compact van made out to look like a florist's delivery truck that Bowenger had supplied. Thinking about him as Sherlock Holmes did not help; then she would have expected a horse-drawn cab. One of her two consolations was the fact that she could not be hurt in an accident; being dead had its advantages, aside from its devastating effect upon one's sex life. Her other consolation was the fact that Holmes seemed to be a very good driver.

"Where should we look first?" Jenny asked.

"Well, I have been thinking about that," Holmes said as he drove, watching the rows of dark warehouses and dusky, cluttered shops roll past. "I am, of course, working on the assumption that they faced the same requirements that we found when we arrived. I admit that they might be landing their airships elsewhere and then entering the city by more conventional methods. But if they are forced to make a quick escape out of this world, then they must have their own ships at hand. The only way I can conceive that they could have gotten even one of their ships within the city is the way you did, sailing it into the harbor and then parking it inside a warehouse. That of course means a waterfront warehouse, a private one in their case, and the fact that we have been looking for a warehouse known as the Blue Fish seems to support this. I suspect that we will find them not far from our own base."

"That sounds reasonable," Jenny agreed. "Those are some amazing deductions on your part, I must say."

"Elementary, my dear child," Holmes replied, then frowned. "Damn the man. I never used to say that."

"Arthur Conan Doyle?"

Holmes smiled slyly. "It amuses me now to think that he spent the last years of his life looking for ghosts."

"Magic ahead," J.T. warned suddenly. "Still some distance yet, at least at walking speed. As this thing moves, no time at all."

"Then I suppose that we should walk," Holmes said as he directed the van into the nearest parking space. "What manner of magic are we discussing?"

"Mortal magic, definitely," the cat replied. "I also sense something far nastier, but I cannot say just what. Possibly demons."

"What would they want with demons in New York?" Jenny asked.

Holmes shrugged. "Protection against muggers?"

He parked the van against the curb and they all climbed out, trying their best to look inconspicuous. That was not exactly a word that one would have chosen to describe their little group. Holmes looked exactly like Sherlock Holmes, or perhaps David Bowie's older brother. Mira, striding forth with her absurd, congenial arrogance, looked like a cross between a hobbit and Auntie Mame. Jenny was the most normal-looking one of the lot, and she was a ghost. Stranger still, they all appeared to be following a black and white cat. In fact, they were following a black and white cat.

They passed slowly up the street, ignoring the frequent stares they met as they stalked unobtrusively toward their prey. Jenny kept thinking that it was getting about time to quietly retreat and go for help, setting Bowenger and the FBI to discover what information they could, or consulting Dalvenjah and Allan about their next step. But Mira and Holmes seemed so sure of themselves that she could not bring herself to interrupt. Jenny had learned to distrust Mira's judgement some time ago, but Holmes represented a strong second opinion that she could not ignore. They proceeded a full block past old, dusty brick buildings, making their way boldly through a scattering of silent, evil-looking people who watched them like hungry predators. That was what she liked about being in parts of New York where you definitely did not belong; did you ever notice how the eyes seem to follow you? She found herself checking to see if her wallet was still in her pocket, reminding herself that her pants were an illusion.

Holmes stopped suddenly at one corner and pointed. "There, you see? The Blue Fish?"

What he indicated was a small, disreputable-looking bar squeezed tightly between a group of old, run-down buildings across the street. The name of the bar was the Blue Dolphin, complete with one of the animals in question leaping over the waves, all rendered in flickering blue neon.

"Of course," Jenny said. "There are no aquatic mammals at all similar to whales and dolphins in Mira's world. Then could this be the warehouse you were expecting?"

"It could be," Holmes said guardedly, watching the immense warehouse that seemed to fill the entire block on that side of the street just ahead of them.

"There is one way to find out," Mira declared, and turned abruptly to the nearest person. "Yo, homeboy! What be these digs?"

Holmes, Jenny and even J.T. turned away, as if pretending they did not know her.

The young, rather tall man—looking at the moment easily twice as tall as the diminutive sorceress—turned to her. He might have been a reasonable person at all times, or simply too startled and amused at the moment to take offense. "Just an old warehouse. All I know about it is that it's for sale. Has been for years. You looking to buy?"

"So what are you, dude? A real estate agent?" She flipped him a coin. "Hang loose, brother."

Mira turned to the others, who were all giving her their best "Are you quite finished?" look. She shrugged. "I don't want to sound like a tourist. Besides, there is one thing I learned when I was very young. When you're a cute little tiny person full of cute little spunk, you can get away with any shit."

Holmes glanced at Jenny. "She became like this watching television?"

Jenny considered that. "No, she always has been like that. Television only taught her to do it in English."

He turned and glanced up the alley. There was only the harbor to be seen at the far end, and about halfway down the ramp and platform of a loading dock for trucks that could be backed down the alley. Holmes stood for a moment, contemplating this matter carefully. They had their source of magic, obviously a hidden stronghold of the Empire. He could suppose, but he could not know that this was in fact the only stronghold of the Empire, or even the main one. He could bring in the dragons now and have done with it, and possibly never know the truth until it was too late. In spite of his misgivings, he thought that they should go in for a better look.

"Well, I suggest that we see if anyone is at home," Holmes declared confidently, as if that was the most logical thing in the world for them to do next. It was not logical but he did consider it necessary, which possibly meant that it really was logical after all.

Mira shrugged. "Sounds great to me."

"It is a good day to die," J.T. added solemnly, like an old Indian.

Neither Holmes nor Mira cared much for entering the alley, as wide as it was. There were only two ways out, one at either end, and it could become a very effective and dangerous trap if their enemies came at them from both sides at once. J.T. was not greatly worried, knowing that he was small enough to find some way to escape, and Jenny was not at all concerned for herself. Since she was immune to physical attack, able to go anywhere she needed with ease and possessing strong dragon magic, she was considering whether she might return to New York when this was all over and set herself up in the superhero business. Unlike the comic-book superheroes, however, she was still trying to think of some way to make the business pay.

"There is one thing that I've been wondering about for the past couple of days," Mira ventured as they walked quietly along the alley.

"And what is that?" Jenny asked.

"If a nudist accidentally sees you naked, should you be embarrassed?"

"Mira!"

The near end of the loading dock was the flat side where trailers were backed up for loading, so they went around the ramp on the far side and sent J.T. on ahead for a quick look. There was only a single wide door that rolled up overhead, now closed up as tight and silent as a bank vault. Holmes followed the cat to the top of the loading platform a moment later and found that the door was securely locked, although it seemed to his trained eye that the lock was very large and heavy and not nearly as old as the door, as if this one had recently replaced a smaller lock.

"This loading ramp has been used in the past two days at the latest," he said, indicating a small patch of greasy liquid. "That is hydraulic fluid, probably from a forklift or similar machine, and you might notice that very little dust has collected on the surface."

"A forklift," Mira mused. "I've never had any trouble lifting my fork. The problem is knowing when to put it down."

"I also detect a faint scent not unlike mustard," Holmes added.

"What would that indicate?" Jenny asked.

"Hot dogs."

He bent a moment to look at the lock, then took a small leather case from the inside pocket of his jacket that Bowenger had reluctantly given him. He opened it and spent a moment inspecting the small, slender tools that it contained. He had a good theory of the working of locks but, unlike the literary Holmes, he had very little actual experience. Mira stepped up quietly to look under his shoulder.

"Let me give it a try," she said after a moment. "I have had experience with this. Besides, I'm short enough that I don't have to bend over much to see the lock."

"Do you intend to return yourself to full height when you leave this world?" Holmes asked as he gave her the case of tools.

"Yes, of course. I have lots of neat clothes at home that don't fit my present height."

"Like your Alasheran party dress?" Jenny asked, teasing her quietly. The Alasherans had apparently believed that bare breasts had a definite place in high society, and they had adapted their fashions accordingly.

Mira ignored her.

As it happened, Jenny was thinking about something else. To be specific, she was thinking that it would be very easy for her to step through that door and unlock it from the inside . . . if it could be unlocked. At the same time, she was hesitant to point out anything so obvious to the faux Sherlock Holmes, as hard as he was trying to live up to his image. And as for Lady Mira, bent over only slightly while she picked and prodded at that lock, Jenny simply did not have the heart. Instead she aimed her own dragon magic at that lock, imagined herself making the proper gestures of command, and the lock made a very loud and satisfying click.

"Ah-ha!" Mira declared, and stepped back.

J.T. glanced up at Jenny; being a familiar, he was never fooled by the use of magic. For once, however, he chose to keep his mouth shut, as much as she knew how he would have liked teasing his mistress.

"Now, perhaps we will have just one quick look at what is inside," Holmes said. "Very quietly, now. Guards with guns and big dogs would be the least of our troubles, if we are caught."

He took hold of the handle in the center of the door and slowly lifted it all the way up, with only a minimum of creaking and clanging. The effort was wasted, unfortunately. There was a dragon just inside the door. It was not particularly large as far as real dragons went, although it was a giant compared to even the largest of the faerie dragons like Allan and Kelvandor and it must have weighed twice as much. Its legs were shorter than those of the rangy Mindijaran and it was more massively armored, deep metallic silver in color.

Holmes turned to Mira and Jenny. "Is this anyone you know?"

Jenny shook her head. "That's a male Karravethi, a silver wyvern, the largest of the breeds of wyverns. You sometimes see them in the world of the faerie dragons."

"Indeed? What is the difference between dragons and wyverns? It cannot be size, unless faerie dragons are really wyverns."

"Well, some do argue that Mindijaran are an intermediate

form between the true dragons and wyverns," Jenny explained learnedly. "Wyverns are civilized, meaning that they live together in communities, they make things and in most cases they even read and write. Most dragons, except of course for our very urbane faerie dragons, are too predatory to live like that."

"Is that a fact?" Holmes turned to the bemused wyvern. "New York is a strange place for such a fine fellow as yourself. Why in the world would you be in the pay of the Empire?"

"Pay is exactly the word," the wyvern said, curiously in English. "These Alasherans think a great deal of dragons, even wyverns, and they are willing to pay fortunes for your service and they don't even expect you to serve the Dark. If you want to get ahead, you need a good hoard."

."Indeed. Well, it has been very good to meet you." Holmes reached up for the handle of the door. "Please excuse us."

He pulled down the door very quickly until it slammed loudly shut, and Jenny reversed her previous spell to lock it.

"And what do you suggest, Mr. Holmes?" Mira asked.

"I do believe that we should run like hell."

It seemed like very good advice. Holmes jumped down from the flat end of the boarding platform, logically selecting that end because it was the closest to the street, then paused a moment to lift Mira down from the top. They would have probably been better off using the ramp. Holmes stepped back onto J.T.'s tail, causing the cat to protest rather shrilly, which in turn caused him to drop Mira. A moment later a large wooden crate exploded through the center of the door and hit the brick wall of the building across the alley, exploding in a shower of splintered wood and skateboards.

"Skateboards!" Jenny exclaimed. "What would agents of the Empire want with skateboards?"

"I doubt very much that the contents of that crate were anything the Empire had intended for its own needs, but goods placed in this warehouse for some other owner," Holmes said. "But they might now offer us a means to escape, since we can hardly run all the way back to the van. I suggest that we each procure a skateboard."

"A person could die waiting for you to say what you mean," Jenny complained. In fact, the wyvern was at that very moment ripping the door apart from the inside. "The rest of you go ahead. I have to fight that wyvern."

"Dear child . . ." Mira protested, but Jenny interrupted.

"I am a dragon, remember," she said as she assumed her dragon form. "I am also a ghost, so I am in no danger. Go get the cavalry."

On skateboards? Jenny thought to herself. Get real.

Holmes selected a skateboard, aimed it down the alley, then leaped aboard and pushed away. If he did not exactly look graceful, at least he was competent, although Jenny suspected that he had never ridden a skateboard in his considerable life. She had spent an entire year of her childhood learning to do as much. One sight you certainly do not see every day is an elf riding a skateboard. Mira followed as well as she was able, with J.T. standing upright on the board behind her and holding tightly to her right leg, although she needed levitation and magical enhancement of her strength and balance to keep herself going.

Jenny turned her attention back to her own problem. The wyvern would be coming through that door at any moment, and wyverns could generally move much faster than skateboards. A faerie dragon was more than a match for any wyvern, but Jenny had never tested her ability as a fighting dragon, much less the ghost of a fighting dragon. About the only effective weapon she had at her command was her flame, which was something even a dragon's ghost could do. Since everything about her appearance was entirely arbitrary, she increased her size until she was larger than the wyvern. Perhaps, between bluff and her immunity to damage, she could hold her own. She could sense at least a dozen wyverns inside that warehouse, now that they were no longer hiding themselves.

The warehouse door peeled inward in two different directions, pulled by the powerful hands of wyverns, and the armored head and long neck of a wyvern appeared through the opening. Jenny arched her own neck and released her best flame, just to show what she could do, and the wyvern afforded her a very startled look. Unfortunately, he did not look particularly frightened.

* * *

Holmes came to the end of the alley and brought his skateboard to a reasonably smooth stop, pausing a moment to look along the street in both directions. Mira saw no reason to hesitate, or at least there was nothing she was able to do about it. She shot across the street at full speed and just in front of a large truck, the cat clutching her leg screaming in terror, and disappeared into the alley across the way. Holmes gave his skateboard a kick and started after her, but Mira returned a moment later. He caught her by the arm, swinging her around in a circle three times before he was able to get her stopped.

"What about Jenny?" Mira insisted. "This might be a trap for her, if they know they have the wrong body."

"Why would they want her?" Holmes asked. "They would be after you to give your body to the Sorceress Darja, and simply throw Jenny's away. For now, I suggest that we get back to the van, before anything else happens."

It was a little late for that. Even as they stood there in the middle of the street, the large front doors of the warehouse were thrown open with a crash and the nose of an airship rolled out into the street. It really was not a very large ship, at perhaps forty feet only a fraction of the size of even a schooner like *Wind Dragon*. Nothing larger than that could have navigated the streets of New York, rolling on its struts, even with its lift vanes folded against its hull, although the stabilizers in her bowsprit were rigged for flight. Worse yet, there were half a dozen archers in her bow.

"Time to go," Holmes said. "Hold on, Lady Mira. I am going to try to get us away from here by employing a little elfin magic."

"What are you going to do?" J.T. asked. "Make cookies?"

Magic no longer came quite so easy to Holmes as it once had. If nothing else, he had not practiced what little was left of his magic in a great many years. A great many centuries, as a matter of fact, but it worked. Using levitational magic much the same way that airships did for forward propulsion, he began to move forward with increasing speed, pushing Mira before him. She had all she could do to stay on the skateboard, its wheels buzzing and snapping on the pavement.

"Mr. Holmes, this was a very stupid idea," Mira shouted, certain that she was going to fall at any moment.

"Do you want to hear another stupid idea?" J.T. asked. He was holding to Mira's leg, looking back. "I believe that we need to go a lot faster. An airship is trying to pass us."

An arrow suddenly skipped off the pavement to one side, and Holmes glanced back only for a moment. The airship was slowly gaining on them, now less than thirty yards behind. The archers were lining up on her bow for some serious target practice, and at this range they would not continue to miss for long. He increased their speed just a little, then glanced back when he saw their white van flash past. It was too late for that under any circumstances, although he did not at all care for a running chase through the streets of New York all the way back to the FBI warehouse, certainly not on skateboards. He had just one thought. While his own mode of transportation was hardly very maneuverable at high speed, an airship was even less so. The ship behind him was the size and weight of a large truck, but without power brakes, power steering, and with its pilot trying to control the vessel from the rear.

"Left, Mira," Holmes warned with an uncharacteristic economy of words.

Mira looked horrified at the thought, and J.T. obviously liked it even less, but it was too late to protest. At the next intersection they executed as wide a turn as they could manage into the next street, which had the added disadvantage of being one-way in the wrong direction. There were only three cars and those moved quickly to one side of the street as Holmes aimed their skateboards right up the middle. That was just as well for the cars, since the airship hurtled around the corner a moment later, moving so fast that the two inner wheels lifted briefly from the pavement. One archer, preoccupied with aiming an arrow, hit the top of his head on a traffic light and put himself out of the action.

"Right, Mira!" Holmes warned at the very next intersection.

He was hoping that his rapid and unpredictable changes of direction would cause the ponderous airship to overshoot its turn or possibly even overturn itself. His best hope, he knew, was to lose the airship in traffic, but there was a disgusting lack of traffic at that moment. Holmes had a sudden thought and brought their skateboards around in as tight a circle as he could manage as they entered the intersection, ignoring the screams of the frightened cat, until they were facing back the way they had

come. Holmes at least had to crouch low to pass beneath the
hull of the airship, and then they were clear. He remembered
Mira saying that airships were tricky to steer running backwards, and that their thrust vanes gave very little power in reverse. He suspected that they would go around the block before
they would try backing up even a short distance.

Holmes turned them back onto the first street with every
hope that it would soon take them back to the Navy warehouse
and the faerie dragons. The sound of a very loud horn immedi-
-ately behind them was nearly enough to cause all three to leap
from their skateboards, and they glanced back just long enough
to see a large and rather impatient truck coming up quickly behind them. It was actually not all that fast for a truck, but by
skateboard speeds it was very fast indeed. Worse yet, there were
two large wyverns a hundred yards or so ahead, ready to grab
them as they went past. It seemed certain that the truck would
get them much sooner.

"Bend down very low," Holmes ordered.

"Only J.T. can bend down low enough to go under that machine," Mira said, but she still complied.

"That is not what I have in mind."

The truck closed the distance very quickly, and its bumper
connected with Holmes's protruding rear end. The result was
surprisingly similar to hitting a tennis ball with a hammer, and
the skateboarding trio hurtled through the grasp of the waiting
wyverns, who then had to move very quickly to get out of the
way of the truck. Holmes kept them moving along quickly with
his magic; he was as surprised as anyone that they had managed
to stay atop their skateboards after that little exercise. It was just
as well, since at that moment he could not have run. For that
matter, he doubted very much that he would be able to stand up
straight for a while.

"That was certainly using your head," J.T. remarked facetiously.

"Do you, perhaps, know the meaning of the term *sacrificial
lamb*?" Holmes asked him politely. "Under the circumstances,
it involves throwing a smart-mouthed cat to the wyverns."

"Yarg!" Mira exclaimed.

It was a very forceful and well-intended *Yarg* and it got their
attention immediately, and they suddenly became aware as

Mira had that the bowsprit of an airship was moving into the intersection just ahead of them. The airship that had been following them must have been forced to its best possible speed to move ahead and cut them off, in spite of their assistance from the truck. It was just as well that they were already crouching, for they passed beneath the bowsprit with only inches to spare. The truck that had been following them, of course, did not have the capacity to crouch, and it impacted into the hull of the turning airship with a tremendous crash of breaking timbers. The ship's forward right strut was broken off in the impact and the bow collapsed heavily to the pavement, an added strain that broke the ship's hull completely through at the point where it had been hit by the truck.

But they were not out of the woods yet, meant of course only as a figure of speech. The two wyverns were coming back and this time they were in the air, hurtling between the tall building to either side of the street. This time Holmes could envision no easy solution to the problem; the wyverns had the supremacy of air power on their side. He was beginning to think that it was about time to abandon the skateboards when three of the faerie dragons dived suddenly at the pair of wyverns and sent them into a very rapid retreat. Kelvandor circled back to follow the three on skateboards, shouting down words in Mira's language as he passed. His English was the most imperfect of all the dragons.

"He said to turn right at the second intersection," Mira translated without being asked.

Easier said than done. Holmes had been concentrating on making them go forward as fast as he could and he now had them moving along at a fair clip, but he had never given a thought to the matter of stopping. At least by the time they came to the street the dragon had indicated, they had slowed enough to make the turn with some difficulty. He had noticed by then that all traffic on the streets had come to a stop, and there was no one to be seen walking in that immediate area. By the sounds of sirens, seeming to fill that entire side of the city, all of New York was under attack. Of course, the eternal battle of Good and Evil is not just another gang fight.

As they came out between the buildings, they saw *Wind Dragon* sitting on the waterfront before them, her vanes rigged for flight. Dooket and Erkin, once again in armor, were standing in the bow of the airship with their crossbows while the two FBI agents, Bowenger and Wallick, held rifles and wore bulletproof vests. Dalvenjah leaped from the helm deck as they approached, spreading her wings to slow her fall.

"What? Dalvenjah Foxfire was flying *my* airship!" Mira exclaimed. Then her skateboard hit a crack and she was sent rolling, having fortunately waited until they were nearly stopped before she decided to fall.

"Get on board," Dalvenjah said simply, then picked Mira up and tossed her over the siderail. She treated the cat similarly. "Mr. Holmes, you have been busy. We just wanted to know where they were and what they were up to. Now there are wyverns and airships all over this end of the city."

"And I still do not know what they want," Holmes admitted. "Perhaps if I were to go back to that warehouse . . ."

"Not just now," Dalvenjah said as she lifted him up and tossed him over the rail as well. Then she leaped to the top of the rail and hurried over to the helm wheels. "I will have to find Vajerral to fly this ship, since I know that neither of you can presently command the necessary magic. I still do not know where Jenny is in all of this confusion."

"The last we saw, she was still at the warehouse fighting wyverns," Mira said, watching with considerable concern as the faerie dragon took the airship back into the sky.

Holmes was still dusting himself off, obviously very surprised about something. Apparently the act of being thrown onto an airship by a disgruntled dragon was a fairly instantaneous cure for the effects of skateboard crouch. All the same, Mira knew that she would not want to have his butt in the morning. Then she entertained herself for a moment by rearranging the meaning of those words.

Jenny returned at that moment. She was still wearing her dragon form, but there was no question that it was her. She passed right through the middle of the ship before drifting over and landing gently on the helm deck. She glanced briefly at J.T., who was sitting in one corner weeping silently. He had seen many horrors in the past, but it seemed that skateboarding through the streets of New York was the worst.

"Did you know that demons can bite ghosts?" Jenny asked.

"No, but it does not surprise me," Dalvenjah said. "Demons are not alive as we know it, neither are they ghosts. Something between the two. Did it hurt?"

"No, that is not exactly the word, but it did not feel good. Since I have not felt anything since I became a ghost, it came as something of a surprise. It did no damage that I could tell, but I knew that I should be afraid of letting a pack of them get me down. I think that they could have turned me into a more permanent type of ghost."

"Just what manner of demons were they, and how many?" Dalvenjah asked.

"Oh, those nasty flying demons that you just can't kill. I saw about two dozen, but I cannot promise that there were not more. Demons, wyverns and airships are still coming out of that warehouse."

"Then you take control of this ship," Dalvenjah said. "Allan and I are the only ones who can manage demons. Kelvandor is a fine fighting dragon but his strengths are the more obvious ones, not subtle magic. And all I can say for Vajerral is that it is a good thing that dragons do not wear shoes. Her laces would never be tied. She is younger than she likes to admit."

Wind Dragon hesitated a moment as Jenny's own magic took over control of the vanes, but she kept her Mindijaran form as she moved behind the ship's wheels. Dalvenjah leaped over the side without a single glance back, flying quickly along the waterfront in the direction of the warehouse, the one with winged demons circling above it like crows.

"Well, now what?" Mira asked. "New York needs us."

"If New York was lacking anything, it was you alone," Holmes remarked. "I wonder what they must think now?"

Jenny was already moving *Wind Dragon* directly toward the warehouse, still several blocks ahead. Dalvenjah and Allan probably could handle the winged demons by themselves, as the dragon insisted, but there were other problems needing attention as well. They still had no idea why the Empire was in this world in general, and New York in particular, and Dalvenjah Foxfire was the one most likely to find that answer. There were spears and arrows aboard *Wind Dragon* magically enhanced to be deadly to demons, and Mira's exploding bolts could make short work of enemy airships, as they had proven in

Mira's world. Then Jenny saw that a fair number of the winged demons were headed toward *Wind Dragon* with intentions of their own, and two large airships were moving in quickly across the water.

"Rig the ship for battle, Mira," Jenny said. "We're destined to have a fight on our hands no matter what. And put those two FBI agents on the catapults. Those guns are going to be little use against airships, and no use against demons."

"Considering our past experience in battle, you should be happy with one thing," Mira said as she hurried forward.

"And what is that?"

"That spell of mine can no longer make your clothes disappear," the sorceress called back. "You don't wear any."

"Those ships are as big as our own," Holmes said as he watched over the rail. "They are coming straight across the harbor from New Jersey, so they obviously had another stronghold somewhere. I should have known."

"Catapults, Mira!" Jenny called. "And get those arrows out right away. We are going to be up to our poop deck in demons any moment now. Mr. Holmes, I might need a little help back here. How are you with a bow?"

"Why, funny you should ask, my dear," he said as he hurried to the front of the ship. "You have heard me play the violin."

Jenny rolled her eyes. "First he thinks he's Sherlock Holmes, and now he's Groucho Marx."

She looked over her shoulder—dragons had good necks for that—and saw that perhaps a score of the demons were closing very quickly. She had found herself in this position before; she was less vulnerable than the last time she had been flying *Wind Dragon* during an attack of winged demons, but there were also more demons. Holmes and Mira both returned within moments, the first carrying a bow and a carefully sealed package of spelled arrows while the other had an assault rifle.

"I suddenly realized that the damned bows are now too big for me to draw," Mira explained. "I cast the same spells on the ammunition that we use on our arrows, so the guns might work about as well."

"And what do you know about guns?" Jenny asked.

"Well, pilgrim, I'd say I know about as much as a cowboy needs to know," the sorceress drawled in a very bad imitation of

The Duke. "At least I can shoot the gun. My arm isn't long enough to pull an arrow, and I'm too short to aim the catapults."

Jenny glanced at Holmes. "And you want a bow?"

"I've never shot a gun in my considerable life," he said. "But I was a master of the bow thousands of years before the mortals of this world stole the technology from the elves."

The first of the demons were coming up quickly behind the ship. Holmes took an arrow from the pack and, in a single move almost too quick to be seen, shot it directly into the mouth of the nearest winged demon. The arrow went all the way through—Jenny missed seeing how that happened—and embedded itself in the chest of a second. Both demons disappeared in a sudden flare of blue flames.

"Yo, pilgrim!" Holmes declared. "Tally up a point for the elf with the bow."

Mira propped the barrel of her gun on the ship's rail, took careful aim and let off a shot, which caught a second winged demon in the head and dispatched it neatly. It was an amazing shot for someone who was not only firing a gun for the first time, but had never even heard of firearms until only a month ago. No one who knew her had ever doubted Mira's abilities, only her judgement, her sense of propriety and her taste. Of course, the weapon that she had been given by the FBI agents was a rather small, lightweight version of an automatic assault rifle, convenient to carry but with a kick like a mule. Mira suddenly found herself sitting on the deck, looking immensely surprised.

"That never happens in the movies," she complained.

"Mira, you could hurt someone," Jenny told her.

Mira's unexpected response, after a look of sudden alarm, was to aim the weapon directly at Jenny's head and fire two rapid shots. The winged demon that had been about to close on her neck fell screaming onto the ship's rear deck, then vanished in blue flames. Jenny jumped straight up, entirely a reaction of alarm, leaving the ship's wheels free to turn on their own for a moment. She grabbed the wheels and brought *Wind Dragon* quickly back on course, glaring at Mira the entire time.

"How did you know that would work?" she demanded.

"I was thinking about what you had just said," Mira explained patiently as she picked herself up and returned to stand watch at the rail. "When you said that I could hurt someone, I immediately thought that it would hardly be you, since bullets would go right through. But I did remember you saying earlier that the bite of the demons did hurt you, and that it might be dangerous to you. So when I had to shoot through you to get the demon, I naturally assumed that the bullets would be less likely to hurt you than the bite, especially if the damned thing took you by the neck."

"Excellent reasoning, Sorceress," Holmes congratulated her.

"Elementary, my dear Holmes."

"Of course, the bullets that you had spelled to be deadly to demons might also have been harmful to her," he added.

"A calculated risk, old boy," she said, and shot another demon that was closing on the ship. "The moment was so brief, I never thought of that."

"Mira, those other ships are turning away," Wallick called from the front of the ship.

Jenny lifted her head to the full extent of her neck to look ahead. The two Imperial airships had not turned away from *Wind Dragon* as much as they were trying to cut across and well below her bow, almost skimming the waves. Both ships had increased their speed, moving probably as fast as they could be pushed, nearly equal to *Wind Dragon*'s best speed. It obviously was not fear of Mira's schooner that had frightened them, but a pair of police helicopters coming up behind them, still some distance behind but closing quickly. Most helicopters could outrun even the fastest airships. Apparently the captains of the Imperial ships were not aware that police helicopters were not likely to carry any weapons that could seriously harm an airship, which is for the most part several tons of heavy wooden planks. An old-fashioned cannonball would have probably bounced off their hardwood hulls like *Old Ironsides*. Shotguns and assault rifles would, at best, ruin the finish.

"I think that we should help them out," Jenny said. "If they realize that those helicopters are unlikely to do them any harm, they might turn. And those fool pilots, like most modern folk, are not going to realize that an arrow can damage an engine or pierce a Plexiglas windscreen."

"They are heading into town," Holmes said, as if musing aloud. "Uptown, unless I miss my guess, and the largest buildings in the city. Will the span of their lift vanes clear the streets?"

"Barely, but I think so," Jenny answered. "*Wind Dragon*'s span is shorter, to reduce drag. The vanes are broader, to make up for the lack of length, and that of course makes them stronger. Do we go after them?"

"You are the pilot, and Lady Mira is the captain," he pointed out.

Mira looked at Jenny. "I can't fly this ship. If you feel capable of flying *Wind Dragon* up Fifth Avenue, then have at it."

"If a seven-story balloon in the shape of Bullwinkle J. Moose can do it, so can we," Jenny decided. "We might even be able to catch them before they get there, if the boys are as good with those catapults as they were over the mountains. I do have one good question for Dalvenjah, next time I see her."

"What is that?" Mira said.

"Who is flying their ships? You're one of the best sorceresses of your world and you can hardly get *Wind Dragon* off the ground, and their sorcerers come from the same world."

"That is curious," Holmes agreed. "I wonder why I did not think of it."

Jenny was already pushing *Wind Dragon* to her limits, even though the ship was bucking and shaking against the strain. She worried about causing the main spar to break, ripping the lift vanes from the hull; it was something that did happen, and the fact that *Wind Dragon* had been built solidly for speed did not mean that she would survive every punishment. Jenny was thinking very hard about what they might do. She doubted that she could encourage the Imperial airships to break off their run and turn to fight; they acted too frightened of the helicopters still half a mile or so behind *Wind Dragon*. But she did believe that she could get the ship close enough to launch a brief attack on the slower of the two.

"Question, Mira," she said at last.

"What is that, child?"

"Do you suppose they can shield themselves against arrows and bolts, as we have seen them do in the past?"

"I hardly know," the sorceress admitted. "J.T.!"

"How should I know?" the cat demanded.

"Can you tell whether a mortal, a faerie or a dragon would be flying those ships from the magic?"

"I know that Jenny's magic feels different when she is flying

Wind Dragon from your own," he said, then he sat for a moment with his head raised as he sniffed the air. "Definitely mortal. Just like every other Imperial ship we have fought. And yet it is focused, as if artificially enhanced in some way."

"Do they have some manner of amplifier that could boost the strength of their own magic?" Holmes asked.

"Not in the way I think you mean," Mira said. "This is probably more like surrogate magic. There are great crystals, like the Heart of Flame that we destroyed in Alashera, that can store tremendous amounts of magic and then release it at command to enhance a sorcerer's abilities."

"That must be what they are doing," J.T. agreed.

"Then can they shield themselves?" Jenny asked again.

"I imagine so."

"But would they bother until we come within bow range?" Holmes asked, as if he was musing over an idea. "Mira, can you keep the winged demons away for a minute? I must talk with those two FBI agents."

"Oh, fine thing!" Mira muttered in disgust, turning her attention back to the winged demons that were about to close on *Wind Dragon* from behind.

Jenny turned her head to look back. "Does it seem to you that there are even more of them?"

"Yes, damn it," Mira agreed, staring back for a moment. "There must now be four, perhaps five dozen demons, and they're all after us. I wonder what those dragons are doing?"

"If I know Dalvenjah, they are probably in even more trouble than we are," Jenny said. "How much ammunition do you have?"

"This box," she answered, showing Jenny what she had.

"Then put that gun on automatic if they come at you all at once. Just remember to be very sparing. A gun like that will go through its ammunition much quicker than in the movies."

Mira braced her gun on *Wind Dragon*'s siderail and took careful aim, picking off the nearest demons with surprising accuracy. It generally took her three or four shots for each demon, but those were fairly good odds; at that rate, she would run out of demons a long time before bullets. Apparently Mira's abilities with the bow and crossbow had translated well into this new weapon.

Jenny could spare no more of her attention to what lay behind. *Wind Dragon* was closing slowly on the second of the two Imperial airships, following by no more than five or six hundred feet. If Holmes had any plans in mind, then he needed to do something soon. She lifted her head as far as her neck would allow and then a little bit more; being a ghost had many advantages, but she sometimes felt like a Looney Toons character. What she was able to see was the two FBI agents Wallick and Borelli crouched down like sharpshooters behind the rail to either side of the bowsprit while the Trassek twins stood ready at the crossbows mounted on their stands a few paces behind, all of them intent upon the nearest of the two Imperial airships. Holmes was standing patiently in the center of it all, directing whatever attack they seemed about to launch, as stern and noble as Caesar leading his armies into battle, calm and certain of victory.

Jenny hoped that Holmes intended to do something very quickly, since they would be over land in a matter of seconds and she would rather not send an Imperial airship crashing in flames on the West Side of New York. The mayor was going to love them for this. Alas for New York, Jenny reflected. What had New York done to deserve this? There was always Staten Island or New Rochelle. Something like this would have put Poughkeepsie on the map. Why did bad things always happen to New York?

"Helicopters, Jenny!" Mira shouted suddenly.

"What?" Jenny looked around quickly and saw that the two police helicopters had closed the distance very quickly, coming up on *Wind Dragon*'s stern very quickly. "Comfustication! The damned fools don't know that we're the good guys. Bowenger!"

"Jenny?" he called back.

"Do you have any sort of radio?"

"Yes."

"Tell them to clear the sky. Those helicopters are coming after us." She glanced over her shoulder and saw the barrel of a rifle aimed right at her from an open side window. "Mira, get to cover."

A bullet passed completely through Jenny and splintered the rail to her left; Mira needed no more encouragement than that to duck behind the siderail. At least Jenny was herself in no danger, but she worried about other members of her crew. Did the policemen in those helicopters have the slightest idea of what was really going on, or was the police department simply responding the best it could? Jenny had to bring *Wind Dragon* around sharply when the two Imperial airships turned suddenly and dropped down to pass hardly fifty feet over the street, right between some of the tallest buildings on that side of the city. She could see that the vanes of the ship ahead of her were clearing the walls of some of the nearest buildings with perhaps two feet of space on either side, and *Wind Dragon*'s span was only slightly narrower. It would have been bad enough at a crawl, and these ships were moving at better than fifty knots.

The helicopters followed them in for a short distance, but gave up the chase after a moment and climbed above the buildings. Now that their deadly blades were gone, the demons renewed their attack on *Wind Dragon*; Jenny was almost surprised that the demons had even the simple intelligence to recognize and respect the danger. Since Mira found it easy enough to keep them away with her rifle, Jenny turned her attention back to the Imperial airships. They were locked on a very straight course as long as they stayed low between the buildings, which was perfect for the purposes of whatever plan Holmes might be contemplating. She forced *Wind Dragon* just a little faster, closing the distance to the second ship.

Wallick and Bowenger shot their rifles, only one shot each, at almost the same instant. Jenny lifted her head to look, but she could not see anything at first except that the two agents both rose, standing at the bowsprit and staring ahead, and Holmes stepped forward to stand between them. A long moment passed, and then the airship ahead of them slowly nosed over and then began to fall with increasing speed, so that Jenny had to take *Wind Dragon* up sharply to avoid its masts. Finally it hit the street below with a noise of breaking wood and the ringing crashes of metal that seemed to go on forever; the ship had not crashed as much as it had crash-landed, sliding along the street on its keel even after its skips had sheared away, wrapping its vanes around light poles. Its shattered hull grated to a stop after sliding the better part of two hundred feet, taking a couple of dozen parked cars with it in death but doing no more damage than that.

Jenny had left her neck stretched out invitingly in the air for too long, and a winged demon suddenly dived in and fastened itself to her. She thrashed and fought, but she dared not throw herself around too hard or dematerialize for fear of *Wind Dragon* catching a vane on a building. There was no pain such as she might have expected from a bite, but a tremendous feeling of pressure that increased steadily, bringing with it a growing sense of panic. The ship's forward left vane grated against the side of one building, in spite of her best efforts, but the impact only nudged the ship clear again. Mira had been there the whole time, trying to get a clear shot, but Jenny's previous fear and Holmes's warning about possible danger had made her hesitant. At last fear of what the demon's bite might be doing to Jenny forced her to fire anyway, shooting twice through the dragon's chest. The demon released its grip at last, arching its neck in a mortal scream of fury before it dissolved into blue flames, still clinging to Jenny's back.

"Are you well?" Mira asked.

"Perfect," Jenny insisted, already giving *Wind Dragon* her full attention.

Mira looked back at the wreckage of the Imperial airship, then paused to brace her gun on the rail and shoot two more demons. "What happened?"

"Holmes had Wallick and Bowenger shoot her pilot," Jenny explained. "With no one to fly the ship, or at least channel the latest magic that was giving power to her vanes, the ship simply lost lift and fell."

"Was he not shielded?" Mira asked.

"Under the circumstances, he probably could not channel the magic both to fly the ship and shield himself. He had a soldier in armor standing behind him with a shield, which would have stopped all the arrows we could throw at them. Not being of this world, he did not know the power of rifles. One of the agents shot the soldier, through both the shield and his armor, and the other got the pilot."

Jenny found that things always seemed to happen quickly when she was flying *Wind Dragon* in battle. She was just beginning to close on the remaining Imperial airship when two helicopters, no doubt the ones she had already met, moved slowly out from between the buildings a couple of blocks ahead. At least this time they seemed to be trying to help, but roadblocks generally do not work in three dimensions. The Imperial ship immediately lifted its bow and began to ascend toward open sky. Jenny did not hesitate to follow, but *Wind Dragon*, although a faster ship, had a smaller lift-to-weight ratio and could not climb as quickly. She was not used to having the disadvantage, and the other ship was slowly moving away.

As soon as *Wind Dragon* came above the tops of the buildings, Jenny was able to see that they were not alone. Five more airships were ascending from the city along with a dozen wyverns and about twice as many demons, all that were left, all converging together as they moved out over the harbor. The four faerie dragons were close behind, but *Wind Dragon* was otherwise alone in the pursuit.

"We seem to have the better of them," Holmes said as he hurried to the helm deck, although the ship was climbing at such an angle that he had to move carefully. "I suppose that they are returning to their other base. Wherever they are going, we cannot allow them to escape us."

A spark of flame appeared suddenly a couple of hundred yards ahead of the leading Imperial airship, expanding rapidly into a circle of fire that opened upon a pit of blackness. With nowhere else to run, the Imperial forces were escaping into another world. The wyverns were already disappearing into the Way Between the Worlds, but the demons were circling back to engage the faerie dragons, covering the retreat of the airships.

"Push *Wind Dragon* as hard as she will go," Mira told Jenny. "If we are close enough behind them, they won't be able to close the passage until we come through."

"No, something about this is wrong," Holmes said.

Just then Dalvenjah circled in close behind the ship's stern. "Hold off! They want us to follow them."

"My thought exactly," Holmes agreed. "This was all a great farce with no purpose except to get us too involved in chasing them to stop."

"An astute observation," the dragon remarked.

"Not at all. Their intentions seem obvious enough if you just watch what they are doing with a level head."

"You are right," Dalvenjah said. "After you blundered into the middle of their first trap, I am grateful that you were more cautious about the second. Chase them to the very edge of the passage, but do not follow."

She turned then and streaked away, evading a small pack of five demons that had suddenly decided that she looked good enough to bite. Holmes and Mira shot at the demons as they passed, picking off four of them.

"Well, I like that," Holmes declared, although he was not offended. He knew that Dalvenjah was teasing him, and that he deserved it.

"You are only an imitation Sherlock Holmes," Jenny pointed out. "She is the real Dalvenjah Foxfire."

❧ PART FIVE ❧

Thinking Caps

Jenny brought *Wind Dragon* down in the water just outside the naval warehouse, and Mira immediately ordered the Trassek twins to fold back the lift vanes and unstep the masts. Another running battle was over and this time they had brought her ship out unharmed, which was to say that they were improving. Or at least getting luckier. Wallick and Bowenger were standing in the bow and looking as if they felt required to offer their help, knowing as well that they did not know the first thing about an airship's rigging. Even Wallick looked a little bewildered, and he was a veteran of Dalvenjah's battle with the steel dragon Vorgulremik. Demons were enough to get on anyone's nerves, like some venomous creature that can kill with only one bite. The winged demons were the smallest of any type that Jenny had ever seen, but they were swift—something most demons were not—and they were nasty, and there had been a small army of them.

Jenny did not even want to think about the damage there might have been on the ground. She certainly did not want to think about trying to explain it all. That was what Bowenger was for. With Imperial airships wrecked on the streets, she doubted that this could be simply covered up. There had probably been film crews crawling over the hulks of those ships quicker than the police could get there.

Mira was quietly hiding her assault rifle in one of the weapons lockers built into the deck, no doubt wondering if anyone would ever think to ask for it back. Mira collected the damnedest souvenirs.

"I wonder if we won or lost," Mira remarked.

"We won," Jenny said. "We did not follow them into their trap."

"So now what do we do?" the sorceress asked.

"Now we start all over again, oh joy of joys and delights everlasting."

"Holmes!" Mira called. "What do we do now?"

"I am surprised that you would ask me," he said as he climbed the steps from the middle deck. "My deductions seem to be amiss."

"Dalvenjah seemed to think that your abilities were of great worth," Mira reminded him. "She brought us all the way here to find you."

"We will have to review all we know and start over again," Holmes said. "I hesitate to know how to begin without Dalvenjah's assistance."

"Ready to go in!" Dooket called. "Mr. Bowenger says to hurry."

Jenny began easing *Wind Dragon* forward, moving slowly until she felt the ship's wheels push against the ramp. She was perfectly willing to hurry; an off-world airship in the middle of New York Harbor on a bright morning was not a wise or safe place to be, especially after a running battle with wyverns and demons. At the same time, she was beginning to worry quite a lot about this old ship, especially her struts and backbone. *Wind Dragon* had taken a lot of abuse, and she probably had a lot more ahead of her. Jenny wondered if she could talk Bowenger into getting some people in to look the ship over for stress.

She moved *Wind Dragon* into the warehouse, and the doors were closed as soon as the stern was clear. She felt a little better as soon as that was done, as if it protected her from prying eyes. She was still in her dragon form and that made her even more nervous, and yet she had no intention of changing her appearance. Her dragon form was secure and familiar, for reasons she could not understand. Dalvenjah Foxfire had been a bad influence on her.

Holmes was already releasing the boarding ramp. "Hurry along, Bowenger. I must get back to that warehouse, and I need transportation."

"What did you do with that van I loaned you this morning?"

Bowenger asked, returning from the bow to help lower the ramp.

"I left it parked about a block from that warehouse," he said. "If you want me to drive it back, then you must take me there."

"Then I am going," Mira declared. "I happen to be the greatest expert in this entire world on the Empire and the Alasheran culture. In fact, I happen to be one of the greatest experts in my own world. How are Dalvenjah and Mr. Holmes supposed to make brilliant deductions from what they find if they do not even know what it is?"

Bowenger had no time to answer. Sir Remidan appeared, dressed in full armor and carrying his weapons, and looking as if he was going into battle. Actually, he looked more prepared for murder than for war. He stopped at the bottom of *Wind Dragon*'s ramp and stood glaring up at Mira.

"Why did you people go into battle without me?" he demanded in his poor but improving English.

"How should I know?" Mira asked.

"Because he was in the shower at the time," Wallick suggested quietly.

"Because you were in the shower at the time," Mira repeated, louder. "They could hardly wait for you to get into your armor. It was nasty out there."

"Well, I could hardly bathe in my armor," the knight insisted. "It might be magical and not subject to rust, but you just do not take chances. What good does it do you, anyway? I can get into my armor in moments."

"Dalvenjah would not wait," Wallick reported.

"Hey, blame that Dalvenjah Foxface," Mira declared. "She was the one who jumped aboard my airship and took off without even asking, and you know how she is. Time waits for no man, and neither does the dragon."

"Well, it's just not fair," Sir Remidan muttered. "I am a knight, after all."

"Stop complaining, or I'll leave you stranded in this world," Mira warned. "Then you would have to make your living in Hollywood, and spend the weekend with the SCA to get your jollies."

Sir Remidan made a vile face.

"Are you going with us to the warehouse?" Mira asked.

"Under no circumstances." He turned to walk away.

"He misses his horse," Mira explained to the others. "Shall we proceed with our investigation?"

Although it was against his better judgement to take this troupe back out into the city, Bowenger loaded them into a car and took them back to the warehouse. At least he was spared the problem of having to deal with Jenny, who now seemed reluctant to leave her dragon form; she declared that she would meet them at the warehouse and simply disappeared.

They had only just started when Holmes announced that they must first see the wreckage of the airship that had been hit by the truck, only a few blocks along the waterfront from their own base at the naval warehouse. The police were there in force and had already blocked off the area, but they had made no attempt to clear the wreckage. Indeed, they seemed reluctant to go anywhere near the damaged ship; fire trucks were standing by, common enough in the presence of a downed aircraft, but the lack of fuel seemed to confound them. They were willing enough to let Bowenger through when he showed his identification. Holmes and Mira attracted a fair amount of interest and J.T. even more so, but no one wanted to follow them aboard. Bowenger stayed behind to talk with the police.

J.T. disappeared into the ship ahead of the others, and the cat came leaping back out of the interior of the hull as soon as the rest were all aboard.

"There is nothing here," the cat insisted with vague impatience. "I suggest that we get ourselves to the warehouse before those dragons muck everything up."

"That particular possibility does not greatly concern me," Holmes said as he assisted Mira in climbing back down. "I am only worried that the dragons might find some important lead and choose to follow it before we can arrive. Perhaps we should not have been so quick to have *Wind Dragon* stowed away."

Bowenger saw that they were returning and hurried them back to the car. They were on their way to the warehouse only moments later.

"It would have made things much easier for us to have live, talking prisoners, but we have been unlucky there," he explained. "One archer from this ship hit his head on a stoplight several streets back and they have him at the hospital now, but he is unlikely to wake up and remember who he is any time soon enough to be useful to us. The other members of the crew of this ship simply disappeared after the wreck. There were no survivors from the crews of the other wrecks."

"What about wyverns?" Mira asked.

"The wyverns seemed to have kept a safe distance from the dragons during the fight," Bowenger answered. "The dragons didn't take any of them, and we certainly didn't see any from *Wind Dragon*."

"I suspect that they were only here to provide distraction," Holmes said. "Having done their part, they fled. They were only mercenaries, and the one I spoke with seemed a decent enough chap. Indeed, I suspect that they were never meant to fight the dragons in the first place."

Getting into the warehouse proved to be much more difficult. As it happened, the New Jersey National Guard, convinced that a foreign invasion had landed, had commandeered boats to cross the harbor in force. The fact that they had no jurisdiction in the state of New York had not bothered them in the slightest, considering that they also assumed that they had the authority to declare martial law. For reasons that never were discovered, they had descended upon this warehouse as a suspected den of communist infiltrators and had refused to let anyone in, from the New York police to the FBI, declaring that they were the highest military authority present and that they would remain on guard until a representative of the regular military arrived to take control of the situation. Fortunately an officer from the naval base arrived at that same time to take the rather young and inexperienced leader of the guardsmen aside and explain certain realities to him, including the fact that he had better get his troops back across the water before New York declared war on New Jersey.

"Have you ever noticed that when really stupid things happen in New York, New Jersey always seems to get the blame?" Bowenger asked no one in particular as he led the others down the alley.

Everything seemed to be very much as they had left it. The overhead door at the top of the boarding platform looked as if a truck had run through it, and the wreckage of wooden crates and skateboards littered the alley.

Bowenger drew his gun. "Be ready for anything. We have no idea what could be waiting for us inside."

They all drew the guns that they had been given, Bowenger on one side and Holmes on the other with Mira and J.T. in the middle, and they leaned forward to look inside through the break in the door. The room inside was large, dark and mostly empty except for a few crates and cardboard boxes. Then they all jumped back as a large, shadowy form, not unlike one of the wyverns, seemed to glide quickly past the door. They glanced in cautiously, their guns ready, and discovered to their vast and everlasting astonishment that it was one of the faerie dragons riding a skateboard. In fact, it was Kelvandor. Allan and Vajerral hurtled around the corner on a skateboard of their own a moment later and ran right into him, sending all three of the dragons flying.

"You see," Allan said as he picked himself up. "Once you learn how, you never forget."

"You seemed to have forgotten something," Kelvandor complained. "Steering comes to mind."

"I never said that I learned it very well."

"I had to believe this to see it," Bowenger said quietly, too confused to realize what he had said. "The New Jersey National Guard invades New York to stand guard over a waterfront warehouse full of skateboarding dragons. You know, my mother wanted very much for me to be a gastroenterologist like my cousin Andy. To think how close I came to missing sights like this to spend my life looking up assholes."

"How did you get in here?" Holmes asked as he climbed through the door.

"Jenny saw that most of the demons had come out of a door in the roof," Allan explained as he righted his skateboard for another attempt. "Dalvenjah wanted to have a look around before anyone else came in here, so it was easy enough to enter from above."

"And where is the esteemed Dalvenjah Foxfire?" Holmes asked. "There should be at least one mature mind trying to make sense of this business."

Dalvenjah arrived almost at that very moment, whipping around the corner on a skateboard of her own. Her skateboard suddenly shot out from beneath her and flew across the room, and the worthy sorceress was thrown onto her tail. A dragon's tail is a mixed blessing in the fine art of skateboarding; it was an awkward bit of weight to upset one's balance, but it did wonders in breaking a backward fall.

"The voice of wisdom and maturity approaches with dignity and restraint," J.T. observed succinctly.

"There you are, Mr. Holmes," Dalvenjah said and she rose and tucked her skateboard under one arm, obviously intending to keep it as a prize. "I would like very much for you to look through this building and see if you agree with my conclusions. I have discovered the most amazing thing."

"And what is that?"

"Absolutely nothing!" she declared. "There is every indication that they have been waiting for some time, several months at least. But there is not even the smallest hint that they were doing anything but simply waiting for us to arrive."

"I expect that your judgement is correct," Holmes said. "That is going to make our next move much more difficult to determine. Where is Jenny? Did she ever arrive?"

"Quite some time ago," the sorceress replied. "Just now she is looking between the walls and beneath the floor for hidden clues. She does that very well, you know."

Holmes set about his own search of the warehouse for clues, assisted by Mira and J.T. Being a familiar, J.T. did possess certain advantages where the investigation of all things magical was concerned, and he generally kept his comments to himself. Mira was less helpful than she imagined herself to be, but she was always eager. Insatiable might have been a better word. And she did prefer the company of Holmes to that of Dalvenjah Foxfire, one of the few forces in the universe that she respected and feared. Especially so, now that Mira had shrunk to the size of three good bites for a dragon.

"Mr. Bowenger, I must go to New Jersey," Dalvenjah said as soon as the others were gone. "Have you heard anything about the location of the base where those larger airships were hidden?"

"The last time I called in, they had a very good idea," he answered. "I can get an exact location as quickly as I can arrange transportation, I am sure. Will all the dragons be going?"

"If we find more demons, you will need all the dragons you have."

"I see your point. Let me find a phone and call back to the naval warehouse. The delivery truck can be here in minutes."

Dalvenjah waited as he climbed out through the hole in the door, then sat back on her tail. "Jenny!"

Jenny appeared only a moment later, her dragon's head and neck lifting straight up out of the floor. "No hidden passages that I can find. There are the remains of an ancient pier down there, but nothing that concerns us."

"Very good," Dalvenjah said. "We will be on our way to New Jersey as soon as Mr. Bowenger returns with the truck. Do you wish to meet us there?"

"Unless I know where you are going, it is not that easy for me to find you again," Jenny said as she pulled herself out of the floor. "Being a ghost is very liberating, but it does not make one omnipotent."

Their day had been a very busy one, and it was four tired little faerie dragons who retired to the naval warehouse that evening. The fifth dragon was immune to being tired, but she was in no better mood than the others. Those dragons who were still interested in such dainties were nibbling dejectedly on rolls with venison and cheese and washing it down with root beer from plastic bottles, while they sat with the others and watched television. The local news could make little sense of what had happened during the day, and the national news did only slightly better; the press was noticeably reluctant to say anything about dragons. As Bowenger had observed earlier, New Jersey was getting most of the blame. One particularly inventive source even speculated that an unknown cargo plane had accidentally dropped replicas of wooden sailing ships on the city. The government, the military and the FBI all seemed to be taking the approach of waiting to see if the press would talk itself into a mundane explanation.

Mr. Holmes was in a high state of dissatisfaction over the affair, and he was too busy contemplating the future to worry about past disasters. He was marching back and forth almost furiously on the far side of the room, just behind the television where the others could see him pass easily. From time to time he would stop and stare at his violin, sitting in its open case on a table beside the television, and the others would hold their breath until he resumed his nervous pacing.

Dalvenjah made a gesture at the television and the sound became inaudible, as if she had used some magical remote control. She glanced up at Holmes. "You look like an elf with an idea."

"I have a theory," he said. "I have a suspicion supported by little more than innuendo and the process of careful elimination. I have nothing more than a hunch, but I can foresee no alternatives."

"You have a nasty habit of talking like a thesaurus," Allan observed. "And just what is this hunch, this theory, this educated guess?"

Holmes turned abruptly to the dragons. "Why did the Empire come into this world in the first place? There are three major reasons."

Dalvenjah nodded. "First, this world served as a stopping-off place or transfer point to some other world, their actual destination. Not a very supportable theory, as far as it goes."

"No, not at all," Holmes agreed. "That would mean that the force they left behind to meet us was a decoy. Why would they do that? The decoy only called attention to the fact that they had been here. The best way to cover their trail was to have left nothing here at all."

"Secondly, the decoy was itself the end to the means," Dalvenjah said. "It did seem to me that we were being invited to follow their retreating forces. Perhaps we were being led into an ambush."

"That idea does have some merit," Allan agreed. "We were not expecting any danger from sorcerers in this world, where no magic except for dragon magic works very well. They might have expected that we would be careless and pursue them into a battle in a place of their choosing, a place where we would not have otherwise gone, and against greater forces than we had expected."

"Perhaps," Holmes agreed cautiously. "That still seems like quite a lot of trouble. In your experience, Lady Mira, would the Empire behave in that way?"

She shook her head. "No, hardly. They might be decadent in

their tastes, but they have always been fairly obvious and simple in their strategies."

"Unless the trap was meant to capture Mira," Kelvandor added. "They might know by now that the Dark Sorceress Darja has the wrong body."

"But their base in this world has been here for several weeks, certainly before they captured Jenny," Holmes pointed out.

"Then that leads us finally to the theory that they are looking for something in this world," Dalvenjah concluded. "We had discussed that question before and rejected it. They would not want technology as a weapon of either attack or defense because technology can always be defeated by magic."

"But they would want power in the form of magic?" Holmes asked.

"Certainly."

"And that is the very thing that they hope to find. I submit that the decoy was to lead us back out of this world before we could discover the true purpose for their presence. They are trying to claim the lost magic of this world."

The others looked so surprised and mystified, especially the dragons, that Holmes could see that they had not followed his logic at all. As far as that went, he could hardly blame them; he was not entirely certain that his reasoning was completely sound. He paced the room three more times, as if to recapture lost momentum, and turned to face the dragons. "In all that you have ever heard or read, has a world that once possessed strong magic ever lost that magic?"

"There has never been a hint that any world has ever lost its magic," Dalvenjah said. "According to accepted theory, that is impossible. Magic simply is. It should never evaporate or run short. That is the very thing that has always intrigued me about this world."

"Exactly the point," Holmes agreed. "And yet this world is different. According to our most ancient legends, this world has not always had magic. It came into being long ago, bringing forth the age of faerie, and the slow loss of magic destroyed the age of faerie, a process that is only now coming to completion."

"That is only a legend," Dalvenjah observed. "You are discussing a time that must be at least several million years old."

"Very old, as a matter of fact," he agreed. "There are certain supporting facts that make it a very compelling legend, however. The bones of the legend state that some one hundred million years ago, a race evolved slowly from the creatures that we would now call dinosaurs, or perhaps pterodactyls to be more precise. A race that was known as the Dragon Lords. Now at that time they possessed very little magic but they were a proud and predatory people and in their way quite wise. In time they discovered a place that they called the Fountain of the World's Heart, a vast cavern or pit, and a group of Dragon Lords descended into that place to explore. No one knows what they found, but they somehow released reserves of magic into the world so vast that it changed the shape of the world forever, destroying much of what had existed before but bringing forth new orders of creatures both mortal and magical. All of this happened some sixty-five million years ago."

"I see what you mean," Allan agreed. "So much for the meteor theory."

"Exactly," Holmes agreed. "Now the dragons were always apart, for they had existed before the coming of magic and they were never completely a part of the Realm of Faerie but different in subtle ways. They were really not at all like the dragons of Saint George or Siegfried but more like the Chinese dragons, immensely wise and enormous in their capacity for life, as quick to laugh as to anger. But they were not civilized as I understand faerie dragons and wyverns to be. They lived in the mountains and made nothing of their own except for some small things they needed. They had no lords or kingdoms but traveled as they pleased."

"Would it be possible to find a dragon?" Dalvenjah asked.

"I doubt that very much. I believe that the last dragons died long ago."

"That is no great problem," she said. "I have spent quite a lot of my time lately trying to talk to dead dragons."

"I am a dead dragon," Jenny added quietly. That was not, of course, entirely true. She was disembodied, not dead, although the effect was very much the same.

Dalvenjah frowned, an expression that worked extremely well on a dragon's face. "I agree with you. We must find this Fountain of the World's Heart."

"Oh, I know where it is," Holmes insisted. "The Fountain of

the World's Heart is said to be on a great island of rock and ice, known in the faerie language as Dhulamarie, or to mortals as Thule."

"Iceland?" Allan asked, surprised.

Dalvenjah bent her long neck to look over her shoulder. "Mr. Bowenger?"

Clark Bowenger peered around the corner a moment later. "Sorceress?"

"We are about to do you a tremendous favor. Call Mr. Wallick and tell him that we will be leaving for Iceland immediately."

"Immediately? I mean, Iceland?" he asked. "Why? What do you expect to find in Iceland?"

Dalvenjah considered that briefly. "Ice?"

"Fair enough. If I were then to ask just how many of you are going to Iceland, would I get a straight answer?"

"We will all be going, I suspect," the dragon replied. "And I suspect that we will be leaving in the middle of the night when *Wind Dragon* is less likely to be seen, anticipating your next question."

Clark Bowenger would not be going on with *Wind Dragon*. His purpose had been to serve as their guide and liaison in New York, and New York was where he would stay. The fate of the world might well be resting in the hands of the Dragon Sorceress Dalvenjah Foxfire and her brave companions, and he knew that he would sleep better at nights if he did not have to see it. For better or worse, Dave Wallick would be going across the great blue waters on Lady Mira's little airship. His duty was to relay messages for Dalvenjah in the event she needed anything, such as NATO.

They were all generally happier to have left mortal civilization, even the mortals in their group. The dragons obviously enjoyed being free to move about when and where they wished rather than hiding in warehouses fearful of being seen. Sir Remidan had been in a bad mood the entire time they had been in the city, since his own talents had been fairly worthless to their task and his command of the local language had been so poor that he had been left very much to himself. Mira was contemplating that she might soon find enough magic to allow her to reinstate the spell that made her taller. Dooket and Erkin were of course as content as stones wherever they might fall, but they always seemed to respond especially well to traveling.

They were well out over the ocean by daybreak and Jenny was, as always, at the ship's wheels. That was just as well, since all the other dragons were incapacitated. Mira had taken a turn in the galley that morning and she had attempted what she considered an improvement upon one of the local dishes, preparing pepperoni, bean and sauerkraut burritos. That had, for some reason, hit the dragons especially hard. They were lined along the downwind side of the deck, bloated like toads and passing enough gas to float a blimp. Being a ghost, Jenny had not eaten and it seemed that, like spiders and snakes, Mira was immune to her own poison.

Which was not to say that Mira was going to survive her catastrophic meal. She suspected that the dragons were going to kill her for certain, and that they would do so just as soon as they could stand themselves. Four sad and weary shapes were hanging their long necks over the rail in the front of the ship. Mira had joined Jenny on the helm deck, as far away as she could get. Holmes sat on the rear rail, contemplating the waves.

"I am seeking out the company of ghosts, since I am about to become one myself," the little sorceress lamented.

"Nonsense," Jenny insisted. "If nothing else, you are too valuable to the Prophecy."

"Yes. Well, I have been thinking about that," Mira said. "If Dalvenjah Foxfire skins me alive and eats me, then the Dark Sorceress Darja can never get my body and the Prophecy will be safe. That dragon is a clever one. I'm sure that she figured that out a long time ago."

Jenny laughed. "Dalvenjah would never eat you. She would just toss you overboard."

"No, she would put me in a bottle and give you my body," the sorceress decided. "An imperfect solution, since you now seem to be a dragon. When did you come to that conclusion?"

"It became inevitable during our visit to New York," Jenny explained. "They say that you can never go back again. Ever since I learned that I have always been a dragon in the appearance of mortal form, I have begun to feel a distance between myself and mortals. Indeed, I find that I actually like being a dragon. Is that wrong?"

"No, I doubt that," Mira said. "Do you recall when we were fighting the Imperial airships and you were hit by an arrow? The damned thing went right through you. That would have been very serious damage to a mortal, but you took it very much in stride and recovered in a couple of days. Only a dragon, or something that was essentially a dragon on the inside, could have endured that so well."

They paused a long moment, trying very hard to keep a straight face as the dragons in the front of the ship began another volley of explosions of excess gas. Jenny had grown up in the company of faerie dragons, and even she had been unaware that they were capable of so much noise.

"We, who are about to die, pollute you," Jenny remarked very quietly, her ears laid back. "Every time they let loose another round, I have to steer into the direction of the fart. We could line them up along the back rail and have the first rocket-propelled airship. I'm amazed at their capacity. They should be swollen like balloons. How do they do it?"

Holmes looked up. "Alimentary, my dear child."

"You've waited a hundred years for that line, haven't you?"

"I have to resist the urge to put matches under their tails," Mira said. "Then we would see them breathe fire out of both ends."

"Dalvenjah really would throw you overboard."

"That alone restrains me. How long do you expect until we arrive?"

"Not until late tomorrow," Jenny said. "We might be following about the same path that Lindbergh took, but at only half the speed. The *Hindenberg* made better time than this. And with your cooking, this ship is just as likely to explode."

They arrived a little ahead of Jenny's schedule, since a strong following wind had added speed to their flight that had not registered on the airship's indicator. Jenny had stood at the ship's wheels the entire time, tireless in her present metaphysical state. Indeed, she was quite noticeably stronger than she had been only days before. Her magic was more powerful and more precise, while her ability to interact with the physical world had been steadily increasing to the point that no one would have known her for a ghost, she seemed so real and solid. At least someone might have taken her as alive until she did something like lengthen her neck to see ahead of the ship, or pass through the deck.

They passed inland until nightfall, then landed for the first time since leaving New York to make camp. Holmes had spent some time with maps and books about Iceland and he decided that the Fountain of the World's Heart, if it looked anything the way legend described, could not be found in the hospitable regions to the west and south of that large island or it would have already been discovered by the mortals of that land. He expected to find it in the northeastern third, and his plan of searching was in two parts. The four dragons would look for it on the wing, covering as much ground as they could by sweeping out large areas in careful patterns, while J.T. would try to locate it by its magical presence as *Wind Dragon* moved in larger, slower circles.

"This is Iceland?" Mira asked as she kicked at the deep grass. All she had seen was a wet, green but treeless land of rough, often tumbled terrain of deep valleys, ridges and mountains. "Where are the Eskimos?"

"There are no Eskimos in Iceland," Wallick told her. "And no polar bears or penguins, for that matter."

"Iceland is in most ways a part of Scandinavia," Holmes added. "Even though most geographers consider it, with Greenland, to be a part of North America. For that matter, you might consider that Greenland has little green but a considerable amount of ice and that Iceland has a lot of green but very little ice."

"Fine," Mira commented sourly. "Nothing in this world is named the way it looks. We just spent several days in New York and New Jersey, and neither of those places looked particularly new. Beratric Kurgel will have a thing or two to say, if he ever has the chance."

Jenny lifted her head. "We must be getting closer to a source of magic. Mira has not invoked the mythic name of Beratric Kurgel in weeks, and I will swear that she must be half an inch taller as well."

"I will dispute any claim that Mistress Mira is taller," J.T. declared. "But there is magic somewhere in this land. I will admit that I have not felt this good in weeks, but it is a long way from what I would call normal."

"Can you find this place?" Dalvenjah asked.

"Some distance northwest of us," the cat said, pausing to lick his hind leg. "If I might amend our plans, I would say that we should proceed in that direction with the dragons sweeping out the area to either side. As we come nearer, I should be able to locate our destination with increasing accuracy."

Wallick frowned. "Where did you learn to speak English like that?"

"From listening to Mr. Holmes, the same as those dragons."

Holmes looked up from the map he was scrutinizing. "I learned English in the most precise manner. I have been around through a very large part of the evolution of the language."

"You've been around for a very large part of evolution," Wallick remarked. "Do you mind if I ask a few questions?"

"Oh, why not?" Sir Remidan demanded. "All we ever do is talk and talk. We never do any fighting."

"Well, you missed the last one, tin-britches," Mira told him, and turned to the others. "He missed out on getting a skateboard for himself."

"If you come through this way again, my government will gladly furnish you with skateboards, bobsleds and little red wagons," Wallick assured the knight.

"Why does he rate such consideration?" Mira asked.

"He was the only member of your little expedition who in no way made a spectacle of himself either on or over the streets of New York," the agent said. "My first question is about this mysterious magical place you consider to be so important. The last time anyone went down into this thing, it brought the dinosaurs to extinction and changed the shape of the world?"

"That is what they say," Holmes agreed.

"But no one knows what is down there?"

"Not that I have ever heard."

"But you propose to take four dragons and this hardwood blimp into this place?"

"We must go."

"This next question is the big one," Wallick said. "Can you possibly avoid a repetition of what happened the last time? Or would you be offended by my asking if that is exactly what you have in mind?"

"No, I would not be offended," Holmes replied pensively. "As the only representative of both your government and your species, you would be remiss in failing to confront that question. The answer is quite simple. The age of faerie that I knew is past, and returning magic to the world will never bring back all the things that used to be."

"The survivors of the Realm of Faerie went into exile long ago," Wallick reminded him. "Dalvenjah Foxfire sent the last of them out of this world when I first met her several years ago. You could bring them back."

"If anything, the choice is mine to make," Dalvenjah said. "Mr. Holmes is very clever but he has very little magic left to him, only a fraction of what Allan or myself can command. Might does not necessarily make right, but it does convey a certain authority. The dragons will decide what will happen, and I see no advantage in restoring magic to this world. Indeed, we must go into the Fountain of the World's Heart to prevent the very catastrophe that you fear."

"You see what I mean?" J.T. asked. "Mr. Holmes is contagious. He has us all talking the way he does."

Wallick ignored him. "What do you mean?"

"I have every reason to believe that the Emperor Myrkan has already taken the Dark Sorceress Darja into the Fountain of the World's Heart," Dalvenjah explained. "I cannot guess exactly what they will do, but I do know that they want vast amounts of magic for their own purposes. Whatever they plan to do will almost certainly not be to the benefit of your world, at least as it exists now."

"I thought that all the magic had gone out of this world," Wallick protested. "You seem to be saying that there are vast amounts of magic somewhere near."

"That would seem to be the case," the dragon said. "Emperor Myrkan and Sorceress Darja certainly believe it to be true. There was no magic for most of the history of this world, until the Dragon Lords revealed it. That seems to indicate that there is magic there somewhere, and that it can be found."

"You make it sound as if it can be turned on and off like a faucet."

"I doubt that it is that simple, but it does seem to be controllable."

They were under way early the next morning, keeping at a low altitude as the airship's swift shadow chased over the ground just below them. The land was green and deeply carpeted in grass at first, just as it had been the day before, washing over a strange country of deep valleys and towering cliffs. But as mid-day approached, they began to move deeper into the volcanic regions near the center of that large island, leaving the grass behind for a land of cinder cones and deep flows of cold lava. This was how the whole world might have looked before the coming of life, a cold and barren place of broken rock and black lava, tortured by constant vulcanism and movements of the land. As Dave Wallick reminded them at one point, the Apollo astronauts had trained here because of the resemblance of this place to the moon.

J.T. stood in *Wind Dragon*'s bow, his nose twitching almost constantly as he stared ahead. He would frequently share his observations with Dalvenjah, who would then convey navigational instructions back to the helm deck. Allan, Kelvandor and Vajerral were overboard most of the time, flying ahead of the ship, although they had little enough to report. Kelvandor returned to the ship quickly in the middle of the afternoon and came down for a landing on the helm deck, having finally perfected the technique after months of practice.

"There are two little air machines about three miles north of us," he reported quietly, as if fearful of being overheard. "Very little ones with cloth wings like kites."

"Ultra-lights, I believe they are called," Holmes said, returning to the upper deck. Most crewmembers left the flight deck while dragons were landing. "I doubt they could match our speed."

"Allan recognized the symbols on their wings," the dragon added. "He says that they are from the Cousteau Society."

Jenny lifted her ears. "Should we consider ourselves warned? We are not fish."

"Allan thought that you might be interested."

"Why, did he plan to make introductions?" Jenny asked. "What a concept! Jacques Cousteau and Sherlock Holmes have tea with dragons."

He frowned fiercely. "Why do I even bother?"

"Because you love me," she told him, flirting outrageously. "It was your misfortune to want me for a mate."

"I was just after your body," Kelvandor insisted.

"Everyone has been after my body, but someone else got it. What did you want with it, anyway? It was the wrong type."

Kelvandor decided that it was a very good time to jump over the side.

Later that afternoon, J.T. called back that they must be getting where they were going in a hurry and that they should slow down or else they would soon be looking in the wrong place. Jenny understood what that meant, which was to say that she ignored every part of that message except the part about slowing down. Dalvenjah went overboard for a closer look, and soon after the other three dragons were seen circling back. Allan circled around again and fell in beside his mate, while Kelvandor moved around behind the ship. Holmes and Mira took one look and descended the steps to the middle deck. Jenny was a ghost and had nothing to fear from being crushed beneath a falling dragon.

"Go to the top of that plateau," he instructed. "There is something very strange about this place."

Jenny brought *Wind Dragon* up somewhat higher and steered a course for the middle of the top of the plateau. The strangeness of the place became apparent as soon as they could see the top clearly. For one thing, the top of the plateau was not level but in the shape of the top half of a large, oval doughnut, sinking in the middle into what appeared to be the neck of a large volcano. That in itself was not especially strange; volcanoes throw themselves up and erode down into any number of shapes. What was strange was that the dull grey stone that formed the entire mesa was weathered granite, not a rock that regularly came out of volcanoes and, not incidentally, a rock that was unknown in Iceland, oh fair land of pyroclastics.

Jenny landed *Wind Dragon* on her struts on the highest, most level ground she could find, leaving the ship's wheels retracted for fear that she might roll in either one of two disastrous directions, and Mira had the Trassek twins fold away the lift vanes as an added precaution. The dragons had been flying circles around the opening during that time and they had looked it over from every angle, but none of them was willing to descend inside. Holmes and Wallick were standing as close to the edge as they dared. There was no actual, broken-off edge; the ground just got steeper in a hurry until it was going straight down.

Mira and Jenny joined Holmes and Wallick at the rim, and the three dragons flew down to meet them a moment later. The opening was more than a thousand feet across and descended straight down as far as they could see, disappearing into darkness after several hundred feet.

"Well, here we are in the wilds of Iceland, brave explorers looking down into a deep, dark hole leading to the center of the Earth," Wallick said. "Jules Verne must be laughing at us from somewhere in the realm of departed souls."

"Give me a few minutes and I'll find out," Jenny said.

"If it was that simple, I would have you find the dragons who went down here the first time," Dalvenjah said. "Perhaps they could tell you how deep this hole is and what they found at the bottom."

Wallick stared into the pit. "And you intend to go down there?"

"I really have no choice," Dalvenjah said. "You might not have noticed, but a short distance from where *Wind Dragon* is parked you will find six sets of scratches on the rocks consistent with marks made from the three sets of landing struts from a very large airship. And there are the marks of three additional airships nearby. The Empire has been here already, and I would suspect that they have already descended into the pit in force."

"A reasonable deduction," Holmes agreed.

"How could they have taken such a large ship into that hole?" Vajerral asked. She remembered the Imperial battleship she had seen when the Emperor had taken Jenny's body.

"An airship is very easy to control," Jenny explained. "Even the largest airships are only about six hundred feet in length, perhaps half the width of this tunnel or a little more, and the extended vanes are even narrower. It would be simple enough to take an airship down in a descending hover."

"You will have every chance to prove that in the morning," Dalvenjah said, watching Jenny's reaction. When the young dragon still did not seem at all concerned, she decided that it really must be simple enough, at least for an experienced pilot.

"Then I should get on the radio and call our base at Keflavik," Wallick said as he turned to walk back to the ship. He would be accompanying *Wind Dragon* no farther, but would establish a base here. The dragons could call for help on the radio if they needed it, assuming that the radio still worked, and he would also be on hand to do something if Imperial airships came out first.

Dalvenjah noticed that J.T. was staring into the depths and stepped over to join him. "What do you sense?"

"Disturbance and distortion," the cat said. "Like a storm of magic. I hope that Jenny can manage the ship."

✄ PART SIX ✄

Islands in the Sky?

A group of large military helicopters arrived early in the night, landing in a loose cluster not far from the airship. Dave Wallick and the officer in charge took aside all the personnel who had flown in and had a good, long talk with them about certain things they were going to see, and then they were all introduced to Jenny. This group had been carefully selected and told what to expect before they had left, but it seemed to bear repeating. And if someone still found it a little much to accept, Jenny had the proven ability to take bullets from high-powered rifles without a scratch. There was quiet industry all night long, and morning found a couple of buildings sheltering anti-aircraft guns and small missile launchers aiming into as well as away from the opening of the pit from all directions. If the Empire contemplated leaving or sending down reinforcements, they were going to be in for a surprise. Dalvenjah had obliged by casting spells on the weapons that would protect them against magical deflection or tampering.

Wind Dragon was rigged for flight, her ropes and lines tight and all goods stored or lashed down for rough travel. Wallick came over to make his farewells, and to receive his final instructions from Dalvenjah.

"If we do not return, I hardly know what to tell you," the dragon said. "I doubt that there is anything you can do for yourselves. If you go down there or if you throw in bombs, you are likely to get the very results that you do not want."

"You do not think that closing the passage will help?" Wallick asked. "That is exactly what this outfit is prepared to do, if things begin to look bad. But the decision is not yet final."

125

She shook her head slowly. "I honestly do not know. I doubt that it would do any harm, except perhaps locally. This passage has kept itself clear since this world was new. Then again, it might work. I would save that for really big last-resort type stuff, though. How do these fine people propose to fill a bottomless pit, I ask you?"

"If we had any smart ideas, we wouldn't be contemplating the stupid ones, would we? I would throw garlic and wolfsbane down that hole, if I thought it might work."

"You will have to rely upon dragons, midgets and cats."

Dalvenjah went off to check on the airship a final time, and Wallick turned to Holmes. "WIll you ever come back to New York?"

"That remains to be seen," he said. "But I have learned one important lesson already. Never again will I open my door to anyone who inquires for Sherlock Holmes."

Wallick regarded him suspiciously. "Would you have really missed this?"

Holmes considered it carefully, and shrugged. "I suppose not."

There was a great deal of interest from those on the ground, at least from cautious distance, as *Wind Dragon* lifted from the stone and drifted slowly out over the dark opening of the Fountain of the World's Heart. The dragons had been over it often enough to know that there were no dangerous air currents in the tunnel, although there was a lazy updraft during the day and a downdraft at night. It was just barely enough to stretch the canvas of the sails behind the ship's vanes, providing a small amount of braking and added stability. Jenny edged the airship out just over the center of the opening while the dragons flew around for a final check, but there was plenty of room to spare. She turned around to face the wall of the tunnel behind her, knowing that she would be fine as long as she kept the same distance between herself and the side of the passage.

"Has it occurred to you that this is another false lead, and that we are going down into nowhere?" Mira asked quietly.

"Do be quiet," Holmes said sharply. "This is simply not the time to be thinking about such things."

The dragons circled around a final time and began coming aboard, a much simpler matter when the airship was not mov-

ing. Dalvenjah was the last to return. "You can begin taking the
ship down when you are ready."

"What speed?" Jenny asked. "I would suggest a reasonably
quick rate or we might never get there."

Dalvenjah nodded. "As fast as you dare without risking control of the ship. The rest of us will watch below, to warn you of
obstructions and other dangers."

With their long, supple necks, the dragons were very well
suited to hanging their heads over the side. J.T. was also on duty
to sense magical dangers before they became visible, assuming
of course that such danger would ever become visible under
present circumstances. Darkness became a problem almost immediately, so that magical lanterns were lit on the deck of the
ship and two more were lowered on ropes for some distance
from either end of the ship. They could still see nothing except
the rough surface of the wall of the tunnel, rippled and occasionally barklike, but so straight and regular in width that it
might have been bored by machine. As it happened, it was not
entirely natural in origin, although it certainly had not been
made by a machine.

"We are coming down into a region of stronger magic fairly
quickly now," J.T. reported, with a look of consternation on his
feline face. "I never thought that magic would behave in that
way."

"We may be able to rewrite the books on the nature of magic
after this," Holmes said. "I have been trying for half a century
to determine how magic figures into the Einsteinian view of
physics and the universe. Unfortunately the equations just keep
getting longer, and I never was entirely brilliant at mathematics
in the first place."

"Lights below!" one of the dragons warned.

Everyone except Jenny leaned well out over the side. There
seemed to be a light mist or fog several hundred feet below, visible by its own pale light even though it had not yet come within
range of their lamps. Jenny was prepared to slow the ship to a
crawl, knowing that they would have to put out poles and tap
their way down like a blind man if she could no longer judge
their distance from the walls visually. But as they came nearer,
the others could see that they would not actually pass into the
fog, which did not fill the tunnel but which clung to the walls in

a thin sheet. As soon as *Wind Dragon* had passed completely into this new tunnel of mist, the entire ship began to shudder and roll slightly, while Jenny fought to maintain her control. More alarming to the others was the fact that they suddenly found themselves in free fall, clinging to the rails to prevent themselves from drifting away. Their first thought was that *Wind Dragon*'s lift had failed and she was plunging into the depths, but they quickly noticed that the airship was actually floating in place.

"What is it?" Dalvenjah called as she flew toward the rear deck with slow, careful strokes of her wings.

"We seem to be in an area of no gravity," Jenny said as she returned both of the ship's wheels to even. "I had to cut our lift or we would have started back up."

"I had wondered about this," the dragon remarked pensively as she held to the rail, her drifting tail curling like a snake. "This tunnel is actually a passage leading to some other world or perhaps to some nether region of magic, such as the Realm of Demons. I suspect the latter."

"Are we in danger?" Holmes asked.

"Not immediate danger, although I am only guessing." Dalvenjah turned her long neck to look at Jenny. "Do you have any control over this ship?"

Jenny nodded. "I could fly her without upward lift without any problem, as long as we are moving forward fast enough to get enough airflow over the rudder and elevator in the bowsprit to give steering control. The only thing I cannot do is rotate the nose of this ship down, at least not without taking us into the mist of the tunnel that is now in front of us. I suspect that we want to avoid that."

"Yes, I believe so," Dalvenjah agreed.

"Do you suppose that you dragons could fly up to the bowsprit and push the nose of the ship over with your wings and lift magic?" Jenny suggested. "It should not be hard."

It was not quite as easily done as said; the dragons pushed the ship's nose over easily enough, but just getting themselves there was a problem. Everything they knew about flying was designed to work against the pull of gravity, while a realm of perpetual neutral buoyancy was a very new experience in which tremendous wingspans and long, slender necks and tails became liabilities. The dragons quickly learned to propel themselves with small, quick snaps of their wings that looked more like swimming than flying. All four of the dragons positioned themselves along the length of the bowsprit and pushed, their forms glowing briefly with the pale light of lift magic, and the nose of the little airship rotated downward. Fortunately Jenny had been thinking ahead and applied thrust to begin moving the ship forward fast enough to get some wind over the stabilizers, correcting the ship's roll by angling the elevator. Otherwise *Wind Dragon* would have been left doing slow somersaults in the middle of the great magical nowhere.

"Why are you not drifting?" J.T. asked Jenny as he held tightly to the rail with his claws.

"I am a ghost," she reminded him. "The magic that Dalvenjah used to allow me to exist independently permits me to respond to gravity easily, but I am still not subject to it. The only reason that I don't always float through the air like a real ghost has been for the sake of appearances."

"Did anyone leave any fires burning below?" Mira asked aloud. "You know, if you went to get yourself a drink, there would be nothing to entice the water to leave the cask."

Dooket and Erkin looked at each other, then began to pull themselves toward the hatch leading below. Mira sent them back to their stations with a sharp wave of her hand, somehow getting a sharp rebuke worked into that simple gesture.

Several members of the crew suddenly crashed to the deck, all except for Holmes and J.T., who had kept themselves held in a normal standing position, and for Jenny, who felt that she was above the laws of common physics. The curious thing was that Vajerral and Kelvandor, who had been holding loosely to the ship's upper rigging, stayed just where they were.

"In spite of what just happened, the ship itself is still in free fall," Jenny reported.

Dalvenjah had observed the odd reactions—or lack thereof—of the two dragons in the upper rigging right away. She jumped up lightly, her wings partly extended to catch herself, and dropped back to the deck immediately. Then she jumped higher, and kept going right up the mast to join the others in the rigging.

"The ship itself has become a source of gravity," she called back. "It reacts normally at very close range, but you push yourself free of it very quickly and easily."

"Indeed, it seems that all objects have become a source of gravity, but all things now possess equal gravitational attraction regardless of their size in the real universe," Holmes amended. He stepped over the siderail and stood on the side of the ship, at a right angle to the others on the deck. "The ship is simply so much more massive that it washes out all smaller sources of gravity, but the cumulative effect does not increase either its intensity or its range."

"Things are finally getting themselves straightened out," Sir Remidan commented.

"In a normal universe, the mass of this ship would generate so little real gravity that it would be hard to measure, even in a weightless environment," Holmes continued. He had returned to the main deck and now tried to walk up the mast, but he failed that completely. "Ah, I see that I must correct my earlier observations. It is not true that all objects generate gravity here, only that all objects above a certain mass generate the same gravity. It seems that the laws of physics are rewritten in this place."

"Is that not what magic is all about?" Allan asked.

"No, you know that yourself. The laws of the physical universe are the framework within which magic works. In either physical or metaphysical terms, you need far less energy to counteract natural forces such as gravity than you need to negate such forces, if indeed you could ever command enough magic to negate a major natural law. The vanes of this ship lift it, but they do not make it immune to the effects of gravity."

"In that sense, antigravity would be more trouble than it is worth since it would probably require so much energy?" Jenny asked.

"You are on the right track," Holmes said. "However, gravity itself is a nonpolar force, unlike magnetism or electromagnetic energy. Magnets have north and south poles, while electricity travels between positive and negative poles. Gravity simply is, regardless of the direction from which you approach it, and therefore it has no negative or antigravity. Think of the consequences if a planet's gravity operated in a polar manner like its magnetism. The planet would always be trying to turn itself inside-out in a vast convection along its line of polarity."

"Then what is happening here?" Mira asked. "Are we in a place where the laws of physics are different?"

"Perhaps. Or else the magic of this place is so strong that it simply overwhelms the common laws of physics. Supersede or supplant the laws of physics might perhaps be a better term."

"Actually, we are in a magical singularity," Dalvenjah said as she dropped down to join them. Holmes stared at her, and she shrugged. "Mindijaran have discovered places like this before. They are like pockets of magic in the real universe, some so large that they seem to be universes in themselves. When the Imperial sorcerers summon demons, they came from a place like this. That is why they seem so unnatural, for they are the product of the laws of an unnatural environment. Of course, you usually have to open your own passage into a magical singularity. This is the first one that I have ever heard of that had a permanent natural opening."

"This must be a very benign one, in most ways like the real universe," Jenny added.

"Why do you say that?" Holmes asked.

"Because we—or perhaps I should say the rest of you—are still alive," she explained. "Singularities are environments unto themselves, and not often very conducive to life as we know it."

"Look! There are images in the mist!" J.T. shouted in alarm. He belonged to a school of thought that believed that magic was more an art than a science, and so he had been paying more attention to their surroundings than to that learned discussion.

The tunnel of mist had begun to glow gently in great patches or streaks of various soft colors, and now distant scenes could be found illuminating some areas of the mist. There were dim, faded visions of forests, mountains and deserts, of seas that were both calm and restless, at night or day and in all seasons and climates. Some of those scenes were of cities or civilizations, always distant and impersonal. The first were familiar enough, scenes of recent history processing steadily backward in time until they had come to an age before the rise of mortal civilization. For a time they looked upon only more sea and landscapes, and then they began to catch glimpses of a far more ancient time, cities that were curious in form and lit with magical lights. They saw the feasts of elves and of centaurs in deep forests, the hidden realms of gnomes buried within their mountains, misty places of coral and shell under the waves, and dragons singing to the stars on cold peaks.

"The Realm of Faerie!" Holmes exclaimed. "We are seeing visions of the Realm of Faerie. These are not mere illusions, for I recognize many of these times and places."

Mira looked surprised. "You recognize these times? Just how old are you, anyway?"

"Far older than I care to admit."

"How long do faeries live, anyway?" she asked.

"Until someone gets sick to death of their eccentricities and hits them over the head with a large stick," J.T. commented drily.

"Then do you know where we are going?" Dalvenjah asked.

Holmes shrugged helplessly. "I cannot guess. We seem to be moving back through time, or at lest through the images of times past."

The dragon lifted her ears. "I wonder if we are to be allowed visions of the Dragon Lords and what they did when they released the magic of this world the first time. That would be a very useful thing to know before we get there ourselves."

"We can only hope," Holmes told her. "These visions seem to be entirely random rather than events of any historical importance. I would suppose that the chances of seeing any single historical event that you want are not that good."

"It is important enough to try."

But Jenny was becoming aware of a certain problem of her own, and she was beginning to suspect that they were headed into serious trouble. "Dalvenjah, something ahead is drawing us forward."

"Is it serious?" Dalvenjah asked.

"I am no longer using any forward thrust, and we are still moving ahead as fast as ever and even accelerating slowly. If we double our present speed, I will have trouble holding this ship to the center of the passage. If our speed triples, we might be in danger of losing our vanes. And you might have noticed that the passage is beginning to narrow."

The others had been so preoccupied looking at the images that they had not seen that the tunnel of mist was now perhaps two-thirds of its original width of about a thousand feet. Dalvenjah looked up with an impatient gesture when she saw

that Vajerral and Kelvandor were still clinging to the rigging.
"You two young idiots get down on deck immediately. I suspect
that we will be coming into some very rough running, and I do
not want any of us getting separated because of such foolish-
ness."

Looking thoroughly chastised, the two young dragons pulled
themselves down through the rigging to the deck. Kelvandor
was actually the oldest dragon of the group; even though
Dalvenjah was his aunt, he was still more than two hundred
years her senior. Age among dragons was most often a measure
of authority than actual years, and in that accounting Dalvenjah
Foxfire was a fossil.

Wind Dragon continued to accelerate, and Jenny was soon
engaging all the limited reverse thrust that the ship had to offer
in a hopeless attempt to keep their speed under control. Worse
yet, the tunnel of mist continued to draw slowly narrower, and
now the ship was beginning to encounter turbulence as strong,
fitful winds began to move through the passage. She would
have considered these winds a nuisance in an open sky, but they
made it nearly impossible to keep *Wind Dragon* centered in the
tight passage. No matter how quickly she turned the wheels, the
system of ropes and pulleys was always slow to adjust the angle
of the stabilizers in the bowsprit. She would have felt better
about allowing the airship to weave and bob in this way if she
could have known whether or not there was still rock on the
other side of the wall of mist.

"Can we turn the ship?" Dalvenjah asked. She was desperate
for any glimpse of the Dragon Lords, and the images were now
moving past so quickly at the same time that the winds were
pulling at the walls of mist tearing and distorting the visions.

"I could never control the ship," Jenny said. "The only hope
I see is to ride the winds straight down the passage until it ends.
Do you suppose that we will be going back in time to when the
Dragon Lords released magic into the world, or all the way to
the beginning of the world? If it takes this long just to get back
a few million years, just think how long this passage must be if
we have to ride out four billion."

"I might be able to assist you somewhat," Holmes said, and
hurried to the front of the helm deck. "Mira! Do you have any

spare sails? Any large sheet of canvas should do. And I need some long, sturdy lengths of rope."

"There is a trim sail in a deck locker there on the helm deck, just behind you," Mira shouted back. "And there is two hundred feet of rope or more that we left at the back rail when we pulled in the lantern."

"Excellent!"

Holmes tied the rope to one corner of the sail, then attached the other end to a stout mooring pin in the rear of the ship. The sail rattled and snapped like thunder in the wind as he released it overboard behind the ship, feeding it out slowly to the full length of the rope. The twins brought him the running sail as well, usually reserved to provide extra speed when the airship had a strong following wind, and Holmes deployed that at the end of a slightly shorter rope. The length of the two sails at the end of their long ropes acted very much like a sea anchor behind an ocean vessel, or perhaps like the tail of a kite, their drag both slowing and steadying the ship.

"Does that help?" Holmes asked.

"Enough to keep us going a while longer," Jenny answered.

"Very well." He turned to the others. "All eyes overboard, if you take my meaning. If we are to be given a glimpse of the Dragon Lords and their mysteries, then it will be coming up any moment now."

Unfortunately, the moment never came. *Wind Dragon* began to roll slowly to starboard, even though Jenny tried desperately to control the roll by applying thrust with the starboard lift vanes against the direction of rotation. It was as if the airship had been caught in a powerful vortex that they could not see. At least down always remained the deck of the ship, and that was perhaps the only thing that kept everyone on board and reasonably intact. Even so, the ride was so rough that no one except Jenny could have remained at the wheels fighting to keep the ship under control. As long as she had something that she could hold onto, the fierce winds that might have otherwise blown her away like tissue paper passed right through her. The others simply held on to anything they could find, except for J.T. He had hidden himself in an empty sail locker and closed the lid.

Wind Dragon was plunged into sudden darkness as she was thrown through the core of the vortex into what appeared to be a raging storm. Lightning flashed frequently in the distance, briefly illuminating the banks of clouds that never broke, and sheets of cold rain or sleet would occasionally sweep across the deck. At least Jenny was finally able to bring the ship under reasonable control, even though it continued to weave and pitch unpredictably. The fact that down remained the center of the ship helped to keep the crewmembers on the deck, but Jenny was still flying in a free fall and that made controlling the ship all the more difficult. If nothing else, gravity was a convenient source of orientation and it was a constant and predictable force that always pulled on the ship from the same direction, adding stability. Now, when the ship was blown in every direction, there was nothing to stop it from going in that direction forever, like a three-dimensional billiard ball.

And if that was not bad enough, Jenny was flying blind with no place to land and no way to find it if there was. She suspected that she had flown right out of the frying pan and into the fire.

"How did an Imperial battleship survive that?" she asked.

"If there was no storm on this side at the time they came through, they might have had a very easy time of it," Holmes said. "Of course, they might have also smashed their ships to splinters on the way through, and we would never find the wreckage."

"That might explain why the Emperor had such a start on us but has not seemed to have done anything so far," Dalvenjah added. "What would be the best way to ride out the storm in this hulk?"

"Assuming that the storm ever ends," Jenny muttered. "All I can do is to ride the winds to keep them from tearing this ship apart, and maintain enough speed to keep the control surfaces responsive. Mira?"

"Yes, Jenny?"

"Can you take the boys below and check the main lift vane spars? Both sets, but especially the rear vanes, seem to be flexing a little more than usual."

"We don't need the lift for flight," Mira reminded her. "It would not give us much trouble if a spar did fail."

"They might not give us lift, but they are very essential to stability," Jenny said. "I've been using lift on first one side and then the other almost constantly to keep us from rolling. Wait, I have another idea. Have the boys pull in the canvas sails behind the lift vanes. Since they were designed to support the full weight of ship and cargo, it must be the sudden jerks of this wind changing direction that has damaged them. Then check those spars and do what you can to brace them."

"Right away."

"What if a spar breaks?" Dalvenjah asked.

"I can maintain control, as long as it's only one," Jenny said. "I would still have one lift vane on either side of the ship. I would still prefer to have a whole ship at my command if we run into any more trouble. We need to find shelter."

"I am not certain that there is any shelter to be had," the dragon said. "I certainly would not know how to find it. We can hardly see beyond the ends of our lift vanes. If we did find shelter, we would likely run into it."

"Why did it never occur to me to get radar from Wallick?" Jenny looked over at Dalvenjah. "Do you have any magic that would do the same thing?"

"I will have to think about that."

Jenny turned to Holmes. "Is there something in your vast experience and wealth of knowledge? Can you build a radar out of Vajerral's boom box and a large piece of aluminum foil?"

"All-you-men-ee-um," Holmes corrected her in his most English voice. "And no, I am not an electronics expert. Can you teach a bat to fly ahead of us and lead the way?"

Jenny found land sooner than she had expected, and in a way that she did not want. The snapping of the top of the mast brought her attention overhead, and she was very surprised to see that it had snagged in the top of a tree. Jenny had just one thought, that by no means was she about to crash this ship upside-down in a place where gravity could not be predicted, and she rotated *Wind Dragon* completely over as quickly as she could manage. What she could not have anticipated nor avoided even if she had known was how quickly the unseen land came up that was now beneath the ship. *Wind Dragon* shuddered violently as her landing struts contacted hard ground and were crushed trying to bring the ship's tremendous weight to an abrupt halt, slamming her hull against the rocks hard enough to break her back in a thundering, ripping crash of breaking timbers.

The impact had not only ripped Jenny from the ship's wheels but thrust her halfway through the deck, one half of her metaphysical self on either side of the unbroken deck planks. She pulled herself out and made a quick survey of the damage. Most of the crewmembers were already picking themselves up, even if most of them were moving very slowly. At least none of them were making any injured noises, which was encouraging.

"Land, ho!" she announced with little enthusiasm.

As it turned out, the crew had survived the unscheduled landing in better shape than they deserved. The dragons had all gone overboard while Jenny had been rotating the ship over, and they had circled around and landed in their own good time. Dooket and Erkin had been kicked over the side by the impact, but they were young and made of rubber and had bounced with only scratches and light bruises. J.T. the cat had also gone over the rail and was the worst of the lot with a broken leg, but he was also knocked unconscious and not to be found for some time. The combination of events left him in a predictably bad mood, and the broken leg kept him in a bad mood for a very long time. Sir Remidan insisted that his armor broke his fall. Lady Mira was so close to the ground that the fall had not bothered her. Holmes had been holding to the rigging and had not even fallen.

"What do you mean, your armor broke your fall?" Mira demanded impatiently.

"Well, the magic came back, you know," Sir Remidan explained happily, and even hopped up and down a couple of times. "Do you see what I mean? It hardly weighs anything again."

Mira was certainly not pleased, and having Sir Remidan all but giggling about his magical suit of armor did not make her any happier. *Wind Dragon* was wrecked in about the worst imaginable place, the weather was the pits and the cat was missing. Even though the wind was still driving occasional sheets of wet sleet, she had the Trassek twins drop the boarding ramp and took them overboard for a look around. Curiously, the vanes that Jenny had been so worried about had survived intact, even though their internal spars had been broken and they now sagged heavily to the ground. Unfortunately, the hull was splintered from bow to stern, and the struts had been reduced to kindling. She glanced up as Dalvenjah shuffled around from the other side of the ship to join her.

"Well, we seem to be stranded," Mira observed.

"You seem to be stranded," Dalvenjah corrected her. "Some of us can fly."

"You are indeed a wicked thing," Mira complained. "Do you, by any chance, have insurance?"

"No, of course not."

"Then it's a good thing that I do. If this weather breaks any time soon, I can get Jenny to venture an opinion on what she can salvage."

"Mira, I just found your cat," Kelvandor called from the other side of the ship.

"Is he alive?"

"Dead cats do not use that kind of language."

Mira was involved for the next hour or so in setting and splinting J.T.'s broken leg and restoring what she could of his fractured temper, both things accomplished easily using magic and generous doses from the bottle of liqueur that Holmes had brought along. At last he was taken to his bed in a cabinet that served at his cabin, not yet actually asleep but gurgling and cooing between crude attempts at singing. When Mira came back on deck later, she was surprised to find that the storm had disappeared completely, revealing a blue sky but no sun and a scattering of floating islands like the tops of hills that had been broken off and thrown up to hang suspended in mid-air. They were in form like irregular disks, thickest in the middle, bare grey stone on the bottom but green and even forested on the top. Curiously, they were all oriented with their green sides facing in the same direction, giving a false direction of up.

Mira was so preoccupied with looking up that she bumped into Holmes, who was leaning over the rail. She lost her balance and nearly fell, but Holmes caught her.

"How is your cat?" Holmes asked.

"He is presently a very pickled puss. Your bottle was very appreciated, I can tell you. My only regret is that the bottle won't last for the weeks that he will have to wear that splint." She looked around quickly. "Where are the dragons?"

"They went off on a reconnaissance as soon as they could see where they are going," he explained. "Since there is no gravity only a few feet above the islands, the dragons can fly effortlessly. Their wings do not have to support their weight and they are not pushing against gravity when they sweep their wings, so they do not tire quickly. Indeed, you will find it very easy to fly yourself, with only a small effort in lift magic."

"Have you tried it?"

Holmes drew himself up regally. "My dear woman, flailing about in mid-air is hardly dignified."

"Oh, certainly," Mira said, knowing that he was teasing her. "Is Jenny anywhere around here, or did she go off with the other dragons?"

"No, she is down below somewhere."

Mira descended the boarding ramp and walked slowly around the shattered hulk of her ship. *Wind Dragon* looked every bit as bad in the clear light of day, even if daylight here was noticeably softer than in the real world. The airship's lift vanes were being removed and set safely aside. She found Jenny still in the process of removing the forward port vane, the last of the four, her arms and long neck reaching through the planks of the hull to detach the vane from the spar. A living person would have been stuck having to climb in and out of the ship several times to remove each lift vane.

"Will she fly again?" Mira asked.

Jenny removed her head from the hull. "This ship will fly only slightly sooner than pigs will. She might not look so bad from the inside, but this hull has been shattered from front to back. The keel and ribs are splintered, and I hesitate to tell you what the bottom looks like."

"We had stressed the ship to the point that something was due to fail even before this happened," Mira said. "What do you think?"

"I sent the dragons out to look for trees," Jenny explained. "I believe that the best plan is to get this ship off the ground so that I can cut away the bottom of the hull and the keel as extra weight and mount the top of the ship on a large raft made of several tree trunks laid side to side. That also means attaching the lift and thrust vanes to the raft, since no remaining part of this ship can carry the strain."

"How do you plan to lift the ship?"

"The other dragons and I can levitate it, I am sure." She

turned her head to look at the sorceress. "Why don't you and Mr. Holmes take a walk? Give this island a good looking-over and see if you can find anything useful."

"Yes, something to eat," Mira speculated.

Now Mira knew quite well that she was being given an excuse to make herself scarce, just to keep her out of the way. That was probably for the best all the way around. For one thing, Jenny had a college degree in engineering and had proven herself to be quite clever in building things, and she could instantly arrange in her head complex mechanical schemes that most people could not have put together even on paper. Besides that, Mira had suspected for some time that the girl harbored secret wishes to take the little airship apart. Given time and the proper tools, two things they did not have, Jenny could have rebuilt *Wind Dragon* exactly the way she had been. On the other hand, even though Mira was herself quite handy, they both knew that it was best if she did not stand around and watch her ship being cut up like a side of beef.

Sir Remidan gallantly declined to accompany Mira and Holmes on their walk about the island, pointing out that he must be on hand to lead the Trassek twins in the event that danger threatened. Mira would have said that the twins needed someone around just to tie their shoes for them, but she decided to keep such comments to herself. Sir Remidan was in an exceptionally good mood now that the magic had come back to his armor, and she did not want to spoil that. She was led to wonder if the reason that he had been in such a bad mood during their visit to New York had been because his armor had grown so heavy once the magic had left it. That, and the fact that the reruns of *Mr. Ed* had made him so lonesome for his own talking horse. She knew now that it was a mistake not to have encouraged him to watch more *Yogi Bear*.

Their investigation of the island soon brought out two important facts. First, they had landed near the highest ground, on the slopes of the low, shieldlike mountain that dominated the center of all the larger islands that they could see. Second, the island they were on was a rough oval some five miles or more wide by three across. They crossed to the nearest edge, a walk of more than a mile in itself.

"I do wonder what the formula is for determining the circumference of an oval," Holmes mused. He was beginning to speak more and more in Mira's own language, having learned both it and the language of the faerie dragons in good time. He would still resort to English, however, when talking to himself or when he needed big words. Holmes seemed to be addicted to big words, and he would get nervous tremors if he was not allowed to exercise his expansive and frequently arcane vocabulary with a certain regularity. Something just like that, you see.

"What was that?" Mira asked.

"I was wondering how long it would take one to walk along the edge of one of these," Holmes explained. "Do you realize that the area of an island of average size, such as we can see from here at least, is quite large enough to support a small village and its surrounding farmlands?"

"Are you going into real estate?"

"No, just wondering if this strange environment might be inhabited," he said. "There is certainly life here, both plant and animal."

"I suppose that you could raft them together," Mira speculated.

"No, I doubt that. Either these islands are held in place by forces we cannot see, or else they repel each other by some means. Otherwise these islands would have started bumping into each other from the first, breaking each other to bits and forming by their curious gravitational attraction into a small planet. That must be why they are still flat."

"I beg your pardon?"

"The gravitational attraction of this one island is equal to that of an entire terrestrial planet," Holmes explained. "That much force should be acting to pull these islands into a more spherical form. Perhaps it is the case that this curious gravity only acts between objects, but a single object is not affected by its own gravity."

"That seems very simple to me," Mira said. "These islands are not just one big piece, but made up of rocks, and sand and soil grouped together. A rock that you might be standing on can be placing tremendous force on the rock just beside it, but it has no effect on rocks even a short distance from it. The effect of gravity here is not cumbersome . . ."

"Cumulative," Holmes corrected her.

"Cumulative, so there is no larger force acting to collapse the entire island."

"By George, that is right! My word, you are indeed a clever one." Holmes stopped short, already musing upon the next mystery. "Of course, what made the islands flat in the first place?"

Mira looked even more mystified. "Who is George?"

They came at last to the edge. Mira had been expecting something a little more dramatic, but Holmes was not surprised. The edge of the island was gently rounded and the grass simply dragged over the side until halfway through the curve, to the point where it circled back beneath the island. One of those little mysteries that Holmes had been contemplating was the fact that all the islands were oriented facing upward directly toward the source of light, even though there was only more blue sky and no actual source of light to be seen, so that the only shadows were those under objects. There would have been vegetation on the lower sides of the islands as well, except for the fact that the undersides were always in the shadows. Another thing was that the edge, which looked paper-thin on the other islands, was actually several yards deep.

Mira began to realize that Holmes was secretly fascinated with the curious gravity within the magical singularity, not just as a scientific peculiarity but also as a great, delightful toy. He walked right over the edge without the slightest hesitation until he came up standing upside-down on the lower side of the island. Mira joined him somewhat more cautiously and they spent some time exploring the mysterious dark side, which was not as barren as it looked from a distance but covered with grey and brown moss and by whole vast communities of mushrooms. It was also noticeably cooler in the perpetual shade.

"Does it ever get night here?" Mira asked as they made their way back to the edge."

"Not that I can tell so far," Holmes said. "There is simply no mechanism to allow it."

"What about the islands? Have you been watching them?"

"Yes, I have."

"Do they move?"

"I saw no evidence of motion even just after the storm had ended, so they were not affected by the winds. If they are in motion, then they are all moving exactly together in fixed positions."

"Like traffic."

"Essentially."

"Do you ever get tired of people asking you questions all the time?"

"It goes with the job."

Mira preferred to ask questions, since it took her mind off the fact that she was in extreme torment. She was on an upside-down island of mushrooms with no way to know if any of them were poisonous, and she had never been more hungry in her life. Actually, she had been this hungry from time to time, but when the stomach lust hits hard and heavy then it seems like nothing could have ever felt so bad. As soon as they reached the top, she headed for the nearest shade tree, took off her pack and sat herself down.

"I say, Holmes old boy, it does seem to be time for lunch, doesn't it?"

"I suppose." He consulted his watch. "Actually it seems to be half past one in the afternoon in the wilds of Iceland, if that means anything."

"It means that I am starving."

Holmes sat down beside her, then leaned over for a quick look inside her pack. "There seems to be nothing in there but food."

"That's right."

"You did eat right before we left," he reminded her.

"That's right." She handed him a granola bar.

"Did you expect to be gone for several days?"

"No, not at all. Can you keep a secret?" She looked around quickly, as if expecting to see the long, narrow faces of dragons peering out at her from every bush. "Am I beginning to show?"

Holmes was so surprised that he nearly stood up. "My dear lady! Don't tell me that you are pregnant?"

"No, of course not!" Mira insisted, pale and shaken at the very thought. "No, I've just reinstated the spell that makes me taller. It does have one serious disadvantage. I can hardly stoke it in fast enough to keep up with my rate of growth."

"I had noticed your discomfort," Holmes remarked. "You

might almost say that your growing pains are all in your stomach."

"Almost."

"And how soon will you be back to the height you desire?"

"Five days," she said. "The first time I did this, I allowed it two weeks. I dislike having to rush it like this, but I want to have the better part of my height back before we get into a fight. I packed extra food for my own need."

She took a cup from the pack, placed a tea bag inside and filled it with water from her bottle, them made a few quick gestures with one hand. The water began to steam almost immediately. As she waited for her tea to brew, she glanced at Holmes shyly, an expression that she did not practice often. "Mr. Holmes, could I ask you a rather personal question?"

"I am blushing in anticipation. Please do."

"You are an elf, and several hundred years old."

"Several thousand, to be more precise," he told her.

"Well, I have been wondering about this from time to time, and having lunch like this brought it back to mind." She bit her lip. "When a person lives that long, what do you do after you wear out your teeth?"

Holmes flashed her a toothy grin. "Like the rest of me, my teeth are magically protected against wear, aging and disease. Even if I should happen to lose one, and in all the time that I have lived I have had the occasional unexpected accident catch up with me, then the tooth grows back."

They had only just finished packing up again from lunch when Holmes, whose elvish eyes had also not deteriorated with time, looked up to check the positions of the nearby islands and saw a distant shape moving slowly toward them. Although he could not yet determine what it was, he considered it a very good idea to return to *Wind Dragon*. They hurried as much as they were able, the problem being that Mira's legs were really not any longer than they had been. They were unable to see the mysterious object during most of their journey back because of the forest, so they did not yet know what it was or if it might have already arrived, but Holmes was certain that it was moving slowly but directly toward the wreck of the airship. They had not speculated so far about what manner of people they might find living within the singularity, but it was certainly possible that such beings would most likely be creatures of faerie or the higher magic such as dragons.

What they found when they reached *Wind Dragon* was certainly strange enough but not immediately threatening. The faerie dragons had returned, and they had brought with them something unusual that they had picked up somewhere. It was all shiny steel or aluminum, in shape somewhat like a submarine or the body of an airplane with a large tail and small, downswept wings located near the front. To be a little more precise but somewhat less technical, it looked like a big metal shark with the top of a gunboat built on its back, except that it had been wrecked, damaging its wings and lower rudder, and reducing the propulsion units to an unrecognizable ruin. The only frightening thing about it was the fact that it was even larger than *Wind Dragon*, and that the dragons, who had been pulling it with ropes, were now trying to figure out how to get it onto the ground and those last tricky couple of feet when it responded to gravity.

"How much do you suppose it weighs?" Dalvenjah called down.

Jenny regarded the hulk speculatively. "Does it have any engines or other pieces of heavy equipment on board?"

"No. It is just the hull, frame and decks."

"Is it steel or aluminum?"

"Aluminum, I am sure. It does not weigh as much as you would expect when you pull it."

"That is mass, not weight," Jenny muttered. "That makes it the weight of an aircraft body of about the same size, without engines or other equipment. Say, a B-1. Twelve to fifteen tons, then."

"Are you certain?"

"No, I really have no clear idea. That is just an educated guess."

"With a degree in engineering, your educated guess is worth something. All we can do is give it a try. The five of us can levitate this, I am sure."

For all of that concern, landing the ship was accomplished without the slightest problem. Jenny made a curious purring noise and leaped aboard the ship with every intention of looking that hulk over inside and out from front to back and top to bottom including all the places where only she could look without first dismantling the ship. The other dragons watched her for a long moment, as if wondering if she would ask anything of them, but she disappeared inside without a sound except for one last contented purr.

Dalvenjah turned to Mira. "If I had been thinking, I would have had it gift-wrapped for her."

"What is it?" Mira asked.

"With any luck, it might well be the hull of your new airship," the dragon explained.

"Really?" Mira gave the thing another appraising stare. "It looks like a great silver shark. Do you think that Jenny would take exception if I painted eyes on it?"

"There is a general conspiracy to keep you away from everything when you have a paintbrush in your hand," Dalvenjah said. "Did you possibly leave anything for four hungry dragons to eat?"

Mira stared at her. "You know?"

"You are beginning to show, dear," Dalvenjah told her solicitously. "Just don't hurry things along too fast, now. You might get stretch marks."

"Oh, you are good," Mira exclaimed, escorting the dragon to the wrecked ship. "Did I ever tell you about Adenna Sheld?"

Mira joined the dragons in a second dinner, for she was already starving from her need for even more bulk to turn into added size. She did check on J.T. in the event that the convalescent cat was ready to join them, but he was still well under the effects of his own brand of anesthetic and probably would not recover for several hours more. At that time he would very likely awaken feeling just as bad as when he had taken that particular painkiller. Curiously enough, Jenny hurried over to join them as soon as they sat down to eat, when they would have expected that she had decided to haunt the curious little ship permanently. As it happened, she had a very good reason for abandoning her inspection. She was curious.

"Where did you find this amazing little miracle of a shell?" she asked impatiently.

"We found it abandoned on an island only half the size of this one, about fifteen miles from here," Dalvenjah explained. "If you will allow, I will now anticipate several of your next questions. My suspicion is that the ship's whirlyblades were wrecked in a storm . . ."

"Whirlyblades?" Mira asked.

"Vectored fans, we call them in the mortal world," Jenny explained. "By what I can tell, the ship was moved by large, flat-bladed propellers inside metal cylinders that directed the stream of air. The fans could be rotated to aim the thrust down to lift the ship or back to move it forward."

"Anyway, the ship was adrift," Dalvenjah continued. "When she came down on that island, she slid in under some trees where she could not be seen. The crew survived, obviously, since they stripped provisions and furnishings from the ship. They must have moved to a remote part of the island, since they were unaware that we were stealing their ship until after we were gone. They shot a couple of arrows at us, but we were already out of range."

"What she means to imply is that we did not know they were still around until they shot at us," Allan added. "It was a surprise for us all."

"Arrows?" Jenny asked. "You were lucky."

"And how is that?" Dalvenjah asked.

"Well, I looked inside one of the motors," she explained. "I found it curious that there were no fuel or power lines. It works on much the same principle as our lift vanes, except that applying lift causes the armature to spin just like an electric motor."

"Ingenious," Holmes remarked quietly.

"It gets more so," Jenny said. "That little ship is no freighter. She has the smooth, lean lines of a ship made to run fast and no real cargo holds. And she also has guns. They use a linear application of the same principle as the vector fans to kick projectiles down a tube. I doubt that it gives the projectiles much of a kick compared to gunpowder, and probably very little speed or range. But the accuracy of the thing must be frightening, since there is no gravity to arc the trajectory."

"Can we fight them?" Mira asked.

"With the catapults and the exploding bolts," Jenny said. "That gives us slightly less range but about the same punch. They use exploding projectiles with both pressure-sensitive triggers when they hit their target and a timer to self-destruct. You don't want these things drifting about in free fall like way-

ward mines. In certain respects they are more like inertia torpe-
does than artillery shells."

"And what plans are you hatching in your ethereal mind?"
Mira asked. "Can you get that ship flying again?"

Jenny sat back on her tail, looking very much like a young
dragon who was extremely pleased with her thoughts. "These
people never learned how to project fields from large vanes.
They use small vane segments to produce strong local fields of
force. In spite of appearances, I doubt this ship could manage
forty knots. *Wind Dragon*'s thrust vanes will move her at better
than sixty. I intend to mount the lift vanes where the vector fans
used to be. Once the ship is in flight, the lift vanes can be rotated
back for extra thrust. I cannot begin to predict the top speed that
might give us, but bursts of a hundred and fifty knots would
hardly surprise me. We'll need that when we go against the Emperor's battleship and fleet."

"Unpleasant realities intrude upon this idyllic scene," Mira
complained softly. "What can we do?"

"You can keep the twins and Sir Remidan away from that
ship," Jenny said. "The rest of you do what you can with the interior of the ship. Lining the inside of the hull with planks from
Wind Dragon will do a lot to contain the damage and keep
pieces of metal from flying about if we are hit. I will do the mechanical work."

The work took the better part of three days, Iceland Time, according to Mr. Holmes's watch, or only a day and a half in local
time. Contrary to what he had predicted, darkness fell rather
quickly only a short time after the dragons had returned, and it
stayed dark for the next twenty hours. Another unpredictable
matter was the weather. Without gravity to stratify the atmo-
sphere by pressure, clouds moved about indiscriminately like
grazing cattle rather than in layers and groups. They would
sometimes have to pause in their work while a cloud moved
across their island in the form of a thick, white fog, departing as
abruptly as it would come. The winds generally moved up and
down, relative of course to the tops of the islands, in a fitful convection that was driven by the mysterious source of light and
heat in this universe of floating islands.

J.T. awoke at last, looking and feeling like something the cat
had dragged in. His head hurt so much that he did not even no-

tice his leg, so in a strange way the alcohol was still working to relieve the pain. As it was, he hurt so much and felt so weak that he could not work himself into a seriously bad mood as he would have wished. Holmes offered him a taste of the hair of the dog that had bit him, to see if that would help. The term so offended the cat that he swore off drinking entirely.

Jenny's part of the repairs was slowed down slightly when she decided that she had to build herself a forge for metalworking. Magic served to give her all the heat she required for her work, and being a ghost she had no need to protect herself. The others were often amazed and unnerved to see her doing things like holding red-hot pieces of metal in her bare hands while she swung a hammer with the other, and Dalvenjah quietly reminded her to be careful about picking up any bad habits that might prove to be dangerous when she was returned to her body.

As it was, Jenny actually finished her part of the rebuilding before the others. They came to realize that the ship had not been stripped as much as they had originally thought; the machine had to be very light so that the four ducted fans could kick it the short distance to get it clear of an island's gravity. The thin aluminum of its construction hardly weighed a thing, but it was not very strong in some places; even an arrow would have pierced it. Planking the interior of the ship actually made her frame a great deal stronger, especially after Jenny showed the others how to lay the hardwood boards between the metal ribs and braces in a way that added the most strength.

Jenny recovered *Wind Dragon*'s wheels and skids and attached these to new struts that she had mounted onto the hull of the metal ship, removing its two forward, downswept wings in the process. Then she cut each of the lift vanes into two equal lengths and mounted these inside short, thick wings, using the wings that she had taken from the front of the ship for the forward pair and making a second set from aluminum panels that had been taken from inside the ship where they were no longer needed as walls. These wings were then attached at the sockets where the ducted fans had been, the internal frame and pivoting mechanism already being strong enough to bear the weight of the ship. The wings themselves did not rotate, but the lengths of lift vanes inside the wings could be turned to direct their thrust.

When the ship was not in flight, the wings were hinged to be folded up against the side of the hull for storage like the forward fins of a submarine. Magic gave Jenny the ability to easily build anything she could design.

Soon enough the new ship was ready for flight, and there was nothing to be done but to take her up for a trial run. Mira, who had come from a less technical world, had some doubt that metal flaps could work as effectively as canvas sheets in steering the ship. Sir Remidan had much stronger doubts that a metal ship could fly; he was certain that it would never float. At least this place was a test pilot's dream, since the only thing that could go wrong short of deliberately flying the ship into an island was stupidly flying it into the ground on landing. Any mechanical failure or insufficiency could be easily controlled by simply stopping, since the ship was not going to fall.

Jenny and Mira took the ship up for the first time, since they had the most experience in flying airships. Jenny of course could not be injured, and Mira could jump overboard if things went wrong. Conditions being what they were, she could swim through the air with some effort and even drop back to the ground without harm. The twins had discovered fairly quickly that there were some places where a person could jump, such as off the top of a large stone, and not come down again.

Jenny took the ship up a couple of hundred feet and brought it to a stop, cutting off all lift from the vanes. The ship remained mostly where it was, drifting at the barest crawl with the light wind. Jenny began to ease the ship forward. "She certainly flies stable enough."

Mira stood up to look over the protective flaring that lined the forward edge of the helm deck, located high above the center of the ship rather than in the stern. Mira had been growing quickly in the last few days and was now only a few inches below her previous height. "Steering is the only part that I'm worried about."

"We can try that right away."

Jenny began putting the ship through a series of maneuvers. The ship was certainly stable enough to satisfy her at any speed, but she did not like the steering. There were three wheels compared to *Wind Dragon*'s two, with rudder and elevator in the tapered stern and ailerons for pitch control in the wings, a necessary matter in a place without gravity. The wires and pulleys that altered the control surfaces were designed so that small turns of the wheels caused large movements in the flaps, biting hard into the air at the lower speeds the ship had been limited to. Under her new speeds, that overreaction of the controls made her very difficult to steer precisely. Jenny knew that she would have to design a better control system as soon as possible. For now, however, they had to be under way immediately.

Keeping to lower speeds, Jenny was able to maneuver the ship in for a landing easily enough. "Well, your ship is ready to fly. Do you have a spare bottle of wine?"

"Why is that?" Mira asked.

"We need to dedicate your ship," Jenny said. "What is her name? Is she still *Wind Dragon*?"

Mira frowned. "I guess that I'll have to think about that."

❧ PART SEVEN ❧

A Most Unfriendly Altitude

Jenny wanted nothing more than to let the little airship loose and see just what it could do, but she did not trust the ship's handling enough to push it past sixty knots. That would have been a very respectable speed indeed for the old *Wind Dragon*, but Jenny was only using power from the forward lift vanes. That seemed to be the most stable application of power, pulling the ship like front-wheel drive rather than pushing it from behind with the thrust vanes. Jenny had already wrecked one ship in the last few days and she had felt guilty enough because of that. Building a new, better ship had helped her to feel that she had paid a part of the debt that she owed Mira for the loss of *Wind Dragon*.

Besides that, they simply could not afford the delay of another extensive repair. The Emperor's fleet was ahead of them by at least several days and possibly several weeks, and they had to begin making up that lead in a hurry. After some thought on the subject, Dalvenjah and Holmes had agreed that they did not need to track the Emperor and the Dark Sorceress Darja, something they could not figure out how to do anyway. They could possibly save a great deal of time and trouble by proceeding directly to the very center of the magical singularity, the source of all magic. That was more easily said than done. Some argued that the center of the singularity must be the source of light and heat, but Dalvenjah found that answer a little too easy.

The Dragon Sorceress had a surprisingly simple answer to the problem of determining the direction to the source of magic, although it sounded so silly that all the others had assumed that she was teasing. All except for Mira the reconstituted, who was

153

fond of silly ideas. They took Jenny down into the ship's main
hold, the largest single cabin aboard, shut the door and placed
wet towels around the cracks. Then Jenny was told to allow herself to drift, an exercise that had always before left her hanging
in mid-air for hours at a time. This time, however, she drifted
slowly toward the floor, no matter how many times they repeated the experiment. If they turned the ship upside-down, she
would drift toward the ceiling. As Dalvenjah then explained,
Jenny was now a creature entirely of magic with no physical
presence at all, and she was reacting to the source of magic.

The trick now was trying to decide whether Jenny was being
pulled toward the source or pushed away from it, indicating
whether the source of magic was also the source of light or in
the opposite direction. At least the choices had been narrowed
down to only two. Holmes argued that the source of light had to
be driven by some other force, most likely the source of magic.
Dalvenjah agreed that he was probably right, but not necessarily
so. At last Jenny made herself very small and held herself as
straight and stiff as a board, and Mira set her spinning rapidly
end over end. Holmes called for heads and Dalvenjah for tails.
They had to wait some time while Jenny's faint resistance to the
air slowed her to a stop, and she came up with her tail pointing
mostly toward the ceiling. Since no one was satisfied with that
answer, even Dalvenjah who had called tails, they proceeded
immediately toward the source of light.

Determining their exact course was a piece of ingenuity of
Jenny's making, since the compass and altimeter from *Wind
Dragon* did not work in this place and there was no actual
source of light to be seen in the middle of that great blue sky.
There was a slender metal pole, obviously a flagstaff, in the
bow of the ship that was straight up relative to the deck. Jenny
tied a piece of cord to the base of the staff, measured out a short
distance and attached the other end to the exact center of the
deck so that the cord made a line down the long axis of the ship.
As long as the shadow of the staff lay on top of the cord, they
were moving directly toward the source of light.

Looking at the tops of the passing islands, with their forests
and plains and low, flat mountain in the center, it looked as if
the airship was standing on her tail. Mira seemed to find that
disconcerting every time she looked. The sorceress insisted

upon remaining on the helm deck at all times, even though Jenny served as their only pilot and was all for practical purposes in complete command of the ship. Jenny was the only one who really understood how the more complex arrangement of thrust vanes and control surfaces really worked, and she was certainly the only one who could keep the ship's rather obvious idiosyncracies under control.

"Have you noticed that it does not get any brighter or hotter as we move toward the source?" Jenny asked. "Of course, the distance might be so great that we simply have not come far enough yet to make a difference."

"It is nice to have the helm deck somewhere that you can see where you're going," Mira observed. "There are no masts or rigging or bowsprit to get in the way of your forward view. How is she handling, by the way?"

"Well enough," Jenny said. "I do want to put down on one of the islands soon and made some adjustments on the steering before we find ourselves in any strong winds."

"Sir Remidan should be pleased with that," Mira said softly. "For some reason, flying the ship through these drifting islands makes him very nervous. He almost looks airsick when we go past a close one."

Jenny glanced at Mira, then did a quick double-take. "Lady Mira, you seem to be getting shorter again."

Mira made a disgusted face. "Oh, piffle! I am getting shorter. I realized just a while ago that I got the magic wrong when I started putting on my height. Now I have to start over again."

Jenny suddenly lifted her head straight up, her ears perked. "What is that?"

Mira listened for a long moment. The ship itself made hardly any noise, less so even than the old *Wind Dragon* with her crude aerodynamics and the wind humming and whistling in her rigging. "I honestly don't hear a thing. I just don't understand it. Your ethereal ears seem a lot more sensitive than the material ears of the other dragons."

"That might be why," Jenny replied. "My shape is arbitrary, so I don't really have ears. I respond to sounds in a more direct manner."

Mira just looked confused. "That sounds complicated. How

do you ghosts manage to hear without real ears or see without real eyes?"

"What worried me more is how I think without a brain," Jenny told her. "I think that you should yell for Dalvenjah to come up here, and have her bring the World's Greatest Elf Detective with her."

Holmes and Dalvenjah came up to the helm deck immediately, and Jenny had them turn an ear to the wind. Mira could still not hear a thing, but she had to admit that elves and dragons had better hearing. Dalvenjah engaged one of her moderately fierce dragon frowns. "What is that?"

"Nothing within the normal experience of a dragon," Jenny explained. "But I would bet my ectoplasm that we are hearing a bank of very large ducted fans, much larger than the blades that were on this ship. My guess is that we are somewhere near a ship that is either quite a lot larger than this one or built for far greater speed. Proceed with caution."

"This worries you?" Holmes asked.

"This little ship had obviously been built for fighting, since it had guns and not much else. My personal suspicion is that no one is in the habit of building and operating military machines unless one has a present or possible future enemy to handle. If we meet another ship, it could be either a friend, an ally or an enemy. We have no way of knowing what their response will be until it comes. And since we have no flags or colors of our own to fly, we could be treated as pirates or smugglers."

"Imagine trying to control smuggling in a place like this," Mira mused.

"The point that I am getting to is simple," Jenny continued. "If we run across the natives, we might not like it. What should we do?"

"Can we evade a hostile ship?" Dalvenjah asked.

"The handling is a little squirrelly," she said. "We might be able to do sixty or seventy knots, but the *Hindenberg* could do that. I can't promise that we would be able to outrun everything we might find. That is exactly why I want to adjust the steering of this ship."

"I suspect that the question just progressed from a matter of speculation to one of greater immediacy," Holmes remarked.

It took the others a moment to figure out what he was trying to say. By that time, they could see for themselves. Coming across the top of a large island to their left was a ship that looked vaguely similar to their own, a curious mixture of submarine and dirigible with the superstructure and gun turrets of a battleship on top. One important difference was that this ship was at least nine hundred feet long, nearly eight times the length of their own. The massive metal cylinders of four ducted fans lined each side of the ship, each one twenty feet or more in diameter. Jenny was uncertain about the speed of this behemoth. Even though it seemed to be crawling, she estimated that it was pushing thirty-five knots. But judging by the heavy droning of its fans, it was laboring.

"Watch her guns," Jenny warned, looking over her shoulder. "If any of them swing around in our direction, I will need time to evade."

Dalvenjah, Mira and Holmes just stood and stared at the larger ship, which had so far maintained it course and speed, giving no indication that it was even aware of their presence. Jenny bent her neck around and stared at the others. "Hello, there. Any thoughts on the subject? Did you want to turn around and have a word with Mighty Mo, or do we just keep going?"

"I was hoping for some indication of their attitude toward strangers," Dalvenjah said. "I wonder if they realize that we are not one of their own. They might not have taken a good, close look at us yet."

"Or they might be just as slow as us in making up their mind," Mira added.

Whatever the reason, the battleship was some time in responding. The deep, rumbling drone of her engines eased back suddenly to a low idle and the flaps of her wings and fins were adjusted to bite into the wind. Jenny could see from the set of her flaps that they were trying to bank the ship and bring her around to follow, although the sharp reduction of her speed suggested that the gesture had not been intended as hostile. The fact that the guns of her two forward turrets continued to remain inactive supported that suggestion.

"It does seem that they want to talk," Jenny told the others, wondering if they would agree with her judgement. The battleship was only now beginning to respond to her sudden change in direction, swinging her long nose around in a slow, graceful arc. "Is that an indication of their attitude?"

"I suppose that it is," Dalvenjah agreed. "I suggest that we circle around and discover what they have in mind."

"What if they want us to pay for this little ship that you just happened to find?" Jenny asked.

"That is simple enough," the dragon declared. "It is Mira's ship."

Mira rolled her eyes and afforded the faerie dragon a very impatient expression. "Piffle."

Jenny began to coax the little ship into a turn, banking sharply in a copy of the maneuvers of the larger vessel. Banking was something that the old *Wind Dragon* could not do easily, and Jenny was interested in experimenting with it. Tilting the top of the ship into the direction of the turn did counteract the ship's tendency to want to slide through a turn. Unfortunately, the ship seemed to have some very definite ideas of her own. Only a third of the way into her turn, the ship suddenly overreacted and spun around out of control to stand on her tail.

"Yarg!" Mira declared, picking herself up from the deck. "I cannot tell you how happy I am that we didn't do that under normal gravity."

"I'm rather pleased with that aspect of the situation myself," Jenny said as she moved the ship forward fast enough to get it under control and bring it around. "Mira, you might consider having the boys stand by with catapults and your dandy exploding bolts, somewhere that you can't be seen but could have your weapons on deck in a moment. Hit them in the fans and control surfaces. Dalvenjah, you might warn the Air Force to stand by."

"What can dragons do with metal?" she asked.

"Thin aluminum will burn like paper under direct flames. Fireballs might be more effective than regular flames."

"Jenny!" Holmes warned sharply.

"Oh, fardles!" Jenny exclaimed when she saw the hull of the larger ship rising before them much sooner than she had expected.

She had only a moment to wonder why she had been so inattentive, pushing the ship much faster than she had intended and forgetting to watch where she was going. Such a lapse of attention might have been normal for a person with a tired mind, but she was a ghost. She spun the wheels to execute a sharp turn, but the little ship overreacted once again and stood straight up on her tail, hurtling belly-first toward the hull of the larger ship rising like a silver wall before them. The controls were unresponsive in that position and Jenny struggled to engage the lift vanes. But she found that her magic, although it seemed stronger than ever, was erratic and strangely resistant to her own control, and her surprise at herself made things all the more difficult. She brought the ship to a dead stop in mid-air at the very last moment, and began returning the wheels to neutral to move away.

What she had forgotten was that the battleship was turning in that very direction. The two left landing struts of their ship impacted almost at the same instant with force enough to pierce the metal plates, the hull of the battleship echoing like a drum from the collision, and the two right struts slammed against the hull of the larger vessel a moment later with slightly less force. Jenny stood ready to move her ship away as soon as they were thrown clear by the impact, but the airship clung tightly to the hull of the larger ship, her left struts locked in the broken plates. The fans on the battleship were shut down a moment later.

Mira lifted her head and looked around. "I don't see that I have to pay for this one."

"I must be losing my mind," Jenny muttered, watching the blades of one immense fan roll slowly to a stop not twenty feet away. "Mr. Holmes, will you please go over the side and check those trapped struts for damage? Tie a rope to yourself, so we don't lose you. If they prove to be unfriendly, and heaven knows that they have no reason to feel very friendly toward us, then I will have to pull straight out and run for it. Mira? Do you want to go up to the top and speak with the good people? Politely?"

Mira made a very unhappy face. "What about Dalvenjah?"

"She's a dragon."

"Well, I know that," Mira said impatiently. "Is that meant to indicate some special draconic privilege, or just her inability to be polite?"

"They who dominate have no need to be polite," Jenny told her. "I want to keep the dragons discreetly out of the way until we know more about what we have here."

"Yes, very well. Very well," Mira grumbled as she entered the hatch that led through the armored wind baffle to the forward deck. "Who died and left you in charge?"

"I did."

Mira walked up to the front of the forward deck, which soon brought her level with the deck of the battleship. Her new ship was by no means small; indeed, its actual hull length was nearly as great as that of *Wind Dragon*'s hull and bowsprit. The battleship was so much larger that the ship fit diagonally up the height of her hull, with only a couple of yards poking over the top and the last four yards of her tapered stern and tailfins below. Mira reflected that as long as they were in this position, at least those big guns could not be brought to bear on her little ship. At the same time, repelling a boarding party would be hellish.

A tall, distinguished-looking gentleman, ruggedly handsome with a greater emphasis on handsome than rugged, looked over the edge of the battleship's deck at her. "Hello, there. Are you in need of assistance?"

Mira was so surprised that she took a step backward and sat down on the deck."

"He spoke English," Jenny said quietly.

"I heard Mindijaran," Dalvenjah reported. "That is an aspect of the magic of this environment."

"Duke Telmar, Lord Admiral of the Imperial Fleet of Acquessa and Captain of the Fortress *Harrier*," the tall gentleman proclaimed himself.

"Ah, Mira. Lady Kasdamir Gerran, Captain of the *Star Dragon*," Mira said somewhat breathlessly, finally giving her new ship a name in the process. "My friends call me Mira."

"Oh, no, it's going to be one of those," Jenny said softly. "Mira can be very susceptible where these suave, sophisticated types are concerned, and this fellow reminds me too much of her last boyfriend."

"What was that?" Allan asked as he came up to the helm deck.

"The High Priest Haldephren."

"He looks human enough," Dalvenjah observed. "I wonder if his kind came down from the surface at some time."

"Not unless they fell in," Allan said.

Mira talked with their host for a while before she hurried

back to the helm deck. She cast a final glance above, but Captain Telmar and his crew had drawn away from the edge. "I don't much like this, I do admit. That fellow reminds me too much of Haldephren."

Jenny looked surprised. "I would have never thought that good sense and caution would have ever overcome your lusty impulses."

"I've been teaching myself not to act on impulse. It hurts," Mira said.

"Are you certain that it is not Haldephren?" Dalvenjah asked.

"Fairly certain. Haldephren was always too smooth. This Telmar is very full of himself. He's trying to keep me under control by charming me with civility and concern, but I doubt that he would go so far as actual seduction. I've been losing my height again in a hurry, and he obviously considers himself above a midget. No pun intended."

"What does he have in mind?" Dalvenjah asked. "Does he expect you to pay for appropriating this little ship?"

"Finders keepers, apparently. But he is very interested in our propulsion systems. He wants to keep us around to talk to us about secrets," Mira said. "I told him that we seem to be having steering problems, and he has asked us to follow him home so that we can make repairs."

"Have these people seen anything of the Emperor's fleet?"

"He says that a group of strange ships moved through an area quite some distance from here about a month ago. They seemed to be lost, or looking for something. Since they have been attacking anything they see, and since their ships are faster and their magic too strong, the Eolwyn have given up trying to fight them and just stay out of their way. I assured him that we are not a part of the Emperor's fleet."

Holmes climbed back over the side to join them. "Very good news. We seem to have sustained no damage from the impact at all, and the other ship has only light damage. We can pull free and be on our way any time."

"Is there any reason why we would want to stay around?" Jenny asked, her own suspicions obvious.

"Three that I can think of immediately," Dalvenjah said. "If these people have been under attack from strangers, then why was this Telmar so friendly with us, even before he knew that we are not associated with the Emperor's fleet? I suspect that there is more going on here than he is willing to admit. I want to know the truth about their actual standing with the Imperial fleet, and I also want to know more about them and whether they will interfere with our business. I want to discover what they know about the nature of their own realm of existence, if they know what and where the source of magic is and if they have told the Emperor."

Jenny looked from Dalvenjah to Mira and back again. "Why do we always have to do it the hard way? We find someone we don't trust, and we allow them to take us home for dinner. That's what got us in trouble last time."

"We have to take the chance," Dalvenjah insisted. "We have been guessing what we need to do, but the time we lose if we are wrong will be disastrous. If we can find out when the Imperial fleet came through here, where they are going and possibly even what they expect to do, then a delay of a day or two would be worth it. Besides, if you can redesign the ship to run faster, then we will make up the time. You have threatened to do that anyway."

Jenny agreed reluctantly; she might be allowed to give orders when the ship was in flight, but Dalvenjah Foxfire was still very much in charge of the expedition. She seemed prepared to be sullen and argumentative over the whole matter, behavior that even she knew was uncharacteristically childish for her, but she was hardly given the chance. She was directed to pull *Star Dragon* away from the *Harrier*'s side, dragging her struts clear with only a little more damage to the hull. In terms of strength of construction, these ships were much closer akin to dirigibles than battleships, possessing tremendously strong frames but thin shells. Jenny brought *Star Dragon* around and landed her on the battleship's rear deck, being very careful to bring the struts down on hard points supported by underlying framework. There was no danger of crushing the larger ship, since the two ships were in fact attracting each other only at the area of contact, and the *Harrier*'s deck was supporting only a ton of *Star Dragon*'s total weight.

Captain Telmar was under the impression that *Star Dragon* was in a much poorer state than she actually was, and both Dalvenjah and Mira encouraged him to maintain that belief.

Both he and quite a few members of his crew gave the little ship a good looking-over as soon as it was aboard. Her thrust vanes were obvious enough but the lift vanes were completely hidden within the two pairs of short wings, but Telmar restrained himself from asking and no one volunteered that information to him. *Star Dragon* was strapped down to the deck and they were under way almost immediately. Mira added power from the thrust vanes to boost the *Harrier*'s eight massive fans, which made enough noise and vibration to make a pleasant cruise impossible. Mira took the watch to free Jenny to work on the steering, and she deliberately kept her own contribution of power to a minimum to avoid revealing just what the vanes could do.

Jenny's earlier estimates about the speed of these ships had been fairly precise. Even though Lord Captain Telmar was in a hurry to get home with his new friends, the air-speed indicator on *Star Dragon* refused to budge past thirty-five knots even with the smaller ship pulling her own weight and giving a little more besides. Jenny, as curious as ever, made herself invisible and undertook a close inspection of one of the *Harrier*'s engines, located directly on the driveshaft in the central hub just ahead of the fan. Even though it was almost the size of a radial aircraft engine of about two thousand horsepower, she assumed that it was putting out only a third of that force. Power was provided by magic-users of fairly low grade, one to each engine; Jenny did not wish to dignify them with the word sorcerers.

Very soon they began to pass among inhabited islands, where the usual stands of trees had mostly been cleared for fields and pastures. There was, however, one important thing about these places that several of the others noticed almost immediately. These were not island-villages, each one supporting its own population of rustic farms. These were large, well-organized and efficiently run plantations, or in some cases groups of islands forming a single large plantation. The core of each plantation was a fortresslike manor house, its massive dome like a stone umbrella providing the stoutest defense turned toward the sky, the most likely direction of attack. Storage and servant quarters were either carved into the stone of the islands itself or in the form of long, lightly fortified buildings like barracks.

All of this provided two important hints about the structure of the local society. This was a nation frequently at war, not necessarily with itself, and subject to sudden if not unexpected attack. This was also apparently a feudal society, where lordlings ran their own pocket-sized empires with armies of serfs or slaves.

After some three hours, Lord Telmar led Mira, Holmes and the dragons to the bridge of his ship, set high in the central superstructure for the view it gave of the rest of the ship. He was still trying a little too hard to be congenial, treating them all like old friends and pretending that the faerie dragons, creatures unlike any that he had seen in his life, were in fact so familiar to him that he took no notice. It sometimes strained him considerably to force himself to take no notice. Somehow, he had acquired the notion that Mira, Homes, Dalvenjah and Allan were lords of rank, while Jenny, Vajerral and Kelvandor as well as Sir Remidan and the Trassek twins were peons. Of course, the boys *were* peons.

"There she is!" Telmar exclaimed gallantly, pointing ahead to the largest island that they had seen yet. "That is Acquessa, my home. There are, you must understand, only eighteen continents in all the Eolwyn Empire. Acquessa is more than two hundred and fifty miles across by nearly two hundred wide."

"My word, is all this yours?" Mira exclaimed in her best "little ol' me" southern belle manner.

"Duke Telmar Vanryekess of Acquessa, at your service," he replied with a heroic sweeping bow. Whether he knew it or not, he had the southern gentleman role down fairly well. Depressingly enough, it probably came naturally. "You must understand that Acquessa is the third largest industrial center in the Empire. The continents differ from the islands not only in size but in the fact that they have the only large deposits of metal, particularly aluminum needed to make our ships. Needless to say, that also gives us almost all of the gold, silver and gemstones as well. Each Duke is given his own territory to govern, and it is his responsibility to protect the islands in his domain. To that end, we collect taxes from the islands in our domain for the building of our navies. The Dukes, in turn, give over a portion of our ships and their maintenance to the Imperial fleet. In that sense, the Imperial fleet is our offensive navy, while the ducal navies are entirely defensive."

"One would guess that you are at war," Mira ventured cautiously. The magical translations they heard were fairly precise;

in this case, Duke was not a rank of aristocracy but the title of supreme war leader.

"I fear that it is so," Telmar admitted. "We have been at war with the Quentarah for as long as our history records, and the Empire is more than twelve thousand years old."

"Why have you been at war for so long?" Mira asked.

"There can never be, I must admit, any hope of peace between ourselves and the Quentarah." He frowned, and continued softly. "They are not our kind, you see. Not as different from ourselves as you and your dragon friends, but still they are another creature entirely. They are small, for one thing, and they are ruled by their females."

"That might be inconvenient," Mira commented. She did not have to remind him aloud that she was both small and female.

"It really is all a matter of their attitude," Duke Telmar was quick to explain. "They are alert and industrious little beggars, I will grant you that. But you can't get decent work out of any of them you take captive, and the next thing you know they disappear. They all have so much magic that it is almost impossible to keep them under control. The best thing you can do is kill them when you can."

If this was his idea of being discreet, then they knew that they were in for some real surprises. These boys would get along with the Alasheran Empire quite well. Holmes, of course, liked to keep things in perspective. Because these people built all-metal, engine-driven flying ships, it was easy to jump to the conclusion that they were fairly advanced. But he had yet to see anything on the ground to support that conclusion. The policies and attitudes that Duke Telmar expressed would have been fairly typical and even expected in the mortal world that he had just left, even within that very democratic and civilized country where he had been living, within what was to him very recent times.

Since their destination lay well toward the center of the continent, they still had a flight of some three hours yet ahead of them. Night had fallen by that time; Holmes and Dalvenjah watched the process carefully this time, and they still did not have a clue about how it was done. Holmes decided that it was time to approach the question of what this place was like, and the matter of day and night where there was no sun was a good place to start.

"Oh, that is simple enough," Telmar explained. "Our world is in the shape of a sphere if you are looking from the outside, but the shape of a vortex or cone as you come nearer the center."

The others quickly realized that when Telmar was describing his world, he meant not just the inhabited islands but all the empty space between. By his definition, his world and his universe would be the same thing. He just had the advantage in that his universe, as far as Holmes could translate the distances, was about twenty thousand miles across and completely filled with air. Curiously, the distance from the outside to the middle, at least as far as the Eolwyn had ever dared to go, was about sixteen thousand miles. The Eolwyn were not particularly curious about anything that did not turn a profit, and they had found nothing profitable about exploring the mysteries of their world.

"What about the change of night and day?" Dalvenjah asked.

"That is all a matter of magic," Telmar said. "When magic radiates from the center, it causes a region of the air surrounding the center to glow with light and soft heat. But the center of the world rotates, or perhaps the world rotates around the center. As the center turns away, and so directs the flow of natural magic away, the the air ceases to glow."

Dalvenjah put on a face that only a dragon could wear. "My head hurts."

"Wait until we go down the middle," Holmes reminded her quietly.

The city of Acquessa was not as impressive as they had expected, certainly not the members of Mira's group who remembered Alashera. Of course, the Alasherans had possessed both the wealth and the security to indulge their decadence, while the Eolwyn appeared to be under the threat of constant attack and had to build defensively. The city was built largely into the slopes of the low but rather steep peaks, one of several in the rugged terrain near the center of the continent. The main castle that dominated the top of the peak was certainly massive enough to deserve that name, intricate if not beautiful in its sprawling design, it spiral-topped turrets and vast domes meant to turn an attack from above.

Since *Harrier* was the Duke's own ship, she passed the military shipyards to land at the castle. *Star Dragon* was cast off first and Jenny landed the smaller ship on the pavement a short distance away, a matter that suited her just fine since it would make sneaking away much easier if the need arose. Four sets of long, wide rails were swung down on struts from the battleship's lower hull and locked into place, so that only the lowest three feet or so of her rounded hull was actually within reach of gravity from the ground, perhaps thirty tons to provide a stable anchoring platform to keep the otherwise weightless upper portions of the hull from being blown about by the wind. Jenny finally realized that the immense ship was not built so lightly so that it could lift itself; in the real world, it could never fly. The fighting ship was as light as possible to make it agile in turns, quicker to accelerate, and to minimize inertia. She soon discovered that the freighters, which were built with sturdy steel and carried thousands of tons of cargo, needed several minutes to come to speed and miles to make a turn.

Duke Telmar wanted to take his guests up to the castle for a welcoming dinner immediately. According to local custom, the list of those he considered his guests was limited to those he considered to be of aristocratic rank, meaning Mira, Holmes and the two dragons Dalvenjah and Allan. Vajerral went along in the guise of Dalvenjah's personal servant, and Sir Remidan, still in his armor, was explained off as Mira's bodyguard. The others were expected to stay with the ship, to await the pleasure of their masters. Jenny preferred that arrangement just fine. She still needed to complete her modifications of *Star Dragon*, and the Duke granted her authority to requisition anything she wanted from his own supplies. That also left a sizeable guard aboard *Star Dragon* to discourage spies.

"That was surprisingly generous of the Duke," Kelvandor observed. "What can he be trying to do?"

"He already thinks of *Star Dragon* as his own, of course," Jenny explained. "He plans to learn all that the others will tell him voluntarily, then put them in prison to extract the rest by force."

"Should you warn the others?"

"Dalvenjah already knows," she assured him. "Duke Telmar has been very free in giving out his own secrets, since he believes that we will not benefit from them. As soon as she knows enough, we will be on our way. I must have this ship ready to run at full speed within the next six hours. Dalvenjah has given me that long, since we must be under way before light."

The Eolwyn went to bed as soon as it turned dark, since they had been awake and working for the last twenty hours of light. By their own habits, they would sleep for a few hours, work through the middle of the night and go back to bed for a few hours more until light returned. Dalvenjah thought that they should wait until some time near dawn before they should leave without saying good-bye. At that time nearly everyone would be back in bed for the second time, resting up for their next twenty-hour marathon of delightful serfdom. Light would be returning soon after that, giving Jenny a clear view to run the ship at full speed. Whacking the bottom of an island at a hundred and fifty knots would make ghosts of them all.

"I've sent word ahead that we should like some dinner before retiring," Duke Telmar reported as he led his guests to the castle. "I am back a day early from my patrol and my return was not anticipated, so I fear that we will have to take what we can find for dinner."

"I would assume that you do not fly with your ships often," Holmes said. "Your other duties must be numerous."

"The *Harrier* is my own ship, and I am her only captain," Telmar explained. "That is a traditional duty within the Empire. I must admit, however, that I can only take her out on a three-day patrol every fifteen days. Not so much for the value of the patrol itself, but to have a personal look at the state of all the islands in my domain. In the event of an attack, of course, I will usually take *Harrier* out immediately."

Eolwyn architecture looked very much on the inside as it did on the outside, thick walls and ceilings of heavy stone reinforced by many buttresses and wide columns. Not to support the weight of the stonework, because the gravity was not cumulative, but to give strength against impacts during an attack. As it was, the place looked like bunkers for heavy cannons. The Eolwyn were also not given to ostentation. Since the climate was mild and the season never changed, there was no need to make provisions for heat or cold, and storms were frequent but never lasted for long. The biggest problem with the weather, aside from wind damage and lightning, was that the winds would often pick up debris from other islands. Since it would not fall, it might be carried by the winds for days, long after the storm had passed, before it just happened to find an island in its way. One could never know when sticks or stones might come hurtling out of the sky, often with force enough to break one's bones. After one of the larger storms, whole trees might be set adrift in the winds.

It also seemed that the Eolwyn did not have much wealth to spare for furniture and decoration, even in the Duke's own palace. To Holmes at least, that indicated a society that was not as advanced as it looked, was not very productive, or else had to channel a large part of its wealth into the military. Duke Telmar spoke of the war as if it was nothing more than petty skirmishes from the Quentarah and counterattacks, but he was beginning to suspect that large amounts of ships and property were lost regularly.

They were taken to their rooms to wash up, as Duke Telmar pointed out to them rather plainly with his usual awkward excuse for discretion, before he led them downstairs to the dining hall. This was actually the lesser dining hall, since the main dining hall seated a hundred and fifty without bringing in extra tables and could have doubled as a hangar if only it had a door big enough. The lesser dining hall was much more cozy, with all the charm of a missile silo.

Dalvenjah sat back on her tail at her place at the table, dragons being unable to sit properly on a chair because of the rather sizeable appendage that was attached in that location. She regarded her plate and saw that it held a fairly large piece of some animal that had been properly cooked. At least Telmar had not served her raw meat, something that was known to happen with people who were not familiar with dragons.

"Do not eat anything," a voice said very softly into her ear. "It has been poisoned."

She lifted her head in surprise. "What?"

"I will explain in a minute."

Dalvenjah looked around quickly, but there was no one there. Duke Telmar looked up at her. "Excuse me, Sorceress? Is there something you require?"

"No, not at all."

"Please eat, by all means," Telmar said, watching her closely. Dalvenjah was beginning to think that invisible words of advice might be correct.

Allan had been cutting up his own meat into manageable slices and was just about to attack with draconic ferocity, when he paused and sat in silence for some time, obviously listening to something that no one else could hear.

"Your ships have intrigued me, I do admit," Holmes was saying. "How long have you been building such ships?"

"Oh, some seven thousand years now," Telmar answered. He was seated at the head of the table with Mira and Holmes on either side, acting as a buffer between himself and the dragons. "The engines we use serve well enough, but we would certainly like to find a better, more powerful system."

Hint. Hint.

"What did your people do before you had those engines?" Holmes asked, to move the subject into safer territory.

"Oh, like some of the primitives still do, we would have used sails when the wind was right, which is really most of the time. And as many primitives are still required to do, our ships used to be rowed."

"Rowed?"

"Well, yes." Telmar seemed to think that the word had no meaning to these strangers. "Groups of slaves would move long shafts that had large fans on the end, pushing enough air to make the ship move. That is slow, of course, and generally reserved for tight maneuvering."

"How do they launch and land such ships?" Holmes asked.

"Launching is the easy part; I've seen it myself. They slide their ships along ramps that carry them out past the edge of the island, or off a cliff. Landing is the tricky part. They just sort of thump down into their cradles, which is less rough than coming down on solid ground. Hitting the cradle can be a bit difficult, so they throw ropes overboard and people on the ground pull them down."

"Sorry to leave you hanging, but I had to warn Allan," the voice said, and Dalvenjah recognized it as Jenny's. A piece of meat suddenly teleported itself from her plate. "You were the one who made him such a big dragon, so you know how he can shovel it in. Anyway, I thought that if I were to follow His Nibs

Squire Telmar around while none of us were in his company, especially after we first landed, then he might say a few things worth hearing that we would not get from him otherwise. He decided right away that the dragons are too dangerous to try to control as prisoners, so he is determined to do away with you and get the information he wants from Mira and Holmes. I saw him poison the meat himself. I warned Vajerral earlier, since she and Sir Remidan are to be fed in the kitchen with the hired help.

"It gets even more interesting. His Nibs had a talk with his admirals or secretaries, whatever they were. To make sense of this situation, you have to realize that this Empire has no Emperor as such, but the Duke who commands the most power, prestige or respect gets to tell the others what he thinks should happen in this council they have. Well, Emperor Myrkan approached the Eolwyn some time ago and dazzled the yokels with the speed of his ships, some twenty-five knots better than the best battleships can manage, even though they are only wooden ships. The Eolwyn thought they had the upper hand at first, and they were surprised. Anyway, His Nibs here thinks that he can capture us and our ship because we are not a part of the Alasheran fleet and no one cares piddly squat what happens to us. Once he gets our secrets, he intends to adapt his own ships in a hurry, put the Alasherans in the place where he believes they belong, capture control of the council because his ships would be faster than anyone else's, eradicate the Quentarah very easily after several thousand years of war, and make a bundle selling improved propulsion systems to his buddies all at the same time."

Another piece of meat teleported itself into oblivion. "So I was thinking that if it appears that you have eaten your dinner, then His Nibs is going to be caught off guard when all the dragons don't suddenly fall over dead but go on living as though nothing ever happened. He might even learn to be a little afraid of us."

"I am happy to hear that someone has everything figured out," Dalvenjah said very softly.

"Thanks much," Jenny said, ignoring any possible sarcasm. "Anyway, I want to come back after dinner and find out what the Duke's reaction will be when certain dragons don't die."

"I do want to be out of here as soon as it is light enough for you to see," Dalvenjah added. "When poisoning fails, Duke Telmar might try something a little more direct."

"Oh, I can see well enough right now," Jenny insisted. "I don't actually see the way you do. Do you know how, when you are flying at night, your magical awareness will tell you where there are trees and such? My awareness is so acute that I can distinguish shape, detail and even color as well as you can see, and the lack of light is no problem. That is how I see what things are like from the inside, you know."

"Then we can leave now?"

"Well, not right now. I have *Star Dragon* dismantled. I will be back in touch with you soon."

"Isn't that right, Lady Dalvenjah?" Mira interrupted her suddenly.

"I beg your pardon?" Dalvenjah responded, looking around quickly. She had been sitting with a blank expression for some time while she had spoken with Jenny. Mira was watching her with quiet concern, while Holmes had a speculative expression suggesting that he had an idea that something was up. Telmar was staring at her with wide, fearful eyes, as if he expected her to roll over on her back with her legs in the air at any moment.

"I was telling Duke Telmar that most of a dragon's flying speed comes from magic."

"Yes, that is so," Dalvenjah agreed, realizing that she was expected to give that very answer for some reason.

Realizing that Holmes and Mira were up to something, Dalvenjah decided that she should pay better attention. The subject was *Star Dragon*'s method of propulsion, and the two of them were filling Telmar full of misinformation. Although they would say nothing definite, they were encouraging him to believe that only dragons could fly an airship, since the principle was similar to their own lift magic. There was no question to the exact moment when the full realization of their implications sank in; Telmar suddenly looked up at the two dragons with an expression of incredulous surprise. Dalvenjah was determined that, if he had the audacity to offer them an antidote, she was going to force-feed him the leftovers.

Duke Telmar soon decided that it was time to retreat and regroup, to see if he could make sense out of this mess and contemplate new tactics. He really was not quite as stupid and incompetent as he seemed, but he was short on subtlety and completely overwhelmed by the opposition, with Holmes attacking him on one front with logic and Mira attacking on the other front with illogic. The poison that he had given the dragons was supposed to have a delayed effect, so that they would have died quietly in their rooms some time soon after dinner. Now that he wanted them alive, he was afraid to let them out of his sight. But he needed time to think even more, and at last he seemed to have decided that if his dragons really were going to die, then he would feel better about the loss if he did not have to see it.

His tactic for controlling his guests during the night was simple: divide and conquer. As long as they were shuffled off into different rooms, then they would not be talking among themselves and hatching up ideas of their own. And since it would have made Holmes and Mira suspicious when the three dragons fell over dead, it seemed easier all the way around if they simply did not know. Since they were in a transitory state between guests and prisoners anyway, it was also a simple matter to put guards in the halls outside their doors. The chambers were large, even lavish in size and, at least by local standards, in appointment, with massive beds and various items of furniture that appeared to have been cobbled out of timbers, although the workmanship was solid, and rather unimaginative carpets both on the floors and doubling as hangings on the walls. The windows in their rooms were too narrow for them to climb out and escape by walking down the outside of the wall, a very real concern here. No one would build windows very large here, partly for the sake of defense and partly because this would have been a cat burglar's paradise otherwise.

At least an hour passed before Jenny put in her appearance. "It's now eight hours past nightfall and well past a third of the way into the night. Unfortunately, the night shift just came on duty down at the docks, the same people who work the day shift as a matter of fact, so there is no getting away until nearly everyone goes back to bed later."

"What about Duke Telmar?" Dalvenjah asked.

"Oh, His Nibs is a tired little trooper and he was just tucked into bed. He tried to work on his schemes, but all he managed was to get moderately sotted instead. He is absolutely overwhelmed with curiosity about when you are going to die and he wishes very hard that you do not, but the only way he can think of to find out is when he invites all of you down for the midnight feeding. It never occurred to him that he could simply have someone walk around the wall and peek in the window at you."

"You don't like him very much, do you?" Allan asked.

"The only thing worse than evil is incompetent evil," the ghost explained. "Perhaps he really is not as stupid as he seems, but he is scared to death of us. It seems that these people are not very capable sorcerers, even the best of them, which puts them at a disadvantage with many of their enemies. And whatever the Emperor Myrkan did when he came through here, it scared these people half to death. Duke Telmar is rattled, and he actually hides it very well. I might add that deductive reasoning is something that these people do not do well at all, whether it's inherent in themselves or simply something that was never adapted well into their culture. That might be because none of them have a very strong sense of individuality, even His Nibs. He's trying to handle this situation according to what is expected of him by tradition and duty, not so much his own initiative. That might be why these people needed thousands of years to come up with the few tricks they do have."

"They probably stole the technology they do have," Allan added. Then he grinned. "It sill amuses me to think that there are whole fields of magic-based technologies. The two words magic and technology seem that they should be mutually exclusive."

"There are some who believe that they should be," Dalvenjah said in her best holier-than-thou voice. "Magical technologies are a crutch for people who are magically challenged, or just plain lazy."

"Like Mira?" Jenny asked.

"Mira is socially challenged in ways that defy description."

Jenny returned the final time about an hour before daylight with the announcement that it was time to leave. That left only one little problem: trying to figure out how. Jenny at least had the advantage, since she had already taken a look outside and knew not only the exact number of guards but where they were located. She did not, however, immediately know what to do about it. There were no less than forty guards watching six people in three suites, and no one was going out those doors until something happened. She sat down together with the dragons to check their mental file cabinets under D for damned good ideas.

"How do you kill forty guards all at the same time without making enough noise to bring more guards?" Vajerral asked. She had been installed in the suite's adjoining servant's chamber, just as Sir Remidan was in Mr. Holmes's suite, and she had come over to join the others.

"His Nibs seemed to remember that he left the rest of us with the ship, and that we might get ideas of staging a rescue," Jenny said. "The guards are all in groups outside of the doors, with no less than twenty guards outside of this room, ten on either side. That makes sneaking up on them hard even for a ghost, since they would notice and make noises if they started falling over."

"What about noise?" Allan asked. "If all of us come out that door spitting fireballs in ever direction, we can probably run right through any limited opposition we might find and be on our way before the natives can get themselves organized."

"That would certainly work," Dalvenjah agreed. "I would still prefer to save that for our last resort. Old faerie dragon proverb: sneaky is safer. Ideas like that work much better in adventure stories."

"I wonder if there is some way to make them all go to sleep," Jenny mused. "I seem to remember something like that in an episode of *Star Trek*."

Allan looked at her. "What do you plan to do, go around pinching all of their necks with your little invisible hand?"

"Something only slightly like that," she said, and turned to Dalvenjah. "What is the quickest, quietest way to put someone to sleep by magic? The bubble?"

"That is not particularly quick, making someone breathe their own air until they pass out," the sorceress mused. "The only advantage is that any fool can work a bubble. A remote shock to the brain is quick and quiet, but very hard to do. If I tried to do it to forty people, even one at a time, something will go wrong soon enough. Are these people exactly human?"

Jenny shook her head. "No, they seem to be closer to elves,

although they are not true immortals but grow old. They also
have tails."

Vajerral looked surprised. "What? Tails?"

Jenny shrugged. "Little hairless tails. They keep them inside
their trousers. I can't blame them for that. They are such pitiful,
worthless tails."

"How did you find out about that?"

"His Nibs took a bath after dinner," she explained. "He also
had three of his favorite bimbos in the tub with him. They all
had tails."

Dalvenjah looked disgusted. "Three at once? I had thought
these Eolwyn too Spartan for such self-indulgence."

"Well, it was a very big tub." Jenny paused as she considered
something. "You know, that gives me an idea. I'll be back in a
minute."

She disappeared before anyone could say a word.

"Well, I like that!" Dalvenjah said, hardly knowing whether
to be annoyed or amused. "It has turned out to be rather useful,
having a ghost about. And there I was, thinking that magic was
the most useful thing in the world."

"If we were all ghosts, we would have been out of here already," Vajerral observed. "I still don't recommend it."

"No, Jenny has the advantage of having a body out there
waiting for her when she finishes with being a ghost," her
mother said. "I do know the magic that would move you right
out of your body in a moment, but do you want to leave it here?
It would be the end of your sex life."

"Don't tease the poor girl," Allan said. "She hasn't been laid
in weeks, and she can't get Kelvandor to take pity on her. He's
devotedly waiting for Jenny to get her own body back, and I'm
sure that he's made reservations."

Vajerral seemed to be trying very hard to blush. Having a
dragon's armor made that very difficult.

"What about that business with tails, though?" Allan continued. "Do you suppose she was making that up?"

"No, I don't think so," Dalvenjah answered. "She seemed to
have a hard enough time believing it herself. It's not the sort of
thing you see every day."

Allan grinned wickedly. "It's not the sort of thing you normally go about looking for. Having a little hairless tail hanging

down in the middle seems very awkward for the gentlemen, don't you think? I mean, if you happened to see them without their pants on, but only from the waist down, you wouldn't know if they were coming or going."

"Allan!" Dalvenjah exclaimed softly. "J.T. is right, you know. We are all beginning to talk like Holmes."

"Sure, and it's a blessing that Sherlock Holmes wasn't an Irishman, isn't it now?" Allan asked.

Jenny returned at that very moment. "Well, what do you know? It worked, and on the very first try at that. Mira would die, if she knew. She always did have such trouble with that spell for dispatching demons."

Dalvenjah regarded her patiently. "Would you be willing to explain your brilliance right away, or do you wish to be wheedled first?"

"Oh, something you were saying earlier brought it to mind," Jenny said. "When you mentioned *Star Trek* and bubbles, I just put the two together and came up with the most wonderful idea."

"You mentioned *Star Trek*," Dalvenjah reminded her. "You also brought up the subject of bubbles. What the deuce does Captain Kirk have to do with being forced to breathe your own air until you pass out?"

"That made me think of warp drives, and I was wondering if I could use magic to bend time and space in a very localized and controlled environment. It seemed to me that if you could make it work, then you could do very much what you want with it on the inside."

Allan looked very startled and alarmed. "You were playing with advanced physics in a place that has its very own laws of relativity?"

"Well, I never thought of that," Jenny admitted. "I suppose that I could have been the first person to make my very own black hole."

"Don't count on it," Dalvenjah said. "So where did you go? I suppose now that you have thoughts of making *Star Dragon* do warp factor nine?"

"No, I don't use it to go anywhere," Jenny insisted. "I just use it to phase myself outside of normal physical reality."

"What, you were here the entire time?" Allan asked, trotting out his most surprised expression one more time.

"Yes, and I heard everything," she told him. "I rearranged the furniture, and none of you saw or heard a thing. It was almost as if everything in the warp field with me had become a ghost."

Dalvenjah lifted her ears and looked around. The bed, two heavy wardrobes and a large writing table had been piled in one corner of the room. "Well, I'll be a dinosaur!"

Jenny's little discovery opened up whole new realms to the time-honored art of being sneaky. Dalvenjah had decided already that she needed to find something else to call this little trick, since it seemed like too much trouble trying to explain *Star Trek* and quantum physics to dragons who might not care for the idea that the universe is a mathematically precise structure. Jenny extended the field around them all and they left by simply walking through the door and right past the unsuspecting guards. She left the three dragons in a safe place and went back to collect the others. By the time she had them all assembled, she was unable to sustain the field any longer.

"I'm sorry, Capt'n. She canna' take no more," Jenny said. She would have been panting, but that was irrelevant to her condition.

"That must take tremendous effort," Dalvenjah agreed. "You cannot expect to go around bending the universe and get away with it. We probably do not need to walk through any more walls, so we might try ordinary invisibility. Mr. Holmes, are you able to make yourself invisible?"

"I do know how," he said. "Regretfully, I have not had much practice in the use of my magic in the last few thousand years."

"Then I will cover you, Vajerral can protect Mira, and Sir Remidan can go with Allan," she said, then noticed that the knight was holding a bottle. "Sir Remidan, have you been drinking?"

"Mr. Holmes and I have been chipping away at that bottle all night, and you know how long the nights are," he insisted defensively. "It seemed like too nice a bottle to leave behind."

"Suit yourself. Just try to keep your armor quiet."

They made themselves invisible and were on their way again. Now the real problem with being invisible was that they were also invisible to each other, and that made it very hard for them to keep from bumping into one another all the time. At least there was no danger of them getting separated from each other; they were making to much noise for that.

"I've never been invisible before," Sir Remidan observed quietly. "At least not that I ever recall. This would have been very handy, when I was a squire for Sir Tesdramode. I wonder what the old boar is doing these days."

"He was Queen Merridyn's Ceremonial Protector for a while," Mira told him.

"Yes, I knew that. Did he retire?"

"Well, some have greatness thrust upon them; for Sir Tesdramode, it was retirement," Mira explained. "You see, Sir Tesdramode has been getting rather blind lately, but he refuses to have anything done about it. He's always had this curious prejudice against magic, you know. He seems to think that if everyone isn't allowed to have magic, then nobody should have it."

"He was always rather suspicious of magic," Sir Remidan agreed. "I never knew that he had carried it that far."

"Anyway, Queen Merridyn had gone off to a party hosted by a wealthy merchant who was hoping for some government contracts, and she was wearing rather startling pants and tunic completely covered with shiny silver disks, like the scales of a fish. Well, Sir Tesdramode had been out of town and had returned to the palace that night, but with the Queen away he retired to his room. Quite some time later, he was wandering about the halls for some reason when he heard someone ratting about the Queen's chambers. It was Merridyn herself, of course, but the old knight was so blind that all he saw, or thought he saw, was someone wearing bright chain mail in the Queen's own chamber, and he assumed that it must be an assassin. He chased the Queen down the hall, out the door and across the yard until three squires tripped him."

Sir Remidan made an apprehensive face. "I can imagine how that went over, the Queen's own protector chasing the Queen herself across the yard in the middle of the night. I also remember Merridyn when she was younger. If she'd had a sword of her own, she'd not have run."

They fell silent, and everyone stood perfectly still for a long moment while a pair of guards marched past.

"Anyway, Queen Merridyn had just about forgiven him when he struck again," Mira continued. "I don't know if you recall Dame Gherdys Caldeben, but she had passed away about a year ago. Well, Sir Tesdramode somehow got it into his head that it was his Great-Aunt Gherdys, his grandfather's youngest sister by some twenty years who had married Sir Bethmond of Oshglaid and who was damned near a hundred years old. So there they were at the funeral, with Queen Merridyn walking up the aisle amid two thousand mourners from the aristocracy and the leading merchant families, with Sir Tesdramode at her side as her protector. They bowed low before the casket, then Sir Tesdramode took one look inside and exclaimed, 'That's not my Aunt Gherdys!' in that great, deep voice of his."

"The two of you can gossip until your ears fall off as soon as we get to the ship," Dalvenjah snapped. "Right now, I want a little quiet or I'll leave you here and you can wander these halls invisible, like Bilbo Baggins."

"Who is. . . ." Mira started to ask, but then she was sure that Dalvenjah was glaring at her, or at least trying to, and she closed her mouth.

They soon came to the main ramp leading down to the ground floor of the castle. Ramps were very popular here, since the direction of gravity would shift and the surface always seemed perfectly level to the person walking it; a ball placed on the ramp, as steep as it was, would not roll. Below was the main entrance foyer of the castle, a long chamber of considerable size, rising up through six levels of the castle and serving as a junction of various ramps and doorways, the main outer doors on the far side. Fortunately it was all very dark just now, and it seemed to be deserted. There was no sound at all, except the clanking of Sir Remidan's armor.

The moment they reached the bottom, however, several lights were uncovered and they found themselves surrounded by a couple of hundred soldiers that had been hiding in the shadows. To make matters worse, a large portion of them had crossbows that would pierce even Sir Remidan's armor, much less that of the dragons. To make matters even worse yet, these were not the local guards but a battalion of Alasheran Legionnaires. Then, just to make things really nasty, an abrupt surge of magic caused their spells of invisibility to collapse, revealing them all as they stood just below the base of the ramp. All except for Jenny, who was invisible by nature.

A tall, almost boyishly handsome young man in bright Imperial armor stepped out to confront them. He was practicing a truly evil smirk, the type that could only be acquired by embracing true evil. "Well now, faerie dragons. I assume that I am in the company of Dalvenjah Foxfire. Duke Telmar has told me that he tried to poison you, and it didn't work. Now why would he want to poison such a lovely golden lady as yourself?"

"He wanted to get the secrets of our propulsion vanes for himself before you arrived," Vajerral said, stepping forward and speaking in a voice that was an overly dramatic imitation of her mother's. That would allow Dalvenjah, the most dangerous magic-user of their group, to remain unobtrusively in the background, and the tactic seemed to work. "He seems to be afraid of dragons, and he thought that my mortal friends would be easier to control. No doubt he meant to make some excuse to you."

"Duke Telmar is a daring fellow," the Alasheran said. "Frankly, he can do what he wants with your friends. I am here to make certain that you do not attempt to interfere in the Emperor's errands in this quaint place, and the only way to insure that is with your death. So you see, our good friend Duke Telmar was very much on the right track."

Vajerral looked surprised. "Your Emperor does not mind if the Eolwyn try to steal your technology?"

The Alasheran laughed. "We plan to give it to them. We do all think very much alike, don't you agree? If Duke Telmar had ever met with us in person, he would have known that. Your information appears to be based upon what he believed, and his own information was somewhat lacking."

Vajerral shrugged. "If it was easy for me to be perfect, your Emperor would be dead already. You certainly got here quickly enough."

"My ship and I had stayed behind as emissaries to the Eolwyn not twelve hundred miles from here. And it seems that you do not know about the magical message-sending equipment the Eolwyn have, not unlike the radio in that world we passed through on our way here."

One surprise after another. They had not known about that

because there had been no such equipment in *Star Dragon*
when they had found her. If there had been such equipment, it
had been taken from the ship by the survivors of the wreck. And
it had not worked, or they would not have still be stranded.

"Duke Telmar was in contact with us immediately after you
made contact with him, or rather will his hull," the Alasheran
continued. "So you see, he was not really trying to betray us,
just to profit by the whims of fortune. We can appreciate that."

"You also don't have the strength to punish him if you
wanted," Vajerral added. "Then again, you might very well be
the best of friends. As you just pointed out, you are much
alike."

"Now why do I suspect that I have just been insulted?" He
laughed again, then bowed gallantly to Mira. "It is very good to
see you again, Lady Kasdamir Gerran, although I must say that
you have come down in the world."

Mira stared at him. "Just who are you?"

"Oh, I don't expect that you recognize me," he told her. "You
might have changed, but I have changed even more. I am in a
new body, to be precise. I am Ellon Bennisjen."

"What?" A thundering, disembodied voice shook the stone
walls. Jenny appeared in the middle of the room, wearing her
dragon form about five times normal size, staring down at one
very frightened Alasheran. "Did you say Ellon Bennisjen? You
slimy little son of a bitch!"

"Ah . . . I beg your pardon?" Ellon looked as if he might wet
his armor.

"You don't recognize me?" she demanded. "I've changed
even more than you have. I'm Jenny Barker."

"But you're dead!" Ellon insisted.

"That's right, bucko!"

Jenny drew herself up on her hind legs and began to move
slowly toward Ellon, her long arms and claws extended menac-
ingly. Ellon drew back in alarm. He did not know what to make
of this thirty-foot-high faerie dragon who claimed to be someone he knew to be dead, but it was thoroughly terrifying. Dozens of crossbows snapped, but the bolts only passed through the
immense dragon without harm. She reached out with one large
hand and lifted Ellon from the ground, shaking him sharply a

few times just to hear his armor rattle. Ellon was making some frightened noises of his own.

In the next instant, Jenny's form suddenly dissolved from that of an immense dragon to that of a swirling vortex of mist, shot through with flashes of white and red, while sheets of lightning rippled over its surface. Ellon disappeared, screaming his terror inside the vortex, and a long moment passed before pieces of his armor began flying out in every direction. The tail of the vortex whipped around sharply and took the bottle from Sir Remidan's hand. With a final flash of lightning and explosion of thunder, Jenny returned to the form of the large dragon. The glass bottle lay on the ground before her, its top fused shut.

"So, who wants to be next?" she demanded, her voice echoing.

The Alasheran soldiers all decided that they should leave in a hurry, dropping their weapons as they ran for the door. As soon as they were all gone, Jenny returned to her normal size and turned to the others, grinning wickedly.

"Special effects by Steven Spielberg," she said. "I think that we can leave now without any problem."

"What did you do with Ellon?" Mira asked.

"I'm tired of these people popping up again every time you kill them," she explained as she collected the bottle. "I stuck his spirit inside the bottle and closed the top permanently. Having spent some time inside a bottle, I can assure you that it makes a most fitting punishment."

They encountered no further opposition on their way out, although they had been concerned that Ellon might have sent other soldiers to guard *Star Dragon*. Jenny had indeed been busy during the night, or at least she had been keeping Kelvandor and the boys busy. She had enclosed the helm deck with a metal roof and glass windows along the side. A large portion of the rear deck had been enclosed as well, although the second half of the roof slid back under the front to open the deck. If this ship could run as fast as she anticipated, the ship needed a roof to prevent members of the crew from being blown away. She had also covered wheels and struts in streamlined flarings. Kelvandor and the twins had the ship ready for flight.

"Eolwyn battleships have been moving out from the island for the last few minutes," Kelvandor reported as he helped Mira on board. "I suspect that they are maneuvering to bring their guns to bear as soon as we leave. There's an Alasheran airship landed on the other side of the castle."

"Allan, I believe that we should eliminate that ship," Dalvenjah said. "Jenny, take this ship to safety and wait for us to return."

The two dragons spread their wings and flew away into the night.

"Kelly, I need for you and the boys to stand by the catapults," Jenny instructed. "Mr. Holmes, will you help Mira to crank up the wheels as soon as we leave the ground? We will be going to full speed immediately. Oh yes, and can you find a very safe place for this?"

Kelvandor looked closely at the bottle Jenny had given him. "What is this, spirits?"

"No, just one."

Jenny quickly checked out the controls of the ship, then released the brakes and rolled the ship forward across the court. She engaged just enough lift to kick the ship clear of the ground, sailing out over the parapet at the outer edge of the court and moving *Star Dragon* into clear sky. Now that they were free of gravity, she rotated the ship's nose straight up and began to accelerate rapidly. Even though it was still night, she was able to see through the heavy darkness easily. No less than nine Eolwyn warships, including two of the massive battleships, were spread out in a loose formation overhead. But it seemed that the Eolwyn could not see well in the dark at all, since the ships were moving slowly with what seemed to be a great deal of concern for running into each other, their recognition lamps brightly lit. *Star Dragon* was a relatively small ship with no lights, and without moonlight or starlight to reflect from her metal hull she was nearly invisible.

"All strapped down?" she called to Kelvandor.

"Ready," he assured her.

"Have everyone hold on, and tell the boys not to hang their heads out the windows. We're going to see what this heap can do," she said.

She pushed forward the lever that rotated the lift vanes into the horizontal thrust position, then she began teasing all of the vanes until they were giving nearly full power. *Star Dragon* accepted the power, accelerating smoothly and responding with very acceptable precision to her controls. The rebuilt air-speed indicator moved to a hundred knots and climbed quickly beyond that. At a hundred and fifty knots the ship still had power to spare, but the deck canopies that she had installed, although they smoothed down the ship's aerodynamics overall, were beginning to give buffeting from the drag of their open ends. Jenny decided that she had all the speed she needed without fighting that drag until she was more familiar with the way this ship handled at speed.

Star Dragon was past the Eolwyn ships within moments, but Jenny kept them going at speed until she thought that they must be outside of reasonable range of the guns, the distance when friction with the air would slow even projectiles from the most powerful guns. Then she cut speed and began to circle. The two dragons had done their work, leaving the Alasheran airship drifting as she burned rather violently in the night. They passed completely unseen through the Eolwyn fleet and were back on board *Star Dragon* shortly, testing their own generous speed in free fall. Jenny had already clocked Vajerral as the young dragon completed a level flight over a mile's course in only twelve seconds, giving her a speed of about three hundred per hour.

"That was smartly done," Dalvenjah commented as she joined Jenny on the helm deck. "Your command of magic seems to be growing tremendously."

"I don't know about that," Jenny said as she eased *Star Dragon* back up to her new cruising speed. "I was just thinking about something. I suppose that finding Ellon brought it to mind."

"What would that be?"

"Well, it was back on the Island of Alashera, there inside the volcano when Ellon and the High Priest Haldephren held me captive," she explained. "Haldephren knew that I was important to their prophecies, but I just realized that even he did not know how. He was trying to subvert me to evil. Since all that I, or perhaps Mira, was supposed to do what to provide a body for the Dark Sorceress Darja, his efforts to subvert me were absolutely pointless."

Dalvenjah considered that. "Yes, that does seem right. I

would suppose that he did not know the exact meaning of the Prophecy because Emperor Myrkan had never told him. Myrkan has existed only for the pursuit of power for the past two thousand centuries, and he seems to have always been a suspicious sort. He once sent Haldephren after me, knowing certainly that Haldephren would not survive the encounter. Haldephren is often played for a stooge by his own master, and he has not figured that out in twenty centuries."

Jenny smiled. "I do recall that he was devious enough when he was making the rules, but he seemed simple and shallow trying to deal with surprises. But why would the Emperor keep such an important secret?"

"By not revealing the full nature of the Prophecy to anyone, perhaps he meant to insure that it would never come about unless he was there himself to make it happen. It was the Emperor himself who gave your body to Darja. At least now we know that the Emperor has been loitering about securing allies rather than pushing directly toward his goal. Why? He knew that I might be close behind him. Did he really think that the Eolwyn could stop me, or even slow me down that much?"

"What course do I strike, then?" Jenny asked. "Do we look for the Emperor or do we go straight in? If we get there first, we can defend it against him when he arrives."

"On to the center for now, but we will have to consider that," Dalvenjah said. "The source of magic is their most logical destination, but it might not be that simple. The Emperor might still be out here because the source of magic is not his goal after all. I wish that Ellon had gloated just a little longer before you killed him. He was a mine of information."

Jenny thought about that for a moment. "I might just have a way to answer that question for us."

❧ PART EIGHT ❧

Friend or Fur?

Jenny brought the bottle out of the small wooden box where Kelvandor had hidden it, packed in rags to protect it against breakage. She laid the bottle gently in the center of the lower rear deck, then stepped back until she could lower her head to look down at it comfortably. The bottle was firmly capped, the glass melted until the lip had fused completely shut, and there was a small amount of liquid still in the bottom. All such things were certain to make its inhabitant's stay very unpleasant.

"Is he still in there?" Kelvandor asked.

"Oh, yes," Jenny answered softly. "And he will stay in there until the bottle is broken, something that he does not have the power to do for himself. Nor can he see or hear outside the bottle, unless I make that possible. His personal universe consists of a disembodied mind and the inside of a bottle that he cannot touch. Distilled eternity. Open this bottle in a few weeks and you will find only the essence of madness. There is no greater torture than utter and complete boredom. Soon he will begin to welcome insanity as the only relief for his pain."

"Enough, Jenny," Dalvenjah admonished her gently. "Just open him up and talk to him. If it is as terrible as you say, and I do not doubt you, then a couple of hours in that bottle should have left him in a more receptive frame of mind. Assuming that his sanity survived what you did to him."

Jenny had not considered that possibility. She did not remember having been left disembodied herself, only that she had suddenly found herself inside Vajerral. She had ripped Ellon Bennisjen bit by bit from his body, and he had still been screaming when she had sealed him inside the bottle. She did not actually open the bottle itself; she just made certain changes that permitted him to see and hear something of what was happening outside. She knew from her own stay inside a bottle that being able to see and hear outside took away from the boredom only slightly, but added greatly to the frustration of being trapped. Having Ellon at her mercy pleased her more than she would have ever thought possible.

"Ellon Bennisjen, are you in there?" Jenny asked, then waited a moment for him to answer. "Ellon, I know that you are in there. Talk to me, or I must assume that you have lost your mind and I will put this bottle in the bottom of the ship until I can find a safe place to hide it."

"Bottle?" a thin voice demanded incredulously. "What bottle? What have you done with me, you fire-breathing bitch?"

"Temper, temper!" Jenny warned him in a sweet voice. "Do you know who I am? The name is Jenny Barker, object of prophecy and one sexy chick. You wanted my body very much at one time, but then so did your Emperor and the Dark Sorceress Darja. A silly mistake, as it turns out, since I was really a dragon in mortal form. Now I am a dragon's ghost, so I know what it's like to be stuck inside a bottle."

"You put me inside a bottle?" Ellon asked.

"It seemed like the best thing to do with you," she explained. "I was not about to kill you again and let you come back on me as a recurring infestation of crab lice. I put you into the bottle where I could keep an eye on you, as it were. Boring as shit, isn't it?"

"You must let me out of this thing," Ellon insisted, his voice already sharp with panic. "What can I do to convince you to let me out of this?"

"Well, I can tell you right now that I am not about to let you out until our little adventure is over. But there are a few things that I want to know for now, and I am willing to bargain. If you will talk to me, then I will release you into true death, to whatever awaits mortals when they pass away into the next realm, as opposed to loitering about in this one. If you will not talk, then I will seal this bottle inside solid stone where you will never be found and you will never see the light of day for a hundred million years when erosion will finally wash you out to sea. And with your luck, the bottle would just be buried again in the silt, and there you go again for yet another hundred million years."

"You do have a way with words," Ellon remarked sourly. "You seem to think that you will win. All I need to do is to wait for my companions to defeat you and I will be rescued."

"And who is to know that you have taken up residence inside a bottle of sky-island brandy?" Jenny asked. "You're magically isolated inside the bottle, so no one will sense your presence and you cannot call out. Now, would you like to reconsider doing things my way?"

"Yes, very well."

"Trouble!" Mira declared.

"Oh, brother!" Jenny declared. She gave the bottle to Kelvandor for him to pack into the wooden box, then she hurried to the central helm deck.

The problem was obvious enough, once Jenny had a chance to look about. She had left Mira and Sir Remidan to watch the helm while she had been having her little talk with Ellon of the flagon, and Mira had blithely flown *Star Dragon* into the middle of a fleet of Eolwyn warships. Mira did not yet trust her new ship enough to take it up to speed, cruising at what would have been only a brisk pace for the old *Wind Dragon*, and the larger ships were moving in quickly to intercept them. There were already ships above and below them as well as to each side and more were moving in behind, so there was no easy direction of escape. Jenny suspected that their intentions were to capture their prey, since their present tactics made it impossible for them to bring their weapons to bear for the danger of hitting each other.

"How did they get ahead of us?" Mira asked.

"Ellon said earlier that they have a system of communication that must be not unlike radio," Holmes explained. "Apparently they took note of our direction and prepared an ambush."

"We have to make a hole in that fleet before they can move in against us," Jenny mused, speaking mostly to herself. Then she lifted her head to look at the other dragons. "This is our fight. Fireballs into the very center of their fans, directed from the front. I will do what I can about their control surfaces."

"That leaves me with the ship," Mira observed. "Should I have the boys stand by with the guns?"

Jenny shook her head. "Only you can work the guns. There are projectiles in the chambers, so just aim the ship when you're ready. But save it, to get you through if something gets in your way. Have the boys stand by with their catapults and the bolts with the exploding heads. Have them aim at the fans, and not at the dragons."

"Where am I going?" Mira asked.

"Hold back for a time to give us a chance to attack some weak point in their assault, then follow us through quickly. We will do what we can to clear the way, but you might have to follow up our attack with all of your own weapons and throw them into confusion just before you break through. And keep in mind that they will feel free to shoot at you when you come out the other side."

Jenny led the dragons overboard, using the greater speed they commanded flying without gravity to dart toward a group of larger ships almost directly ahead. Mira was not immediately reassured about their choice of targets until she realized that the larger ships were too slow and heavy to maneuver, their massive turrets too ponderous to turn quickly enough to track a swift target like *Star Dragon*. The smaller vessels could support each other, moving to fill any hole as quickly as the dragons could make one. Mira turned *Star Dragon* in the other direction, circling wide well inside the wall of the Eolwyn ships but still moving fast enough to discourage attack.

The faerie dragons concentrated their first attack on one of the immense Eolwyn battleships, darting quickly in and away to avoid any small weapons that were being turned on them from the deck of the ship. They soon discovered that a single blast from one of their potent fireballs was usually enough to disable one of the large ducted fans. The magically activated motors were, like the rest of the ship, made almost entirely of aluminum and were packed in large quantities of thin oil to contain the heat of friction that would have otherwise weakened the light metal. Engine fires were apparently a frequent problem, since the fans of the larger ships were built with ejection devices that kicked the burning fan from its pivoting axle and away from the ship. As Jenny had reminded the dragons earlier, aluminum was perfectly willing to burn while exposed to flame; fires had to be controlled quickly.

The dragons had divided themselves into teams of two, each pair going after a large ship. For her own part, Jenny was attacking ships where they were most vulnerable: from within. All of the cables from the rudders and elevators in the tail of each ship came down from the bridge and then back through a wide conduit through the center of the hull. The cables were thick but they were also braided aluminum wire, burning through as easily as rope under her flames. She could hamstring a ship in this manner in half a minute, leaving it only limited up-and-down motion by pivoting its fans. And with the others picking engines off ships like nuts from a tree, they could have disabled the entire fleet within minutes.

Mira had already discovered that they did not have that much time. Small ships, most no larger than *Star Dragon* and quite possibly of the same make as her original hull, had separated from the main fleet and were moving in, trying to get into a position where they could safely use their smaller guns. Mira took just enough time to scratch her head twice and decided that the dragons had already created enough confusion to buy her the time to get her ship through the Eolwyn line. Burning fans that had been ejected from disabled ships were burning lazily with thick, black smoke; the lack of gravity prevented natural convection to feed the flames with fresh air. About a dozen ships had already been disabled to various degrees, many drifting without their ducted fans while others dared not move because of their inability to turn. This seemed like a very good time to be on their way.

Unfortunately, Jenny's little plan for making a diversion had not worked out quite as predicted. With an entire section of their fleet crippled, other ships were moving quickly to strengthen that line. Mira spun the wheels and turned *Star Dragon* sharply, heading back toward one section of the line of Eolwyn ships well removed from the fight and, according to her own reasoning, not paying very strict attention. In this case, as indeed happened with surprising regularity, Mira's curious and imperfect logic actually paid off. *Star Dragon* slipped between a loose collection of medium-sized warships that did not even begin to respond until she was streaking past. Dooket and Erkin took advantage of the moment to take out fans on two of the nearest ships with their exploding bolts.

Mira expected that they should have been free and clear, leaving the Eolwyn warships far behind. Perhaps it was fair to assume that nothing was ever supposed to be simple; there would be no purpose in life if it was not complicated enough to be worth doing. Even as *Star Dragon* was moving toward open sky, an Eolwyn ship turned to follow and began to accelerate with unexpected speed. Looking back, Mira saw that the ship was unusual in design, about half the length of one of the battleships but very narrow and tapered of hull, a slender rail to serve as a platform for six pairs of large fans and over-sized fins and wings for agility. This beggar was built for running.

Mira knew that she had the faster ship, but she did not yet trust running *Star Dragon* at full speed and she was less certain that she could match the maneuverability of the Eolwyn cruiser. She urged her ship to a little more speed, seeing that the cruiser was actually closing the distance between them, and steered a heading for open sky. The problem was that the sky islands were small and very thickly clustered in this region, no doubt the reason why it had been selected by the Eolwyn for their ambush. Mira knew that she should not try to fight unless she had no choice, or unless she had an advantage that she could not ignore. It was better to run for now and wait for the dragons to come to her rescue, since their speed of nearly three hundred knots would allow them to make short work of the chase.

Just because they were needed, fate had its own way of making certain that the dragons were slow in coming to the rescue. Mira began to wonder if her unexpected change of tactics had gone unnoticed, and if they might still be waiting for her to bring *Star Dragon* through their own hole in the Eolwyn line.

Mira looked up to see something pass only a few inches over the roof of the helm deck, and she realized that the Eolwyn ship was shooting at her. She glanced back at the long, slender ship, and she was dismayed to find that it was gaining on her. While it had only light weapons, it did have the speed and maneuverability to use them very effectively. Whether she liked it or not, she was going to have to push *Star Dragon* a little faster. Mira spun the wheels to strike an evasive course, trusting that her little ship was still the more agile of the two, and *Star Dragon* turned only just in time. A moment later, a shell from the Eolwyn guns tore completely through the tapered rear hull just above the main thrust vanes, the delayed fuse exploding the shell about twenty feet from the left rear wing.

"Kill it, Mira!" Holmes warned, already on hand to survey the damage. "The thrust vanes are about to rip loose. Convert your thrust to the directional vanes inside the wings."

Mira urged thrust out of the vanes located in *Star Dragon*'s two sets of wings, and the right rear vane began to shake and buckle almost immediately. She looked over the side at the wing, seeing that it had been ripped through at several points by fragments of the exploding shell. Either the main spar inside the wing was about to fail, or the pivoting hinge for the vanes had been damaged. The only thing she could do now was to shift all of the ship's thrust to the two forward vanes, the only remaining pair, although the ship seemed to steer very loosely with only the forward vanes pulling the greatest part of its mass. And with two of the three sets of vanes down, *Star Dragon* no longer had the speed to evade the Eolwyn cruiser.

Mira considered her options and mentally flipped a coin, which only came down on the side she wanted anyway. The daring plan might not be the best, but it was certainly her style.

"Stand by the crossbows, boys!" she shouted as she banked the ship and spun the rudder wheel. "We can't run, so we have to fight!"

The Trassek twins shouted something that she hoped was approval; they were committed to doing this anyway, so it would be better for them if they thought it was a good idea. Mira brought *Star Dragon* around as tight as she could manage while maintaining her speed, completing the turn with the two ships standing bow to bow only a hundred feet apart. And at their combined speed, they were coming at each other very fast indeed. Mira had only a moment to align her ship before she activated the first bow gun. For having never done this before, she was lucky; the nearest fan on the Eolwyn's port side exploded into flames. Mira turned *Star Dragon* out and then back in again, bringing the other gun to bear on the second fan; this time she was luckier than she deserved to be. Unfortunately, she was also out of loaded guns. She steered straight down the length of the other ship's hull, close in and slightly below, and Holmes and the twins took out the three remaining fans on that side with the exploding bolts from their crossbows.

Mira turned *Star Dragon* straight down, the only direction in which the disabled ship was unable to shoot at her. Her one intention now was to make herself and her little ship very scarce, disappearing among the maze of sky islands before any other Eolwyn ships found her and tried to follow. The dragons appeared only a few minutes later, hurrying to the rescue as fast as they could fly. Mira was still relieved to see them, so later really was better than never.

Jenny circled around the little ship twice, surveying the damage before she came aboard. She looked far from happy with the situation, but at least she had the decency to keep her comments to herself. Mira understood the matter perfectly well; if she had not been afraid of *Star Dragon*'s full speed, the ship would have evaded the attack easily.

"Mira, can you watch the ship a little longer?" she asked. "I want to put as much distance between ourselves and this place as we can before we put up for repairs. If I can tie down those rear thrust vanes, we might be able to double our speed."

"We were fortunate that the shell passed completely through the hull before it exploded," Holmes said. "How does it look to you?"

"Not bad, really," Jenny said. "It should be a simple matter to rebuild the frame and brackets under the thrust vanes, and I have enough sheet metal to repair the hull. The difficult part will be opening up the wing to repair the spar. Perhaps, since I can dematerialize myself and work from the inside, I will not have to take very much apart to get at it."

"And what do you need for now?"

"Rope, Mr. Holmes. When I said that I am going to tie down the thrust vanes, I meant it."

Jenny realized that they could not safely land the ship without the rear set of lift vanes as well, so she cut a couple of wooden braces to hold the damaged wing in place. *Star Dragon* was still lame either way; the ship could fly forward on the propulsion of the front lift vanes and the thrust vanes, but the rear vanes could only be engaged for lift since they were braced only in that direction. Jenny took command of *Star Dragon* after that—as if she had not been giving the orders all along—and she brought the ship back up to speeds that Mira had not dared at the best of times.

The days were long in the world of the sky islands, and by nightfall they had crossed the better part of fifteen hundred miles according to the log on *Star Dragon*'s air-speed indicator. They had come within sight of one of the floating continents, which seemed like a very good place to spend the night to some members of the crew and not a good idea at all to others. The continents were the most likely to be inhabited. At the same time, Jenny saw that this place had forests deep enough to hide *Star Dragon* and her shiny hull. Since Jenny was driving, she got to choose where they parked.

Mr. Holmes came out at dawn the next morning for a good look around. He had been the most resistant to landing here, since he was certain that any of the larger pieces of real estate were probably occupied. It seemed to him that the very essence of logic would be to find out for himself if anyone was about before someone found them. First he thought that he should see how Jenny was doing with the repairs, just in the event that they should have to leave in a hurry. He walked around *Star Dragon*'s bow and found that Jenny was just about finished with her work.

Then he noticed that there was something wrong with the young dragon. Admitting that she was a ghost, her form had always looked solid enough. Now her image was blurred and indistinct. She spun herself around as if he had startled her, understandably enough. Then she lowered her long neck and lifted her crest, and in his limited familiarity with faerie dragons he still knew that for a posture of attack. She glared at him, as if she saw only an enemy.

"Who are you?" she demanded, her voice soft but threatening. "It seems that I have seen you before."

"You know me well enough," he told her, keeping his own voice calm and even. "I am your friend and companion, Sherlock Holmes."

"There is no Sherlock Holmes!" Jenny declared, drawing herself up as if to strike. "Sherlock Holmes is just a story."

"Yes, that is so," he admitted. "I am in truth the Elf Lord Alberess, but I am sometimes called Sherlock Holmes. That is how you have always known me."

Jenny hesitated, and her rage collapsed in an instant. She

shook her head and her form became more real and solid. "Please excuse me, Mr. Holmes. I don't know what happened."

"You have been working hard all night," he assured her gently. "Perhaps you are just tired."

"I'm dead," she reminded him. "I don't get tired."

"You are disembodied," Holmes said. "I imagine that you have been concentrating very hard all night. Your mind can still grow tired, I suppose, and likely to play tricks on you. How is the ship?"

"Everything works, so we can leave in a hurry if we must. I've cut the new sheet metal for the hull and wing, but I've waited until morning to rivet them down because of the noise." She bent her neck around to look up, seeing that J.T. was peering over the top of the siderail. "Good morning, cat. I see that you have decided to rejoin the living."

"That's a funny remark, coming from you," the cat said. "My hind leg finally stopped hurting enough for me to get around. I thought that I should make my presence known before things get entirely out of hand. They tell me that you have been running things."

"It amuses Dalvenjah Foxfire for her to permit me to command this ship," Jenny replied. "Perhaps because it amuses her less to think of Lady Mira in control."

"Then should I talk to you or Mira?" J.T. asked. "Someone is coming. About a hundred someones, to be precise. They already have us surrounded."

"You might have come to the point a little sooner," Holmes admonished him.

"I would have, if it had been important. These ladies mean us no harm, as long as we can make a good accounting of our trespass. Remember that we are flying what looks to be one of the ships of their enemies. I suggest that a certain dragon should show herself, to give them something to think about."

"Show myself?" Jenny asked. "I'm already naked."

"Cute, dragon. Just do it."

Jenny turned to face the forest that surrounded the ship, lifting her neck and standing well up on her hind legs. Fortunately, Dalvenjah and Allan came out on deck at that moment, and Vajerral was close behind. Seeing that Jenny and Holmes were watching the forest expectantly, they also lifted their heads to look around.

Apparently knowing that they were expected was enough to convince J.T.'s someones to show themselves also, and they were certainly worth looking at. They were furry little female persons, their bodies those of small women, none of them more than four and a half feet high and covered in a short, thick pelt of brown or tan fur. Their faces were more feral than human, with large, dark eyes, blunt snouts with black button noses, and long, pointed animal ears poking out of long manes of black hair that was the same color as their bushy tails. They all wore armor that looked vaguely Greek or Roman, with fringed skirts and short sleeves of stiffened black leather and full breastplates that appeared to be aluminum, and they were armed with small bows or long, slender spears. They were certainly spunky little things. Although the dragons could have dispatched them easily, they appeared coldly determined to stand their ground.

"These must be the Quentarah that Duke Telmar mentioned, the dire enemies of the Eolwyn," Holmes said. "We can hope that the fact that we share a common enemy predisposes them to be our friends. In spite of their fierce attitude, they do have the look of reasonable people."

"They look like Amazon Chipmunks," Jenny remarked softly.

The leader of the Quentarah, or so they assumed, stepped out from the group of warriors to face Holmes and Jenny. Her armor was gold-trimmed, and her cloak was black rather than deep red that the others wore. Jenny felt quietly envious of her beautiful tan fur; Mindijaran were the only mammalian dragons, so there was no reason as far as she was concerned why they should not be fur-bearing as well. She shook her head, realizing that her mind was wandering.

"Travelers," the little warrior said, stopping several paces away. "I am Hadera, Captain of the Citadel Guard. You are on land that belongs to the Quentarah. Have you come as friends?"

Simple and direct. Perhaps Mr. Holmes was correct. Since she had brought them here, Jenny thought that she should explain. "We are travelers from a very distant place. We came here pursuing enemies who have since allied themselves with the Eolwyn. When our ship was destroyed in a storm, we rebuilt it from the wreckage of an Eolwyn scout. Unfortunately, our ship was damaged when we tried to evade an ambush."

"Are the Eolwyn pursuing you?" Hadera asked.

"If they are, they will be a long time in finding us," Jenny said. "The ambush took place yesterday more than fifteen hundred miles from here, and we left more than half of their ships disabled."

"Your little ship must be fast indeed. What weapons do you have that you can fight an Eolwyn fleet?"

"Dragons, actually," she explained. "Dragons fly ten times as fast as an Eolwyn battleship under their own power, they breathe fire, and there are five of us. Given time, we could take on every ship the Eolwyn have."

"Don't boast," Dalvenjah said very, very softly. "They might take it to be a promise."

Apparently that was food for thought to Hadera, who spent a good, long time chewing it up. "I do believe that you are good people, and you look reasonable."

Mr. Holmes looked startled, but said nothing. The leader of the Quentarah glanced at her sisters, who put away their bows and spears and gathered around to stare in open curiosity at the dragons. Hadera bowed. "You would honor us greatly with a brief visit, if you could spare the time from your journey. We will prepare a feast in your honor, and our queen would certainly wish to speak with you."

There was no help for it, although the Quentarah would have certainly let them continue on their way without a fuss. Jenny could not think of anything to be gained by staying; she still felt tired, and she seemed to have a hard time concentrating. But both Dalvenjah Foxfire and Mr. Holmes wanted more information about where they were going, and these little furry ladies were in the mood to be helpful.

Getting *Star Dragon* to the Citadel of the Quentarah was not as easily done as said, since the ship was not yet in perfect flying condition. Having observed that the airship had wheels, that being something of a novelty in itself locally, the leader of the Quentarah patrol suggested that they simply drive. After following the warriors down a path through the forest for hardly a hundred yards, admittedly with some trailblazing to clear a path for the ship, they came upon a wide road that led to the capital city of the Quentarah Empire only twelve miles away; Jenny's search for a secluded place to make repairs had nearly landed *Star Dragon* in their laps. In spite of their weapons and armor, the Quentarah were actually more advanced than the Eolwyn. They had attached their magical motors to a transmission and had built themselves great, lumbering trucks. The warriors packed themselves into two of these machines, and they were away.

Needless to say, *Star Dragon* drove like a trawler on roller skates and Jenny was greatly relieved when they arrived. The last little bit was the most difficult part since they had to make their way through the wide streets of the Citadel. It had been built very much on the style of the Eolwyn city, buildings of heavy dressed stone with thickest defensive portions facing upward against attack from above. Jenny was certain by this time that it would have been easier to fly. *Star Dragon* had never been meant to drive like a truck; her size was ungainly, her acceleration was uncertain and her brakes were inadequate to her weight, so her handling was more a matter of taxiing her like an aircraft. Mira still seemed to be spooked of her new ship and that left Jenny to do all the driving, even though she still seemed to have trouble concentrating.

The city and its curious inhabitants were certainly interesting enough. The favorite article of fashion among the Quentarah was the short skirt, no doubt because it gave their tails someplace convenient to go. The skirts were very short and usually split up the back to accommodate their tails and the flaps often stood open, so it seemed that the Quentarah were not in the habit of wearing clothes out of any sense of modesty. But they still never seemed to go naked, although their short but very thick fur made any clothing irrelevant. They seldom wore shoes except for the light sandals that the warriors wore as a part of their armor.

All in all, they kept a very clean and orderly society. Their city reminded Jenny of much of what she had seen of Mira's world, late renaissance but with a growing industry based upon magic-based machines and industrial technics, in some respects quite advanced technologically. Unlike Mira's people and more like immortal races such as elves or the faerie dragons, all of the Quentarah possessed magical abilities to some degree. None of them looked old, a fair indication that they were immortal. Living closer to the center of their universe and the source of their magic might have had some influence in their inner essence.

Since all of the Quentarah warriors were female, the visitors had naturally wondered if theirs was indeed a matriarchal society, as Duke Telmar had listed as a chief cause of complaint of the Eolwyn. As it happened, both sexes of their society lived on a very equal basis, the only difference being that there were very few males, no more than one in twenty. They never married but wandered in and out of relationships, reproducing enough to keep the population going. This demanded a lot of each male, keeping his statistical twenty females properly entertained, but they possessed the amorous inclinations required of them. The male Quentarah reminded Jenny curiously of Pepe Le Pew, the Looney Toons skunk with the wayward libido. The females found them quaint and amusing for a few weeks at best, when they could no longer stand their concupiscent males and tossed them out. Which was just as well, or Quentarah society would have never worked.

Star Dragon was parked in the yard of the Inner Citadel, and Hadera conveyed them into the presence of Beradoln, the Queen of the Quentarah. Now Beradoln was a very canny lady indeed. All Quentarah behaved as if they were nobility, from the Queen herself to the lowest shepherdess, and they treated each other as equals in rank and dignity. While Beradoln was the queen of a considerable realm, she was also as alert and crafty as a clever merchant in the middle of a tough bargain, generous but never foolish in her trust, cold and calculating to her enemies. She listened to Hadera's report of the abilities of the dragons and their curious ship and immediately saw for herself the value of having such allies. She wished to reserve for herself the judgement of whether to welcome them as friends.

"We have all manner of enemies," she said. "We know their manner well, and we have heard every lie that ever crossed a villain's tongue. There is no sense of that about you."

With introductions aside, that was very much the end of it for that time. Queen Beradoln was a busy person and they had arrived at a bad time; there was the morning's business to be attended to before she had time for anything unexpected, at least anything that would keep until later. Jenny was allowed to go back to *Star Dragon* to complete her repairs, attended by Kelvandor and the Trassek twins, while the others were shown to rooms within the Citadel. At least this time they did not worry about having to sneak away in the night, nor did Jenny feel the need to snoop about invisible.

Hardly an hour had passed, however, before Holmes, Dalvenjah and Lady Mira were summoned to a private meeting with Queen Beradoln. She had quite literally squeezed them into her schedule. As Queen, she was also war leader of the Quentarah; she set aside two hours each morning for gymnastics, archery and spear-chucking, and she invited the others to join her. This gave them a chance to endear themselves to the Quentarah. Dalvenjah was impressive enough in herself. Mr. Holmes was an archer of prodigious talent. And Mira, who had dropped back to her natural height, was of a size that the little furry ladies could relate to. She was also a competent archer in her own right.

The Quentarah went to the practice field naked, in the legendary manner of the ancient Spartans. That was Dalvenjah's natural state and Mira hardly cared less; she was smaller even than the Queen, and she simply looked diminutive and cute. Mr. Holmes, a proper English gentleman, made his one concession to nudity by removing his jacket.

"Your arrival has been most timely," Beradoln said, flipping another arrow into her target. "We have heard that the Eolwyn have recently made a treaty with strangers, wizards from outworld by what I am told. You can do much to help us, even if all you can offer is information and good advice. You are from outworld yourselves?"

"We are all from different worlds," Dalvenjah explained cautiously, unsure how much she should try to explain and fearful that the Quentarah would know if she was holding back. "Mira comes from the same world as these wizards from outworld, and we have pursued them now across four worlds."

"Three," Mira corrected her as she stepped up to face the target and drew her bow.

"Four, if you include this one," the dragon said, moving away with less than perfect discretion. "Your new enemies are Emperor Myrkan of Alashera, his High Priest Haldephren and the Dark Sorceress Darja. We believe that Darja is the one to watch out for. She has Jenny's body, for one thing. You might have noticed that Jenny is a ghost."

"Jenny? The distracted one?" Beradoln asked, although her identification startled Mira. "Then Darja is also a dragon?"

Dalvenjah rolled her eyes and sighed. "That gets a little complicated. At the time, Jenny was wearing another form. Like Mira's people, only taller. Of course, most of Mira's own people are taller."

"Watch it, lizard."

"The Dark Sorceress Darja is the key to some ancient prophecy," Dalvenjah continued. "She is to somehow provide the Emperor with tremendous power, all the magic he needs to conquer whole worlds. Now we do not know what this source of magic will be, but his trail has led us here. Our suspicion is that Darja can give them access to the source of magic at the center of your world, since that is the only relevant source of magic here."

"Their new alliance with the Eolwyn is not enough in itself?" Beradoln asked.

"The Eolwyn are fairly irrelevant to the Emperor's plans." Holmes said. "Jenny was not boasting when she said that *Star Dragon* and the five dragons in our company could, given time, defeat the Eolwyn fleet. Whatever the Eolwyn themselves may believe that they are receiving in this alliance, I suspect that the Emperor is only using them to delay us long enough to complete his quest. The curious thing is that the Emperor has been wasting his time here in the outer world rather than pressing his advantage of time in reaching his goal ahead of us. If only we knew what they are planning."

"Perhaps we do," Mira remarked, then looked up at the dragon. "We still have Ellon packed away in that bottle, and Jenny was about to talk to him when we flew into the middle of the Eolwyn ambush. Perhaps we should continue that little talk."

"Who is Ellon?" Beradoln asked. "One of your enemies?"

"Another ghost in our keeping," Dalvenjah explained. "We are keeping him in a bottle, as a matter of fact. Ellon was the henchman of the High Priest Haldephren, and neither of them seems to have a clear idea of what is happening with the Prophecy so they have been running about doing general mischief.

You must also understand that the Alasherans have an especially nasty habit. They are mortals, meaning that they grow old and die in a relatively short period of time, at least as you or I would view it. They compensate by having their spirits transferred into new bodies, dispossessing the rightful inhabitants. If you kill them, they come back. Jenny interrupted the process for Ellon by imprisoning his spirit inside a bottle."

Queen Beradoln twitched her ears one after the other, the same gesture of consternation that Dalvenjah was fond of using. "You know some very nasty people. Perhaps we should talk to Ellon immediately, if you know how."

And that was the end of morning archery practice. They hurried to where *Star Dragon* had been parked, only to discover that the ship had been moved to the Citadel's military yard where Jenny could find the tools she needed to complete her work. The young ghost did not notice them at first as they came up behind her; she was busy drilling out old rivets. The hinge mechanism that rotated the lift vanes within the damaged wing had failed during the first test, having been more severely damaged than she had thought. Holmes tried tapping her on her bent back, but his hand passed through. Jenny did not even feel it, although the Queen was certainly impressed. The Quentarah were not especially superstitious, but she had not known what to make of the news that Jenny was a ghost.

"Jenny?" Dalvenjah said softly.

She jumped, startled, and spun around to face them, holding the drill as if it were a gun. Holmes's insatiable curiosity was immediately captivated by the tool, a cordless power drill. "How do you recharge that?"

"I never worry about recharging it," Jenny said. "I have another way of making it work."

"Oh?" Holmes had to contemplate that for a brief moment. "Well, of course. How stupid of me not to have figured that out for myself long ago. I might have saved a tidy sum on my electric bill."

"I like my sums big and messy," Mira commented.

"Where did you get that?" Dalvenjah asked.

"I found it aboard *Wind Dragon*, after the wreck. I assume that Lady Mira stole it from the naval shipyard in New York, along with two assault rifles, a boom box, five disposal lighters, an Arnold Schwarzenegger poster, a Little Mermaid pop-up figure book, and assorted power tools."

Mira grinned sheepishly and blushed furiously at the same time. "What can I say? I like Arnold. I need something that big to satisfy my ambitions."

"We have this saying about your eyes being bigger than your . . ." Holmes thought about what he was saying, and he blushed as well.

They seemed to have Beradoln's full attention. As they were to discover later, the Quentarah talked about their recent sexual experiences with the same candid delight that tourists would compare their travels; apparently the males were not the only libidinous members of their race. The furry little Queen was quietly curious about the mating habits of the dragons, thinking that it must be splendid. Of course, such speculations had often entertained Mira as well.

Jenny saw that Mira was wearing Quentarah armor and light sandals. "Where are your clothes? You don't have so many clothes that fit. Don't you plan on stealing that, unless you expect to stay that size."

"I might just grow fur and stay here," Mira said defensively. "Besides, she has my clothes."

Jenny noticed for the first time that the Queen was wearing Mira's jean jacket and Muppet Babies shirt. Since the pants were not designed to accommodate her tail, she was still naked from the waist down. She had a very pert little bottom, if furry.

"We wanted to continue our talk with Ellon," Dalvenjah said firmly. "Do you believe that he might be at home?"

"I suspect that he might be somewhere about the bottle," Jenny answered. "I will have to ask him if he is receiving visitors today."

Ellon Bennisjen was indeed receiving that day. He refused to believe that it had only been little more than a day since the last time they had spoken to him, swearing that it must have been long, cruel weeks. As Jenny had predicted, the absolute nothingness of his disembodied existence had left him desperate to escape the bottle, even if the only way was through death. He wanted out of the bottle as soon as possible, no longer willing to wait even had he known that his masters would eventually rescue him; death had become preferable to him to another day of this torment. He was so fearful and wretched that the others were moved to pity him. All but Jenny, whose vengeance was boundless. Dalvenjah let him know that he could buy his release, and he would have done anything to please her.

"I must know what the Emperor and the Dark Sorceress Darja are doing in this place," Dalvenjah told him. "What are they going to do? Have they gone on into the center?"

The bottle almost seemed to shake. "Pity me, Lady. You are my mistress now, and I belong to you. I would give you anything you ask of me, as long as it is mine to give. I do not have the answers to your questions. Such matters were never for my ears, as close as I have stood in the High Priest's favor."

"Perhaps you know more than you think," Dalvenjah said, speaking softly to sooth his fears. "Do you know why the Emperor made an alliance with the Eolwyn when he might have gone directly to his goal?"

"He feared that you would follow," Ellon insisted. "The Emperor fears you greatly, Dalvenjah Foxfire, and Haldephren has told me that the Emperor has feared nothing since the end of the last war. He fears only you, and he knew that he must first have great power to defeat you. He also wants this pocket universe swept clean of all life before he tries to make peace with the new god. The easiest way to accomplish that was to seed war."

"What new god?" Dalvenjah demanded.

"I thought you knew about that," Ellon told her, eager to please.

"Who is this new god? Darja herself?"

"That I do not know. All that I have ever heard is that the new god is to awaken, and that the Dark Sorceress is going home."

That was all the information that Ellon had to impart, although Dalvenjah questioned him long and carefully and he tried to answer her as fully as he could manage. His mind seemed distracted and remote from everything except his own torment and desperation.

"Release him," Dalvenjah directed Jenny at last, then seemed to think the better of it. "Give him true death. I suspect that you will not be satisfied unless you have destroyed his spirit."

"He is evil," Jenny declared, seething with cold fury. "He deserves it."

"That he does not!" Dalvenjah told her sternly. "True death is the greatest of equalizers. He will not remember the evil that he became in this life nor the evil that he has done, if you will free him of the evil that binds his spirit to his masters."

Jenny was not happy, but she did as she was told. Queen Beradoln walked slowly back to the Citadel with Dalvenjah, with Holmes and Mira close behind. Most of the Queen's subjects did not seem to recognize her, and those who did were obviously curious that their Queen was walking about strangely dressed in the company of these unusual visitors.

Beradoln could not easily comment on Ellon's contention that there was a new god lurking in the center of her world. For one thing, the concept was very confusing to her. The Quentarah, like all other races of their world, knew that great power in the form of magic emanated from the center of their world, and that it was the source which had created and still controlled all aspects of their existence. But they had never considered that the source might be a person or a conscious entity in any sense; it simply was, like the sky and the land.

"There are two things to know about our world that might be important," she continued. "Our world becomes steadily more magical as you come closer to the center, as you may have noticed already. On the fringe are the mortal barbarians. Farther in are the Eolwyn, who are human but immortal, although magic is inconsistent in their race. As you come closer to the center, the races become less human and more fanciful. Of the civilized races nearest to the center, the Quentarah are most removed from human in form, but our magic is the strongest. The Eolwyn consider us the first of the true monsters."

"There are monsters nearer to the center?" Holmes asked.

Beradoln nodded emphatically. "Going inward, you will come to a region where the sky is clear and the islands do not exist. Then you will come into the region of darkness, where the monsters dwell. They are true monsters in form, fanciful and complex in their design, no two the same but all of them horrible to behold. I fear that we will soon be monsters ourselves."

"The region of darkness is expanding?" Dalvenjah assumed, then saw that Holmes was staring at her. "It only makes sense, you realize. There always used to be a balance of magic between the singularity and the outer world, but something has stopped the dissipation of latent magic into the outer world for the past several thousand years. That has to have had some effect here."

"We know of the outer world," the Queen added. "Others have come before, if rarely. And we know that the balance between the two worlds must be restored, or else our entire world will in time become a place of monsters. Can you help us?"

"I cannot promise that until I know the cause of your problem," Dalvenjah said. "It might be that the solution to our problem will also solve your own. I will do what I can. It seems inevitable to me that we must soon go into the center of your world."

"We have never been able to penetrate the Region of Darkness, and we do not know what lies in the center," Beradoln said. "No doubt your dragons and your fast ship will carry you safely past the monsters."

That the spunky little Amazon Chipmunks had found the Region of Darkness to be too dangerous was not encouraging news. It hardly seemed that they would have been afraid of much, and if they were afraid then there must have been a very good reason.

That evening, the Amazon Chipmunks threw a party as only they could throw a party. There were wilder parties to be had throughout the various levels of existence, and some that might have better food, drink or entertainment. But no other parties in any world had the Quentarah. It was a matter of endless fascination and delight to watch them. They were so bold at the same time that they were careful to maintain their pride and reserve. They possessed a boundless love of life, but they worked so hard at guarding their dignity. Their flirtations were a meticulous game of manners, and yet they seemed to have a serious problem staying in their clothes . . . as if it really mattered. Observing the meticulously balanced choreography of their social manners was almost enough to make one dizzy.

Complicating the festivities was the matter of the guests, in particular their appearance and the behavior of certain members of their party. Mira was the belle of the ball in her Quentarah armor. Jenny had gone one better by taking the form of an Amazon Chipmunk, but she had some trouble remembering to stay fully materialized and her armor kept falling off. She had turned

herself into an extremely voluptuous Quentarah, and Queen
Beradoln, who was certainly no slouch herself, was still wear-
ing Mira's clothes without the pants, so they made quite a pair.
To make matters worse, Jenny's behavior was extreme even by
Quentarah standards; she could teach the amorous Chipmunks a
thing or two about flirtation.

Fortunately, matters were not likely to get out of hand. The
females found her cute and the males thought that she was
lively and witty, returning her flirtations on her own terms but
shying away at the last minute. They all knew by now that she
was a ghost, which had aroused their curiosity but little else.
They assumed that she was playing and responded accordingly.
And that was just as well, since Jenny was not physically able to
perform if she had gotten lucky. The worst part of her behavior
was her thoughtless cruelty to Kelvandor, who loved her. He
was left to seethe quietly until, like most of her companions, he
began to realize that something was wrong. This was by no
means her normal behavior.

The travelers worried that a party like this could go on the
better part of the night, and the local nights were twenty hours
long. As it happened, things were over sooner than they had expected; the Quentarah were Spartan in many of their habits, including going to bed early. The handful of males were snapped
up in a hurry. The remaining females talked about fighting and
warfare and began wandering away. That gave Dalvenjah,
Allan and Kelvandor a chance to get Jenny started in the direction of *Star Dragon.*

Jenny had returned to her dragon form, but her mood was increasingly hostile. They had convinced her to go back to the
airship to stand guard; *Star Dragon* was the only thing that always held her complete and devoted attention. The others left
quietly, returning to the rooms that they had been given within
the Citadel. Then they paused, hearing that the two dragons
were in the middle of a serious argument.

"If you want love, tell me," Kelvandor responded to something Jenny had said very loudly, but which they had not caught.
"I will do the best for you that I can."

"But you can't touch me!" Jenny lamented. "Don't you understand? I can't feel it. I don't even remember clearly what it is
like! All I have left is the excitement of teasing, and even that is

hollow. You have been so solid and understanding, I will admit. But even you treat me like I'm already dead."

"You are dead, and I hardly know what to do. Tell me what you want of me, and I will give it."

"Kelly, you're my own half-brother," Jenny reminded him.

The others waited for a long moment, but their conversation after that become so silent that even the dragons could not hear. Allan shook his crest, as if suddenly shy about their eavesdropping. "Jenny and Kelvandor share the same father, Dalvenjah's brother Karidaejan. Such matters are irrelevant to dragons, but Jenny was human most of her life."

"What is wrong with her?" Mira asked in a voice softer and more uncertain than they had ever heard her use. "Is she just frustrated with being a ghost?"

"I wish that it was that simple," Dalvenjah said. "In a sense, each of us is two beings existing in perfect harmony. The spirit is the essence of being while the mind is the source of conscious thought. We make the mistake of believing that our memories, our character and our self-awareness is our true identity, but those are only the transitory aspects of physical life. Jenny no longer has a mind, but her spirit remembers her mind and has existed for a time with the illusion that her mind still exists. But the spirit of a dragon also possesses the instinct to seek rebirth, and the first step toward rebirth is to lay aside the memories and habits of the previous life."

"And that is happening to Jenny?" Mira asked. "She is forgetting what it was like to be alive?"

"Unfortunately, that is only the cause," Dalvenjah explained. "The slow loss of her identity, all the trappings that turned her base spirit into the person that was Jenny Barker, is destroying her mind. And her mind is very vulnerable, since it is only an illusion maintained by her spirit. This has happened much sooner than I had expected, perhaps because she has been so active. I could have kept her spirit in stasis, preserving her mind. That is surely what the Emperor has done with the spirit of Karidaejan, who has been dead for years. But we needed her to find the way for us, through her link to her former body. That is why I have allowed her to be our leader."

"Can we get her body back to her in time to save her?" Allan asked.

Dalvenjah shook her head sadly. "The damage is done. Indeed, the damage was done long ago. We could give her back her body, but that will not restore her mind. We would have the Jenny that we knew before, doomed to a lifetime of insanity. And dragons live a very long time. It would be better for us to let her go, to start again."

Mira turned away suddenly. Putting her arms around Sir Remidan, she began to weep. She had always been so tough and practical that the others were surprised and moved by her distress. But Remidan had known Mira for a long time, and he knew that she had loved Jenny as her own child. Lady Mira was pragmatic enough that she gave her love sparingly. But when she did, her devotion was absolute.

"I cannot make it right," Dalvenjah said sadly. "I never had the opportunity to make things right for her. I fear that she will not be with us much longer. But even then, I have made such arrangements as I can."

The next morning was one of surprises. The Amazon Chipmunks were quite taken with the fashion trend that Lady Mira had accidentally started, and they had been busy with their needles through the night. By morning, all of the Quentarah within the Citadel who were not in armor or uniform were sporting their own versions of the wardrobe that Mira had given to Beradoln, light jackets and shirts decorated with drawings of unusual creatures, mostly faerie dragons. They were all otherwise bare from the waist down, not including their rather discreet coat of thick fur. And because Mira had made off with the Queen's sandals, they were all barefoot as well. It seemed that the only good that the Quentarah saw in clothing was in satisfying their delight in dressing up, to whatever degree they happened to find desirable.

The travelers were beginning to think that this world had not been at all conducive to Jenny's continued mental health; between the painfully obvious duplicity of the Eolwyn and the perky eccentricities of the Quentarah, they were all feeling a little confused. At least Mira's loss of stature had left her wearing the children's clothes that Dr. Rex and Marie had brought her, as strange as it was. Bare-bottomed, bushy-tailed chipmunks were bad enough; the very thought of what they had done with

Mira's usual gaudy fashion sense boggled the mind. It gave Allan a horrible vision of an entire race of spunky little chipmunk women all dressed like Rosalind Russell.

The morning was still young when the Queen sent messengers to collect the various members of *Star Dragon*'s crew, discounting the ones there was no point in trying to talk to. Mira arrived to find that Dalvenjah, Allan and Mr. Holmes were already waiting in the Queen's council chamber; she would have been there sooner herself if she had not been soaking herself in the heated pools at the practice field. Beradoln had also gathered more than a dozen of her captains, all of them dressed for battle. They were all wearing serious expressions, but the Quentarah looked up with quiet curiosity when Mira entered wearing her black-and-white panda jogging suit, courtesy of the children's department at J.C. Penney. New Chipmunk fashion trends were in the making, and Mira found herself a reluctant guru of vogue. But when it came to pants, she had been a complete failure.

"Ah, there you are," Beradoln said, seeing that Mira had arrived. She was in one corner of the room folding up the royal Muppet Babies shirt so that she could put on her own armor. "An Eolwyn fleet is approaching, and they are led by a group of large wooden airships with wings of canvas. Dalvenjah believes that it must be the Alasheran fleet."

"I wonder how the Emperor managed to get an entire fleet through the outer world and down that volcano," Mira remarked. She was also wondering why the Queen seemed to value her opinion so highly. Probably because she was the owner and theoretical captain, at least now that Jenny was incapacitated, of *Star Dragon*, the new secret weapon in the Quentarah fleet. It could not be entirely due to her fashion sense.

"They might have opened a Way Between the Worlds there at the volcano, once they knew what they were looking for," Holmes said. "They might have brought through any number of ships. The descent should have been easy enough for them. We were just unlucky enough to emerge in the middle of a storm."

"That is not an encouraging thought," Mira remarked. "Just how close are they?"

"About two hundred miles," the Queen said. "By the best speed of the Eolwyn fleet, they are still at least ten hours away."

"But the Alasheran airships could be here in only four hours."

"I have sent Allan and Vajerral out to take a look," Dalvenjah said. "They will fly as fast as they can, so they could be there and back again in as little as an hour and a half. Vajerral has seen the Emperor's flagship before and perhaps she will know if he is here."

"Will that make a difference?" Beradoln asked.

Dalvenjah was wearing a big dragon frown. "As I see it, there are certain questions that I would like to have answered. Is the Emperor with the fleet? If so, does that mean that he already has the power that was promised to him in the Prophecy, or is he coming to face the problem that we represent to him first?"

"If he has that much power coming to him, why risk a fight with us first?" Holmes asked. "Is it only because he already knows what will be involved when he takes the Dark Sorceress Darja into the center, and that he will be vulnerable for that time?"

"That is the only thing that makes sense to me," Dalvenjah agreed.

"Because time is short, I must speak candidly," the Queen said. "What are your own plans? Will you try to reach the center before the Emperor, if you find that he is here? Will you stand and fight with us? And whether we fight alone or together, what are our chances of winning? I will admit that I do not have the forces gathered here to win this battle, not from the reports that I have about the size of that fleet."

"The fight is because of us," Dalvenjah said. "Therefore we will fight. Better I think to force this battle here and now. I believe that the Emperor has not yet found the power granted to him by the Prophecy. If he commanded such power, then we would have become insignificant to him. He is putting himself to a great deal of trouble, and that must mean that he expects to have a fierce battle on his hands. But he has never fought faerie dragons, and I believe that he does not know what we can do. And *Star Dragon*, with a crew of Quentarah gunners, is a formidable ship in herself. But only if you will learn that you must not be afraid of her speed. That speed is your ship's defense, as you discovered the hard way in our last battle."

"I want to practice first," Mira said.

"For the rest, they are very vulnerable to us," Dalvenjah continued. "We have proven that dragon-fire is very effective against the fans of the Eolwyn ships, and the Alasheran airships are only wood, rope and canvas. I suggest that the dragons should strike at portions of their fleet at a time, moving through quickly with *Star Dragon* and the Quentarah ships to follow us in and destroy the ships that we have disabled."

"There is just one problem," Mira reminded her. "The Alasherans have always used winged demons in the past to keep our dragons busy."

"That is so," Dalvenjah agreed. "If that happens, the dragons will attack the demons. *Star Dragon* and the Quentarah will have to take on the fleet, and I fear that their task will be harder. We must teach the Quentarah the spells that will make their arrows and spears dangerous to demons."

Mira was still far from satisfied, and she looked it. "What about Jenny? Will she be in the fight?"

"I do not see how we could stop her," the dragon said. "We have benefited greatly from her cleverness on this journey. She has become fierce lately, and I do not trust her judgement enough to permit her to fly *Star Dragon*. But her magic is as strong as ever, and she is still cunning. Above all else, she is absolutely invulnerable."

There was nothing to be done for now except to prepare for battle. The Quentarah put out the call throughout that region of their realm for ships and troops. Not just those that had a chance of arriving in time for the battle but others that could not arrive until later, providing reinforcements if the fight turned into an extended siege. Fortunately the Quentarah possessed the same magical communication devices that the Eolwyn used, so that warships were already on their way, and they could be directed in flight to join the main fleet at the scene of battle. The Queen was cautious and canny, having the garrisons send in only a tithe of their ships so that other portions of the realm would not be undefended.

The Quentarah were more clever in the construction of their ships than the Eolwyn. The ducted fans of the Eolwyn were

simple, but they were also vulnerable and not especially efficient in getting a ship off the ground. The Quentarah ships
looked more like aircraft, if only vaguely so. The hull was wide
and flat, with a pair of short wings at either end and a long, tapered tail giving stability. The ship took off and landed by the
means of retractable landing gear that expanded mechanically
to lift the entire ship well above the pull of gravity or drop it
back down again, needing only small directional fans to maneuver the ship. The Quentarah ships were more heavily armored
and could carry more cargo. And their larger, more powerful engines were embedded within the hull like jet engines in a
fighter, protected by the ship's armor.

The Quentarah ships were much faster; even their largest battleships were capable of cruising at more than a hundred miles
per hour with short-range bursts of nearly twice that. The only
problem was that the Quentarah could not build as many of their
ships, which were far more complex and required greater resources which they had only in limited supply. They also had to
devote a large number of ships to their extensive patrols, leaving only a few for defense, and they gave a fair number away to
their most trusted allies. Their interest in *Star Dragon* was not
for her speed but for her absolute silence and the simplicity of
her operation.

For Mira, the next couple of hours were spent learning to fly
Star Dragon at high speed. Jenny took the airship up first for a
quick test, satisfying herself that everything was functioning
normally. Mira was trying very hard not to think that she was
being taught to fly a ship that had been repaired by someone
who was fading in and out of sanity. It was more than a matter
of her own peace of mind; she did not want Jenny picking up
her thoughts, as the girl had been likely to do in the past. It was
disquieting to think that Jenny was really only a magical spirit
maintaining an illusion of physical and mental presence. There
was really less of her left than it seemed.

Complicating Mira's driving lessons were about two dozen
Quentarah who had come aboard as *Star Dragon*'s new gunners
and boarding party. Jenny and Mira had retreated to the helm
deck, letting the warrior women settle themselves into their stations.

"Mira, your ship is overrun with Amazon Chipmunks," Jenny observed.

"At least they have the skirts on their armor," Mira said. "I admit that I was afraid that they would take the skirts off their armor, all because of my little fashion trend. Every warrior shot through the butt would have been my fault."

"This lot looks like they would never let fad and fashion interfere with business," Jenny remarked very softly. "This is a special squad of their best warrior women, you know. They all have PMS."

"Be kind, child."

"They do have nice legs," Sir Remidan remarked as he stepped up quietly behind them. A slightly mischievous smile was peeking out from behind his mustache.

"They have muscley legs," Mira commented sourly.

Allan and Vajerral returned as predicted, making the round trip of some two hundred miles each way in about an hour and a half. That was a long, hard pull for a Mindijarah, even flying in this place of no gravity. They might have sent Jenny, who was faster than any of the others and did not tire, but Dalvenjah kept in mind what she had done to Ellon and feared how she might react to the presence of the High Priest Haldephren. Jenny was rational most of the time, but she was finding it harder and harder to keep her mind focused and when she lost it, she went right over the edge.

The two dragons returned directly to the Queen's council chamber, where they were expected. The Queen herself was out at that moment, taking stock of exactly how many ships her people could get into the sky, but an aide hurried to fetch her. Dalvenjah and Mr. Holmes were there at about the same time, all of them arriving so quickly that Vajerral was still panting in one corner from her exertions. Mira was, of course, learning to fly her little ship like a madman. She had a qualified teacher.

"Something very strange is happening," Allan reported immediately. "The combined Eolwyn and Alasheran fleets are approaching at the best speed that they can manage, little more than twenty knots. I counted eight Alasheran warships of considerable size, the largest wooden ships that I have ever seen. There were also about eight hundred Eolwyn ships, although I am not sure of the exact count. Half are larger ships and half are scouts."

Beradoln frowned. "We cannot fight that ourselves. I doubt that we could have three hundred ships on hand in time."

"You might not have to fight anyone," Allan told her. "The Alasheran ships are flying black flags above their own colors, and the Eolwyn ships are all making a great mess of smoke from burning pots at the ends of long poles suspended from the sides of their ships. That suggests to me a desire to parlay. Perhaps they are arrogant enough to call for our surrender, but I hope that the Emperor wishes to keep this fight between ourselves."

"How many fires to each ship?" Beradoln asked eagerly.

"Quite a few, on some of the larger ships," the dragon answered.

"There will be no fight, unless this is a trick," the Queen said. "The burning of the fire pots makes a ship deliberately visible, the smoke during the day and the light of the fire at night. One fire in the stern is a signal to parlay. Several fires is a signal to surrender. The smoke obscures the aiming of the turrets, and the light blinds the gunners at night. It is a gesture of putting yourself at a disadvantage."

Dalvenjah sat back on her tail, then laid her head on the floor and sighed. "Surrender. Why would they offer a surrender? In the game of traps, that is an ineffective one at best and the Emperor would not underestimate me. What could they possibly have in mind?"

"Do you advise that we should go out to meet them?" Beradoln asked.

"Meet them, certainly. And I suggest that we should move out to meet them soon. If it does turn into a fight, we must give ourselves time to work that fleet over at our own pace. Their smaller or faster ships will likely try to outflank us, causing us to divide our forces."

"We can get nearly all of our ships into the sky within the hour," the Queen said. "Only seven of our ships need repairs that could keep them on the ground, and we can get even those flying at need."

There was certainly little danger in flying a malfunctioning ship. Once it cleared the pull of gravity, it could hardly crash.

Dalvenjah turned her head, seeing that Holmes was watching her. "Can you suggest anything?"

"Nothing, except caution. You know these people best." He paused a brief moment. "I do not recommend speculation as a basis for drawing conclusions, but it does occupy the mind and suggests solutions until more facts become available. What do you suspect?"

Dalvenjah sighed again. "If the Emperor does mean to surrender, then he has gone ahead of us and he knows that the Prophecy has turned against him. Perhaps that power has been lost to him. Perhaps the Dark Sorceress cannot get him the power he wants. But that power must be available to us. He is afraid, and he wants peace between us while it is still to my advantage to make peace with him."

"Under those same circumstances, he would desire most to destroy you and your allies," Holmes reminded her.

"Unless he knows that he cannot win," she said. "Our fight with the Eolwyn ambush might have shown him what dragons can do. Remember also that he must know by now that the spirit of Jenny is still with us, and he will have heard what she did to Ellon. Perhaps she is the one he fears."

"Perhaps we should discover the answer to this question for ourselves," Queen Beradoln suggested. "We can take our fleet and meet them at a time and place of our choosing."

❧ PART NINE ❧

Cthulhu Dawn

The only complaint that the Quentarah had with their new allies was the surprising and unsettling fact that they proposed to send their males into battle. They were not exactly shocked or appalled, but they obviously thought that it was a very bad idea. Being Quentarah, of course, they were not about to insult their friends by making an issue of it. They were fond of saying, "Opinions are like assholes: everybody has one, and they all stink."

"There really is no problem," Dalvenjah assured Queen Beradoln quietly. "We have enough males that we can spare the losses. I can think of at least two of our own males that we could easily afford to lose."

"Oh, it is not that so much," the Queen insisted. "We would allow our own males into battle if we thought that we could trust them. Their judgement is bad enough at the best of times. When they get excited, they have absolutely no sense at all."

The dragon laid back her ears. "I have that same problem with Vajerral."

The Quentarah fleet began assembling into formation within an hour after Allan and Vajerral had returned from their reconnaissance. They practiced until they were prepared for the worst, but they still had the better part of three hundred ships to get into the air and that took half an hour. Most of their ships were scouts and cutters of less than a hundred feet, and those could be launched into the sky in flocks. But there were also ninety of the larger ships, most of them five to six hundred feet in length. These vast machines moved rather ponderously at low speeds and they needed room to get themselves up to the speed at which they would begin to handle predictably.

In the end, the Quentarah had seven larger ships that had a motor or two down for repairs but which were otherwise fit to fly and even fight, if they were needed. Once in the air, their ships were quieter than those of the Eolwyn, who used over-sized fans rotating at relatively low speeds to make up for the lack of gearing on their motors. The Quentarah engines used a powerful high-speed motor running a series of compressor blades not unlike those of a jet engine, but there was no burning of fuel within the engines and they were buried deep within the armored hull, muffling their sound.

Even so, the Quentarah quietly coveted Mira's little ship and they were enormously pleased that she was willing to share the secret for making thrust vanes. *Star Dragon* was only slightly faster than their own ships, but the vanes could maintain full speed indefinitely and needed little maintenance due to the fact that they were magical solid-state, with no moving parts. They were also absolutely silent and, in the arrangement that Jenny had designed for *Star Dragon*, tremendously versatile, able to direct thrust for vertical takeoff or quick maneuvers.

Once the fleet was in formation, *Star Dragon* was installed in the lead beside the Queen's own flagship and they accelerated smoothly to cruising speed at about a hundred knots. The cutters ringed themselves defensively about the larger ships, and the scouts moved out in small groups to guard against sudden attacks, moving through the clusters of islands to insure that no enemy ships might be lurking in hiding waiting to fall in behind the fleet. Quentarah scouts had been watching the Eolwyn armada very closely, arriving in increasing numbers soon after the first patrol had found the enemy fleet. So far, the Eolwyn had kept to a tight group with every appearance of surrendering, sending out no vanguard or scouts of their own, following the wooden Alasheran airships dutifully. Of course, their torches were making so much smoke that it was hard to tell if they were trying to hide anything in the middle of their fleet.

Queen Beradoln, speaking from the experience of several thousand years of war with the Eolwyn, found it hard to believe that they were interested in a permanent surrender of their hostile plans of conquest. The Eolwyn were not a very complex or subtle people, whatever they might wish to believe about themselves, but they were greedy and violent. Even if the Alasherans were honest in their desire to surrender, the Eolwyn were only going along with it out of expediency; meaning that they were afraid to cross the Alasherans, the faerie dragons, or a possible future combination of those two forces joined in an overpowering alliance. Beradoln's suspicion was that the Eolwyn would play along only until they discovered the secret of the lift vanes.

The Quentarah moved their fleet into position a short distance ahead of the Eolwyn armada and stopped at a place of their choosing, an open space in the sky islands where they could see clearly for several miles. The Eolwyn came into view a few minutes later, the Alasheran airships in the lead, and their entire group drew to a stop almost immediately. Their intentions known, they extinguished nearly all of their torches and the smoke cleared quickly to reveal nothing unexpected. Then the Emperor's own flagship moved forward into the center of the clearing. Several Eolwyn battleships followed at a discreet distance.

Allan and Dalvenjah flew out to the Emperor's airship, never landing on the deck but standing off to one side. After a minute they hurried back, and Dalvenjah flew directly to the Quentarah flagship. Queen Beradoln was waiting on the forward deck.

"The Emperor is waiting on his ship, but the High Priest Haldephren and the Dark Sorceress Darja are not here," the dragon reported quickly. "They have no weapons out and they could not defend themselves if we attack. The Emperor wants to talk with me, and he is willing to come alone to *Star Dragon*. I am inclined to speak with him. Will you come?"

"In the company of dragons, I feel no cause for concern," Beradoln said. "I will accompany you."

Mira brought *Star Dragon* close enough alongside the Quentarah flagship for Queen Beradoln and two of her captains to jump aboard, the lack of gravity allowing them to cross the space between the two ships easily. The transfer was less simple when *Star Dragon* went out to meet the Emperor's flagship, an immense airship that was dark of hull with vanes and stabilizers that were as black as night. Lines were thrown between the two ships and *Star Dragon* was hauled in until the two ships were side by side, the smaller ship rotated slightly so that her wings settled on the rail of the battleship's center deck to form a bridge between the two. Emperor Myrkan, nothing more than a tall, slender figure in a dark, hooded robe, was assisted to the top of the rail, but he walked across the wing by himself. The lines were loosened and *Star Dragon* moved off a short distance.

Dalvenjah hesitated only a moment before she reached down and lifted the Emperor over the siderail and set him on the deck. Myrkan bowed his head to her politely, then he pushed back his hood and smiled. His features had been changed tremendously by the magic he commanded, his deeply lined face almost that of an animal, in its way more alien than even the Quentarah. His mouth and nose had merged nearly together into a blunt canine snout, his eyes deeply set but large and bright, his brows heavy. His bony hands looked half again as long as normal. And yet his smile was warm and pleasant and completely without guile, that of a kindly old man who was pleased with his world and honestly happy to see them. The crew of *Star Dragon* stared in wordless amazement. This was hardly what they would have expected of a man who had been the embodiment of evil for two thousand years.

"This is a fine world in its way. A very pleasant place indeed. Never hot nor cold, and the view is always spectacular," he said, looking up at the sky. Then he turned to Dalvenjah. "So we meet at last, Dalvenjah Foxfire. I hope that I have not disappointed you, but I have lost my will to fight."

"If you are sincere, then you certainly will not find me disappointed," she assured him.

"Then you will not be disappointed," he told her. Then he turned to Lady Mira and nodded. "Sorceress Kasdamir Gerran. Even among your enemies, you hold a reputation as a sorceress of tremendous stature."

"Oh, piffle," Mira complained. "Even among my enemies, all I get is short jokes. Now you understand what I like about the Quentarah."

Myrkan laughed. "Your forgiveness, Sorceress. I feel very good, I do confess. I think that I have never felt so good in all my life."

"Perhaps we might go below and have a little talk about whatever it is that has made you so happy," Dalvenjah suggested. "I confess that I would like to hear something to be happy about as well."

Jenny was left on the helm deck to watch the ship, the assumption being that she was safer there than in the company of the Emperor where she might hear something that would set her off. Her extended out-of-body experience had resulted in an out-of-mind experience that left her untrustworthy. Vajerral was left to keep her company and to serve, if necessary, as a secondary conscience and a calming voice if anything went wrong. Dooket and Erkin stayed at their posts with the Quentarah gunners, and Sir Remidan was asked to keep watch on deck. In other words, none of the ship's cabins were very big and Dalvenjah had to think of every excuse she could to expel several would-be participants and make them like it.

The Emperor was given a comfortable chair in one corner of the large cabin that had been serving as a combination galley and meeting room, and Mira put on water to make tea. Under the circumstances, she cheated by casting a spell on the teapot that heated the water instantly, and she was able to pass out cups about as quickly as everyone was seated. The two dragons, of course, sat on their tails, a peculiar habit of their kind. Emperor Myrkan sat back in his chair and stirred his tea, smiling pleasantly like someone's old uncle come over for a visit and a game of bridge.

Mira reminded herself once again that this was the most evil, ruthless man that her world had ever known. She had always heard rumors about his appearance, and he looked more than half like the demons his followers were fond of summoning. But his manner was so unexpected and bizarre that she was inclined to believe that he must be pretending. She felt herself compelled to say that he seemed to be doing much better now that they had changed his medication, but by force of will she was able to keep that to herself.

Dalvenjah ignored the tea and got herself a mug of mead, which she had learned to like cold after spending several weeks in Allan's home world several years back. She had actually learned to tolerate cold beer, since mead had been rather out of fashion there for some time, but that had given her the idea for cold mead.

"May I introduce my associate, Mr. Sherlock Holmes,"

Dalvenjah began. "And this is Queen Beradoln of the Quentarah."

"My pleasure, Your Majesty," Emperor Myrkan said, bowing his head to her politely.

"I hope that you will not mind if we get down to business right away," the dragon said. "To tell you the truth, I will feel much happier very quickly if you will answer certain questions that I have. Feeling happy was to be the subject of our conversation, you might recall."

"Yes, I do recall," the Emperor assured her. "We might begin by making it perfectly understood that, while my mood has improved, I have by no means lost my wits. I have not become simple, nor am I insane. Do not think that I could have brought the Eolwyn here to surrender, much less my own people, if they had thought me foolish. Now I suspect that I do not have to say this to you, Dalvenjah Foxfire, but it must still be said."

Dalvenjah nodded. "That is understood. My first question, if I may. Have you been to the center of this place?"

"Yes, I have."

"And that made you very happy?"

"No, that was rather disappointing," the Emperor said, and frowned. "Perhaps it would be easiest and quickest if I anticipated your questions in order of occurrence, and leap all the way back to the beginning. Now, it all began several thousand years ago."

"This sounds like the beginning of a very long story," Mira said to herself.

The Emperor laughed. "I will be brief, I promise you. As you may already know, the source of magic of this place was once the source of latent magic for the world above as well. Several thousand years ago, the bridge between this world and the one above became weaker, so that the latent magic failed to dissipate into the outer world. When that happened, the latent magic became increasingly concentrated here, overflowing as it were at the source. A part of that excess magic eventually became a god, an entity of immense powers. Such occurrences happened often, but these beings almost always move away, exploring the ways of their new existence before any serious disruption of magic occurs. This one was stupid and obstinate, or perhaps just excessively cautious, staying in the vortex thousands of years growing stronger."

"I have heard of such entities," Dalvenjah agreed. "They will generally lose interest in mortals and quasimortals like you and me when they grow out of their childhood."

"Yes, but that childhood may last many thousands of years," the Emperor said. "Two thousand years ago, my followers and I were seeking the power we needed to command our entire world. We sought the source of all magic, and I realize now that in a rudimentary way we learned to open a Way Between the Worlds. But there is no place like this in our own world; the magic escapes too freely. Our efforts to bridge a way to the source of magic led us instead to this place. It was here that we met the immortal one."

"Your people have been through here before?" Queen Beradoln asked. "We have never heard of visitors from outworld going into the center before this."

"We were being sneaky, you understand," he told her. "No one around here was interested in going into the center, and we were not about to generate any interest in that direction. We never wanted anyone else to go talking to our god, you know."

He sighed heavily, setting aside his cup and saucer. "We were fools in those days. We worshipped evil with absolute devotion. We had found a virgin god and we pledged ourselves to him, if he would only become a god of evil. That poor creature hardly knew what we were talking about, his experience was so limited. The entity would not leave this place, and we could convince him only to agree to send a surrogate consciousness in the form of the Sorceress Darja to observe life in the real world, gather knowledge and experience, and then return with her experiences. When Darja merges with her parent entity, then everything that she has become will form the basis of his new consciousness."

"But Darja has not been able to merge with the entity," Dalvenjah said.

"Fortunately, no," the Emperor admitted. "Something prevents it. Now you must destroy Darja before it can happen."

"Your news reassures me tremendously," the dragon told him. "I do not believe that it will ever happen. You see, something went fatally wrong with your prophecy long ago, and it was your fault. As I understand it, the Dark Sorceress Darja did not survive the great defeat of your Empire nearly two thousand years ago. Her spirit needed a new body. But unlike you and your followers, she needed a very specific body, and you waited a very long time to find it."

"Yes, that is so."

Dalvenjah cocked her head. "You gave her the wrong one."

Emperor Myrkan looked both frightened and then relieved, as if realizing for the first time how close he had come to disaster was honestly important to him. "But, how can that be? The Prophecy clearly indicated the girl Jenny."

"The Prophecy also indicated Sorceress Kasdamir Gerran," the dragon said. "Did you dismiss that aspect because it made no sense to you? There were two choices, one right and one wrong, and you made the obvious choice. You were guided by the Prophecy of Maerildyn, which makes only a passing reference to Mira's existence. The Prophecy of the Faerie Dragons only seemed to confirm what you already believed. You also knew, even at the time when you first bound the spirit of Darja with Jenny's, that she was in truth a faerie dragon in mortal form. Perhaps you thought that was all the better, for dragons are not mortal. You forgot that dragon magic is something apart from the latent magic that you know. Jenny's body leaves Darja incompatible with the entity, and she cannot merge with him. Your greatest mistake was in assuming that the prophecies existed for your benefit."

"Yes, I see that now," Myrkan agreed. "I also understand the danger in having you point out my mistakes to me, the danger to you and to myself, and I cannot believe that you have not realized that for yourself. You know that I will not be going back."

"Going back where?" Holmes asked, speaking for the first time. "I was under the impression that you have brought the Alasheran fleet here for the purposes of surrendering."

"The High Priest Haldephren is not yet accounted for," Dalvenjah reminded him. "Perhaps this has something to do with whatever left you disappointed enough to abandon your plans."

"That is exactly the point," the Emperor agreed. "My journey has been a very enlightening one. Darja is everything that I once would have expected of a god of evil. She belongs to the Dark.

And I have come to realize that I have been betrayed in ways that I had never expected. I had dedicated myself and everything that was mine to the service of Evil, and now I have learned that Evil simply does not care. The Dark consumes everything and never gives any lasting reward. Evil never creates except for the purpose of even greater destruction. That was never what I wanted. I wanted to rule. I wanted the Dark to be the absolute power throughout the universe. Now I have learned that the ultimate aim of the Dark is to destroy until nothing is left except Evil itself. I worshipped the Dark but I value accomplishment and prosperity above all else, and so you see why I looked upon the true face of evil and was bitterly disappointed. Then I realized that perhaps I was not as evil as I had always believed."

"Is it really all that simple?" Mira asked, looking profoundly surprised. "Those of us who reject the Dark understand that almost instinctively."

"That is true," the Emperor agreed. "Unfortunately, some of us cannot see that so plainly. And I fear that some, like Haldephren, can never understand that simple truth."

"Haldephren, of course, did not agree with your decision to betray the Dark," Mira observed. "He always was too shallow to appreciate such subtlety of thought."

"I played him for the fool for hundreds of years, and he never realized that," Myrkan said. "From his way of thinking, I was the betrayer. But I will not try to deceive you. I have followed the Dark for a very long time. Too great a part of what I am has been given over to the Dark, and too much of the Dark has entered into what is left of me. I see the deception, but I am not cured of its influence. That is why I have come to you."

"I cannot sever your ties to the dark," Dalvenjah told him.

"Indeed you can, although the cure is a desperate one," Myrkan told her gently, his smile warm and reassuring. "My followers and I have come to you because you surely must know how to free us from the Dark. We want you to help us to die, finally and in a way that the Dark can never again claim us. And it must be soon, before the Dark finds some new use for us and attempts to seduce us to return. You can help us, can you not?"

The others turned to Dalvenjah, who looked troubled. "Yes,

it can be done that way. Indeed, Jenny has already freed Ellon, that self-important little boy-thing of Haldephren's, and he never willingly renounced the Dark."

The Emperor looked surprised. "Jenny? But I took Jenny Barker's body for Darja some weeks ago."

"True, but her ghost has been haunting us ever since," Dalvenjah said, and she smiled wickedly. "We came prepared."

Emperor Myrkan watched her suspiciously for a moment, then he sat back and laughed. "There was never any profit in evil with people like you about. You have been too clever, and too lucky."

The Emperor returned to his ship in the company of Dalvenjah Foxfire, and they retired to his cabin with a bottle of his favorite wine. They talked and laughed together for a couple of hours, and in the end only the dragon returned. Dalvenjah was, as always, grimly efficient.

There remained many other troublesome matters to be concluded. Some three dozen of the Emperor's closest followers, in particular his chief advisors, captains, sorcerers and dark priests, all needed to follow their master into peaceful death, their courage and resolution fortified by his example. The dragons attended to that matter. All except for Jenny, who found this whole matter disquieting, and also for Vajerral, a proven and capable warrior but whose mother deemed her too young to be dispatching people who wanted to die and certainly needed to. The crews of the Alasheran fleet were given two of their ships and sent home. These poor folk were not true servants of the Dark; being Alasherans, they had only been behaving as they believed they should. The curious fact remains that Evil has very few devoted followers, but a great deal of hired help.

The last problem was the Eolwyn fleet, which had been standing off in tight formation that suggested morbid fascination. Dalvenjah had wondered at first why the Emperor had found it so necessary to bring them along, and all the more why they had agreed to come. They were greedy and often cruel people but not true servants of the Dark, whatever they pretended to the Alasherans. They had been enormously impressed with their visitors, especially the cold, complex evil of the Emperor in the days before he had found the enlightenment of disillusionment and his consequent happiness. They had been even more impressed and also very frightened when Emperor Myrkan had returned from his visit with an evil god ready to denounce the Dark and escape its command upon him through death. The Eolwyn had seen the light, but Queen Beradoln knew from long experience that it would not last.

In that, the Queen was probably right, and Emperor Myrkan had known it as well. This mass surrender served three purposes. They had seen that Myrkan's determination to escape the Dark was absolute, which would serve to reinforce the lesson. He had brought them to make their capitulation to the Quentarah, their chief enemies, a serious political and strategic embarrassment that would seriously damage their influence throughout their world. And they would see for themselves that the Quentarah would be receiving the magical secrets of the outworld airships, a matter of vastly important military implications. These things were meant to break the Eolwyn Empire and prevent them from ever again being a serious threat. Dalvenjah decided that the best she could do was to leave the matter in the hands of the capable and cunning Queen Beradoln, who was already thinking of countless ways to exploit this situation to advantage.

That still left Dalvenjah with the most important of problems to solve for herself. The High Priest Haldephren and the Dark Sorceress Darja—servants of the Dark are enormously fond of their silly titles—were already at the center, where Darja was trying to turn a magical entity into a god of evil by booting herself up like software. At least she knew now that the matter would probably keep until she could get there, since she doubted that Haldephren was capable of figuring things out for himself and Darja was too abstract to take much notice.

Dalvenjah was still walking around shaking her head. Later that day, as *Star Dragon* was finally able to turn back to the Quentarah Citadel, she was finally able to sit back on her tail in the middle of the helm deck and shake her head to her heart's content.

"He looked into the face of Evil, and it did not live up to his expectations," she said, and looked up at Mr. Holmes. "He was disappointed, and an Empire that might have conquered worlds comes to an end. It all sounds very stupid, when you think about it."

"Then pray don't think it," Holmes told her. "Count your blessings and be on your way, and may all of your enemies be conquered so easily. How do you suppose I feel? You brought me along to assist with matters of logic, and there is precious little logic to be found in any of this."

Dalvenjah sighed, and shook her head yet again. "What is happening? We are making progress, but have we been clever or just very lucky?"

"A fair amount of both, I should say. We have just been very lucky, and a major victory has just fallen into our laps. Our next battle will be our last and we will have to be very clever."

"Can they get Darja to merge with the entity?" Mira asked.

"If they identify the problem," the dragon answered. "Knowing that it is Jenny's body that causes the incompatibility could lead them to think about ways to force the merger directly between the entity and Darja's spirit."

"Well, what was so special about my body that Darja needs it?"

"Absolutely nothing. Your Alasheran friends get certain mystical ideas in their heads that have no reality. Darja needs a mortal body. Any mortal body would serve."

"Oh, my." Mira realized certain frightening implications; Haldephren could transfer Darja to any mortal body at hand and get what he wanted. "But why was Darja called the Consort?"

"Jiminy Cricket, how should I know?" Dalvenjah demanded, turning her head to glare. "The Emperor certainly never intended to marry her, you can be sure of that. Of course, Haldephren never knew what she really is until recently. Myrkan was a suspicious sort who kept certain secrets to himself. Perhaps the title Consort was meant to be misleading."

Queen Beradoln offered to send a fleet of her best ships to accompany *Star Dragon* into the center, and it was a generous offer indeed. Even the fearless Quentarah had never dared to penetrate the Region of Darkness and its population of nasty things, but they would go eagerly for Dalvenjah Foxfire, whose wisdom they admired, and for Lady Mira, who had taught them to dress in a sophisticated manner. But Dalvenjah knew that Beradoln needed every ship she had to prevent the Eolwyn from getting sneaky ideas, especially now that the dragons and their airship were leaving. The Eolwyn had respected the Emperor, and they feared the Mindijaran after the ambush that had cost them a dozen of their best ships in half as many minutes. Now the Quentarah would have to deal with them alone.

As it happened, Queen Beradoln had solved most of her problems by the next morning. She had spent a large portion of the night negotiating the surrender of the Eolwyn, and she had arrived at terms that left both sides feeling that they had won. The Eolwyn actually preferred farming and simpler crafts; they had established their empire to protect themselves from pirates so that they could pursue their first loves of agriculture and carpentry. Their giant ships flew so slowly in part because they had a nervous fear of flying and were subject to motion sickness. They were also not very clever about administration and bureaucracy, and they seemed to know it. On the other hand, the Quentarah loved their ships and they delighted in adventure and travel. They were very good with machines but were rather indifferent to farming and other forms of puttering.

The Queen's idea, which the Eolwyn agreed to with hesitant optimism, was to allow everyone to do exactly what they did best. The Eolwyn would farm and produce handcrafted products to their heart's content. The Quentarah merchant ships would move their products about the entire world quickly and efficiently while their fighting fleet would protect the Eolwyn and each of their respective allies from pirates and primitives. Queen Beradoln had already talked the Eolwyn into surrendering their ships for refitting; in this way, she had insured that they would no longer have the means for making war even if they decided to return to their old habits. The observation that the Eolwyn were not very bright had already been made, and the negotiations had been seriously influenced by the fact that the Amazon Chipmunks had stopped wearing their skirts.

Dalvenjah was still shaking her head when *Star Dragon* set sail the next morning. Jenny was at the helm for the first few hours, but she was becoming increasingly distracted. Mira relieved her some time later, and after that she spent most of her time hanging her neck over the side or sitting in the bow letting the wind blow through her metaphysical substance. J.T. would often join her. Although he would not be back to normal for the remainder of their journey, his leg had improved to the point that he could tolerate it, and his mood had improved to the point that the others could tolerate him. Actually enjoying his company was a rare event at the best of times.

The sky islands became smaller and farther apart during that first day of travel. The islands of the Quentarah were among the closest to the center of their world, although without gravity it was hard to say whether they were highest or lowest. *Star Dragon* laid over for the night on one of the last of the small sky islands; without Jenny to navigate through the darkness with her remarkable ability to see, flying at night presented too much danger of running into something dark and hard. There was also no reference for navigation that even Jenny could have seen. She had been able to navigate at night because the tops of the sky islands, the sides with trees, had always pointed upward, or inward. It was all a matter of perspective, but they had also run out of islands.

They left the last sky islands behind the next morning, which meant that they now had to find their way toward the center using the string-and-shadow arrangement that Jenny had devised. The sky was a bright deep blue, completely open and featureless in every direction. Mira pushed the ship to its fullest stable speed, well over a hundred knots, although she blew J.T. and Jenny both off the forward deck and nearly rebroke the cat's leg in the process. The Quentarah had reported that there was about six thousand miles of open sky to cross before *Star Dragon* came into the Region of Darkness, admitting that it might have expanded a mile or two since the last time they had checked. Mira wanted to cross that distance as quickly as they could, even if it meant flying *Star Dragon* in the dark. As it happened, Mr. Holmes had regained enough of his magic and the control to make it useful, and he was now able to take turns with Mira at the helm.

After the third day of open sky, they made the transition into the Realm of Darkness rather suddenly. For one thing, the Realm of Darkness was not dark; the sky turned as black as night, but the source of light remained and they were able to navigate with the same string-and-shadow trick. Dalvenjah explained that they had already reached the center of the singularity and had now taken a dimensional right turn, and were now proceeding down through the center of the center itself. Holmes understood what she meant readily and the other dragons had a fairly good idea of the mechanics involved. Curiously, Mira had little trouble with the concept. Of course, her sense of reality was skewed at the best of times. Because they had approached during the day, they knew that the way was open before them by the simple fact that light was coming out of the vortex. Dalvenjah and Holmes both expressed a keen interest in staying around until night to see what the back of the vortex looked like, but their two most popular theories on what they would find argued that they would see nothing at all or else an infinite amount of nothing. That sounded boring in either case, so they just kept going.

Because the Quentarah had been so adamant that the Region of Darkness was full of monsters, Mira decided to cut *Star Dragon*'s speed to about seventy knots. That, she explained, was to give herself time to change course so that they would not run into any. Although they were flying toward the source of light, the effect was not at all the same as looking toward the sun and they were able to see ahead fairly well, if there had actually been anything to see. They certainly did not see any monsters in their first full hour. J.T. yawned and announced that he was going below to look for monsters under his bed. All the same, everyone stayed off the open bow deck and the moveable roofs were kept closed over the center and rear decks.

When they did find a monster, it was everything that they had been led to expect. And Mira very nearly did run into it. The thing was so big and complicated in its form, and it moved so quickly, that they never did get a very good look at it. Because the monsters had evolved in an environment without solid land or even gravity, they lacked the need for legs or any other support and their build lacked any specific orientation. And because there was precious little about to eat, they were largely designed around abilities to feed themselves. The first one they met had certain aspects of a squid, but with a large beaked head at the top rather than below and similar beaks at the ends of each of its ten long tentacles, although these lesser beaks were apparently meant only for biting and not actual eating, with a cluster of smaller tentacles surrounding each beak to form a crude hand.

The thing took one good look at *Star Dragon*, which was only about four or five times its own considerable size. It raised all of its tentacles as if to give this community of beaks a chance to take a good look as well, and each of the hungry little mouths licked its chops. Then the monster attacked with surprising speed and no obvious method of propulsion except for magic, making a great shrill, roaring noise that had to be heard to be believed and even that stretched credibility.

Mira turned sharply to one side and advanced *Star Dragon*'s speed in an effort to avoid the monster. The object was to continue their journey by getting the ship to the other side of the monster, but the great, ugly beast was just fast enough to make that difficult. Mira was certain that she could manage it, but she was never given a chance to try.

Jenny suddenly leaped into the bow of the ship by simply passing through the deck. She lowered her neck and arched her back, challenging the monster with the half roar, half bark of the Mindijaran. As small as she was in comparison, the monster seemed to recognize her immediately not as prey but as something akin to its own kind, and a threat to its possession of the great aluminum delicacy that it had selected for its dinner. Then Jenny leaped into battle with a speed that no living dragon could have matched, darting rapidly in and out to tease the monster with her flame and snap at the beaked tentacles. Mira cut speed quickly and prepared to circle back, but Dalvenjah was there on the helm deck immediately.

"No, just go on," the dragon said. "Jenny is in no physical danger. The beast cannot harm her, and her magic is stronger. But she has lost all wit and reason at the moment, and she is as much a danger to us as to our enemy. If her sanity returns, then she will follow."

"Can't you do something for her?" Mira demanded, although she obediently turned the airship back on course.

"What could I do, except place her inside a bottle?" Dalvenjah asked. "You know the dangers of that, after seeing Ellon, and placing her spirit inside one of the dragons would only endanger both. I believe that she will return, but perhaps it would be best if she did not. The spells that I cast upon her spirit to confine and protect her as a ghost have begun to deteriorate rapidly since we have entered the Region of Darkness."

"You could renew those spells," Mira insisted.

"I have been renewing those spells all the time," the dragon explained. "That no longer has any great effect. Soon now Jenny will lose all sense of identity from her past life, and she will know only the instinct to seek rebirth. There is only one thing more that I can do for her."

Whatever that was, Dalvenjah did not say; she left the helm deck at that very moment and went below. Jenny did return within the hour, unharmed, although she would not speak of her battle. Considering her mindless battle fury and the disquieting inclination for cruelty that Jenny had displayed lately, Mira did not doubt that she had destroyed the monster. Would she give battle to every monster they found? Mira wondered if the girl was possessed by some will for self-destruction, forgetting that she was dead already. Jenny sat alone in the very stern of the airship, sitting back on her haunches with her tail wrapped around her long legs, staring into the starless night. She would not be with them for very long now, perhaps no more than a few hours more.

Holmes came up to the helm deck a short time later, and he saw that Mira had been weeping. He was not surprised, for he could guess the reason why.

"I have to keep thinking that it was my fault," she said. "It was my idea to rush off to Alashera, putting her into the reach of her enemies. I knew better, I really did. I used to be so damned sure of myself, when I was younger and taller. We were supposed to be too smart to let ourselves get caught."

"The Prophecy had to take its course, so perhaps your judgement had been influenced by forces you did not expect," Holmes told her. "Although the cost has been Jenny's life, that sacrifice was necessary to force Darja to reveal herself and lead us to the entity. And that is a matter that must be resolved at any cost."

He paused a moment as if listening, then stared down at the deck. "Is it my imagination, or is this ship swaying slightly from side to side? Have we encountered any crosswinds?"

"That is not the wind," Vajerral said, coming up on the helm deck. "Allan and Dalvenjah went below some time ago. They seemed to think that they had something important to do."

"Are they making something?" Holmes asked.

"If they are making anything, then it will be a little dragon," Vajerral explained succinctly.

That certainly came as a great surprise. Holmes and Mira had observed that Allan and Dalvenjah enjoyed a purely platonic relationship. Vajerral and Kelvandor, who knew them better, realized that they enjoyed a largely platonic relationship with occasional attacks of raw, fiery lust.

"What a time for those two dragons to decide to go frolic in the autumn mists," Mira remarked with obvious displeasure. "Even my own animal passions respond to some sense of propriety."

"And what about your height?" Holmes asked, as if he saw some need to change the subject. "I had assumed that you would make another attempt to restore yourself to your desired stature, now that you have returned once to your original height."

"Not in this place, I'm not," Mira insisted. "The magic here is too strong and unpredictable. You can imagine the unexpected results I might get if I tried to change my physical structure now."

Mira sent Vajerral and Kelvandor overboard, flying ahead of the ship just far enough to send back warning when they found additional monsters in their path. That gave Mira enough warning to steer a wider course around the great beasts, for she wanted to avoid provoking another attack. The plan worked well enough for the most part, although a few of the most fierce, or at least the most obstinate, monsters chased the dragons. Since they were twice as fast even as the airship, they found it easy enough to lead the monsters away from *Star Dragon* and then leave the creatures behind.

No one was exactly certain when Jenny left them for the last time.

Dalvenjah was not surprised to find that Jenny was already gone. She seemed to believe that the time was right, whatever that could mean, and that it was all for the best. They would be coming to the center soon enough, in no more than two or three days and perhaps as soon as just a few hours, and she quietly reminded the others, especially Mira, that they really did not want Jenny with them at that time anyway. The girl's wits were so far gone that she had become too unpredictable, no longer able to tell friend from foe. Under the circumstances, she might well have been responsive to the will of the Dark Sorceress Darja, for there was a link that remained between the two of them.

Although they had been inside the Region of Darkness for less than a day, the tremendous magic inherent in that place was beginning to have an effect upon certain members of the crew. The mortals remained essentially unchanged but Holmes, who was responsive to the same latent magic as themselves even though he was of a race of faerie, had begun to change quickly. He was no longer the small, slender hawk of a man that he had been for centuries but more like the elves of ages past, taller and younger in appearance, massive in his shoulders but delicate of feature. Mira remarked that he looked like the muscle-bound boys in beefcake calendars, and she had taken to cooing quietly whenever she saw him.

J.T. recovered from his broken hind leg within hours, and his own appearance began to change. His black-and-white patterns of fur became a full, solid black and his size had doubled by the end of the first day. Even the faerie dragons had changed, becoming larger, longer of leg and more slender of build with powerful muscles moving beneath their soft hides. Their eyes of jade green became large and soft, their muzzles longer and more delicate, and their crests of sapphire blue were long and full. Holmes suggested that they were becoming increasingly purer examples of their various races until those very qualities had reached the point of exaggeration, what he called hyper-faerie. He also said that they should do what they needed to do and get out again as quickly as possible, for fear that the process would continue until they became true monsters. Neither he nor Dalvenjah could predict if they would ever return to normal.

Mira thought that it was all very unfair. The others had become taller, stronger and more graceful, while all that she had ever gotten out of this journey was shorter. Sir Remidan was inclined to agree with her. His magical armor was getting slowly larger, and he feared that he would no longer be able to wear it should the process continue for long.

It seemed an awkward time aboard *Star Dragon*. Getting used to the fact that Jenny was no longer with them was a part of it, but several of them were distracted from their own concern and grief by the surprise and even fear for what was happening to themselves. They knew also that they were going to their final confrontation with their enemies, and that the Prophecy would be played out for better or worse very soon now. Time was short, in spite of their assurance that the High Priest Haldephren might not be clever or patient enough to complete the Prophecy for himself. Dalvenjah was not greatly concerned about Haldephren; the two problems that occupied her most were knowing what to do about Darja and the entity itself. Simply killing Darja or expelling her from Jenny's body would only free her spirit to merge with her parent entity, completing her mission to create a god of evil. Darja's spirit had to be contained, and Jenny's bottle trick seemed the best idea until Dalvenjah had the time to destroy her spirit completely. Containing the entity was more daunting, since she doubted that she possessed the magic necessary to compel the entity to get inside the bottle and she did not have a bottle that big in the first place.

Their problems were far from over, even if they had been lucky so far. Dalvenjah honestly did not know how they could win, or even survive. But they still had to try, and she would feel much better for having some idea of how to go about it.

Containing Darja was the important part, and that was relatively easy. Although she did not know just how much magic the Dark Sorceress Darja might command, she was fairly certain that she and Allan could strip her right out of Jenny's body and stuff her down a bottle. As long as Darja could not merge with the entity, then the entity itself presented no immediate danger. She could come back and solve that problem in her own good time, meaning that she could go home and research the matter of destroying juvenile godlings before she gave it a try. And that might in itself solve the problem that the Quentarah had asked of her, the matter of excess latent magic building up within the singularity. What the release of that magic would do to the outer world was a problem in itself, and that made it Dalvenjah's next problem.

Dalvenjah preferred to face her problems in reasonable numbers, no more than twenty at a time.

With all of these problems facing her, Dalvenjah did not need any stupidity. Unfortunately, that was exactly what she got. The Region of Darkness was exactly like the Outer Regions in one certain respect; anything that was thrown overboard did not fall but continued to float exactly were it had been left. Dalvenjah encountered this effect unexpectedly upon returning to *Star Dragon* from a turn patrolling ahead of the ship. She was coming up for a landing on the stern deck, the roof opened to allow room for the dragons, and approaching to the right side of the tail planes so that Allan could come in from the left. As it happened, Dooket and Erkin had just pissed over the side of the ship.

Now in any possible world, it was never, ever a good idea to piss on the esteemed Sorceress Dalvenjah Foxfire, whether one had intended to or not. Mira locked the boys into their cabin for their own protection. Dalvenjah might be willing to forgive and forget, but not any time in the foreseeable future.

Things began to change within the next few hours. The black sky began to be crossed by slender pathways that glowed softly in pale colors, things that the crew of *Star Dragon* assumed must be either optical illusions, arcs of raw latent magic or a simple phenomenon of the local weather. The dragons went out for a closer look and found that the truth was rather more than they had expected. The arcs were actual physical structures, as if the light had solidified in a slender strand. They were indeed caused by arcs of latent magic, although completely benign in nature and safe enough even to touch.

Star Dragon continued on her way, now having to dodge the multicolored arcs as well as the monsters, which were becoming steadily bigger, nastier and uglier. Apparently competition squeezed the little ones to the outside, where the magic they fed upon, at least in part, was not as strong. Although the monsters seemed perfectly willing to try eating dragons and aluminum airships, Dalvenjah and Holmes were both fairly certain that they sustained themselves in some way directly upon latent magic. Mr. Holmes then pointed out that they were not at all certain that the monsters fed upon anything but magic, which also seemed likely. Their only excuse for attacking either the dragons or the ship might have been entirely an attitude and behavioral problem.

Star Dragon proceeded inward toward the center, and two things became obvious over the next few hours. The first problem was that the multicolored arcs were becoming more numerous, eventually forming a vast spider's web that filled the dark sky. The arcs were a hazard to navigation in themselves, but they were also a favorite lurking place of the monsters that were steadily becoming larger and more common. The dragons had to scout very carefully now, finding a path that kept the ship as far as possible from the arcs to prevent ambushes from nasty things that bumped about quite a lot in this perpetual night. When the ship could not avoid the arcs by several hundred yards, then the dragons had to look on the back sides of the arcs to see if anything was bumping about out of sight.

The other problem was that *Star Dragon* was slowing down, which only made the matter of monsters even more dangerous. There was no reason for the problem that either Dalvenjah or Holmes could find at first. Mira was soon giving full power to all sets of the vanes, then had to cut back slightly; the super-abundance of magic caused the vanes to develop too much thrust, and the powerful wing vanes, originally intended to support the full weight of a ship, had made some noises suggesting that their mountings were about to fail. The vanes were reactionless drives that actually produced no true thrust but pushed against the fabric of space, but the effect upon the ship's frame was essentially the same.

When Kelvandor came in to trade his watch with Allan, he reported that the dragons were experiencing the same phenomenon. Of course, the dragons boosted their natural flying abilities with their lift magic, which worked much the same way as *Star Dragon*'s vanes. But when they propelled themselves by their wings alone, they still found themselves moving slowly. Adding to the confusion was the fact that *Star Dragon*'s air-speed indicator insisted that the ship was still making over a hundred and fifty knots, even when it seemed that they were doing barely a fifth of that in real distance. And to confuse matters even more, the dragons found speeds returned rapidly to normal at very close range; they might spend two minutes or more coming up the last two hundred yards behind the ship, then suddenly find themselves hurtled forward the last twenty yards. That resulted in three aborted landings and seven near disasters until the dragons got the feel of things.

That last part was the clue that Dalvenjah and Holmes needed to figure things out sufficiently. It was not speed that was affected, but distance that was distorted. Calculating from the reports of the dragons on their approach runs, Holmes determined an expansion ratio of four point four to one, so that four hundred yards of apparent distance was indeed a mile. Ten hours later, that ratio had become an even five to one. Aside from the fact that it was a great intellectual curiosity, it was also both good news and bad news. The good news was that they had much more time to escape when they found a monster. The bad news was that they had a lot farther to go than they had anticipated, and that distance would become much greater as they came closer. Mira pointed out that they had no idea how far they had to go in the first place, so the matter was irrelevant. That made perfect sense to her.

The first serious problem came suddenly and unexpectedly, although Holmes and Dalvenjah both insisted afterward that they should have anticipated it. Vajerral and Kelvandor had been flying ahead on patrol when the younger dragon flushed a particularly large monster that had been hiding behind a group of the colored arcs. The monster chased her as she had expected, and she had been leading it away from the ship according to their usual plan when she realized that this one was just a little faster than herself. In spite of her partially deserved reputation for bad judgement, she kept her head and continued leading it away from the ship; if she could not outrun the thing, then *Star Dragon* never could. She was much smaller and probably the more agile of the two in the air, since her wings could assist her in tight turns, so she believed that her best bet to lose the beast would be in darting rapidly in and out among the arcs.

Unfortunately, the monster was just too fast for her. When fighting became inevitable, then she elected to turn and fight before she tired herself in the chase. Her fireballs and sustained flame were deadly, but the monster was big and fully as obstinate as it was stupid. Her best defense was the fact that she could circle the monster faster than it could turn its bulk to face her, giving her time and opportunity to attack swiftly and dart away. Kelvandor had realized the problem and was already well on the way to her assistance. Dalvenjah had also become aware of the matter even before Vajerral had turned to fight.

"Allan!" she called urgently, and his head and long neck emerged from the main hatch a moment later. "Vajerral just picked a fight with the largest monster that we have seen yet. I suppose that she needs our help."

Allan lifted his head even higher and looked around. "What possessed her to want to fight? Was the thing too fast for her?"

"Exactly. Kelvandor has gone to assist her."

"Oh." Allan frowned. "I suppose that we should go and help them."

Neither of them wanted to speak too critically of the abilities of the two young dragons, but they seemed to be finding it hard not to. Kelvandor, of course, was not a young dragon but the oldest of them all, more than twice as old as all of their ages combined. He was a very capable and competent fighting dragon and sorcerer in his own right, but he was completely overshadowed in both ability and personality by his aunt Dalvenjah and he knew it. For that matter, Allan and Dalvenjah both possessed stronger fighting magic, their flames were stronger and with greater range, and being smaller they were both swifter and more agile. But in a fight with a monster that was noticeably larger than *Star Dragon*, all four of the dragons would have to work together.

"I suppose that we should be taking *Star Dragon* out of the way," Mira remarked quietly.

"That would probably be advisable," Holmes agreed.

Mira did not want to run. The monsters had so far proven extremely resistant to damage, even flame, and they all knew that four dragons could not easily fight one this large. It was at times like this that they missed Jenny most, particularly her ability to stay in tight, giving full punishment with endless endurance as well as immunity to harm. The living dragons were distracted by the need to protect themselves from a vast creature that may or may not be trying to eat them but which certainly took exception to the fact that they were not yet ghosts. Lady Mira, possessor of truly erratic motherly instincts, wanted to intervene.

Mira gave all the power she dared to every set of vanes, although the ship seemed barely to crawl. The battle with the monster appeared to be no more than a few hundred yards away, but the fivefold distances of this place made that at least five or six miles. Mira thought that it would make very little difference whether she got *Star Dragon* past in a hurry; the dragons could not escape the monster until they defeated it, or at least effected a major alteration in its attitude. Dalvenjah and Allan had not yet even joined the battle, and while Vajerral and Kelvandor were holding their own they were not about to convince their adversary to make any fundamental changes in its philosophies.

Matters took a turn for the worse quite suddenly. Mira was unable to see exactly what happened, except that Vajerral suddenly found herself much closer to the monster than she had intended. The young dragon was either struck or bitten; she let out a barking roar that could be heard all the way to the ship, although the sound took a little time to get there. Kelvandor threw himself into the face of the monster with boundless fury and a complete disregard for his own safety, and his flames and the snaps of his tail were enough to distract the beast sufficiently to give Vajerral a chance to get herself away. He had to hold his own for several long seconds, but Dalvenjah and Allan came to his assistance before he got in trouble himself.

Vajerral was still unable to escape. It seemed that she could not fly, but was bent over in the air holding her right hind leg. Mira spun the ship's wheels, turning *Star Dragon* without hesitation toward the battle.

"Weapons, boys!" she shouted. "Exploding bolts. Mr. Holmes, can you act as our gunner?"

"Yes, I believe so," he agreed cautiously, although he did not yet begin preparing the weapon for battle. "You believe that the dragons will benefit from your assistance?"

"You're damned right!" she declared. "If nothing else, we have to carry Vajerral to safety. Would you not agree that this course of action is our only logical and honorable alternative, Mr. Holmes?"

"Oh, I must concur entirely. I just required the reassurance of knowing that you were aware of what you were doing."

Pushed to her limits, *Star Dragon* was perfectly capable of doing three miles a minute. Even at that speed, she still needed two minutes to cross the distance to the battle of the dragons. Although the Trassek twins and Holmes needed that time to prepare their weapons for battle, Mira begrudged the delay. At least Vajerral was using her wings again, carrying herself farther away from the monster that the other three dragons were harassing to little effect, but she seemed hardly to have the strength to move herself and her right wing appeared damaged as well. Jenny was gone already, and Mira was not about to lose another of those brave, beautiful dragons. She still felt that this was all her fault, resulting from her spying mission in Alashera.

"Fire in the hole!" Dooket called suddenly.

"What?" Mira demanded, wondering where he had picked up that expression. She turned and saw that thin, black smoke was escaping from the main hatch leading below. It did not seem immediately dangerous; since the ship carried no fuel and was made mostly of metal, she was not worried about swift fires consuming her ship. "Check it out."

Dooket disappeared below deck, leaving Erkin to set up the catapults on their mounts. Mr. Holmes hurried to the bow and removed the barrel plugs on the two larger guns built into *Star Dragon*'s hull. By the time he returned, Dooket had also come back up on deck.

"Small fire in the galley," he reported. "Somebody left a large pan of potatoes on the stove to cook. The water boiled out and the potatoes were starting to burn. I cut the fire and secured the pan for a rough ride, but those potatoes are still burning."

"Good enough," Mira said. "Back to your station. We will be in battle in a few seconds."

"But the potatoes . . ."

"Damn the potatoes, full speed ahead!" Mira declared. "Mr. Holmes, stand by the main guns. We will try to get off a shot or two, if we can get a clear aim through those fool dragons."

Mira began easing off the ship's speed at the same time that she set a course directly at the middle of the beast, slowing enough to give Mr. Holmes a chance for a couple of good shots. The charges of the guns were ordinarily no more effective than the fireballs of the dragons, except for the penetrating power of a sharp point backed up by thirty-five pounds of weight accelerated to several hundred miles per hour. Nothing less would be very effective against a monster of this size; Holmes was worried whether it would be enough. Apparently the dragons saw what Mira was planning and elected to oblige her; at least they decided to get out of the way while they could.

As soon as the dragons were clear, Holmes let off both shots in rapid succession. The guns launched their projectiles with no dramatic bang; there was no explosion of gunpowder to set the charges in motion, and the charges themselves were thrown at speeds that were just barely subsonic. Their aim was very good, and both shots hit the monster squarely in the middle of its whatever. But they had not counted upon monsters being made out of rubber, and the shots hardly dented it before their charges exploded. Under those circumstances, the charges did no more damage than the dragons' fireballs.

Mira took in the situation in short order, no pun intended, and came up with a very quick fix. It was probably not one of the very best decisions of her career, but it was fairly typical.

"Brace for impact!" she called.

Holmes ducked down under the wind baffle with his back to the bulkhead, having no time to explain to the sorceress that she was either insane or just stupid. Mira could only hope that the boys had protected themselves; she had completely forgotten that J.T. was somewhere below. Things proceeded very simply and quickly from that point. *Star Dragon* rammed the monster fairly well in the middle, and Mira engaged full power to all the ship's vanes to push it backwards quickly before it could recover from the impact. The collision in itself was unlikely to have done any more damage than the charges had, but Mira pushed up their speed, driving the beast back before it could recover enough to attack the ship.

Mira rammed the creature backwards into one set of arcs with unexpected results, for the arc shattered with a tremendous flash of light and a flare of inert magic that rippled across the monster's hide like chain lightning. This time the beast was harmed, apparently by the magic itself far more than the effects of the impact, for it roared in pain and began to smell especially bad. Mira kept full power to the vanes, hurtling the monster back with even greater speed into a spider's web of intersecting arcs. The arcs did not break this time, although another flare of energy engulfed the monster. Mira was not inclined to stay around at this point. She backed the airship away and turned tightly, then accelerated away at the best speed the little ship could manage. She knew that she could not outrun the monster; she hoped only to put some distance between it and her ship before it could recover enough to turn its attention to a new attack.

Fortunately the dragons arrived at that point, giving the airship more time to escape. Dalvenjah tried something especially clever at this point; noticing that the monster was backed up against the web of arcs, as if to guard its back against attack, she directed all three of the fighting dragons to send fireballs into the web itself around the monster. The results of that tactic were so spectacular that the crew of *Star Dragon* was unable to look back for some time. By the time the flare was beginning to fade, the airship was slowing to come up beside Vajerral. Holmes and Sir Remidan hurried to help the injured dragon aboard. Mira immediately brought the ship back up to full power and returned to their original course.

The other dragons returned within a couple of minutes, although they took Vajerral below without a word. Mira could at least take that to mean that they were no longer in danger, and she eased *Star Dragon* back down to a low cruising speed before they flew blind into another fight. They were flying slow enough now that she could send the boys out onto the airship's long, slender bow to access their damage, now that they had rid the ship of burning potatoes and had vented it to blow out the smoke. Since she suspected that the two barbarians did not really understand the modern metal complexity of the new ship, she asked Mr. Holmes to go along as well.

The report was not bad, but not good. The frame of the ship itself had held fairly well, due in part to the reinforcement of planks and timbers from the old *Wind Dragon* inside the hull. The shell of the hull had suffered buckling and small tears along the first ten feet or so. The only serious damage was in the form of several long rips along the right side of the hull, the worst being a large hole that opened the cabin within. If *Star Dragon* had been on the ocean, she would have already gone down. As it was, the damage was not critical. The only serious problem was that they no longer had Jenny to repair their damage, and Holmes was uncertain about his ability to drill out the rivets of the broken plates and cut new ones. He was called down to assist Dalvenjah soon after that, which did not in itself seem like a good sign.

Mira endured in silence for a good, long time, not daring to interrupt the dragons to discover how Vajerral was doing. Dalvenjah herself came out on deck well over an hour later, looking tired but not greatly concerned. She climbed up the helm deck and lifted her head to look about.

"You are insane, Lady Kasdamir Gerran," she remarked after a long moment.

"But I get results," Mira reminded her. "I will not see another young dragon die on this quest. It still all seems like my fault, you know."

Dalvenjah nodded slowly. "Vajerral will be just fine, although she will not fight again for the remainder of this journey. She was bitten high on her right leg, and there was venom in the bite. Fortunately the venom was magical rather than chemical, easier to nullify, and it caused more pain than true harm. But I do not know how we could have protected her if you had not come when you did."

"Is the monster dead?" Mira asked.

"I am not certain that they can be killed entirely, although the parts that were left were hardly in fighting condition." The dragon paused, and frowned. "I fear that we did lose one member of our crew, all the same. We cannot find your cat. We suspect that he was in your cabin, which was ripped open during the fight. He must have been lost overboard when the ship rammed the monster."

"You looked in all the storage lockers?" Mira asked, and the dragon nodded slowly. She shrugged. "He was a brave cat."

Dalvenjah perked her ears. "Indeed?"

"No, not hardly," Mira admitted, and smiled. "What indeed can I say of this cat? In life, he shared great adventures in the company of sorceresses and precocious dragons, traveling the skies of many worlds in magical airships. Of course, that was never by any plan of his. He would just as well have spent many a long year asleep on a window ledge. Of my cat, I can say only this. Of all the cats that I have met in my travels, he was the most worthless."

Dalvenjah nodded. "He will not be missed."

Mira smiled. "So much for solemn occasions. You must promise me one thing, dragon. If I do not survive this journey, I want a great, gaudy marble tomb with stone cherubs and acorns. And carve this epitaph over the door. *'She was the light of our dreary lives.'* "

"You flatter yourself, Sorceress."

"A nasty job, but someone has to do it." She looked ahead,

standing well up on her box to see over the forward baffle. "I suspect that it will not be long now. Perhaps you dragons should rest yourselves and lick your wounds."

Dalvenjah stuck out her tongue and made a face, that being no expression that faerie dragons were in the habit of using.

❧ PART TEN ❧

This Is All Very Confusing

When they arrived in the center, there was certainly no question about where they were even if it was not at all what they had expected. At that, Mira still found it a little hard to believe. She called the others on deck, for them to take a good look and offer opinions.

What they found before them was a structure of immense size, like a palace or fortress thousands of yards across, seeming to be made of white marble and crystal glowing with an inner light. In truth it more closely resembled a palace, for it looked like an apparently endless assembly of tall, thin towers, vast domes and countless other structures too numerous and varied to identify clearly. It looked too delicate to have been intended as a defensive structure, in no way like the massive stone fortresses of the Eolwyn or the Quentarah with their heavy defenses turned outward against attack. There seemed to be no sky island forming its core, unless the island itself was completely enclosed within the structure. Most likely it was exactly what it appeared to be, a single immense structure floating free in space.

It also appeared to be completely deserted.

Farther beyond the floating palace, the walls of the singularity closed in rapidly into a long, narrow funnel, the glowing arcs of magic eventually becoming so thick and overlapping that they seemed to form almost a solid wall. Mira was reminded more of the web tunnels leading into the lairs of certain spiders. *Star Dragon*'s string-and-shadow guide indicated that the source of light lay beyond the palace somewhere down that tunnel. The only blessing was that there were no monsters in this place, perhaps because they were unable to handle a diet of pure magic so near the source.

"That palace is vast," Kelvandor observed. "Why would anyone build a thing like this if no one lives here?"

"I do not believe that this place is as deserted as it appears," Dalvenjah remarked. "And when you are a god, there might be no such thing as too large or pretentious."

"Maintaining a proper professional appearance must be hell," Mira agreed.

Mr. Holmes had been staring ahead, and he now turned back to the dragons. "Then I beg your indulgence for just one question. Is this floating palace in the very center of the singularity?"

"No, the actual center must be at the point where the walls of this universe merge," Dalvenjah said.

"Then should we not find this virgin god in the center?"

"That is two questions, and you begged me to indulge you for just one," Dalvenjah reminded him.

"Indulge me just a little more."

"I was hoping to avoid another of our long and pointless philosophical debates," the dragon said, and sighed heavily. "No, I would not expect to find a magical entity evolved in the center of a singularity. The force of magic would be too strong and pure. It would have to happen somewhere very close but far enough for eddies to form in the flow, disturbances that break the uniformity of pure magic to permit it to begin to recombine into new and more complex forms."

"Yes, that makes perfect sense," Sir Remidan agreed in one of his most heroic voices.

Dalvenjah glanced at the Knight suspiciously. "There is also the fact that the space for some distance about the palace is completely free of arcs of magic, when this area should be so completely filled with them that we would be unable to fly this ship. Something within this palace has been consuming vast amounts of magic for a long time indeed."

"Well, yes," Holmes admitted. "An illusion. My own suspicion is that an illusion of that palace has been cast to distract us from our true goal."

"An illusion would not require as much magic as I sense disappearing into that place," Dalvenjah insisted. "We will proceed carefully, testing against traps. But this is the place we must look first."

"Airships behind us!" Erkin called from the stern. "At least they must be airships of some type. But there certainly is a whole swarm of them."

The others had already looked back long before he finished his report, and they had seen for themselves. The ships were very unusual in design compared to anything they had seen. They were silent, propelled by thrust vanes much like those of *Star Dragon* rather than magical engines. They were metal rather than wood in construction and they were all like catamarans in design, two long, slender hulls joined by two or three short wings, with steering fins at the ends of each hull. This design was probably meant to enclose a set of lift vanes within each hull, the wide spacing of the pair giving a stable balance. Perhaps it worked better under gravity; here, the ships were bobbing and pitching slowly, as if they were not inherently stable.

Dalvenjah sat back on her tail, her ears laid back. "It seems to be just one thing after another. Now just who do you suppose this is?"

"Those are not Alasheran ships," Mira said. "Nothing from my world has that much metal, except for what some of us wear for clothes."

"I wish we had one of the Quentarah along to tell us if these ships had originated somewhere within the singularity," Holmes said. "I doubt that very much, however. These ships had never been built to fly in free fall, unless they have idiots for designers. I suspect that their basic instability is due to the fact that they are fighting their own lift. Granted, of course, that they might be far more stable at lower speeds. Distances here make things look deceptive, but those ships are moving at better than a hundred knots."

"And if they have followed us, they must have been able to match our best speed," Dalvenjah added. "And it seems to me a fair assumption that anyone who has been following us without making themselves known cannot be any friends of ours."

"Could they be new allies of the Alasherans?" Mira asked. "The High Priest Haldephren might have left them lurking about to intercept us."

"I doubt that," the dragon said. "The Emperor said nothing about any new allies beyond the Eolwyn, and I know that he would have told me. And if they had been ahead of us and waiting in ambush, they should have attacked first rather than let us by."

"Unless Haldephren's ships are on the other side of the palace, and we are caught between the two," the small sorceress pointed out.

"Haldephren has only three ships."

The problem with having Sherlock Holmes along on their journey was that they had gotten into the habit of trying to answer every question by logical deduction. Even Holmes was quick to point out that deduction worked only as long as they had information that could be processed into a logical sequence that provided answers, but he was still as bad as any of them. He was also quick to remind them that he was not really Sherlock Holmes. Sometimes they could only wait for answers to come to them, and such answers certainly seemed to be on their way. The small fleet of unidentified flying catamarans, an even dozen in all, slowed to a stop; a very slow stop indeed, or so it appeared because of the distance distortion. Only the lead ship continued to approach, and that at reduced speeds. Apparently a parlay was in the works.

Mira had been holding *Star Dragon* in place. The other ship looped around wide to come up behind her, perhaps aware and respectful of the fact that her main guns were in her bow, its starboard hull drifting to a stop barely ten yards from *Star Dragon*'s wing tip. From closer range, it could easily be seen that the strange airship was actually fairly primitive in design, closer to the level of technology of Mira's own world for all that it was built entirely of metal. The design of the ship was very simple, nothing more than two very long, thin hulls joined by three wing segments that were rather long and thick and which Holmes recognized as a very basic high-lift design for low speeds, comparable to the wing designs for a late 1930's bomber. If these ships were local then the lift was needed to get the ships away from the gravity of the sky islands but interfered in free flight. The Quentarah solved that problem by lifting their ships clear of gravity, the Eolwyn by having no wings at all, while Jenny had possessed an advantage in designing the aerodynamics of *Star Dragon* by her degree in engineering.

A tall, dark man with sharp features stepped up on the deck of the strange ship. He was dressed richly in a manner that suggested both wealth and command, and he was holding a cat. Several members of *Star Dragon*'s crew were startled by the sight of him.

"A Dark Elf!" Holmes declared. "That is a Dark Elf, the evil equivalent of my own race. I had thought that their kind had died out long ago, but I can see now that some survivors of their race must have taken refuge down here."

"Who cares about that?" Mira demanded. "That son of a bitch has my cat!"

The stranger smiled with amused satisfaction. "You are both perfectly correct. I am Dourkess An-shallestern, Captain of the Dark Elves. Our people and certain of our allies retreated into this place many thousands of years ago, when it became obvious that the outer world was becoming uninhabitable to our kind. It was never a part of our nature to foolishly endure our decline, as certain others of the faerie races did."

"And you assume that this place belongs to you?" Dalvenjah asked.

"Our numbers were small enough from the start, and we have been slow to recover," he explained, suspiciously quick to justify why his people did not rule the entire singularity. "We have been biding our time, keeping ourselves secret so that others would not fear us and bring war upon us before we are ready. We had never assumed that there might be an entity existing within the deepest core of this world. In those days, our ships were not yet up to the standards demanded of this place."

"You still don't know jack shit about shipbuilding," Holmes remarked. His annoyance and distaste was very plain, particularly in his ungentlemanly use of language. Dalvenjah was looking quietly amused.

Dourkess ignored him, with noticeable effort. "Our surprise could not have been greater when the Alasherans established contact with the entity and even made arrangements to make it into an evil god to serve their own purposes. In all that time since, we have been trying to discover some way to undo that. In time we sent our agents to the world of the Alasherans, where they discovered the prophecies that would lead eventually to these very events we face now. Unlike the Alasherans, we unravelled the prophecies to mean that Lady Mira, not Jenny Barker, was the true object of Prophecy. We hoped to use that knowledge to our own advantage, although by no means could we permit the Alasherans to know that. We sent a spy to watch your every move."

He set J.T. on the rail, and the cat bowed his head. "We meet once again, Kasdamir Gerran. I hope that you will excuse me for jumping ship a few hours back, but it seemed like a good time. I knew that my friends were following close behind."

"But . . . you?" Mira stared in disbelief. "You are my familiar. How could you be a spy?"

"Think about how we first met," J.T. suggested. When it was obvious that she did not remember, he sat down and sighed. "Well, you were fairly tipsy at the time. I came to you."

"Oh, yeah!" Mira agreed, understanding matters at last. "Why, you little bastard! You eat my kippers, and then you turn on me. Just like a cat!"

Dalvenjah rolled her eyes and shook her head slowly. "Here we go again. Well, what do you want? Have you come to claim the virgin god for yourselves? That seems to be very popular among the servants of evil these days."

"We may be of the Dark, but we are not servants of Evil," Dourkess was quick to protest, as if there was a real difference. "Those foolish mortals might be satisfied to find themselves a god to fear and worship. We are quite satisfied with ourselves and our own plans of conquest, and we will not work and fight and die for the entertainment of any godling. We have come to destroy the entity."

"Oh, well, that's what we plan to do," Mira observed brightly.

"We can do that just as well, after we destroy you," Dourkess declared. "J.T. has already told us all of your secrets. We know, for example, that our greatest concern now is to keep the Dark Sorceress Darja from merging her own consciousness with that of the entity."

"Yes, but do you know how to destroy the entity itself?" Dalvenjah asked.

Dourkess paused, looking sternly displeased. "Do you?"

"I know who does."

He had to think about that very carefully. "The entity is really of no immediate importance to us. We do want to destroy it eventually, so that the magic will return to the outer world and restore the age of faerie, but we can bide our time. The immediate problem for us is confining Darja and destroying the Alasherans before they do something regrettable."

Dalvenjah sat back on her tail. "Why are you explaining all of this to us? What good does it do you?"

Dourkess smiled wickedly. "Years of secret planning on my part have brought me to sudden victory over you, something that none of your other enemies has ever managed. I just wanted the last laugh."

Dalvenjah lifted her head, her ears perked. "You seem very sure of yourself. Has your cat not explained to you the flaw in your plans? You cannot hope to take us with only twelve ships."

"The ships are a minor concern," Dourkess told her. "I also have three dozen of my own dragons at my command."

He turned and nodded to someone they could not see, and the airship began to move away quickly. At that same moment, J.T. gathered himself together and leaped over the rail, hurtling himself toward *Star Dragon*. Mira reached out and snatched him out of the air, hauling him aboard. Still, she did not seem particularly pleased to have him back; as a matter of fact, she was trying to strangle him. The cat was desperately trying to explain himself, his efforts complicated by the fact that he could not breathe. Holmes and Sir Remidan pulled her hands apart long enough for J.T. to speak.

"I'm a double agent!" he insisted. "I have been for years. I just never told you because I feared that you would react inappropriately."

"You still went overboard and returned to your former associates," Holmes reminded him.

"I knew that they were following and that they would attack," the cat explained quickly. "I had to go to them as arranged to discover what they were planning. Tell the faerie dragons that the creatures that Dork-head called dragons are things that the Dark Elves brought with them down from the outer world. They won't be very effective in a fight against real dragons. They have little enough magic, and less intelligence."

Dalvenjah heard that for herself, and it was all she needed to know. She called Allan and Kelvandor to her and they went overboard immediately, ready to give battle. She had to trust that Mira and Holmes would prepare the ship for battle; whether or not Mira strangled the cat was now irrelevant. The other ship was moving away slowly; it was indeed a local design but powered by large and apparently very inefficient versions of *Star Dragon*'s lift vanes, producing enough power to drive the ship but not enough in itself to lift it. The three dragons made a wide circle behind Mira's airship before Dalvenjah turned and darted forward, flying faster and faster as her entire form began to glow with golden light before she disappeared entirely within a shaft of flame. Mira had often heard of the ability of the faerie dragons to assume their fiery form, but she had certainly never seen it.

The other two fighting dragons turned to follow Dalvenjah a moment later, although Kelvandor seemed to have some trouble assuming his fiery form; this was something that not even all of the Veridan, the Warrior-sorcerers of the faerie dragons, could accomplish easily. Dalvenjah had overtaken Dourkess's airship within the first few moments and she circled it a couple of times as if contemplating what her magical enhancement could do to a metal ship; this was a trick that she had only used against Dark Dragons and wooden ships in the past. She apparently remembered what Jenny had once told her about the inclination that aluminum had for burning and darted in, hitting the starboard hull squarely in the center. That entire portion of the ship disappeared in a tremendous explosion of flames, while the dragon passed completely through the hull and emerged from beneath. She circled around tightly and struck the other hull, and the ship began to break up in flight.

After that the three dragons moved on to decimate the remainder of the enemy fleet, and it became impossible to tell them apart. The matter became irrelevant, beyond the fact that they were all three moving through the fleet with deadly efficiency. The dragons of the Dark Elves were attacking from *Star Dragon*'s other side, and that was quite enough to command Mira's attention for the moment. They were not true dragons, of course; they did have large wings but fairly small bodies and no forelegs at all, just small hind legs, short necks and long, narrow heads. Since they were entertaining or inspiring themselves by making a great deal of loud, obnoxious but fairly insipid noises, they probably were not very intelligent. Mira could imagine that the ship's main guns would be fairly ineffective, since she could hardly turn the ship quickly enough to track such small, swift targets. It seemed best to her to let the boys have their bows and catapults. She opened the weapons locker on the helm deck and took out the two assault rifles that she had snitched from the FBI.

"We don't have a lot of ammunition for those guns," she said, handing one to Holmes and Sir Remidan. "You need to let them come in close and make each shot count. Our dragons should be back around to help us in a couple of minutes or so."

"You know this weapon better than I do," the knight reminded her.

"I can hardly fly the ship and shoot at the same time," she told him. "If nothing else, the kick of that weapon would knock me off my box."

As it happened, she would have never given him a gun if she could have helped it. Sir Remidan's grasp of nonmagical technology had stalled out somewhere between water faucets and remote controls.

The false dragons had a simple but effective tactic for attack. They came straight in at the airship, then turned aside at the last moment and increased their speed to intercept the three dragons. The faerie dragons were still finishing up their own attack on the Dark Elf fleet, although they had dropped out of their fiery forms and were hitting the few remaining ships with fireballs. Mira was left to wonder if their tactic had stolen too much of their strength early on, leaving them too tired to protect themselves. She turned *Star Dragon* about sharply and forced all the speed she could out of the ship before she enjoyed the luxury of swearing furiously.

Her one consolation was that the false dragons were olive green, so dark that they were almost black, not easily confused with the golden Mindijaran. That gave her some reason to hope Sir Remidan or the boys would not shoot their friends by mistake.

Naturally enough, it had to be Holmes who shot one of the dragons by accident, and it had to be Kelvandor who got it. As it happened, it was a reasonable enough mistake; Holmes had shot one of the false dragons in the head and the bullet had bounced off a particularly hard skull, hitting Kelvandor who was in fact some distance away. The dragon took the shot in a place that is not nearly as delicate as most people imagine, although less well padded in dragons, and the bullet had actually lost a good portion of its energy before it had hit. Kelvandor reversed himself very quickly, thinking at first that he had been bitten by one of the false dragons. He was not seriously harmed but he could not have been more surprised; it was hard for those on the ship to hide their amusement and pay attention to the task of shooting false dragons.

The battle was over very quickly, even though Kelvandor returned to *Star Dragon* to attend to his wound. This was the first battle in which the group had been around to witness the aftermath, and they were surprised by the amount of mess. Because of the lack of gravity, everything stayed very much where it had fallen. There was on the one side the wreckage of the airships that the faerie dragons had destroyed, some of it still burning. There were also a fair number of survivors who had dived overboard and were swimming for all they were worth, although that was a very ineffective method of travel. In a gesture of either desperation or extreme optimism, they were headed away from the center, going home the hard way. The remains of the false dragons were drifting about on the other side, quite a few of them done to a turn from dragon flames.

"What a great, damned mess," Mira declared. "I suppose that it will just hang there for years."

"I doubt that," Dalvenjah remarked without looking up from her work. She was tending Kelvandor's wound. "A few monsters should be along in the next few hours, looking to see where all of those idiot Dark Elves are coming from. They might be kind enough to pick things up, at least the bodies. We do serve meat in various stages from rare to well done. The shame is that we never did determine whether or not they actually eat their prey."

She glanced at Kelvandor, who had his neck bent around as far as it would go to watch her. "Hardly more than a scratch. The bullet seems to be already gone somewhere."

"I teleported it out, of course," Kelvandor said defensively. "It was very hot."

"You will be staying with the ship, all the same."

Kelvandor looked more worried than indignant. "I am not so badly wounded. You have said that yourself."

"That is beside the point," the sorceress said, speaking softly. "Vajerral is not doing so well. Jenny's disappearance has depressed her, and this place is not cheerful. She is in no condition to defend this ship herself and yet our companions must have this ship to leave here, even admitting that we could pull or carry them if we must. Do you want to fly two thousand miles with those two barbarians hanging on your tail?"

"You expect to go overboard any time soon?" Mira asked suspiciously. She had already been moving the airship away from the area of their battle.

"I belive that we must go in quickly now," the dragon said. "Our battle will have very likely made the entity aware of our presence here."

"Being a god, he surely knew that we were here the moment we arrived," Sir Remidan remarked.

"That great, worthless creature is not a god," Dalvenjah said sharply. "It is a magical being of vast powers and limited experience, and it probably lacks the common sense to watch out for itself. I felt very certain that we could easily catch it by surprise, but we have now made quite enough magical noise that it has to have become aware of our presence no matter how obtuse it might be."

Holmes frowned. "Considering what you have said about the entity, is it likely to make any difference even if it does know that we are here? It would probably not even recognize the danger, or at least know how to respond if it did."

"Don't complicate things at this point, Holmes," the dragon said. "The time for logic and reason has passed. Let's go kick some ass, so that we can go home."

Actually, things were not quite so easily done. The palace was vast in proportions and, for all they knew, the entire structure was a maze of rooms and passages. Mr. Holmes compared it to trying to find their way about the Smithsonian, the Kremlin and the Palace of Versailles all joined together, without a map or any other means of knowing where they were going. Searching the entire thing was possible but certainly not desirable, not if they could find some clue or make some logical deduction about where to begin. Dalvenjah reminded them that their time would be limited from the moment they landed, so they needed to know where they were going.

As it happened, it was J.T. the cat who provided the solution. He still insisted that he had been a double agent, although the wiser members of the crew suspected that he had not decided finally upon the idea of becoming a double agent until he had realized that the Dark Elves intended to attack *Star Dragon* without the numbers or weapons they needed to win. The Dark Elves were wise, cunning and powerful in their magic; if not for their serious lack of numbers and a racial paranoia that required them to keep themselves hidden, they could have ruled the entire world of the sky islands easily. But their strength was in subterfuge, deception and bluff. Their tremendous arrogance made them terrible warriors, since they invariably overestimated the value of their own abilities, weapons and ploys. J.T. had only been vaguely impressed with them, and that at a time in his life when he simply had not had the experience to know any better.

Of course, J.T. was still a familiar, and his natural talents were his abilities to identify and locate sources of magic. In spite of the tremendous wash of latent magic radiating from the core, he still knew exactly where to find the entity. The only trouble was knowing whether or not to trust him. At this point, curiously enough, Mira was his greatest advocate. She had known him for a long time, and she was certain that his cat-spitting hatred of the Alasherans was real enough. Dalvenjah pointed out that the cat could very well hate the Alasherans but still be devoted to the entity. She also had to agree that his plan was best.

Star Dragon drifted slowly over the palace, and J.T. led them to a point that he thought was about as close to the entity as they could come from the outside. His report was confirmed when they discovered three Alasheran ships parked in the shadows behind some of the larger buildings. Since the ships were not guarded, it seemed that Haldephren had never seriously expected that *Star Dragon* would get through. Mira and the boys went aboard each ship for a quick look about, and they loosened certain bolts that attached the lift and thrust vanes in a way that promised trouble if the ships were taken back into the sky. Mira thought it was better to be safe.

In the few minutes they were gone, the others had made some very quick preparations for their last battle with the Alasherans. Vajerral had brought herself up on deck, her hind leg still splinted because of the broken bone she had received from the monster. She was given a post on the helm deck and a crossbow so that she could defend the ship without stirring herself too much, freeing Kelvandor to fight in the way of dragons. Dooket and Erkin were to stay aboard *Star Dragon* as well, to tend the ship and assist the dragons if they were attacked. Dalvenjah at least was not satisfied with the disappearance of the crews of the Alasheran ships, unless they had been undermanned in the first place or had lost much of their crews on the way down. Mira reported that all three ships had suffered from attacks by monsters.

They were ready to begin within a few minutes. Dalvenjah lifted the cat down from the deck, but she did not put him down again. "I believe that I should carry you, at least until we find what we are seeking and we know how things stand."

"I can walk," J.T. assured her fearfully.

"I do insist," she said, placing one of her large, strong hands on his neck. "How odd. I do believe that a faerie dragon could wring your delicate little neck without the smallest effort."

"Yes, I do believe one could."

"I know that I could. And if you lead us wrong, I certainly will."

J.T. just swallowed nervously.

Dalvenjah smiled; on a dragon, even that looked frightening. "Cheer up, cat. Your reputation will be restored or destroyed very soon now."

"I like your confidence," J.T. remarked sourly. "I keep thinking that the question of my reputation might become irrelevant very soon now."

Because things had been going so generally well for them lately, certain members of their group had been inclined to forget just how dangerous this final confrontation could be. Fighting the sky-island airships, with their slow speeds and ineffective weapons, had been simple enough, especially with the deadly secret weapons that the faerie dragons had proven to be. They had been both lucky and clever in New York, finding Mr. Holmes quickly, and his advice had helped them to avoid the traps and false leads that had been set for them. If it had not been for his knowledge and ingenuity, even Dalvenjah would have never known where to look. And the Emperor Myrkan's decision to defect from the Dark had been a bonus. Although magic abounded in this place, no one had tried to use anything potent against them. Their only real setback had been the battle with the monster in which Vajerral had been injured and the ship damaged.

And, of course, the loss of Jenny. But that had been unavoidable, as it had turned out, and not a direct result of anything that had occurred in the course of their journey.

The odds had become rather more stacked against them now, and Dalvenjah at least knew it perfectly well. Her first hope was that the entity would remain uninvolved in the contest between her people and the servants of the Dark, as blissfully indifferent as ever. Under those circumstances, she expected one of two results. Either they would dispatch the High Priest Haldephren, the Dark Sorceress Darja and their henchmen in due course, or else Darja herself would prove to be rather more than they anticipated and they would themselves come to a bad end. The third possibility was that the entity would take sides against them, perhaps because Darja had already found the secret to merging with it or simply out of loyalty to its old friends. And so it turned out that they were in serious trouble in two chances out of three. Dalvenjah still believed that most of the advantages remained on their side, but she realized how quickly things could turn against them.

Even if things turned out badly, she still had a hidden ace up her metaphorical sleeve; in reality, dragons ran about as naked as Spartans and they were not given to playing cards. The trouble was that her little surprise was very unreliable.

The way in was fairly obvious, once they knew where to begin. J.T. led them to a large doorway—the doors themselves had been left open—and after that they made their way through several wide corridors and descended a series of broad, flowing stairs. The architecture of this place made even less sense on the inside than the outside, as if the designer, or creator, had at least some awareness of appearances but little knowledge of substance. It did become apparent very quickly that practical considerations had not been an important factor, since corridors led to halls without purpose and stairs descended at irregular intervals. There was a general lack of any habitable chambers but whole regions that existed only for the sake of appearances, as if the entity welcomed company but wished to discourage anyone from staying the night. Holmes estimated that at least half and perhaps as much as three-quarters of the interior space was solid stone.

"Movement," J.T. warned suddenly. "There are several beings of fairly strong magical ability moving in to surround us. I suspect that an ambush is being prepared."

As it was, they were in the middle of a very large chamber or hall at that moment. This was not a very good place for an ambush, leaving more than enough room for the dragons to move about for a counterattack, and so Dalvenjah was not immediately concerned. Even so, she was not surprised when the attack began almost that same moment. The initial assault came in the form of magic, a concentrated barrage of magical flames that swept across the chamber to center upon their group. Allan and Dalvenjah drew back hastily, forcing the others into a tight group that they could protect with a force barrier. Black flames poured over the invisible wall they had created, and for the moment they were safe.

Immediately after the first attack had begun, forcing the dragons on the defensive, small groups of Imperial warriors marched out smartly from smaller side corridors, took their positions and bent their bows. The first volley was rather wild, their aim disturbed by the black flames of the Dark Sorcerers. The dragons were quick enough to avoid the arrows, and Sir Remidan saved Mira from one arrow by the simple tactic of stepping out before her. His magical armor rang like a bell, and it was not even scratched. Then Mira and Holmes corrected the situation simply and effectively by stepping out with their assault rifles and spraying the area generously. The survivors broke and ran for their lives, fleeing down the main corridor at the far end of the chamber. The two dragons leaped after them, meaning to put an end to any future threats of ambush.

"No more bullets," Mira remarked sourly, removing the clip

from her gun with some effort. The gun was almost too large for her to handle.

"No more bullets?" Holmes asked, and checked his own clip. "I have only three. Fortunately, our need for these weapons may well be behind us now."

Mira reached into her small pack and produced two more clips, handing one to the elf. "I certainly hope so. This is all I have left. I've regretted from the first my lack of foresight in not stealing more. At the time, three clips each seemed like a bountiful supply, perhaps because of the number of actual bullets that represents. An equal number of arrows is considered to be a generous amount. I never realized what a glutton this weapon can be."

"That is the principle advantage of the automatic rifle: it solves certain problems very quickly, but it demands a price," Holmes said. "I suspect that we should follow those two dragons. They might not need our help, but we could easily need theirs if the Alasherans circle around us."

Following the dragons proved to be easy enough. They had run down the main passage after the Alasherans, catching Imperial warriors and sorcerers one at a time and quickly wringing their necks, then tossing the bodies aside. It all had the look of simple efficiency, made easy by the size and strength of the faerie dragons; J.T. swallowed nervously to see it.

"One would think that they thought it sport," Holmes remarked. "That is what I like about those dragons. When logic and deduction have run their course, they can follow up with mindless mayhem."

"They might be wise and gentle, but they are still dragons," Mira reminded him. "That wildness in their nature makes them such forceful personalities. Dalvenjah is simply more wild than most."

"Vajerral and Kelvandor don't seem particularly wild."

"They can certainly get in touch with it when they want to," Mira said. "I've seen them fight more often than you have."

Their concern now was that the dragons would have to run too far ahead of them, as unlikely as it seemed that they would have forgotten. Dalvenjah was indeed a dragon and given to passionate extremes, but only within the limits of the cold, calculating fury of her kind. Mindijaran were, in their way, the most dangerous of dragons, for their emotions never obscured their keen wits. And even if she ever was inclined to get carried away, Allan was as solid and understated as dragons came. As it happened, the two dragons simply ran out of necks to twist after a few hundred yards, so they stopped to wait for the others to join them.

"Did you enjoy yourselves?" Holmes asked.

"It was very satisfying, as a matter of fact," Dalvenjah said. "I have wanted to break a few necks since that first night in Mira's house. Cat, are you paying attention?"

The cat swallowed loudly. "Yes, ma'am. The High Priest Haldephren is just ahead, not six hundred yards. The Dark Sorceress Darja is just beyond him. Aside from those two, and ourselves, I doubt that there is anyone else alive in this place. Keep in mind that I cannot clearly sense the presence of mortals, especially the more magically inept. Haldephren might still have a few of his apes in leather lurking about."

This passage was clearly the main one, and they had come now into regions that had apparently been intended as more habitable. This area was designed more like a conventional palace, with side passages leading into whole suites of rooms as well as armories, kitchens and storage chambers. After the Outer Regions, this was absolutely homey. Apparently the Alasherans had had some influence in the construction of this place, although the entity had either seen no need to accommodate large numbers or else meant to discourage any major invasions of houseguests. Gods, like dragons, did indeed have a reputation for being antisocial.

The passage ended suddenly in a pair of wide, heavy doors. Before J.T. could give warning, Dalvenjah pushed through the doors without hesitation and marched boldly into the chamber beyond. This was a hall of immense size, an oval dome easily three hundred yards wide by two hundred and perhaps fifty yards high; Mira could have circled *Star Dragon* in this place. The walls were carved in the appearance of great columns and rafters, flowing upward in great smooth arcs, but with so many gathered together into groups that portions of the dome looked almost fluted. It was, all in all, a superabundance of so many long, clean lines that it became cluttered.

"Rococo art deco," Holmes commented. "Who would have thought?"

Dalvenjah raised her head and was looking straight up. The center of the dome was a large flat panel like a single sheet of glass, an oval two hundred feet or more across. There were stars in a black sky. "How very odd."

"It looks perfectly normal to me," Mira said.

"Anywhere else, perhaps. It definitely goes somewhere, since more stars appear from behind the edge as we walk. But we just came from outside, and we know that there were no stars."

Mira shrugged. "When you're a god, you can have any view you wish."

"Such a view requires a tremendous amount of magic," Holmes told her. "It seems strange to think an entire world of faerie died to indulge the whims of a single entity hardly conscious of its own existence."

"The entity has been consuming most of that magic itself," Dalvenjah said. "If it had not been such an absolute lump, it would have gotten itself up and moved on to explore long ago, and your world would have been saved."

"An old friend is waiting just ahead," J.T. warned them.

A second set of large doors stood at the far side of the chamber, above a series of steps that ended in a wide platform. A second, much smaller platform, a tall wooden dais of very recent and rather hasty construction, stood a short distance out from the doors. A large wooden throne stood upon the dais, and upon that throne sat a man. He was a tall man, handsome and strongly muscled, still young enough to be considered in the prime of life. He was no one any of them had ever seen before, but that was hardly unexpected.

He sat back in the throne and smiled, looking sincerely pleased to see them. "Sorceress Kasdamir. It really has not been all that long, and yet I hardly know which of us has changed the most. You look as cute as ever, I must admit. I am reminded of the time many years ago in the golden canals of Serras. . . ."

Mira lifted her gun and pointed it right at him. "Not another word, asshole. That was years ago, and you were operating under false pretenses, Lord Dasjen Valdercon. You owe me. You owe Jenny Barker a lot more, and I mean to make you pay."

Dalvenjah stepped forward. "You owe me something also. I want my brother back."

Haldephren did not look as entirely pleased to see her. "Ah, yes. We still have something to settle. If you win, you can have him back. I have him in stasis, of course. Go to my cabin aboard the flagship. Look for the large emerald on the heavy gold chain."

"Oh, well." Mira reached inside her jacket and brought out the very chain and emerald in question, holding it up for the dragon.

"You little thief," Dalvenjah remarked, taking the emerald. "What has happened to you? Ever since you lost your height, you have become a regular kleptomaniac. Did becoming short again bring out your childhood tendencies?"

Dalvenjah opened the chain and fastened it around her own neck, although it was barely long enough to fit. Presumably she knew what to do with it, since it did not look very much like her brother at the moment.

She looked up at Haldephren. "That brings us to the next question. Where is the Dark Sorceress Darja?"

Haldephren glanced briefly over his shoulder. "She is in there, beyond those doors."

"She is with the entity?"

He frowned, considering the question carefully. "I realize that you must know enough of the truth already. Something has gone wrong with the Prophecy. The new god will talk to us. He will talk to anyone who possesses magic enough to speak directly to him. But he will not permit Darja to merge with him. He insists that he does not yet recognize her, and he seems to think we might be trying to pass off a substitute. Darja is in the inner chamber, but she is not allowed to pass the final set of doors."

"And what are you waiting for?" Dalvenjah asked. "Did you think that you would find your answer?"

"Darja says that Jenny Barker will know the answer. And we have known since your arrival in New York that she is still with you. We have been waiting for you to come to us."

"So you laid your trap to destroy the rest of us," Holmes concluded. "How does the fact that we are still alive affect your schemes?"

"Not seriously," Haldephren said, although he seemed less certain. "Now you will have to fight Darja herself. You are in her element now, and she has the power to destroy you."

Dalvenjah lifted her head. "Can she stop me from first separating you from your present incarnation?"

Haldephren laughed. "If it pleases you, then go ahead. I will be back again, soon enough."

"Then the time has come to complicate your plans," Holmes said. "Jenny is no longer with us. You probably know yourself what would have happened to Dalvenjah's brother if you had not kept him in stasis. She lost her sense of identity and reverted into true death only a couple of days ago."

Whatever response he might have expected, the one that came was very much a surprise. Even while Haldephren was still trying to think of what this must mean, the doors behind the throne were pushed open and a large black dragon stepped forward. She was in form a faerie dragon, slender and long of leg, except that she was as black as utter darkness with silver eyes and a crest of purest white. She was also much larger than a Mindijarah, easily the size of a true dragon. Haldephren rose from his throne and turned to face her, his gestures eager and servile, although the black dragon ignored him completely as she stood with her head raised above him, glaring coldly at the smaller dragon sorceress.

"Is this the truth, Dalvenjah Foxfire?" she asked.

"It is the truth, Sorceress Darja," Dalvenjah agreed. "I see that you have discovered the true nature of the body that you stole."

"The body was stolen for me, but I have adapted it for my own purposes," Darja said. "I have discovered the dragon magic, and I have made it a part of my own essence. I am now like yourself, a being of the dragon magic."

Dalvenjah cocked her head inquisitively. "Is that a fact. There is no going back, once you have changed your inner name to define your new essence."

Darja lowered her head. "It is so."

"Oh, good." Dalvenjah sat back on her tail, and she honestly looked to be relieved. "That means that you can never merge your essence with that of the entity. You have discovered already that the entity will not acknowledge you as the true Darja for as long as you were wearing Jenny's body. Even in human form, she still belonged to the dragon magic, incompatible with the common magic that forms the essence of the entity. Now you cannot succeed even if you abandon Jenny's body because you have made your very spirit a part of the dragon magic."

"Then it's over?" Mira asked.

"Well, everything just became much simpler," the dragon said. "Now at least I have very little concern about the entity becoming the god of evil that the Emperor and the High Priest always intended. Is that why you have been called the High Priest, in anticipation of your new god?"

Haldephren drew himself up proudly. "I am the Emperor, now that Myrkan has proven himself a traitor."

Darja had been thinking things over very quickly and thoroughly in the last few moments, and she seemed to have come to the conclusion that she was not especially upset with the way things had turned out. Merging with the entity would have meant the end of her own existence entirely. That would not have been a matter of any concern to her in the past, when she had little enough awareness of her own existence. But that had changed recently, and she was beginning to think of herself and her own schemes at least as much as of the original purpose of her existence.

After a moment, she sat back on her tail and smiled wickedly. "That is all the better. Now I know exactly how to merge with the entity. I still possess that ancient tie with the entity, and I can use that to draw it to me and make it a part of myself. The entity has little sense of self, far less than I. I can convert the entity's essence from its own magic into dragon magic and make it a part of my own, and then I will be a god."

Dalvenjah stared at her for a long moment, then laid back her ears. "Oh, shit! And just when I thought it was over. I really must learn to keep my mouth shut."

Darja turned and walked slowly back into the chamber beyond the throne, as if she was no longer concerned that she was in the presence of her most dire enemies. Dalvenjah, fearful of what she might intend, hurried after her, and the others followed quickly. The chamber beyond was not as large as the oval dome although the walls and ceiling were adorned with much the same flowing stonework. This chamber was in the form of a long, narrow hall with a high ceiling, thirty yards or so wide but perhaps two hundred yards long. Yet another set of doors stood at the far end of the chamber, and these looked even more massive and secure, appearing to have been cast in some grey metal that looked oily or waxy. Two heavy bars of bright metal prevented the doors from being opened. The entity had a most unsubtle approach to discouraging unwanted visitors.

Darja had spent weeks in this chamber, trying unsuccessfully to force those doors to open. The far end of the chamber was littered with the various books and magical paraphernalia that she had employed, as well as many items that she had collected in her growing awareness of her own comfort.

As soon as the company from *Star Dragon* entered the chamber, some very unexpected things began to happen. The two bars closing the door glowed briefly for a long moment and then shattered as if they had been made of ice, the shards falling away. Then the doors themselves opened slowly, although the only thing that lay beyond were broad steps leading down into the glare of brilliant white light. The entity itself was hidden even deeper within the core of this place.

"What happened?" Allan asked quietly.

"Mira's presence must have made the difference," Dalvenjah explained. "Any mortal body might have served Darja's purposes, at least before she took her new inner name and became a true faerie dragon, but the Prophecy named Mira specifically and the entity recognizes her presence. Having Mira and Darja here together must have confused the thing."

Darja's own reaction to this unexpected turn of events was predictable, considering her last declaration of intent. She rushed forward to the doors and then stopped, obviously thinking things over very carefully. Although she now had access to the entity, she wanted to proceed with that contact under her own terms. Even yet, it might have been entirely a matter of her own instincts that drew her toward that door, aware she had been created for this very moment.

"Yes, good day, everyone. How very nice to see everyone again, myself included."

They turned quickly to discover that they had company in the form of yet another giant faerie dragon, although this one remained in the true colors of her kind, golden with a sapphire crest. She stepped through the outer doors and sat back on her tail, cocking her head as she regarded Darja curiously. The black dragon seemed to captivate her full attention.

"Who is that?" Holmes inquired quietly.

"The ace up my sleeve," Dalvenjah responded. "It could only be Jenny."

"Then she is still alive?" Holmes asked, then frowned. "Still communing with the living, I should say."

"Yes, she is once again with us. I knew that the spells I had used to keep her in the state we knew would last for some time yet, so the fact that she had left us hardly meant that she was finally dead. I also suspected at the time that she would be coming here, drawn by the link she still possessed with her living body. So you see, I had every reason to expect that we might see her once again."

Darja began to pace slowly back from the inner doors, glaring at Jenny with suspicion and growing concern. "Who are you? This is no place for you, and you should not have come. Tell me now who you are."

"You don't know me?" Jenny asked. "I would have thought that you knew me very well. You've been walking around looking like me for the past few months, although I can't say that I like what you've done with me. Would you mind giving me back to myself now?"

Darja was so surprised that she sat back on her tail and stared. "I had expected that it must be you, although they told that you were gone. Your sense of identity seems to have suffered in a most remarkable manner."

"Hey, it's easy to lose your mind when you don't have a brain," Jenny said as amiably as ever. "Being dead is nearly as enlightening an experience as being alive. The shame of it is that all enlightening experiences are given to those who need them the least and hardly ever come to those who could best benefit from a broadening experience. You have certainly improved from having worn me around for the past few months. That borrowed brain you like so much is just full of useful experiences and concepts. Have you thought about what you want to do with that degree in mechanical engineering?"

"I like what I have become," Darja answered obliquely, although she had shown the patience of sitting and listening.

"Then I will make this bargain with you. The damage that has been done to me cannot be undone. I can take back my body and go through the rest of my interrupted life talking like Robin Williams, and that is a frightening prospect when you never grow old. I must pass on into my next life. In fact, I already have reservations. So if you'll promise to be good and help us to destroy the entity, you can have my body."

"I see no need to bargain for something I already have," Darja answered. "Soon I will be a god."

"Well, have it your way," Jenny said, shrugging.

Then she launched herself into the air, hurtling across nearly the full length of the chamber until she impacted with Darja, sending the black dragon tumbling. It was an impossible leap for a real dragon, even one of her present size, unassisted by wings, but Jenny was of course a ghost. She must have learned quite a few tricks about applying the rules of physics to metaphysics, if she could hit a dragon the size and weight of a dinosaur that hard. She came out on top during that initial impact, pinning Darja to the floor. The black dragon twisted, fighting fiercely to escape until she was able to break Jenny's hold. Darja nearly had her by the neck, a vulnerable hold for any dragon, when Jenny simply passed through her enemy and came out on top.

The others drew back closer to the outer doors, giving the two dragons plenty of room for their fight. It was hard enough to say just which of the two had the advantage, even after watching them for a few minutes. Jenny had a certain quickness and invulnerability that came from being a ghost, but Darja seemed to possess the magic to match her abilities. Even Dalvenjah did not know what Darja could do to Jenny, at least as long as Jenny was careful. At the same time, Jenny might not find the opportunity to do anything effective to Darja. Of course, Jenny was more likely to win a long battle, since Darja would tire and the effects of her misfortunes were cumulative.

Holmes looked at Dalvenjah suspiciously. "You are putting me completely to shame, I must say. You obviously expected this."

"I have been paying strict attention to the Prophecy, and there was one last point yet to be played out," she explained. "Dragons gold and dragons black seek to gain what each may lack.

When I saw that Darja had turned herself into a black dragon, I knew that Jenny must be around somewhere."

"And what do they lack?" Holmes asked.

"The only thing that they both have seriously lacked in common was a body. Jenny lacks her own body, which Darja received to make up for her own lack."

"And that is what they are fighting over? Jenny has a very valid reason for not wanting her body back."

"Well, I might not be interpreting the Prophecy with complete accuracy, but I do my best," Dalvenjah said. "Which reminds me."

She released the chain that held the emerald, removing it from her neck, and fastened it back into a loop. Then she took three small, quiet steps forward and threw the chain over Haldephren's head, catching him by surprise while he was preoccupied watching the battle of the two dragons. Before he could react, she threw him to the floor and held him down. Haldephren's form began to glow with a powerful light until his features were hardly to be seen, only a black figure within the core of that brilliance. That figure began to flow, becoming larger and taking a new shape. When the light faded, a male Mindijarah lay sprawled on the floor before Dalvenjah.

She took his arm and helped him to stand. "How do you feel?"

"I feel surprisingly well," he said, rising to stand carefully. "I seem to be back again. The last thing I recall, the Emperor had come to take the body of my daughter and give it to the Dark Sorceress Darja."

"That was exactly what happened," Dalvenjah said. Then she noticed that the others were staring. "This is my brother, Karidaejan. Back from the dead and again with the living."

"Yes, and a very neat trick it was," Holmes agreed. "But what did you do with Haldephren?"

"I could not allow him to escape, and I did not have the time to dispose of him properly. He is in the jewel." She paused, seeing that Mira and Sir Remidan were still staring. "I gave Haldephren's body to my brother, after I had made certain alterations to make it more suitable. I am afraid that it does not look entirely like the original, but that would have been a little much to expect."

"It will be fine, I am sure," Karidaejan assured her. "But what became of Jenny?"

"That is exactly the point," Sir Remidan said gruffly, his displeasure obvious. "It is hardly fitting for a Knight to stand by while a Lady fights a great battle."

"This is not your fight, tin-britches," Dalvenjah told him sternly. "I cannot believe that it will go on for long."

Indeed it did not. Jenny thrust herself forward with her head held low, driving in under Darja's chest and throwing the black dragon backwards against the wall behind her. Before Darja could gather herself together, Jenny was on her again, leaping high and strong to land heavily on the black dragon. There was a sudden, brief flash of light as they hit and then Jenny was alone, once again her normal size, sitting back on her tail as she held something small in one hand. She looked over at the others, and they hurried to join her.

As Dalvenjah came close, Jenny handed her the thing she held. It was a female faerie dragon, adult in appearance but tiny in size, smaller even than J.T., wiggling and straining weakly to free herself. Dalvenjah took the little dragon, careful to hold her diminutive wings closed.

"Something to remember me by," Jenny said. "Sorceress Darja, lately of the Dark. She might as well have my body, since I will not be returning to it."

"Do you expect me to take this home and feed it?" Dalvenjah asked.

"Darja's whole trouble is her attitude. She only just started to be truly alive when she took my body and came under the influence of my character and memories. She needs a little more time to come to terms with life, and she very much needs a positive influence. If she learns her lessons well enough, then you can remove the restraints that I have placed upon her magic and return her to her full size."

"Oh, that poor little thing," Mira said softly, peering at the miniature dragon. She could relate to being shrunk.

"Jenny?" Karidaejan said softly.

She turned to him. "Hello, Daddy! The last time we met, you were the ghost."

"I somehow get the impression that you will not be coming back," he said.

She smiled wryly. "I have been a ghost too long. You can appreciate the dangers of that, better than anyone. Now don't go looking so concerned. You did your best, but they took advantage of you. They took advantage of us all, for that matter. I walked right into their trap, even knowing what they wanted of me. You did your best, even when you were under their power."

"I will always regret that I could not have done better, all the same," he said.

"I am sure that we all regret that we did not do better," Jenny told him. "Except, perhaps, Auntie Dalvenjah."

"I am not in the habit of making mistakes, and so my mistakes annoy me all the more," she answered. "What will you do now?"

"There is still the matter of the entity," Jenny explained, indicating the open inner doors. "He's still waiting for someone to come to him. I intend to merge with him in Darja's place. I believe that I possess the force of will and certain other advantages that come from being a ghost that will compel him to accept me, and then I plan to force him to destroy himself. He has thousands of years of latent magic in reserve, so he should explode in a most spectacular and satisfying manner."

Dalvenjah did not look pleased. "Is this what you want?"

"My life is over," Jenny said. "It ended a very long time ago. I have conserved myself for this moment, so don't think that I'm doing as well as I might seem. At least I can clear the entity out of this hole, and I doubt that you have any other plans for that. Besides, the matter has become rather urgent. I know that the Dark Elves have been here once, and they will be back as soon as they know that the Alasherans are gone."

Dalvenjah did not answer at once, obviously thinking the matter over very carefully. Jenny sat back on her tail, grinning wickedly. "How do you plan to stop me?"

"I don't like this," Mira protested. "Put yourself back inside that lizard that you want to give to Darja. We can do something to help you later. I feel responsible for what happened to you, and I just don't want to lose you."

"I am not going anywhere," Jenny told her. "Other arrangements already have been made, and I will be with you again in a few months."

"You will have to hurry," Dalvenjah added. "Those arrangements will not wait for you much longer."

"I am not entirely pleased with your arrangements," Jenny said. "Take your little bundle of joy and your long-lost sibling and get the hell out of here. I will hold on here for as long as I can, hopefully as much as ten hours, but I can't promise you more than two. Keep reminding Mira that she must not be afraid of her ship and have her push it as fast as it will go. That ship can give a hundred and eighty knots, and you'll need every mile."

"Do you really expect such a vast explosion?" Mira asked.

Jenny grinned madly. "I don't know. I've never blown up a god before. Dalvenjah, you must go."

Dalvenjah closed her eyes, and sighed heavily. "The time has come that we must go. Every extra minute we take in getting back to the ship is three miles closer we will be when the entity is destroyed."

Mira looked back, but Jenny had already solved the problem of forcing her reluctant companions to leave by simply turning and walking almost casually through the inner doors. She descended the steps into the misty white light from below, and the doors closed slowly behind her. And that was very much the end of the matter. Dalvenjah hurried the others out of the chamber, although Mira remained reluctant to go even yet and hesitated at the door. The two steel bars that closed the doors were once again in place, so there was hardly any hope of going after her. For better or worse, Jenny was committed to her plan and no one except herself could stop her now.

They picked up their speed once they were away from the inner chamber, although Allan tossed Mira on his back so that he could run on all fours and she in turn took the cat. Karidaejan was still having some trouble adjusting to having a real body once again, but he was able to keep a pace that made Sir Remidan's armor clang and crash. They returned to the ship within a matter of minutes, and Mira had *Star Dragon* in the air only moments later. In spite of what Jenny had assumed, she had had a fair amount of experience lately in taking the ship up to full speed.

"Do you expect an explosion that great?" Mira asked as she brought *Star Dragon* around on course and engaged the final set of vanes to bring the ship up to speed. The floating palace receded at a frustrating crawl.

"We are discussing tens of thousands of years of latent magic," Holmes reminded her. "The sudden release of that energy will probably distort this region of the singularity, and it takes quite a lot to bend the shape of any universe. Even one this small. The more it bends, the better."

"Why is that?"

"Bending the universe will absorb large amounts of that energy, but the rest will be channeled down the core into the singularity. We will not be able to get out of the way."

"Something is happening," Vajerral warned suddenly. She had stayed up on the deck with Kelvandor to watch; they hardly knew whether to be glad or saddened by the news that Jenny had returned, even briefly.

The young dragon had not actually seen anything, since there was nothing to actually see. What she had sensed was a sudden shift in the latent magic, as if the singularity itself was about to turn inside out. All of the magic flowing out through the spider's webs of arcs reversed, drawn back toward the palace, and tremendous bolts of lightning leaped out from the arcs to ripple across the maze of towers and domes, cracking and exploding stone. The ship's vanes failed as the magic itself was drawn away. The crew of *Star Dragon* watched that terrible display of destructive force, allowed only a single long moment to know that Jenny had failed to contain the entity for the time that she had promised, and that they were about to die in an explosion that would make an atomic bomb look small and weak.

And then the palace simply disappeared.

Dalvenjah lifted her head straight up, staring in disbelief. "She imploded the entity! At least, I suppose that she imploded the entity. Obviously that was no accident. She knew what she was doing, and she knew that it would work or she would not have done it while we are still so close."

"Admitting that her judgement is somewhat impaired," Holmes added, and he was very deliberately being kind, in honor of Jenny's tremendous courage and astoundingly poor judgement. Now that he was better aware of what had just happened, he decided that he had never been so frightened in all his life. And he had stopped having birthdays at twenty-five thousand. "And what do you mean, you suppose that she imploded the entity? Is it possible to cause magic to implode?"

"Oh, yes. Dragons do it to facilitate home canning. I was just wondering where she put it all. Magic can neither be created nor destroyed; it just keeps popping up again when you least expect it." Dalvenjah sat back on her tail, her ears laid back. "I am also worried about what Jenny might have done to herself."

"She was already dead," Holmes reminded her. "Could any force really do her any further harm?"

"That is exactly my concern," the dragon said. "Jenny was a dragon, and a dragon's spirit is tremendously strong. Much stronger and more massive, in fact, than our fragile physical selves, although most of that power and mass is locked in realms of existence that even dragons know only by inference. She would have survived an explosion of any size in this level of existence, but an implosion involves moving tremendous amounts of magic through other levels of existence and turning it inside out at the same time. If Jenny was pulled through with that magic, then I am concerned for her safety. Having parts of her being in several separate levels of existence would, of course, help to anchor her very solidly. Does that make any sense?"

"Damned little," Mira said, staring over her shoulder. "Do you know, in all the months of our association, I've understood less than half of those great, long-winded explanations that you rattle off as if it was all the most simple, logical thing in the world. You make magic sound like the lost laws of relativity."

Dalvenjah looked hurt and confused, her ears laid back. "Well, it is."

"Yes, and it only got worse when you found Mr. Holmes."

Holmes smiled wryly. "Frankly, she sometimes goes right over the top of my head as well. She does have the advantage of the experience of the faerie dragons, while I knew Albert Einstein only vaguely."

"Yes, but what does all of this mean for Jenny?" Mira demanded. "When will we know whether or not she survived?"

"I suspect that we might not know for some months yet." Dalvenjah replied. "My method of restoring her to full life does take some time. And now, I believe that it is time for me to go home and get to work on it."

"Is there anything I can do?" Mira asked.

"You can explain it to Jenny's mother," the dragon suggested hopefully.

Mira turned back to her wheels. "Explain it? I don't half understand it myself."

❧ PART ELEVEN ❧

All's Well That's Finally Over

The blessed event occurred some months later. Dalvenjah Foxfire gave birth to her second child, a tiny female dragonet. And she had not yet eaten it.

Actually, faerie dragons were not tigers and they were never known to eat their young. Most of her friends and acquaintances, however, would have assumed that the esteemed Dragon Sorceress Dalvenjah Foxfire did not possess the parental compassion and almost mindless patience required of motherhood, and they had concluded that it would have been better for the child if she had eaten it. As a matter of fact, Dalvenjah had gone to a great deal of trouble to have this child, she wanted it and she was quietly pleased to finally have it, meaning in part that she was very pleased that she was no longer pregnant. She had been through this once before, and she had in fact proven herself to be a patient and devoted mother. The trouble in that case had come when Vajerral had been mostly a grown-up dragon, with a large bulk of her education behind her and of an age when she should have begun showing signs of becoming capable and responsible.

Dalvenjah had been reminded often enough that she had been judging young Vajerral by a harsh standard, that being her own dauntingly serious and responsible postadolescence. Vajerral was spirited and, like most dragons her age, she was young enough to prefer adventure to cerebral pursuits. That was an unfortunate state, when one shared a castle with Dalvenjah Foxfire and Sherlock Holmes. Of course, with those two now working in partnership, high adventure would probably turn up at the door often enough.

But for now, Dalvenjah had a little dragon in her care, and adventures would probably be postponed for a while yet. Mindijaran did not lay eggs like true dragons but bore their young live and nursed them for the better part of three or four years, although the little dragons would supplement their diets with anything they could catch almost from the start. They could walk almost from birth and fly within a month, and they generally grew very quickly for their first four to six years. They would grow quickly again in their tenth year and a final time at about fourteen or fifteen before they would finish filling out slowly during their mid-twenties, usually at that time in their young lives when their sex hormones either became sated or else gave up in raw frustration. Faerie dragons were fairly notorious among the other races as having sexual impulses as big as their wingspans.

Dalvenjah waited until the young dragon was about half a year old before she called her various companions from *Star Dragon* for a formal presentation and naming of the little one. Faerie dragons took serious exception to having their young referred to as baby dragons; they were dragonets in more formal usage—dragonettes to the gentile—and kits in more common practice. After half a year, the little dragon was becoming fairly alert and intelligent, and she was beginning to speak her first words. Vajerral would sometimes explain, at least until it got her into trouble, that her little sister was learning to speak from her mother and Mr. Holmes, that being the reason why no one could understand her.

That was also, as it happened, the first anniversary of the day that Jenny Barker had destroyed the entity and had herself disappeared. Actually, because of the slight variance between worlds, that same anniversary had already come and gone in other places. It had been three days earlier in Mira's world, and two days earlier in Jenny's own home world.

Calling together all of those Dalvenjah thought should be invited was a difficult proposition, since they were scattered over three worlds. Karidaejan had returned to his own home, which happened to have been not all that far from Dalvenjah's converted fortress. Since the place had suffered from neglect in his twenty years of absence, most of which time he had been dead, his son Kelvandor had gone with him to help in repairs. Vajerral had spent as much time as she could spare from her magical and martial studies to be with Kelvandor, whose company she preferred. Unfortunately, Kelvandor did not prefer her company in ways that she would have wished; they were the best of friends, with frequent attacks of raw lust on Vajerral's part. For his own part, Kelvandor was still loyal to the memory of Jenny, whom he had loved with a devotion that dragons usually found embarrassing.

Mira had taken her own assortment of champions, companions and henchmen back to her own world, where she had spent a great deal of time in the South on the Queen's business, letting it be known far and wide that the Empire was dead, or at least in serious need of revision. As it happened, most of the Alasherans were themselves perfectly willing to make changes. They were all merchants by instinct and inclination, and they generally felt that empire-building and minding other people's business was too expensive and far more annoying than it was worth. There were precious few actual servants of the Dark left in that world; there had never been that many in the first place, and most of those had met their timely ends in the destruction of the Island of Alashera and on the quest into the world of the sky islands.

Stories of the exploits of Sorceress Kasdamir Gerran and her dragon companions had swept through the South quicker than Mira herself could get there, so she found that a considerable reputation had preceded her. Because of her part in the destruction of the Island of Alashera, a fairly solid reputation had already been there waiting. And when Mira arrived in person in her new airship, which the Amazon Chipmunks had been delighted to repair for her, there was no question that she had made a serious impression. Mira let it be known that the North would be building entire fleets of such airships, but she strategically failed to mention that those plans were dependent upon finding a source of aluminum and learning quite a few tricks about advanced engineering.

Certain of Mira's companions did not attend the reunion. Once matters were settled in the South, Sir Remidan and his neurotic horse Staemar had set out on adventures of their own. Remidan still had matters of his own to settle with the Sorceress Queramael, and he had set off with the intention of either defeating her once and for all or else making an honest woman of her. He was convinced that if she was honest then he would be pleased to marry her, and he had now decided that Queramael had turned to evil because he had withheld his affections from her when they were young. Mira had sent him merrily on his way, trusting that he and Queramael deserved each other.

J.T. did elect to go along, partly because he was more fond of parties than he cared to admit and partly because he thought that he had a good idea of how everything had turned out and he wanted to see if he was right. The Trassek twins remembered only too well that they did not stand very high in Dalvenjah's favor, and they wisely decided to stay outside and guard the ship.

The first thing that everyone noticed was that Mira had finally returned to her regular height of spitting distance below six feet. Most of the dragons had hardly known Mira at all before she had lost her enhanced height, while both Vajerral and Kelvandor had gotten used to seeing her short, so it took everyone a little time to get used to her new height. Unfortunately, she was now able to return to her old clothes and a fashion sense that was predatory and often blatantly gaudy. This time, she came dressed for hunting. Holmes, like the dragons, had kept the physical enhancements that they had received during their visit to the core of the singularity, and Mira had been lusting after his augmented physique ever since.

Mira was the first to arrive, brought into the world of the faerie dragons through a Way that Vajerral had opened for her. She sauntered into the room with her old perky, self-satisfied swagger restored to its proper proportions by the lengthening of her legs. Dalvenjah lay on her side on a bed of cushions near the fire, such as faerie dragons preferred for sitting to talk or read. Her little one was drawn up close to her side, the young dragon hardly any larger of body than a small dog. Faerie dragons were born lanky and lean, unlike most babies of almost any type, and at any age they were never as large and heavy as they looked. Her brother Karidaejan and Mr. Holmes sat nearby, the three of them in the middle of some arcane conversation. Kelvandor sat by the bank of large windows that looked out over the valley far below, while Vajerral hurried over to sit close by his side and did her inadequate best to flirt for his attention.

"Well, long time no see!" Mira declared in a voice intended

to wake the dead and get the party rolling. Her definition of the perfect party was the proper balance of intellectual debate and depravity, and the dragons were too fond of the former. "All of you are looking well."

"You have certainly grown," Dalvenjah remarked, frowning. "Lady Kasdamir Gerran, do you know how to spell 'rude'? This is a solemn occasion. And do not ask; I will tell you when the others arrive."

"Perhaps I could show you to the drinks and food," Karidaejan offered.

"Oh, I would never think of interrupting your conversation. Mr. Holmes can do it," Mira insisted. Fire one. Torpedo on target.

Holmes looked over his shoulder. "Everything is there on the table across the room. Please help yourself."

Mira frowned and began maneuvering for another shot. Vajerral watched it all, sighed and bent her neck to rub her cheek against Kelvandor's. Since she was rather overaffectionate in her gesture, she only managed to poke him in the chin with her horn. Kelvandor drew back, fussing and swearing quietly in his own language.

Dalvenjah looked up impatiently. "Why don't you just give her what she wants?"

"I once made the mistake of giving her what she wants," Kelvandor complained. "She keeps wanting more."

"Then please take her away and give her more," Dalvenjah said.

"My, we certainly are peevish today," Holmes observed.

"I have a very good reason to be peevish," the dragon answered. "Peevish is a poor word. Today I must explain certain things to certain unreasonable mortal persons. Lady Mira, you did park you ship in some place that will give my other guests room to land on the ledge?"

"I rolled her back as far as I could manage," Mira said, and turned to Mr. Holmes. "Perhaps you should come out and make sure that *Star Dragon* is out of the way."

Fire two. Torpedo on target.

"Ah . . ." Holmes hesitated, running at full speed for room to maneuver. "Young Vajerral guided you in, and she knew what was expected, I am sure."

Mira corrected course. "Meaning no criticism, of course, but the young dragon's thoughts seem to be on other matters."

"Excellent point," Dalvenjah agreed. "Vajerral, take Kelvandor outside and make certain that Mira's ship is out of the way."

"Mother?"

"Find a cold mountain stream and stick your head in it."

Vajerral certainly did not object to making any brief journeys with the object of her draconic lust, although Kelvandor looked as if he would rather spend the afternoon bathing cats. They were suddenly interrupted by a sound that all of them had heard at some time in their lives, as unexpected as the blades of a helicopter were in the world of dragons. Certain guests would soon be arriving from the mortal world, led through a Way Between the Worlds by Allan. And since magical airships were still unstable in that world, a small helicopter served much the same purpose. The one great advantage of machines was that they would run anywhere. Dalvenjah cocked her ears for a moment, then lowered her head and sighed heavily. Holmes and Mira had long since observed that all dragons were fond of sighing. Their long necks gave them an excellent set of pipes for heavy breathing.

"The last guests will soon be here," she said. "I wish that I could have avoided this meeting, but in all fairness I cannot."

"When have you worried about being fair?" Mira asked, which was of course unfair of her.

Dalvenjah looked up. "I have often been stern, especially in making others do what was required of them, or what was best for them. I have never been unfair when I could help it."

The little dragon had awakened at the sound of the helicopter, opening her small mouth in great, cavernous yawns, before she lay down again and began to suckle. Dalvenjah looked surprised and then uncomfortable; this was not the best of times, and the dragon felt confined and vulnerable at a time when she needed very much to be in control. If nothing else, this called attention to the fact that her breasts were enlarged to ungainly proportions for nursing, although still small by mortal or even elvish standards.

The sounds of the helicopter grew louder even through the heavy stone walls of the old fortress, until the machine finally landed on the ledge just outside. A couple of uncomfortable minutes passed before Allan entered with their remaining guests, the three mortals from Jenny's home world who had known the girl best. Most important were her own mother and Allan's mortal sister Marie, she of the Viking temper, and Jenny's father by adoption, Dr. Rex Barker. The last member of this little group was Dave Wallick, the FBI agent who had helped Dalvenjah in her battle with the steel dragon Vorgulremik during her first visit to his world. His former partner, Don Borelli, had been unable to attend, while the New York agent Clark Bowenger had declined the invitation, having decided that he had seen quite enough of dragons to last a lifetime.

Karidaejan lifted his head when he saw Marie, recognizing her even after all the years, and he took a cautious step back. They had been Jenny's true parents, at the time when Karidaejan had taken the mortal form of James Donner in order to provide a sire for the true object of the Prophecy of the Faerie Dragons. He had supposedly died in a traffic accident, when in fact the High Priest Haldephren had stolen his body and captured his spirit. He feared what Marie might have to say to him, this strong-willed mortal woman who had once been his wife and mother of his second child, and whom he had been forced to deceive in many ways. Even her memories of him had been altered to excuse his disappearance, although she now knew the full truth.

Even Dalvenjah Foxfire respected Marie's forceful temper, although it was fairer to say that Marie was one of very few, and perhaps the only mortal, who could stand up to Dalvenjah's forceful temper. Karidaejan Foxfire did not share his younger sister's boundless personality, and he knew that he had met his match. Even Dalvenjah dreaded this meeting.

Marie guessed who he must be from his reaction. "James?"

"My proper name is Karidaejan," he said. "I suppose that you must know by now everything that happened, and why."

Marie nodded slowly. "I really don't want to hear any more explanations and excuses just now. If there's one thing that I learned from Dalvenjah, it's that you dragons will always do whatever you seem to think is important. You can be cold, determined and proud at the best of times. I could forgive you easier if it was simply your nature, but you do understand the damage that your grand schemes do to a person's life. So I have to ask just one thing. Why didn't you just do what you needed to do and go away?"

"Because I cared," Karidaejan answered simply. "You were the mother of my child and I loved you, in spite of what you looked like. I started something that I did not know how to end. I never expected that things would come out in quite the way they did."

"You brought Jenny to life knowing what you expected for her," Marie said. "You began the chain of events that led to her death."

"He did not begin it," Dalvenjah said firmly. "And Jenny is not dead. She is here in this very room."

Several of those gathered knew already. Several, most of those mortals, could not have been more surprised.

Mira just clapped her hands. "Ah-ha, I knew it! I knew it when I first came into the room and saw that little dragon."

Marie hurried over and looked closely at the tiny dragon, still suckling at Dalvenjah's breast. It was a vision of her worst nightmares. Every member of her immediate family had been turned into faerie dragons; at this rate, she would end up a troll herself and live under a bridge eating goats. She sat down on the edge of the cushion, rubbing her face in her hands and muttering pitiful broken words in Norwegian.

"It's not so bad as all that," Dalvenjah said. "Look at it from my point of view. After Vajerral, I had no intention of becoming a mother once again for at least a hundred years. Since there was no hope of returning Jenny to her past life, the only way was forward. And since she really is a dragon in spirit, the only proper thing was to offer my parental services. The only other choice was to have Mira bear her, and she would have grown up a midget with a confused sense of height and good taste."

Marie looked up. "What does that mean? Am I her mother, or are you?"

"Technically, I am now her mother," Dalvenjah explained. "Under present circumstances, you might consider it a joint effort."

Dr. Rex was scratching his head. "Then when she grows up, she will be the same Jenny that we knew before, except in appearance?"

"That is something that I do not yet know," Dalvenjah admitted. "When a faerie dragon enters a new life, it is not usual for her to keep memories of her former life. Magical efforts can be made to keep memories and personality intact, at least to a great extent, and I took all necessary measures when I first stabilized Jenny's existence. Unfortunately, I never anticipated that she would magically implode the entity. I do not yet know how much she might have damaged herself, and I doubt that I will know for some years yet."

"Then she might be changed?" Marie asked.

"I am not yet certain that this dear child even is Jenny. But that is the name she shall have, all the same."

Marie looked as if she was having a hard time being consoled. The thought that her only child was now a dragon's daughter seemed irrelevant compared to the question of whether or not it was Jenny and if she would remember who she was when the time came. She looked down at the little dragon, who did not yet even seem to be aware of her.

She stared at Allan. "That means that you're her father!"

"Well, it does follow, doesn't it?" Allan admitted, looking embarrassed and slightly bewildered as if he was not yet used to the thought himself.

"Well, yes . . ." Marie began to protest, then stopped and stared when a second tiny dragon trotted into the room. This one was even smaller than Jenny, although she had the proportions of an adult.

"Oh yes, one final member of my loyal band of merry faeries," Dalvenjah said. "The Sorceress Darja, formerly of the Dark. I am now fairly certain that she has mended her ways, although it would be more accurate to say that she has learned for herself what she really wants in life."

"What, to be taller?" Rex asked.

"I will return her to her proper size very soon now, and then I will send her and Vajerral out into the wide world to look for boyfriends," Dalvenjah continued. "She is wearing Jenny's old body, you know."

"But it's a dragon," Marie protested.

"Jenny always was a dragon," Darja explained in her tiny voice as she sat down beside Dalvenjah's cushion. "Since returning to her old body would not repair the damage that had been done to her mind, she graciously permitted me to have it."

"That brings up one question that I've been wondering about for some time now," Holmes said, deciding that it would be best to change the subject for a while. "The Quentarah have asked us to solve their problems by releasing the excess magic of the singularity into the outer world. Unfortunately, releasing that magic into the outer world would create problems of its own."

"Magical creatures would return to our world?" Dr. Rex assumed.

"The results would be rather more complex than that," Holmes said. "The return of magic to the outer world will, in the long run, have certain dire consequences. It is true to say that magical creatures will return to that world. Unfortunately, the laws of evolution are hardly that simple. The same conditions that will permit the return of faerie life will no longer favor mortal life. As magic slowly returns, this time you may very well see mortals fading away into insignificance in the dawn of a new golden age of faerie."

"That does not necessarily follow," Dalvenjah said. "There is the very real possibility that their world will become like Mira's, a world of mortals who have access to strong magic."

"Perhaps, but I think not," Holmes said. "Having once been a faerie world, I believe that it will once again become a faerie world. Although I will grant you that the presence of mortals may predispose matters to keeping it a world of mortal magic-users."

"And you intend to restore magic to our world?" Marie asked incredulously.

Dalvenjah looked momentarily uncomfortable. "I'm afraid that it has been done already. When Jenny destroyed the entity, she also removed the obstruction that prevented latent magic from flowing freely through the singularity into the outer world. The entity, you see, was the obstruction. And now that it has been done, I certainly cannot imagine how we might possibly set things back to the way they were before."

"It's been about a year now, and I have observed no change at all so far," Rex observed. "My assumption therefore is that evolutionary change is slow, even magical evolutionary change. It took thousands of years for the age of lost faerie to come to an end, and it will probably take several thousand years for the new age of faerie to evolve."

"That is essentially correct," Holmes agreed. "A very astute deduction on your part, Dr. Barker."

"Elementary, my dear Holmes," Rex said, enormously pleased with himself. "So it all comes down to the fact that the worst-case scenario, from the mortal point of view of course, is that change will be slow and relatively if not completely painless. And when you discuss magical evolution, I am tempted to assume that you mean that mortals will become magical and eventually faerie, rather than the assumption that mortals will simply die out. So if the situation cannot be reversed, at least it is by no means tragic."

"That is essentially correct."

"Indeed, it might actually be good for us."

Dalvenjah glanced up at Marie. "It comes from being around Holmes for extended periods of time. We all started to talk like him, even the cat."

Marie glanced at the cat, who lifted his head and smiled pleasantly. He was in an exceptionally good mood. Jenny had been one of his favorite people, and he held such a low regard of people in general. It suited him to think that she might very well be back.

"Well, yes," Marie mused, rubbing her nose. "I seem to recall that we were discussing Jenny. I know better than to ask if she is going to stay like this. You were telling us about what her chances might be of remembering her past life, and possibly how soon you might know."

Dalvenjah laid back her ears. "I cannot say. I do not know if the spells of containment I had placed upon her would have held through the implosion of the entity. I do not even know if Jenny's spirit survived. The problem now is that Jenny is a child, and we must wait for her to grow up somewhat before she will be able to tell us what she knows. All I can say is that most young dragons will begin to recall their past memories at some time between the age of four and sixteen. We might have a long wait."

"Is there some way to cast a magic spell and have her tell you?" Marie asked fearfully.

Dalvenjah glanced down at the little dragon. "No, there is

not. At least you might have your answer very soon. Kelvandor will be obliged to wait at least sixteen years or more for what he wants, and he has no assurance that she will even remember who he is."

Kelvandor was still sitting quietly by the window, wearing a long face. All faerie dragons had naturally long faces, but Kelvandor had just about cornered the market in lugubriousness. Of course, part of the reason for his present emotional state was the fact that Vajerral was still trying to encourage an affectionate response from him.

Marie's eyes got very wide. "I hesitate to ask, but just what does that great lump of a dragon expect from her?"

"Well, he loves her, of course," Allan said. It was his turn to break bad news to his sister. "They were mates, although I hesitate to think how they managed that."

"But, I thought that Vajerral . . ."

"No, she just wants sexual favors," he insisted. "It's a vicious triangle. Vajerral lusts after Kelvandor, who loves Jenny, whose present interests are limited to dragon's milk. If Vajerral gets her way, Kelvandor will get in a lot of practice by the time he gets Jenny back."

"My word, what a concept!" Mira agreed eagerly. "Multiple first-time experiences! No wonder reincarnation is so popular."

"Nature never intended that a dragon should remember anything of her past life, and we have that against us as well," Dalvenjah said, affording Mira a hard stare. "Circumstances were such that Jenny never had a chance to enjoy her previous life, and I have done what I could to give her another chance. But you must also remember that it is actually more important to us that the Jenny we knew is returned than it is to her, as long as she is alive. If she does not remember her past, then we must allow her to develop into this new life in her own way rather than expect her to mimic the manners and traits of someone who has ceased to exist. And if this is not even Jenny's spirit in the first place . . ."

"It is," J.T. announced calmly. "It is my business to know such things. I sense beyond any doubt that the spirit of this young dragon is Jenny. What I cannot tell you is whether or not she remembers anything."

"But does she have to be a dragon?" Marie asked.

"It is logical that she should be," Dalvenjah said. "She has the spirit of a faerie dragon, and she was born one this time. Both of her fathers and one of her mothers were dragons, so it's three against one. At least you will perhaps be grateful that I do not insist upon her having a Mindijaran name. I had thought that she should be named Maeridaln."

"Thank heaven for small favors," Marie muttered. "It just needs a little getting used to, that's all. To think that I was once married to a dragon, and that my college-educated daughter is now a baby dragon, and that my own brother is now her father."

The little dragonet lifted her head and looked over her shoulder, blinking at Marie. "Ah, mom! It's neat!"

Everyone stopped and stared for what seemed like a very long time. For those who had been present in their first adventure together, those few words in that tiny, childlike voice reminded them particularly of a very young Jenny of some fifteen years or so earlier, a precocious nine-year-old with a fascination for flying and making herself invisible.

"Well, that would seem to put any remaining questions to rest," Dalvenjah said at last. "If she remembers everything from her previous life, that at least will make educating her fairly easy. Granted that she is probably the only dragonet with a degree in engineering from Colorado State."

"Then she really does remember everything?" Kelvandor asked hopefully. Then he dropped his head and laid back his ears. "I still have to wait."

Vajerral nuzzled him gently. "I know some games to pass the time."

"Young dragon, you will be going back to your studies," Dalvenjah told her firmly. "At this time, your little sister is probably better educated than you are. I never intended that I should raise any ignorant dragons."

"So, things are working out fairly well for everyone involved after all," Mira observed as she helped herself to the drinks. "So just about everyone gets some sort of happily ever after, even if they have to wait."

"I am happy that you think so," Dalvenjah said. "I hardly know if we will survive this double blessing of maternal bliss."

Mira hesitated, then decided that she should pour herself a

second measure of some interesting draconic liqueur. "And just who else here is experiencing maternal bliss?"

"You are, of course."

Mira put down her glass and took a long drink from the bottle, then she turned and glared at the cat. "Did you know?"

"J.T. the Cat knows all," he said smugly. "Remembering how you nearly twisted my neck, I have enjoyed keeping that knowledge to myself. I admit that I was beginning to wonder when you would realize just why you were turning green over your morning tea and kippers."

"Is that a fact!" Holmes was making very little effort to conceal his tremendous amusement. "Sorceress Kasdamir Gerran is due to be our next little mother? Would it be rude of me to ask if you know who the father is?"

Mira looked surprised, and took another quick drink from the bottle. "Oh, my! Oh, my! That steel-plated bastard!"

"You never should have listened to his story about leaving on a dangerous quest and not wanting to die a virgin," J.T. reminded her. "If nothing else, you might have recalled that he has a proven history of getting sorceresses pregnant."

Holmes laughed out loud this time. "You fell for that line?"

"Well, I was tipsy at the time," Mira explained. "Otherwise I would have remembered that spell of contraception. This is what I get for not listening to Beratric Kurgel. He always warned me that Sir Remidan is a little too fond of tipping his lance."

Holmes had risen from his seat and went now to the table where Mira had been making very free with the drinks. He chose a large bottle of fine wine that had been sitting on ice and began removing the cork. "And so, our great quest is done at last and we have not suffered too greatly from our trials."

"Speak for yourself," Mira said sullenly.

"Your present condition is not a direct result of our journey," Holmes reminded her. "You lost your old ship but you received in exchange your new *Star Dragon*, the marvel of your world. Jenny lost her life, but she had been given a second chance at the life that should have been hers. Darja has been saved from the dire fate that she had been created to serve and is now free to embrace a life of her own. Karidaejan lost his own life for the sake of the Prophecy, and it was given back. I have found my lost magic and now I am permitted to once again take part in life rather than watch it pass anonymously. Mira will be allowed to discover the joys of motherhood, and Kelvandor will have a fine opportunity to discover the true meaning of patience."

"And was it worth it all?" Rex asked.

"Indeed it was," Holmes insisted as he poured wine into a whole regiment of long-stemmed glasses. "One world has been liberated from the terror of the Dark, while other worlds have been spared from the danger of the expansion of the Dark. The sky islands are at peace and freed from the threat of being overwhelmed in a flood of latent magic, while faerie magic has been restored to yet another world. These were the goals that we fought to achieve, and we should be grateful that a greater price was not demanded of us."

"Mr. Holmes, I never suspected that you were secretly an optimist," Rex said as he helped to pass out the glasses.

"You must never confuse me with my fictional counterpart," Holmes said. "If everyone of a drinking age has a glass, I would suggest that a toast is in order. Dalvenjah Foxfire, if you would be so kind."

Dalvenjah looked surprised. "This was your idea."

"You were our leader."

"And you know what you want to say. I am in no mood to read your mind."

"Then I will indeed propose a toast," Holmes said, lifting his glass as an indication for the others to join him. "To my dear companions. To old friends and new. To dragons, elves, men and even cats. May our roads never end. May we always fly an open sky. May life be grand and glorious. I ask you now to join me in proposing a toast to Adventure. May we always enjoy it in full and proper measure, and never face the grim specter of boredom."

The others hesitated, wondering if they really wanted to join him in that rash toast.